BY F. SCOTT FITZGERALD

NOVELS

This Side of Paradise
The Beautiful and Damned
The Great Gatsby
Tender Is the Night
The Last Tycoon
   (Unfinished), with a Foreword by
   Edmund Wilson and Notes by the Author

STORIES

The Stories of F. Scott Fitzgerald
   A Selection of 28 stories, with an
   Introduction by Malcolm Cowley
Flappers and Philosophers
   With an Introduction by Arthur Mizener
Six Tales of the Jazz Age and Other Stories
   With an Introduction by Frances Fitzgerald Lanahan
Taps at Reveille

STORIES AND ESSAYS

Afternoon of An Author
   With an Introduction and Notes
   by Arthur Mizener

TAPS

AT REVEILLE

by F. SCOTT FITZGERALD

CHARLES SCRIBNER'S SONS   New York

CONTENTS

TAPS AT REVEILLE

TAPS AT REVEILLE

BASIL

THE SCANDAL DETECTIVES

I

It was a hot afternoon in May and Mrs. Buckner thought that a pitcher of fruit lemonade might prevent the boys from filling up on ice cream at the drug store. She belonged to that generation, since retired, upon whom the great revolution in American family life was to be visited; but at that time she believed that her children's relation to her was as much as hers had been to her parents, for this was more than twenty years ago.

Some generations are close to those that succeed them; between others the gap is infinite and unbridgeable. Mrs. Buckner—a woman of character, a member of Society in a large Middle-Western city—carrying a pitcher of fruit lemonade through her own spacious back yard, was progressing across a hundred years. Her own thoughts would have been comprehensible to her great-grandmother; what was happening in a room above the stable would have been entirely unintelligible to them both. In what had once served as the coachman's sleeping apartment, her son and a friend were not behaving in a normal manner, but were, so to speak, experimenting in a void. They were making the first tentative combinations of the ideas and materials they found ready at their hand—ideas destined to become, in future years, first articulate, then startling and finally commonplace. At the moment when she called up to them they were sitting with disarming quiet upon the still unhatched eggs of the mid-twentieth century.

Riply Buckner descended the ladder and took the lemonade. Basil Duke Lee looked abstractedly down at the transaction and said, "Thank you very much, Mrs. Buckner."

"Are you sure it isn't too hot up there?"

"No, Mrs. Buckner. It's fine."

It was stifling; but they were scarcely conscious of the heat, and they drank two tall glasses each of the lemonade without knowing

3

that they were thirsty. Concealed beneath a sawed-out trapdoor from which they presently took it was a composition book bound in imitation red leather which currently absorbed much of their attention. On its first page was inscribed, if you penetrated the secret of the lemon-juice ink: "THE BOOK OF SCANDAL, written by Riply Buckner, Jr., and Basil D. Lee, Scandal Detectives."

In this book they had set down such deviations from rectitude on the part of their fellow citizens as had reached their ears. Some of these false steps were those of grizzled men, stories that had become traditions in the city and were embalmed in the composition book by virtue of indiscreet exhumations at family dinner tables. Others were the more exciting sins, confirmed or merely rumored, of boys and girls their own age. Some of the entries would have been read by adults with bewilderment, others might have inspired wrath, and there were three or four contemporary reports that would have prostrated the parents of the involved children with horror and despair.

One of the mildest items, a matter they had hesitated about setting down, though it had shocked them only last year, was: "Elwood Leaming has been to the Burlesque Show three or four times at the Star."

Another, and perhaps their favorite, because of its uniqueness, set forth that "H. P. Cramner committed some theft in the East he could be imprisoned for and had to come here"—H. P. Crammer being now one of the oldest and "most substantial" citizens of the city.

The single defect in the book was that it could only be enjoyed with the aid of the imagination, for the invisible ink must keep its secrets until that day when, the pages being held close to the fire, the items would appear. Close inspection was necessary to determine which pages had been used—already a rather grave charge against a certain couple had been superimposed upon the dismal facts that Mrs. R. B. Cary had consumption and that her son, Walter Cary, had been expelled from Pawling School. The purpose of the work as a whole was not blackmail. It was treasured against the time when its protagonists should "do something" to Basil and Riply. Its possession

gave them a sense of power. Basil, for instance, had never seen Mr.
H. P. Cramner make a single threatening gesture in Basil's direction
but let him even hint that he was going to do something to Basil, and
there preserved against him was the record of his past.

It is only fair to say that at this point the book passes entirely out
of this story. Years later a janitor discovered it beneath the trapdoor, and finding it apparently blank, gave it to his little girl; so
the misdeeds of Elwood Leaming and H. P. Cramner were definitely
entombed at last beneath a fair copy of Lincoln's Gettysburg Address.

The book was Basil's idea. He was more the imaginative and in
most ways the stronger of the two. He was a shining-eyed, brown-
haired boy of fourteen, rather small as yet, and bright and lazy at
school. His favorite character in fiction was Arsène Lupin, the gentleman burglar, a romantic phenomenon lately imported from Europe
and much admired in the first bored decades of the century.

Riply Buckner, also in short pants, contributed to the partnership a
breathless practicality. His mind waited upon Basil's imagination
like a hair trigger and no scheme was too fantastic for his immediate
"Let's do it!" Since the school's third baseball team, on which they
had been pitcher and catcher, decomposed after an unfortunate
April season, they had spent their afternoons struggling to evolve a
way of life which should measure up to the mysterious energies
fermenting inside them. In the cache beneath the trapdoor were
some "slouch" hats and bandanna handkerchiefs, some loaded dice,
half of a pair of handcuffs, a rope ladder of a tenuous crochet
persuasion for rear-window escapes into the alley, and a make-up
box containing two old theatrical wigs and crêpe hair of various
colors—all to be used when they decided what illegal enterprises to
undertake.

Their lemonades finished, they lit Home Runs and held a
desultory conversation which touched on crime, professional baseball, sex and the local stock company. This broke off at the sound of
footsteps and familiar voices in the adjoining alley.

From the window, they investigated. The voices belonged to
Margaret Torrence, Imogene Bissel and Connie Davies, who were

cutting through the alley from Imogene's back yard to Connie's at the end of the block. The young ladies were thirteen, twelve and thirteen years old respectively, and they considered themselves alone, for in time to their march they were rendering a mildly daring parody in a sort of whispering giggle and coming out strongly on the finale: "Oh, my *dar*-ling *Clemon*-tine."

Basil and Riply leaned together from the window, then remembering their undershirts sank down behind the sill.

"We heard you!" they cried together.

The girls stopped and laughed. Margaret Torrence chewed exaggeratedly to indicate gum, and gum with a purpose. Basil immediately understood.

"Whereabouts?" he demanded.

"Over at Imogene's house."

They had been at Mrs. Bissel's cigarettes. The implied recklessness of their mood interested and excited the two boys and they prolonged the conversation. Connie Davies had been Riply's girl during dancing-school term; Margaret Torrence had played a part in Basil's recent past; Imogene Bissel was just back from a year in Europe. During the last month neither Basil nor Riply had thought about girls, and, thus refreshed, they become conscious that the centre of the world had shifted suddenly from the secret room to the little group outside.

"Come on up," they suggested.

"Come on out. Come on down to the Whartons' yard."

"All right."

Barely remembering to put away the Scandal Book and the box of disguises, the two boys hurried out, mounted their bicycles and rode up the alley.

The Whartons' own children had long grown up, but their yard was still one of those predestined places where young people gather in the afternoon. It had many advantages. It was large, open to other yards on both sides, and it could be entered upon skates or bicycles from the street. It contained an old seesaw, a swing and a pair of flying rings; but it had been a rendezvous before these were put up, for it had a child's quality—the thing that makes young people huddle inextricably on uncomfortable steps and desert the houses of their friends to herd on the obscure premises of "people nobody knows." The Whartons' yard had long been a happy compromise; there were deep shadows there all day long and ever something vague in bloom, and patient dogs around, and brown spots worn bare by countless circling wheels and dragging feet. In sordid poverty, below the bluff two hundred feet away, lived the "micks" —they had merely inherited the name, for they were now largely of Scandinavian descent—and when other amusements palled, a few cries were enough to bring a gang of them swarming up the hill, to be faced if numbers promised well, to be fled from into convenient houses if things went the other way.

It was five o'clock and there was a small crowd gathered there for that soft and romantic time before supper—a time surpassed only by the interim of summer dusk thereafter. Basil and Riply rode their bicycles around abstractedly, in and out of trees, resting now and then with a hand on someone's shoulder, shading their eyes from the glow of the late sun that, like youth itself, is too strong to face directly, but must be kept down to an undertone until it dies away.

Basil rode over to Imogene Bissel and balanced idly on his wheel before her. Something in his face then must have attracted her, for she looked up at him, looked at him really, and slowly smiled. She was to be a beauty and belle of many proms in a few years. Now her large brown eyes and large beautifully shaped mouth and the high flush over her thin cheek bones made her face gnome-like and offended those who wanted a child to look like a child. For a moment Basil was granted an insight into the future, and the spell of her vitality crept over him suddenly. For the first time in his life he realized a girl completely as something opposite and complementary to him, and he was subject to a warm chill of mingled pleasure and pain. It was a definite experience and he was immediately conscious of it. The summer afternoon became lost in her suddenly—the soft air, the shadowy hedges and banks of flowers, the orange sunlight, the laughter and voices, the tinkle of a piano over the way—the odor left all these things and went into Imogene's face as she sat there looking up at him with a smile.

For a moment it was too much for him. He let it go, incapable of exploiting it until he had digested it alone. He rode around fast in a circle on his bicycle, passing near Imogene without looking at her. When he came back after a while and asked if he could walk home with her, she had forgotten the moment, if it had ever existed for her, and was almost surprised. With Basil wheeling his bicycle beside her, they started down the street.

"Can you come out tonight?" he asked eagerly. "There'll probably be a bunch in the Whartons' yard."

"I'll ask mother."

"I'll telephone you. I don't want to go unless you'll be there."

"Why?" She smiled at him again, encouraging him.

"Because I don't want to."

"But why don't you want to?"

"Listen," he said quickly, "what boys do you like better than me?"

"Nobody. I like you and Hubert Blair best."

Basil felt no jealousy at the coupling of this name with his. There was nothing to do about Hubert Blair but accept him philosophically, as other boys did when dissecting the hearts of other girls.

"I like you better than anybody," he said deliriously.

The weight of the pink dappled sky above him was not endurable. He was plunging along through air of ineffable loveliness while warm freshets sprang up in his blood and he turned them, and with them his whole life, like a stream toward this girl.

They reached the carriage door at the side of her house.

"Can't you come in, Basil?"

"No." He saw immediately that that was a mistake, but it was said now. The intangible present had eluded him. Still he lingered. "Do you want my school ring?"

"Yes, if you want to give it to me."

"I'll give it to you tonight." His voice shook slightly as he added, "That is, I'll trade."

"What for?"

"Something."

"What?" Her color spread; she knew.

"You know. Will you trade?"

Imogene looked around uneasily. In the honey-sweet silence that had gathered around the porch, Basil held his breath.

"You're awful," she whispered. "Maybe. . . . Good-by."

II

It was the best hour of the day now and Basil was terribly happy This summer he and his mother and sister were going to the lakes and next fall he was starting away to school. Then he would go to Yale and be a great athlete, and after that—if his two dreams had fitted onto each other chronologically instead of existing independently side by side—he was due to become a gentleman burglar. Everything was fine. He had so many alluring things to think about that it was hard to fall asleep at night.

That he was now crazy about Imogene Bissel was not a distraction, but another good thing. It had as yet no poignancy, only a brilliant and dynamic excitement that was bearing him along toward the Whartons' yard through the May twilight.

He wore his favorite clothes—white duck knickerbockers, pepper-and-salt Norfolk jacket, a Belmont collar and a gray knitted tie. With his black hair wet and shining, he made a handsome little figure as he turned in upon the familiar but now re-enchanted lawn and joined the voices in the gathering darkness. Three or four girls who lived in neighboring houses were present, and almost twice as many boys; and a slightly older group adorning the side veranda made a warm, remote nucleus against the lamps of the house and contributed occasional mysterious ripples of laughter to the already overburdened night.

Moving from shadowy group to group, Basil ascertained that Imogene was not yet here. Finding Margaret Torrence, he spoke to her aside, lightly.

"Have you still got that old ring of mine?"

Margaret had been his girl all year at dancing school, signified by the fact that he had taken her to the cotillion which closed the season. The affair had languished toward the end; none the less, his question was undiplomatic.

"I've got it somewhere," Margaret replied carelessly. "Why? Do you want it back?"

"Sort of."

"All right. I never did want it. It was you that made me take it, Basil. I'll give it back to you tomorrow."

"You couldn't give it to me tonight, could you?" His heart leaped as he saw a small figure come in at the rear gate. "I sort of want to get it tonight."

"Oh, all right, Basil."

She ran across the street to her house and Basil followed. Mr. and Mrs. Torrence were on the porch, and while Margaret went upstairs for the ring he overcame his excitement and impatience and answered those questions as to the health of his parents which are so meaningless to the young. Then a sudden stiffening came over him, his voice faded off and his glazed eyes fixed upon a scene that was materializing over the way.

From the shadows far up the street, a swift, almost flying figure emerged and floated into the patch of lamplight in front of the Whartons' house. The figure wove here and there in a series of geometric patterns, now off with a flash of sparks at the impact of skates and pavement, now gliding miraculously backward, describing a fantastic curve, with one foot lifted gracefully in the air, until the young people moved forward in groups out of the darkness and crowded to the pavement to watch. Basil gave a quiet little groan as he realized that of all possible nights, Hubert Blair had chosen this one to arrive.

"You say you're going to the lakes this summer, Basil. Have you taken a cottage?"

Basil became aware after a moment that Mr. Torrence was making this remark for the third time.

"Oh, yes, sir," he answered—"I mean, no. We're staying at the club."

"Won't that be lovely?" said Mrs. Torrence.

Across the street, he saw Imogene standing under the lamp-post and in front of her Hubert Blair, his jaunty cap on the side of his head, maneuvering in a small circle. Basil winced as he heard his chuckling laugh. He did not perceive Margaret until she was beside him, pressing his ring into his hand like a bad penny. He muttered a strained hollow good-by to her parents, and weak with apprehension, followed her back across the street.

Hanging back in a shadow, he fixed his eyes not on Imogene but on Hubert Blair. There was undoubtedly something rare about Hubert. In the eyes of children less than fifteen, the shape of the nose is the distinguishing mark of beauty. Parents may call attention to lovely eyes, shining hair or gorgeous coloring, but the nose and its juxtaposition on the face is what the adolescent sees. Upon the lithe, stylish, athletic torso of Hubert Blair was set a conventional chubby face, and upon this face was chiseled the piquant, retroussé nose of a Harrison Fisher girl.

He was confident; he had personality, uninhibited by doubts or moods. He did not go to dancing school—his parents had moved to the city only a year ago—but already he was a legend. Though most of the boys disliked him, they did homage to his virtuosic athletic ability, and for the girls his every movement, his pleasantries, his very indifference, had a simply immeasurable fascination. Upon several previous occasions Basil had discovered this; now the discouraging comedy began to unfold once more.

Hubert took off his skates, rolled one down his arm and caught it by the strap before it reached the pavement; he snatched the ribbon from Imogene's hair and made off with it, dodging from under her arms as she pursued him, laughing and fascinated, around the yard. He cocked one foot behind the other and pretended to lean an elbow against a tree, missed the tree on purpose and gracefully saved himself from falling. The boys watched him noncommittally at first. Then they, too, broke out into activity, doing stunts and tricks as fast as they could think of them until those on the porch craned their necks at the sudden surge of activity in the garden. But Hubert coolly turned his back on his own success. He took Imogene's hat and began setting it in various quaint ways upon his head. Imogene and the other girls were filled with delight.

Unable any longer to endure the nauseous spectacle, Basil went up to the group and said, "Why, hello, Hube," in as negligent a tone as he could command.

Hubert answered: "Why, hello, old—old Basil the Boozle," and set the hat a different way on his head, until Basil himself couldn't resist an unwilling chortle of laughter.

"Basil the Boozle! Hello, Basil the Boozle!" The cry circled the garden. Reproachfully he distinguished Riply's voice among the others.

"Hube the Boob!" Basil countered quickly; but his ill humor detracted from the effect, though several boys repeated it appreciatively.

Gloom settled upon Basil, and through the heavy dusk the figure of Imogene began to take on a new, unattainable charm. He was a romantic boy and already he had endowed her heavily from his fancy. Now he hated her for her indifference, but he must perversely linger near in the vain hope of recovering the penny of ecstasy so wantonly expended this afternoon.

He tried to talk to Margaret with decoy animation, but Margaret was not responsive. Already a voice had gone up in the darkness calling in a child. Panic seized upon him; the blessed hour of summer evening was almost over. At a spreading of the group to let pedestrians through, he maneuvered Imogene unwillingly aside.

"I've got it," he whispered. "Here it is. Can I take you home?"

She looked at him distractedly. Her hand closed automatically on the ring.

"What? Oh, I promised Hubert he could take me home." At the sight of his face she pulled herself from her trance and forced a note of indignation. "I saw you going off with Margaret Torrence just as soon as I came into the yard."

"I didn't. I just went to get the ring."

"Yes, you did! I saw you!"

Her eyes moved back to Hubert Blair. He had replaced his roller skates and was making little rhythmic jumps and twirls on his toes, like a witch doctor throwing a slow hypnosis over an African tribe. Basil's voice, explaining and arguing, went on, but Imogene moved away. Helplessly he followed. There were other voices calling in the darkness now and unwilling responses on all sides.

"All right, mother!"

"I'll be there in a second, mother."

"Mother, can't I please stay out five minutes more?"

"I've got to go," Imogene cried. "It's almost nine."

Waving her hand and smiling absently at Basil, she started off down the street. Hubert pranced and stunted at her side, circled around her and made entrancing little figures ahead.

Only after a minute did Basil realize that another young lady was addressing him.

"What?" he demanded absently.

"Hubert Blair is the nicest boy in town and you're the most conceited," repeated Margaret Torrence with deep conviction.

He stared at her in pained surprise. Margaret wrinkled her nose at him and yielded up her person to the now-insistent demands coming from across the street. As Basil gazed stupidly after her and then watched the forms of Imogene and Hubert disappear around the corner, there was a low mutter of thunder along the sultry sky and a moment later a solitary drop plunged through the lamplit leaves overhead and splattered on the sidewalk at his feet. The day was to close in rain.

III

It came quickly and he was drenched and running before he reached his house eight blocks away. But the change of weather had swept over his heart and he leaped up every few steps, swallowing the rain and crying "Yo-o-o!" aloud, as if he himself were a part of the fresh, violent disturbance of the night. Imogene was gone, washed out like the day's dust on the sidewalk. Her beauty would come back into his mind in brighter weather, but here in the storm he was alone with himself. A sense of extraordinary power welled up in him, until to leave the ground permanently with one of his wild leaps would not have surprised him. He was a lone wolf, secret and untamed; a night prowler, demoniac and free. Only when he reached his own house did his emotion begin to turn, speculatively and almost without passion, against Hubert Blair.

He changed his clothes, and putting on pajamas and dressing-gown descended to the kitchen, where he happened upon a new chocolate cake. He ate a fourth of it and most of a bottle of milk.

His elation somewhat diminished, he called up Riply Buckner on the phone.

"I've got a scheme," he said.

"What about?"

"How to do something to H. B. with the S. D."

Riply understood immediately what he meant. Hubert had been so indiscreet as to fascinate other girls besides Miss Bissel that evening.

"We'll have to take in Bill Kampf," Basil said.

"All right."

"See you at recess tomorrow. . . . Good night!"

IV

Four days later, when Mr. and Mrs. George P. Blair were finishing dinner, Hubert was called to the telephone. Mrs. Blair took advantage of his absence to speak to her husband of what had been on her mind all day.

"George, those boys, or whatever they are, came again last night."

He frowned.

"Did you see them?"

"Hilda did. She almost caught one of them. You see, I told her about the note they left last Tuesday, the one that said, 'First warning, S. D.,' so she was ready for them. They rang the back-door bell this time and she answered it straight from the dishes. If her hands hadn't been soapy she could have caught one, because she grabbed him when he handed her a note, but her hands were soapy so he slipped away."

"What did he look like?"

"She said he might have been a very little man, but she thought he was a boy in a false face. He dodged like a boy, she said, and she thought he had short pants on. The note was like the other. It said 'Second warning, S. D.' "

"If you've got it, I'd like to see it after dinner."

Hubert came back from the phone. "It was Imogene Bissel," he said. "She wants me to come over to her house. A bunch are going over there tonight."

"Hubert," asked his father, "do you know any boy with the initials S. D.?"

"No, sir."

"Have you thought?"

"Yeah, I thought. I knew a boy named Sam Davis, but I haven't seen him for a year."

"Who was he?"

"Oh, a sort of tough. He was at Number 44 School when I went there."

"Did he have it in for you?"

"I don't think so."

"Who do you think could be doing this? Has anybody got it in for you that you know about?"

"I don't know, papa; I don't think so."

"I don't like the looks of this thing," said Mr. Blair thoughtfully. "Of course it may be only some boys, but it may be——"

He was silent. Later, he studied the note. It was in red ink and there was a skull and crossbones in the corner, but being printed, it told him nothing at all.

Meanwhile Hubert kissed his mother, set his cap jauntily on the side of his head, and passing through the kitchen stepped out on the back stoop, intending to take the usual short cut along the alley. It was a bright moonlit night and he paused for a moment on the stoop to tie his shoe. If he had but known that the telephone call just received had been a decoy, that it had not come from Imogene Bissel's house, had not indeed been a girl's voice at all, and that shadowy and grotesque forms were skulking in the alley just outside the gate, he would not have sprung so gracefully and lithely down the steps with his hands in his pockets or whistled the first bar of the Grizzly Bear into the apparently friendly night.

His whistle aroused varying emotions in the alley. Basil had given his daring and successful falsetto imitation over the telephone a little too soon, and though the Scandal Detectives had hurried, their preparations were not quite in order. They had become separated. Basil, got up like a Southern planter of the old persuasion, was just outside the Blairs' gate; Bill Kampf, with a long Balkan mustache attached by a wire to the lower cartilage of his nose, was approaching in the shadow of the fence; but Riply Buckner, in a full rabbinical beard, was impeded by a length of rope he was trying to coil and was still a hundred feet away. The rope was an essential part of their plan; for, after much cogitation, they had decided what they were going to do to Hubert Blair. They were going to tie him up, gag him and put him in his own garbage can.

The idea at first horrified them—it would ruin his suit, it was awfully dirty and he might smother. In fact the garbage can, symbol of all that was repulsive, won the day only because it made every other idea seem tame. They disposed of the objections—his suit could be cleaned, it was where he ought to be anyhow, and if they left the lid off he couldn't smother. To be sure of this they had paid a visit of inspection to the Buckners' garbage can and stared into it, fascinated, envisaging Hubert among the rinds and eggshells. Then two of them, at last, resolutely put that part out of their minds and concentrated upon the luring of him into the alley and the overwhelming of him there.

Hubert's cheerful whistle caught them off guard and each of the three stood stock-still, unable to communicate with the others. It flashed through Basil's mind that if he grabbed Hubert without Riply at hand to apply the gag as had been arranged, Hubert's cries might alarm the gigantic cook in the kitchen who had almost taken him the night before. The thought threw him into a state of indecision. At that precise moment Hubert opened the gate and came out into the alley.

The two stood five feet apart, staring at each other, and all at once Basil made a startling discovery. He discovered he liked Hubert Blair—liked him well as any boy he knew. He had absolutely no wish to lay hands on Hubert Blair and stuff him into a garbage can, jaunty cap and all. He would have fought to prevent that contingency. As his mind, unstrung by his situation, gave pasture to this inconvenient thought, he turned and dashed out of the alley and up the street.

For a moment the apparition had startled Hubert, but when it turned and made off he was heartened and gave chase. Out-distanced, he decided after fifty yards to let well enough alone; and returning to the alley, started rather precipitously down toward the other end—and came face to face with another small and hairy stranger.

Bill Kampf, being more simply organized than Basil, had no scruples of any kind. It had been decided to put Hubert into a garbage can, and though he had nothing at all against Hubert, the idea had made a pattern on his brain which he intended to follow. He was a natural man—that is to say, a hunter—and once a creature took on the aspect of a quarry, he would pursue it without qualms until it stopped struggling.

But he had been witness to Basil's inexplicable flight, and supposing that Hubert's father had appeared and was now directly behind him, he, too, faced about and made off down the alley. Presently he met Riply Buckner, who, without waiting to inquire the cause of his flight, enthusiastically joined him. Again Hubert was surprised into pursuing a little way. Then, deciding once and for all to let well enough alone, he returned on a dead run to his house.

Meanwhile Basil had discovered that he was not pursued, and keeping in the shadows, made his way back to the alley. He was not frightened—he had simply been incapable of action. The alley was empty; neither Bill nor Riply was in sight. He saw Mr. Blair come to the back gate, open it, look up and down and go back into the house. He came closer. There was a great chatter in the kitchen— Hubert's voice, loud and boastful, and Mrs. Blair's, frightened, and the two Swedish domestics contributing bursts of hilarious laughter. Then through an open window he heard Mr. Blair's voice at the telephone:

"I want to speak to the chief of police. . . . Chief, this is George P. Blair. . . . Chief, there's a gang of toughs around here who——"

Basil was off like a flash, tearing at his Confederate whiskers as he ran.

V

Imogene Bissel, having just turned thirteen, was not accustomed to having callers at night. She was spending a bored and solitary evening inspecting the month's bills which were scattered over her mother's desk, when she heard Hubert Blair and his father admitted into the front hall.

"I just thought I'd bring him over myself," Mr. Blair was saying to her mother. "There seems to be a gang of toughs hanging around our alley tonight."

Mrs. Bissel had not called upon Mrs. Blair and she was considerably taken aback by this unexpected visit. She even entertained the uncharitable thought that this was a crude overture, undertaken by Mr. Blair on behalf of his wife.

"Really!" she exclaimed. "Imogene will be delighted to see Hubert, I'm sure. . . . Imogene!"

"These toughs were evidently lying in wait for Hubert," continued Mr. Blair. "But he's a pretty spunky boy and he managed to drive them away. However, I didn't want him to come down here alone."

"Of course not," she agreed. But she was unable to imagine why Hubert should have come at all. He was a nice enough boy, but surely Imogene had seen enough of him the last three afternoons. In fact, Mrs. Bissel was annoyed, and there was a minimum of warmth in her voice when she asked Mr. Blair to come in.

They were still in the hall, and Mr. Blair was just beginning to perceive that all was not as it should be, when there was another ring at the bell. Upon the door being opened, Basil Lee, red-faced and breathless, stood on the threshold.

"How do you do, Mrs. Bissel? Hello, Imogene!" he cried in an unnecessarily hearty voice. "Where's the party?"

The salutation might have sounded to a dispassionate observer somewhat harsh and unnatural, but it fell upon the ears of an already disconcerted group.

"There isn't any party," said Imogene wonderingly.

"What?" Basil's mouth dropped open in exaggerated horror, his voice trembled slightly. "You mean to say you didn't call me up and tell me to come over here to a party?"

"Why, of course not, Basil!"

Imogene was excited by Hubert's unexpected arrival and it occurred to her that Basil had invented this excuse to spoil it. Alone of those present, she was close to the truth; but she underestimated the urgency of Basil's motive, which was not jealousy but mortal fear.

"You called *me* up, didn't you, Imogene?" demanded Hubert confidently.

"Why, no, Hubert! I didn't call up anybody."

Amid a chorus of bewildered protestations, there was another ring at the doorbell and the pregnant night yielded up Riply Buckner, Jr., and William S. Kampf. Like Basil, they were somewhat rumpled and breathless, and they no less rudely and peremptorily demanded the whereabouts of the party, insisting with curious vehemence that Imogene had just now invited them over the phone.

Hubert laughed, the others began to laugh and the tensity relaxed. Imogene, because she believed Hubert, now began to believe them all. Unable to restrain himself any longer in the presence of this unhoped-for audience, Hubert burst out with his amazing adventure.

"I guess there's a gang laying for us all!" he exclaimed. "There were some guys laying for me in our alley when I went out. There was a big fellow with gray whiskers, but when he saw me he ran away. Then I went along the alley and there was a bunch more, sort of foreigners or something, and I started after'm and they ran. I tried to catchem, but I guess they were good and scared, because they ran too fast for *me*."

So interested were Hubert and his father in the story that they failed to perceive that three of his listeners were growing purple in the face or to mark the uproarious laughter that greeted Mr. Bissel's polite proposal that they have a party, after all.

"Tell about the warnings, Hubert," prompted Mr. Blair. "You see, Hubert had received these warnings. Did you boys get any warnings?"

"I did," said Basil suddenly. "I got a sort of warning on a piece of paper about a week ago."

For a moment, as Mr. Blair's worried eye fell upon Basil, a strong sense not precisely of suspicion but rather of obscure misgiving passed over him. Possibly that odd aspect of Basil's eyebrows, where wisps of crêpe hair still lingered, connected itself in his subconscious mind with what was bizarre in the events of the evening. He shook his head somewhat puzzled. Then his thoughts glided back restfully to Hubert's courage and presence of mind.

Hubert, meanwhile, having exhausted his facts, was making tentative leaps into the realms of imagination.

"I said, 'So you're the guy that's been sending these warnings,' and he swung his left at me, and I dodged and swung my right back at him. I guess I must have landed, because he gave a yell and ran. Gosh, he could run! You'd ought to of seen him, Bill—he could run as fast as you."

"Was he big?" asked Basil, blowing his nose noisily.

"Sure! About as big as father."

"Were the other ones big too?"

"Sure! They were pretty big. I didn't wait to see, I just yelled, 'You get out of here, you bunch of toughs, or I'll show you!' They started a sort of fight, but I swung my right at one of them and they didn't wait for any more."

"Hubert says he thinks they were Italians," interrupted Mr. Blair. "Didn't you, Hubert?"

"They were sort of funny-looking," Hubert said. "One fellow looked like an Italian."

Mrs. Bissel led the way to the dining room, where she had caused a cake and grape juice supper to be spread. Imogene took a chair by Hubert's side.

"Now tell me all about it, Hubert," she said, attentively folding her hands.

Hubert ran over the adventure once more. A knife now made its appearance in the belt of one conspirator; Hubert's parleys with them lengthened and grew in volume and virulence. He had told them just what they might expect if they fooled with him. They had started to draw knives, but had thought better of it and taken to flight.

In the middle of this recital there was a curious snorting sound from across the table, but when Imogene looked over, Basil was spreading jelly on a piece of coffee cake and his eyes were brightly innocent. A minute later, however, the sound was repeated, and this time she intercepted a specifically malicious expression upon his face.

"I wonder what you'd have done, Basil," she said cuttingly. "I'll bet you'd be running yet!"

Basil put the piece of coffee cake in his mouth and immediately choked on it—an accident which Bill Kampf and Riply Buckner found hilariously amusing. Their amusement at various casual incidents at table seemed to increase as Hubert's story continued. The alley now swarmed with malefactors, and as Hubert struggled on against overwhelming odds, Imogene found herself growing restless —without in the least realizing that the tale was boring her. On the contrary, each time Hubert recollected new incidents and began again, she looked spitefully over at Basil, and her dislike for him grew.

When they moved into the library, Imogene went to the piano, where she sat alone while the boys gathered around Hubert on the couch. To her chagrin, they seemed quite content to listen indefinitely. Odd little noises squeaked out of them from time to time, but whenever the narrative slackened they would beg for more.

"Go on, Hubert. Which one did you say could run as fast as Bill Kampf?"

She was glad when, after half an hour, they all got up to go.

"It's a strange affair from beginning to end," Mr. Blair was saying. "I don't like it. I'm going to have a detective look into the matter tomorrow. What did they want of Hubert? What were they going to do to him?"

No one offered a suggestion. Even Hubert was silent, contemplating his possible fate with certain respectful awe. During breaks in his narration the talk had turned to such collateral matters as murders and ghosts, and all the boys had talked themselves into a state of considerable panic. In fact each had come to believe, in varying degrees, that a band of kidnappers infested the vicinity.

"I don't like it," repeated Mr. Blair. "In fact I'm going to see all of you boys to your own homes."

Basil greeted this offer with relief. The evening had been a mad success, but furies once aroused sometimes get out of hand. He did not feel like walking the streets alone tonight.

In the hall, Imogene, taking advantage of her mother's somewhat fatigued farewell to Mr. Blair, beckoned Hubert back into the library. Instantly attuned to adversity, Basil listened. There was a whisper and a short scuffle, followed by an indiscreet but unmistakable sound. With the corners of his mouth falling, Basil went out the door. He had stacked the cards dexterously, but Life had played a trump from its sleeve at the last.

A moment later they all started off, clinging together in a group, turning corners with cautious glances behind and ahead. What Basil and Riply and Bill expected to see as they peered warily into the sinister mouths of alleys and around great dark trees and behind concealing fences they did not know—in all probability the same hairy and grotesque desperadoes who had lain in wait for Hubert Blair that night.

VI

A week later Basil and Riply heard that Hubert and his mother had gone to the seashore for the summer. Basil was sorry. He had wanted to learn from Hubert some of the graceful mannerisms that his contemporaries found so dazzling and that might come in so handy next fall when he went away to school. In tribute to Hubert's passing, he practised leaning against a tree and missing it and rolling a skate down his arm, and he wore his cap in Hubert's manner, set jauntily on the side of his head.

This was only for a while. He perceived eventually that though boys and girls would always listen to him while he talked, their mouths literally moving in response to his, they would never look at him as they had looked at Hubert. So he abandoned the loud chuckle that so annoyed his mother and set his cap straight upon his head once more.

But the change in him went deeper than that. He was no longer sure that he wanted to be a gentleman burglar, though he still read of their exploits with breathless admiration. Outside of Hubert's gate, he had for a moment felt morally alone; and he realized that whatever combinations he might make of the materials of life would have to be safely within the law. And after another week he found that he no longer grieved over losing Imogene. Meeting her, he saw

only the familiar little girl he had always known. The ecstatic
moment of that afternoon had been a premature birth, an emotion
left over from an already fleeting spring.

He did not know that he had frightened Mrs. Blair out of town
and that because of him a special policeman walked a placid beat
for many a night. All he knew was that the vague and restless yearn-
ings of three long spring months were somehow satisfied. They
reached combustion in that last week—flared up, exploded and
burned out. His face was turned without regret toward the boundless
possibilities of summer.

THE FRESHEST BOY

I

It was a hidden Broadway resturant in the dead of the night, and a brilliant and mysterious group of society people, diplomats and members of the underworld were there. A few minutes ago the sparkling wine had been flowing and a girl had been dancing gaily upon a table, but now the whole crowd were hushed and breathless. All eyes were fixed upon the masked but well-groomed man in the dress suit and opera hat who stood nonchalantly in the door.

"Don't move, please," he said, in a well-bred, cultivated voice that had, nevertheless, a ring of steel in it. "This thing in my hand might—go off."

His glance roved from table to table—fell upon the malignant man higher up with his pale saturnine face, upon Heatherly, the suave secret agent from a foreign power, then rested a little longer, a little more softly perhaps, upon the table where the girl with dark hair and dark tragic eyes sat alone.

"Now that my purpose is accomplished, it might interest you to know who I am." There was a gleam of expectation in every eye. The breast of the dark-eyed girl heaved faintly and a tiny burst of subtle French perfume rose into the air. "I am none other than that elusive gentleman, Basil Lee, better known as the Shadow."

Taking off his well-fitting opera hat, he bowed ironically from the waist. Then, like a flash, he turned and was gone into the night.

"You get up to New York only once a month," Lewis Crum was saying, "and then you have to take a master along."

Slowly, Basil Lee's glazed eyes returned from the barns and billboards of the Indiana countryside to the interior of the Broadway Limited. The hypnosis of the swift telegraph poles faded and Lewis Crum's stolid face took shape against the white slip-cover of the opposite bench.

"I'd just duck the master when I got to New York," said Basil.

"Yes, you would!"

"I bet I would."

"You try it and you'll see."

"What do you mean saying I'll see, all the time, Lewis? What'll I see?"

His very bright dark-blue eyes were at this moment fixed upon his companion with boredom and impatience. The two had nothing in common except their age, which was fifteen, and the lifelong friendship of their fathers—which is less than nothing. Also they were bound from the same Middle-Western city for Basil's first and Lewis's second year at the same Eastern school.

But, contrary to all the best tradition, Lewis the veteran was miserable and Basil the neophyte was happy. Lewis hated school. He had grown entirely dependent on the stimulus of a hearty vital mother, and as he felt her slipping farther and farther away from him, he plunged deeper into misery and homesickness. Basil, on the other hand, had lived with such intensity on so many stories of boarding-school life that, far from being homesick, he had a glad feeling of recognition and familiarity. Indeed, it was with some sense of doing the appropriate thing, having the traditional rough-house, that he had thrown Lewis' comb off the train at Milwaukee last night for no reason at all.

To Lewis, Basil's ignorant enthusiasm was distasteful—his instinctive attempt to dampen it had contributed to the mutual irritation.

"I'll tell you what you'll see," he said ominously. "They'll catch you smoking and put you on bounds."

"No, they won't, because I won't be smoking. I'll be in training for football."

"Football! Yeah! Football!"

"Honestly, Lewis, you don't like anything, do you?"

"I don't like football. I don't like to go out and get a crack in the eye." Lewis spoke aggressively, for his mother had canonized all his timidities as common sense. Basil's answer, made with what he considered kindly intent, was the sort of remark that creates lifelong enmities.

"You'd probably be a lot more popular in school if you played football," he suggested patronizingly.

Lewis did not consider himself unpopular. He did not think of it in that way at all. He was astounded.

"You wait!" he cried furiously. "They'll take all that freshness out of you."

"Clam yourself." said Basil, coolly plucking at the creases of his first long trousers. "Just clam yourself."

"I guess everybody knows you were the freshest boy at Country Day!"

"Clam yourself," repeated Basil, but with less assurance. "Kindly clam yourself."

"I guess I know what they had in the school paper about you——" Basil's own coolness was no longer perceptible.

"If you don't clam yourself," he said darkly, "I'm going to throw your brushes off the train too."

The enormity of this threat was effective. Lewis sank back in his seat, snorting and muttering, but undoubtedly calmer. His reference had been to one of the most shameful passages in his companion's life. In a periodical issued by the boys of Basil's late school there had appeared, under the heading Personals:

If someone will please poison young Basil, or find some other means to stop his mouth, the school at large and myself will be much obliged.

The two boys sat there fuming wordlessly at each other. Then, resolutely, Basil tried to reinter this unfortunate souvenir of the past. All that was behind him now. Perhaps he had been a little fresh, but he was making a new start. After a moment, the memory passed and with it the train and Lewis' dismal presence—the breath of the East came sweeping over him again with a vast nostalgia. A voice called him out of the fabled world; a man stood beside him with a hand on his sweater-clad shoulder.

"Lee!"

"Yes, sir."

"It all depends on you now. Understand?"

"Yes, sir."

"All right," the coach said, "go in and win."

Basil tore the sweater from his stripling form and dashed out on the field. There were two minutes to play and the score was 3 to 0 for the enemy, but at the sight of young Lee, kept out of the game all year by a malicious plan of Dan Haskins, the school bully, and Weasel Weems, his toady, a thrill of hope went over the St. Regis stand.

"33-12-16-22!" barked Midget Brown, the diminutive little quarter-back.

"Oh, gosh!" Basil spoke aloud, forgetting the late unpleasantness. "I wish we'd get there before tomorrow."

II

St. Regis School, Eastchester,
November 18, 19——

Dear Mother: There is not much to say today, but I thought I would write you about my allowance. All the boys have a bigger allowance than me, because there are a lot of little things I have to get, such as shoe laces etc. School is still very nice and am having a fine time, but football is over and there is not much to do. I am going to New York this week to see a show. I do not know yet what it will be, but probably the Quacker Girl or little boy Blue as they are both very good. Dr. Bacon is very nice and there is a good phycission in the village. No more now as I have to study Algebra.

Your Affectionate Son,
Basil D. Lee.

As he put the letter in its envelope, a wizened little boy came into the deserted study hall where he sat and stood staring at him.

"Hello," said Basil, frowning.

"I been looking for you," said the little boy, slowly and judicially. "I looked all over—up in your room and out in the gym, and they said you probably might of sneaked off in here."

"What do you want?" Basil demanded.

"Hold your horses, Bossy."

Basil jumped to his feet. The little boy retreated a step.

"Go on, hit me!" he chirped nervously. "Go on, hit me, cause I'm just half your size—Bossy."

Basil winced. "You call me that again and I'll spank you."

"No, you won't spank me. Brick Wales said if you ever touched any of us——"

"But I never did touch any of you."

"Didn't you chase a lot of us one day and didn't Brick Wales——"

"Oh, what do you want?" Basil cried in desperation.

"Doctor Bacon wants you. They sent me after you and somebody said maybe you sneaked in here."

Basil dropped his letter in his pocket and walked out—the little boy and his invective following him through the door. He traversed a long corridor, muggy with that odor best described as the smell of stale caramels that is so peculiar to boys' schools, ascended a stairs and knocked at an unexceptional but formidable door.

Doctor Bacon was at his desk. He was a handsome, red-headed Episcopal clergyman of fifty whose original real interst in boys was now tempered by the flustered cynicism which is the fate of all headmasters and settles on them like green mould. There were certain preliminaries before Basil was asked to sit down—gold-rimmed glasses had to be hoisted up from nowhere by a black cord and fixed on Basil to be sure that he was not an impostor; great masses of paper on the desk had to be shuffled through, not in search of anything but as a man nervously shuffles a pack of cards.

"I had a letter from your mother this morning—ah—Basil." The use of his first name had come to startle Basil. No one else in school had yet called him anything but Bossy or Lee. "She feels that your marks have been poor. I believe you have been sent here at a certain amount of—ah—sacrifice and she expects——"

Basil's spirit writhed with shame, not at his poor marks but that his financial inadequacy should be so bluntly stated. He knew that he was one of the poorest boys in a rich boys' school.

Perhaps some dormant sensibility in Doctor Bacon became aware of his discomfort; he shuffled through the papers once more and began on a new note.

"However, that was not what I sent for you about this afternoon. You applied last week for permission to go to New York on Saturday, to a matinée. Mr. Davis tells me that for almost the first time since school opened you will be off bounds tomorrow."

"Yes, sir."

"That is not a good record. However, I would allow you to go to New York if it could be arranged. Unfortunately, no masters are available this Saturday."

Basil's mouth dropped ajar. "Why, I—why, Doctor Bacon, I know two parties that are going. Couldn't I go with one of them?"

Doctor Bacon ran through all his papers very quickly. "Unfortunately, one is composed of slightly older boys and the other group made arrangements some weeks ago."

"How about the party that's going to the Quaker Girl with Mr. Dunn?"

"It's that party I speak of. They feel that their arrangements are complete and they have purchased seats together."

Suddenly Basil understood. At the look in his eye Doctor Bacon went on hurriedly:

"There's perhaps one thing I can do. Of course there must be several boys in the party so that the expenses of the master can be divided up among all. If you can find two other boys who would like to make up a party, and let me have their names by five o'clock, I'll send Mr. Rooney with you."

"Thank you," Basil said.

Doctor Bacon hesitated. Beneath the cynical incrustations of many years an instinct stirred to look into the unusual case of this boy and find out what made him the most detested boy in school. Among boys and masters there seemed to exist an extraordinary hostility toward him, and though Doctor Bacon had dealt with many sorts of schoolboy crimes, he had neither by himself nor with the aid of trusted sixth-formers been able to lay his hands on its underlying cause. It was probably no single thing, but a combination of things; it was most probably one of those intangible questions of personality. Yet he remembered that when he first saw Basil he had considered him unusually prepossessing.

He sighed. Sometimes these things worked themselves out. He

wasn't one to rush in clumsily. "Let us have a better report to send home next month, Basil."

"Yes, sir."

Basil ran quickly downstairs to the recreation room. It was Wednesday and most of the boys had already gone into the village of Eastchester, whither Basil, who was still on bounds, was forbidden to follow. When he looked at those still scattered about the pool tables and piano, he saw that it was going to be difficult to get anyone to go with him at all. For Basil was quite conscious that he was the most unpopular boy at school.

It had begun almost immediately. One day, less than a fortnight after he came, a crowd of the smaller boys, perhaps urged on to it, gathered suddenly around him and began calling him Bossy. Within the next week he had two fights, and both times the crowd was vehemently and eloquently with the other boy. Soon after, when he was merely shoving indiscriminatively, like every one else, to get into the dining room, Carver, the captain of the football team, turned about and, seizing him by the back of the neck, held him and dressed him down savagely. He joined a group innocently at the piano and was told, "Go on away. We don't want you around."

After a month he began to realize the full extent of his unpopularity. It shocked him. One day after a particularly bitter humiliation he went up to his room and cried. He tried to keep out of the way for a while, but it didn't help. He was accused of sneaking off here and there, as if bent on a series of nefarious errands. Puzzled and wretched, he looked at his face in the glass, trying to discover there the secret of their dislike—in the expression of his eyes, his smile.

He saw now that in certain ways he had erred at the outset—he had boasted, he had been considered yellow at football, he had pointed out people's mistakes to them, he had shown off his rather extraordinary fund of general information in class. But he had tried to do better and couldn't understand his failure to atone. It must be too late. He was queered forever.

He had, indeed, become the scapegoat, the immediate villain, the sponge which absorbed all malice and irritability abroad—just as the most frightened person in a party seems to absorb all the others' fear, seems to be afraid for them all. His situation was not helped by the fact, obvious to all, that the supreme self-confidence with which he had come to St. Regis in September was thoroughly broken. Boys taunted him with impunity who would not have dared raise their voices to him several months before.

This trip to New York had come to mean everything to him—surcease from the misery of his daily life as well as a glimpse into the long-awaited heaven of romance. Its postponement for week after week due to his sins—he was constantly caught reading after lights, for example, driven by his wretchedness into such vicarious escapes from reality—had deepened his longing until it was a burning hunger. It was unbearable that he should not go, and he told over the short list of those whom he might get to accompany him. The possibilities were Fat Gaspar, Treadway and Bugs Brown. A quick journey to their rooms showed that they had all availed themselves of the Wednesday permission to go into Eastchester for the afternoon.

Basil did not hesitate. He had until five o'clock and his only chance was to go after them. It was not the first time he had broken bounds, though the last attempt had ended in disaster and an extension of his confinement. In his room, he put on a heavy sweater—an overcoat was a betrayal of intent—replaced his jacket over it and hid a cap in his back pocket. Then he went downstairs and with an elaborately careless whistle struck out across the lawn for the gymnasium. Once there, he stood for a while as if looking in the windows, first the one close to the walk, then one near the corner of the building. From here he moved quickly, but not too quickly, into a grove of lilacs. Then he dashed around the corner, down a long stretch of lawn that was blind from all windows and, parting the strands of a wire fence, crawled through and stood upon the grounds of a neighboring estate. For the moment he was free. He put on his cap against the chilly November wind, and set out along the half-mile road to town.

Eastchester was a suburban farming community, with a small shoe factory. The institutions which pandered to the factory workers were the ones patronized by the boys—a movie house, a quick-lunch wagon on wheels known as the Dog and the Bostonian Candy Kitchen. Basil tried the Dog first and happened immediately upon a prospect.

This was Bugs Brown, a hysterical boy, subject to fits and strenuously avoided. Years later he became a brilliant lawyer, but at that time he was considered by the boys of St. Regis to be a typical lunatic because of his peculiar series of sounds with which he assuaged his nervousness all day long.

He consorted with boys younger than himself, who were without the prejudices of their elders, and was in the company of several when Basil came in.

"Who-ee!" he cried. "Ee-ee-ee!" He put his hand over his mouth and bounced it quickly, making a wah-wah-wah sound. "It's Bossy Lee! It's Bossy Lee! It's Boss-Boss-Boss-Bossy Lee!"

"Wait a minute, Bugs," said Basil anxiously, half afraid that Bugs would go finally crazy before he could persuade him to come to town. "Say, Bugs, listen. Don't, Bugs—wait a minute. Can you come up to New York Saturday afternoon?"

"Whe-ee-ee!" cried Bugs to Basil's distress. "Whee-ee-ee!"

"Honestly, Bugs, tell me, can you? We could go up together if you could go."

"I've got to see a doctor," said Bugs, suddenly calm. "He wants to see how crazy I am."

"Can't you have him see about it some other day?" said Basil without humor.

"Whee-ee-ee!" cried Bugs.

"All right then," said Basil hastily. "Have you seen Fat Gaspar in town?"

Bugs was lost in a shrill noise, but someone had seen Fat; Basil was directed to the Bostonian Candy Kitchen.

This was a gaudy paradise of cheap sugar. Its odor, heavy and sickly and calculated to bring out a sticky sweat upon an adult's palms, hung suffocatingly over the whole vicinity and met one like a strong moral dissuasion at the door. Inside, beneath a pattern of flies, material as black point lace, a line of boys sat eating heavy dinners of banana splits, maple nut and chocolate marshmallow nut sundaes. Basil found Fat Gaspar at a table on the side.

Fat Gaspar was at once Basil's most unlikely and most ambitious quest. He was considered a nice fellow—in fact he was so pleasant that he had been courteous to Basil and had spoken to him politely all fall. Basil realized that he was like that to everyone, yet it was just possible that Fat liked him, as people used to in the past, and he was driven desperately to take a chance. But it was undoubtedly a presumption, and as he approached the table and saw the stiffened faces which the other two boys turned toward him, Basil's hope diminished.

"Say, Fat——" he said, and hesitated. Then he burst forth suddenly. "I'm on bounds, but I ran off because I had to see you. Doctor Bacon told me I could go to New York Saturday if I could get two other boys to go. I asked Bugs Brown and he couldn't go, and I thought I'd ask you."

He broke off, furiously embarrassed, and waited. Suddenly the two boys with Fat burst into a shout of laughter.

"Bugs wasn't crazy enough!"

Fat Gaspar hesitated. He couldn't go to New York Saturday and ordinarily he would have refused without offending. He had nothing against Basil; nor, indeed, against anybody; but boys have only a certain resistance to public opinion and he was influenced by the contemptuous laugher of the others.

"I don't want to go," he said indifferently. "Why do you want to ask *me?*"

Then, half in shame, he gave a deprecatory little laugh and bent over his ice cream.

"I just thought I'd ask you," said Basil.

Turning quickly away, he went to the counter and in a hollow and unfamiliar voice ordered a strawberry sundae. He ate it mechanically, hearing occasional whispers and snickers from the table behind. Still in a daze, he started to walk out without paying his check, but the clerk called him back and he was conscious of more derisive laughter.

For a moment he hesitated whether to go back to the table and hit one of those boys in the face, but he saw nothing to be gained. They would say the truth—that he had done it because he couldn't get anybody to go to New York. Clenching his fists with impotent rage, he walked from the store.

He came immediately upon his third prospect, Treadway. Treadway had entered St. Regis late in the year and had been put in to room with Basil the week before. The fact that Treadway hadn't witnessed his humiliations of the autumn encouraged Basil to behave naturally toward him, and their relations had been, if not intimate, at least tranquil.

"Hey, Treadway," he cried, still excited from the affair in the

Bostonian, "can you come up to New York to a show Saturday afternoon?"

He stopped, realizing that Treadway was in the company of Brick Wales, a boy he had had a fight with and one of his bitterest enemies. Looking from one to the other, Basil saw a look of impatience in Treadway's face and a far-away expression in Brick Wales', and he realized what must have been happening. Treadway, making his way into the life of the school, had just been enlightened as to the status of his roommate. Like Fat Gaspar, rather than acknowledge himself eligible to such an intimate request, he preferred to cut their friendly relations short.

"Not on your life," he said briefly. "So long." The two walked past him into the candy kitchen.

Had these slights, so much the bitterer for their lack of passion, been visited upon Basil in September, they would have been unbearable. But since then he had developed a shell of hardness which, while it did not add to his attractiveness, spared him certain delicacies of torture. In misery enough, and despair and self-pity, he went the other way along the street for a little distance until he could control the violent contortions of his face. Then, taking a roundabout route, he started back to school.

He reached the adjoining estate, intending to go back the way he had come. Half-way through a hedge, he heard foot-steps approaching along the sidewalk and stood motionless, fearing the proximity of masters. Their voices grew nearer and louder; before he knew it he was listening with horrified fascination:

"—so, after he tried Bugs Brown, the poor nut asked Fat Gaspar to go with him and Fat said, 'What do you ask me for?' It serves him right if he couldn't get anybody at all."

It was the dismal but triumphant voice of Lewis Crum.

III

Up in his room, Basil found a package lying on his bed. He knew its contents and for a long time he had been eagerly expecting it, but such was his depression that he opened it listlessly. It was a series of eight color reproductions of Harrison Fisher girls "on glossy paper, without printing or advertising matter and suitable for framing."

The pictures were named Dora, Marguerite, Babette, Lucille, Gretchen, Rose, Katherine and Mina. Two of them—Marguerite and Rose—Basil looked at, slowly tore up and dropped in the waste-basket, as one who disposes of the inferior pups from a litter. The other six he pinned at intervals around the room. Then he lay down on his bed and regarded them.

Dora, Lucille and Katherine were blond; Gretchen was medium; Babette and Mina were dark. After a few minutes, he found that he was looking oftenest at Dora and Babette and, to a lesser extent, at Gretchen, though the latter's Dutch cap seemed unromantic and precluded the element of mystery. Babette, a dark little violet-eyed beauty in a tight-fitting hat, attracted him most; his eyes came to rest on her at last.

"Babette," he whispered to himself—"beautiful Babette."

The sound of the word, so melancholy and suggestive, like "Velia" or "I'm going to Maxim's" on the phonograph, softened him and, turning over on his face, he sobbed into the pillow. He took hold of the bed rails over his head and, sobbing and straining, began to talk to himself brokenly—how he hated them and whom he hated—he listed a dozen—and what he would do to them when he was great and powerful. In previous moments like these he had always re-warded Fat Gaspar for his kindness, but now he was like the rest. Basil set upon him, pummelling him unmercifully, or laughed sneer-ingly when he passed him blind and begging on the street.

He controlled himself as he heard Treadway come in, but did not move or speak. He listened as the other moved about the room, and after a while became conscious that there was an unusual opening of closets and bureau drawers. Basil turned over, his arm concealing his tear-stained face. Treadway had an armful of shirts in his hand.

"What are you doing?" Basil demanded.

His roommate looked at him stonily. "I'm moving in with Wales," he said.

"Oh!"

Treadway went on with his packing. He carried out a suitcase full, then another, took down some pennants and dragged his trunk into the hall. Basil watched him bundle his toilet things into a towel and take one last survey about the room's new barrenness to see if there was anything forgotten.

"Good-by," he said to Basil, without a ripple of expression on his face.

"Good-by."

Treadway went out. Basil turned over once more and choked into the pillow.

"Oh, poor Babette!" he cried huskily. "Poor little Babette! Poor little Babette!"

Babette, svelte and piquant, looked down at him coquettishly from the wall.

IV

Doctor Bacon, sensing Basil's predicament and perhaps the extremity of his misery, arranged it that he should go into New York, after all. He went in the company of Mr. Rooney, the football coach and history teacher. At twenty Mr. Rooney had hesitated for some time between joining the police force and having his way paid through a small New England college; in fact he was a hard specimen and Doctor Bacon was planning to get rid of him at Christmas. Mr. Rooney's contempt for Basil was founded on the latter's ambiguous and unreliable conduct on the football field during the past season —he had consented to take him to New York for reasons of his own.

Basil sat meekly beside him on the train, glancing past Mr. Rooney's bulky body at the Sound and the fallow fields of Westchester County. Mr. Rooney finished his newspaper, folded it up and sank into a moody silence. He had eaten a large breakfast and the exigencies of time had not allowed him to work it off with exercise. He remembered that Basil was a fresh boy, and it was time he did something fresh and could be called to account. This reproachless silence annoyed him.

"Lee," he said suddenly, with a thinly assumed air of friendly interest, "why don't you get wise to yourself?"

"What, sir?" Basil was startled from his excited trance of this morning.

"I said why don't you get wise to yourself?" said Mr. Rooney in a somewhat violent tone. "Do you want to be the butt of the school all your time here?"

"No, I don't," Basil was chilled. Couldn't all this be left behind for just one day?

"You oughtn't to get so fresh all the time. A couple of times in history class I could just about have broken your neck." Basil could think of no appropriate answer. "Then out playing football," continued Mr. Rooney "—you didn't have any nerve. You could play better than a lot of 'em when you wanted, like that day against the Pomfret seconds, but you lost your nerve."

"I shouldn't have tried for the second team," said Basil. "I was too light. I should have stayed on the third."

"You were yellow, that was all the trouble. You ought to get wise to yourself. In class, you're always thinking of something else. If you don't study, you'll never get to college."

"I'm the youngest boy in the fifth form," Basil said rashly.

"You think you're pretty bright, don't you?" He eyed Basil ferociously. Then something seemed to occur to him that changed his attitude and they rode for a while in silence. When the train began to run through the thickly clustered communities near New York, he spoke again in a milder voice and with an air of having considered the matter for a long time:

"Lee, I'm going to trust you."

"Yes, sir."

"You go and get some lunch and then go on to your show. I've got some business of my own I got to attend to, and when I've finished I'll try to get to the show. If I can't, I'll anyhow meet you outside."

Basil's heart leaped up. "Yes, sir."

"I don't want you to open your mouth about this at school—I mean, about me doing some business of my own."

"No, sir."

"We'll see if you can keep your mouth shut for once," he said, making it fun. Then he added, on a note of moral sternness. "And no drinks, you understand that?"

"Oh, no, sir!" The idea shocked Basil. He had never tasted a drink, nor even contemplated the possibility, save the intangible and nonalcoholic champagne of his café dreams.

On the advice of Mr. Rooney he went for luncheon to the Manhattan Hotel, near the station, where he ordered a club sandwich, French fried potatoes and a chocolate parfait. Out of the corner of his eye he watched the nonchalant, debonair, blasé New Yorkers at neighboring tables, investing them with a romance by which these possible fellow citizens of his from the Middle West lost nothing. School had fallen from him like a burden; it was no more than an unheeded clamor, faint and far away. He even delayed opening the letter from the morning's mail which he found in his pocket, because it was addressed to him at school.

He wanted another chocolate parfait, but being reluctant to bother the busy waiter any more, he opened the letter and spread it before him instead. It was from his mother:

DEAR BASIL: This is written in great haste, as I didn't want to frighten you by telegraphing. Grandfather is going abroad to take the waters and he wants you and me to come too. The idea is that you'll go to school at Grenoble or Montreux for the rest of the year and learn the languages and we'll be close by. That is, if you want to. I know how you like St. Regis and playing football and baseball, and of course there would be none of that; but on the other hand, it would be a nice change, even if it postponed your entering Yale by an extra year. So, as usual, I want you to do just as you like. We will be leaving home almost as soon as you get this and will come to the Waldorf in New York, where you can come in and see us for a few days, even if you decide to stay. Think it over, dear.

With love to my dearest boy,

MOTHER.

Basil got up from his chair with a dim idea of walking over to the Waldorf and having himself locked up safely until his mother came. Then, impelled to some gesture, he raised his voice and in one of his first basso notes called boomingly and without reticence for the waiter. No more St. Regis! No more St. Regis! He was almost strangling with happiness.

"Oh, gosh!" he cried to himself. "Oh, golly! Oh, gosh! Oh, gosh!" No more Doctor Bacon and Mr. Rooney and Brick Wales and Fat

Gaspar. No more Bugs Brown and on bounds and being called Bossy. He need no longer hate them, for they were impotent shadows in the stationary world that he was sliding away from, sliding past, waving his hand. "Good-by!" He pitied them. "Good-by!"

It required the din of Forty-second Street to sober his maudlin joy. With his hand on his purse to guard against the omnipresent pickpocket, he moved cautiously toward Broadway. What a day! He would tell Mr. Rooney—Why, he needn't ever go back! Or perhaps it would be better to go back and let them know what he was going to do, while they went on and on in the dismal, dreary round of school.

He found the theatre and entered the lobby with its powdery feminine atmosphere of a matinée. As he took out his ticket, his gaze was caught and held by a sculptured profile a few feet away. It was that of a well-built blond young man of about twenty with a strong chin and direct gray eyes. Basil's brain spun wildly for a moment and then came to rest upon a name—more than a name— upon a legend, a sign in the sky. What a day! He had never seen the young man before, but from a thousand pictures he knew beyond the possibility of a doubt that it was Ted Fay, the Yale football captain, who had almost single-handed beaten Harvard and Princeton last fall. Basil felt a sort of exquisite pain. The profile turned away; the crowd revolved; the hero disappeared. But Basil would know all through the next hours that Ted Fay was here too.

In the rustling, whispering, sweet-smelling darkness of the theatre he read the program. It was the show of all shows that he wanted to see, and until the curtain actually rose the program itself had a curious sacredness—a prototype of the thing itself. But when the curtain rose it became waste paper to be dropped carelessly to the floor.

Act I. *The Village Green of a Small Town near New York.*

It was too bright and binding to comprehend all at once, and it went so fast that from the very first Basil felt he had missed things; he would make his mother take him again when she came—next week—tomorrow.

An hour passed. It was very sad at this point—a sort of gay sadness, but sad. The girl—the man. What kept them apart even now? Oh, those tragic errors and misconceptions. So sad. Couldn't they look into each other's eyes and *see?*

In a blaze of light and sound, of resolution, anticipation and imminent trouble, the act was over.

He went out. He looked for Ted Fay and thought he saw him leaning rather moodily on the plush wall at the rear of the theatre, but he could not be sure. He bought cigarettes and lit one, but fancying at the first puff that he heard a blare of music he rushed back inside.

Act II. *The Foyer of the Hotel Astor.*

Yes, she was, indeed, like that song—a Beautiful Rose of the Night. The waltz buoyed her up, brought her with it to a point of aching beauty and then let her slide back to life across its last bars as a leaf slants to earth across the air. The high life of New York! Who could blame her if she was carried away by the glitter of it all, vanishing into the bright morning of the amber window borders, or into distant and entrancing music as the door opened and closed that led to the ballroon? The toast of the shining town.

Half an hour passed. Her true love brought her roses like herself and she threw them scornfully at his feet. She laughed and turned to the other, and danced—danced madly, wildly. Wait! That delicate treble among the thin horns, the low curving note from the great strings. There it was again, poignant and aching, sweeping like a great gust of emotion across the stage, catching her again like a leaf helpless in the wind:

> Rose—Rose—Rose of the night,
> When the spring moon is bright you'll be fair——

A few minutes later, feeling oddly shaken and exalted, Basil drifted outside with the crowd. The first thing upon which his eyes fell was the almost forgotten and now curiously metamorphosed spectre of Mr. Rooney.

Mr. Rooney had, in fact, gone a little to pieces. He was, to begin with, wearing a different and much smaller hat than when he left Basil at noon. Secondly, his face had lost its somewhat gross aspect and turned a pure and even delicate white, and he was wearing his necktie and even portions of his shirt on the outside of his unaccountably wringing-wet overcoat. How, in the short space of four hours, Mr. Rooney had got himself in such shape is explicable only by the pressure of confinement in a boys' school upon a fiery outdoor spirit. Mr. Rooney was born to toil under the clear light of heaven and, perhaps half consciously, he was headed toward his inevitable destiny.

"Lee," he said dimly, "you ought get wise to y'self. I'm going to put you wise y'self."

To avoid the ominous possibility of being put wise to himself in the lobby, Basil uneasily changed the subject.

"Aren't you coming to the show?" he asked, flattering Mr. Rooney by implying that he was in any condition to come to the show. "It's a wonderful show."

Mr. Rooney took off his hat, displaying wringing-wet matted hair. A picture of reality momentarily struggled for development in the back of his brain.

"We got to get back to school," he said in a sombre and unconvinced voice.

"But there's another act," protested Basil in horror. "I've got to stay for the last act."

Swaying, Mr. Rooney looked at Basil, dimly realizing that he had put himself in the hollow of this boy's hand.

"All righ'," he admitted. "I'm going to get somethin' to eat. I'll wait for you next door."

He turned abruptly, reeled a dozen steps and curved dizzily into a bar adjoining the theatre. Considerably shaken, Basil went back inside.

ACT III. *The Roof Garden of Mr. Van Astor's House. Night.*

Half an hour passed. Everything was going to be all right, after all. The comedian was at his best now, with the glad appropriateness

of laughter after tears, and there was a promise of felicity in the
bright tropical sky. One lovely plaintive duet, and then abruptly
the long moment of incomparable beauty was over.

Basil went into the lobby and stood in thought while the crowd
passed out. His mother's letter and the show had cleared his mind
of bitterness and vindictiveness—he was his old self and he wanted
to do the right thing. He wondered if it was the right thing to get
Mr. Rooney back to school. He walked toward the saloon, slowed up
as he came to it and, gingerly opening the swinging door, took a
quick peer inside. He saw only that Mr. Rooney was not one of
those drinking at the bar. He walked down the street a little way,
came back and tried again. It was as if he thought the doors were
teeth to bite him, for he had the old-fashioned Middle-Western boy's
horror of the saloon. The third time he was successful. Mr. Rooney
was sound asleep at a table in the back of the room.

Outside again Basil walked up and down, considering. He would
give Mr. Rooney half an hour. If, at the end of that time, he had
not come out, he would go back to school. After all, Mr. Rooney had
laid for him ever since football season—Basil was simply washing
his hands of the whole affair, as in a day or so he would wash his
hands of school.

He had made several turns up and down, when, glancing up an
alley that ran beside the theatre his eye was caught by the sign,
Stage Entrance. He could watch the actors come forth.

He waited. Women streamed by him, but those were the days
before Glorification and he took these drab people for wardrobe
women or something. Then suddenly a girl came out and with her
a man, and Basil turned and ran a few steps up the street as if afraid
they would recognize him—and ran back, breathing as if with a
heart attack—for the girl, a radiant little beauty of nineteen, was
Her and the young man by her side was Ted Fay.

Arm in arm, they walked past him, and irresistibly Basil followed.
As they walked, she leaned toward Ted Fay in a way that gave
them a fascinating air of intimacy. They crossed Broadway and
turned into the Knickerbocker Hotel, and twenty feet behind them
Basil followed, in time to see them go into a long room set for afternoon tea. They sat at a table for two, spoke vaguely to a waiter, and

then, alone at last, bent eagerly toward each other. Basil saw that Ted Fay was holding her gloved hand.

The tea room was separated only by a hedge of potted firs from the main corridor. Basil went along this to a lounge which was almost up against their table and sat down.

Her voice was low and faltering, less certain than it had been in the play, and very sad: "Of course I do, Ted." For a long time, as their conversation continued, she repeated "Of course I do" or "But I do, Ted." Ted Fay's remarks were too low for Basil to hear.

"—says next month, and he won't be put off any more. . . . I do in a way, Ted. It's hard to explain, but he's done everything for mother and me. . . . There's no use kidding myself. It was a fool-proof part and any girl he gave it to was made right then and there. . . . He's been awfully thoughtful. He's done everything for me."

Basil's ears were sharpened by the intensity of his emotion; now he could hear Ted Fay's voice too:

"And you say you love me."

"But don't you see I promised to marry him more than a year ago."

"Tell him the truth—that you love me. Ask him to let you off."

"This isn't musical comedy, Ted."

"That was a mean one," he said bitterly.

"I'm sorry, dear, Ted darling, but you're driving me crazy going on this way. You're making it so hard for me."

"I'm going to leave New Haven, anyhow."

"No, you're not. You're going to stay and play baseball this spring. Why, you're an ideal to all those boys! Why, if you——"

He laughed shortly. "You're a fine one to talk about ideals."

"Why not? I'm living up to my responsibility to Beltzman; you've got to make up your mind just like I have—that we can't have each other."

"Jerry! Think what you're doing! All my life, whenever I hear that waltz——"

Basil got to his feet and hurried down the corridor, through the lobby and out of the hotel. He was in a state of wild emotional confusion. He did not understand all he had heard, but from his clandestine glimpse into the privacy of these two, with all the world that his short experience could conceive of at their feet, he had gathered that life for everybody was a struggle, sometimes magnificent from a distance, but always difficult and surprisingly simple and a little sad.

They would go on. Ted Fay would go back to Yale, put her picture in his bureau drawer and knock out home runs with the bases full this spring—at 8:30 the curtain would go up and she would miss something warm and young out of her life, something she had had this afternoon.

It was dark outside and Broadway was a blazing forest fire as Basil walked slowly along toward the point of brightest light. He looked up at the great intersecting planes of radiance with a vague sense of approval and possession. He would see it a lot now, lay his restless heart upon this greater restlessness of a nation—he would come whenever he could get off from school.

But that was all changed—he was going to Europe. Suddenly Basil realized that he wasn't going to Europe. He could not forego the molding of his own destiny just to alleviate a few months of pain. The conquest of the successive worlds of school, college and New York—why, that was his true dream that he had carried from boyhood into adolescence, and because of the jeers of a few boys he had been about to abandon it and run ignominiously up a back alley! He shivered violently, like a dog coming out of the water, and simultaneously he was reminded of Mr. Rooney.

A few minutes later he walked into the bar, past the quizzical eyes of the bartender and up to the table where Mr. Rooney still sat asleep. Basil shook him gently, then firmly. Mr. Rooney stirred and perceived Basil.

"G'wise to yourself," he muttered drowsily. "G'wise to yourself an' let me alone."

"I am wise to myself," said Basil. "Honest, I am wise to myself, Mr. Rooney. You got to come with me into the washroom and get cleaned up, and then you can sleep on the train again, Mr. Rooney. Come on, Mr. Rooney, please——"

V

It was a long hard time. Basil got on bounds again in December and wasn't free again until March. An indulgent mother had given him no habits of work and this was almost beyond the power of anything but life itself to remedy, but he made numberless new starts and failed and tried again.

He made friends with a new boy named Maplewood after Christmas, but they had a silly quarrel; and through the winter term, when a boy's school is shut in with itself and only partly assuaged from its natural savagery by indoor sports, Basil was snubbed and slighted a good deal for his real and imaginary sins, and he was much alone. But on the other hand, there was Ted Fay, and Rose of the Night on the phonograph—"All my life whenever I hear that waltz"—and the remembered lights of New York, and the thought of what he was going to do in football next autumn and the glamorous mirage of Yale and the hope of spring in the air.

Fat Gaspar and a few others were nice to him now. Once when he and Fat walked home together by accident from downtown they had a long talk about actresses—a talk that Basil was wise enough not to presume upon afterward. The smaller boys suddenly decided that they approved of him, and a master who had hitherto disliked him put his hand on his shoulder walking to a class one day. They would all forget eventually—maybe during the summer. There would be new fresh boys in September; he would have a clean start next year.

One afternoon in February, playing basketball, a great thing happened. He and Brick Wales were at forward on the second team and in the fury of the scrimmage the gymnasium echoed with sharp slapping contacts and shrill cries.

"Here yar!"

"Bill! Bill!"

Basil had dribbled the ball down the court and Brick Wales, free, was crying for it.

"Here yar! Lee! Hey! Lee-y!"

Lee-y!

Basil flushed and made a poor pass. He had been called by a nickname. It was a poor makeshift, but it was something more than the stark bareness of his surname or a term of derision. Brick Wales went on playing, unconscious that he had done anything in particular or that he had contributed to the events by which another boy was saved from the army of the bitter, the selfish, the neurasthenic and the unhappy. It isn't given to us to know those rare moments when people are wide open and the lightest touch can wither or heal. A moment too late and we can never reach them any more in this world. They will not be cured by our most efficacious drugs or slain with our sharpest swords.

Lee-y! It could scarcely be pronounced. But Basil took it to bed with him that night, and thinking of it, holding it to him happily to the last, fell easily to sleep.

HE THINKS HE'S WONDERFUL

I

AFTER the college-board examinations in June, Basil Duke Lee and five other boys from St. Regis School boarded the train for the West. Two got out at Pittsburgh, one slanted south toward St. Louis and two stayed in Chicago; from then on Basil was alone. It was the first time in his life that he had ever felt the need of tranquillity, but now he took long breaths of it; for, though things had gone better toward the end, he had had an unhappy year at school.

He wore one of those extremely flat derbies in vogue during the twelfth year of the century, and a blue business suit become a little too short for his constantly lengthening body. Within he was by turns a disembodied spirit, almost unconscious of his person and moving in a mist of impressions and emotions, and a fiercely competitive individual trying desperately to control the rush of events that were the steps in his own evolution from child to man. He believed that everything was a matter of effort—the current principle of American education—and his fantastic ambition was continually leading him to expect too much. He wanted to be a great athlete, popular, brilliant and always happy. During this year at school, where he had been punished for his "freshness," for fifteen years of thorough spoiling at home, he had grown uselessly introspective, and this interfered with that observation of others which is the beginning of wisdom. It was apparent that before he obtained much success in dealing with the world he would know that he'd been in a fight.

He spent the afternoon in Chicago, walking the streets and avoiding members of the underworld. He bought a detective story called "In the Dead of the Night," and at five o'clock recovered his suitcase from the station check room and boarded the Chicago, Milwaukee and St. Paul. Immediately he encountered a contemporary, also bound home from school.

Margaret Torrence was fourteen; a serious girl, considered beautiful by a sort of tradition, for she had been beautiful as a little girl. A year and a half before, after a breathless struggle, Basil had succeeded in kissing her on the forehead. They met now with extraordinary joy; for a moment each of them to the other represented home, the blue skies of the past, the summer afternoons ahead.

He sat with Margaret and her mother in the dining car that night. Margaret saw that he was no longer the ultraconfident boy of a year before; his brightness was subdued, and the air of consideration in his face—a mark of his recent discovery that others had wills as strong as his, and more power—appeared to Margaret as a charming sadness. The spell of peace after a struggle was still upon him. Margaret had always liked him—she was of the grave, conscientious type who sometimes loved him and whose love he could never return—and now she could scarcely wait to tell people how attractive he had grown.

After dinner they went back to the observation car and sat on the deserted rear platform while the train pulled them visibly westward between the dark wide farms. They talked of people they knew, of where they had gone for Easter vacation, of the plays they had seen in New York.

"Basil, we're going to get an automobile," she said, "and I'm going to learn to drive."

"That's fine." He wondered if his grandfather would let him drive the electric sometimes this summer.

The light from inside the car fell on her young face, and he spoke impetuously, borne on by the rush of happiness that he was going home: "You know something? You know you're the prettiest girl in the city?"

At the moment when the remark blurred with the thrilling night in Margaret's heart, Mrs. Torrence appeared to fetch her to bed.

Basil sat alone on the platform for a while, scarcely realizing that she was gone, at peace with himself for another hour and content that everything should remain patternless and shapeless until tomorrow.

II

Fifteen is of all ages the most difficult to locate—to put one's fingers on and say, "That's the way I was." The melancholy Jacques does not select it for mention, and all one can know is that somewhere between thirteen, boyhood's majority, and seventeen, when one is a sort of counterfeit young man, there is a time when youth fluctuates hourly between one world and another—pushed ceaselessly forward into unprecedented experiences and vainly trying to struggle back to the days when nothing had to be paid for. Fortunately none of our contemporaries remember much more than we do of how we behaved in those days; nevertheless the curtain is about to be drawn aside for an inspection of Basil's madness that summer.

To begin with, Margaret Torrence, in one of those moods of idealism which overcome the most matter-of-fact girls, gave it as her rapt opinion that Basil was wonderful. Having practised believing things all year at school, and having nothing much to believe at that moment, her friends accepted the fact. Basil suddenly became a legend. There were outbreaks of giggling when girls encountered him on the street, but he suspected nothing at all.

One night, when he had been home a week, he and Riply Buckner went on to an after-dinner gathering on Imogene Bissel's veranda. As they came up the walk Margaret and two other girls suddenly clung together, whispered convulsively and pursued one another around the yard, uttering strange cries—an inexplicable business that ended only when Gladys Van Schellinger, tenderly and impressively accompanied by her mother's maid, arrived in a limousine.

All of them were a little strange to one another. Those who had been East at school felt a certain superiority, which, however, was more than counterbalanced by the fact that romantic pairings and quarrels and jealousies and adventures, of which they were lamentably ignorant, had gone on while they had been away.

After the ice cream at nine they sat together on the warm stone steps in a quiet confusion that was halfway between childish teasing and adolescent coquetry. Last year the boys would have ridden their bicycles around the yard; now they had all begun to wait for something to happen.

They knew it was going to happen, the plainest girls, the shyest boys; they had begun to associate with others the romantic world of summer night that pressed deeply and sweetly on their senses. Their voices drifted in a sort of broken harmony in to Mrs. Bissel, who sat reading beside an open window.

"No, look out. You'll break it. Bay-zil!"

"Rip-lee!"

"Sure I did!"

Laughter.

> "—on Moonlight Bay
> We could hear their voices call——"

"Did you see——"

"Connie, don't—don't! You tickle. Look out!"

Laughter.

"Going to the lake tomorrow?"

"Going Friday."

"Elwood's home."

"Is Elwood home?"

> "——you have broken my heart——"

"Look out now!"

"Look out!"

Basil sat beside Riply on the balustrade, listening to Joe Gorman singing. It was one of the griefs of his life that he could not sing "so people could stand it," and he conceived a sudden admiration for Joe Gorman, reading into his personality the thrilling clearness of those sounds that moved so confidently through the dark air.

They evoked for Basil a more dazzling night than this, and other more remote and enchanted girls. He was sorry when the voice died away, and there was a rearranging of seats and a businesslike quiet—the ancient game of Truth had begun.

"What's your favorite color, Bill?"

"Green," supplies a friend.

"Sh-h-h! Let him alone."

Bill says, "Blue."

"What's your favorite girl's name?"

"Mary," says Bill.

"Mary Haupt! Bill's got a crush on Mary Haupt!"

She was a cross-eyed girl, a familiar personification of repulsiveness.

"Who would you rather kiss than anybody?"

Across the pause a snicker stabbed the darkness.

"My mother."

"No, but what girl?"

"Nobody."

"That's not fair. Forfeit! Come on, Margaret."

"Tell the truth, Margaret."

She told the truth and a moment later Basil looked down in surprise from his perch; he had just learned that he was her favorite boy.

"Oh, yes-s!" he exclaimed sceptically. "Oh, yes-s! How about Hubert Blair?"

He renewed a casual struggle with Riply Buckner and presently they both fell off the balustrade. The game became an inquisition into Gladys Van Schellinger's carefully chaperoned heart.

"What's your favorite sport?"

"Croquet."

The admission was greeted by a mild titter.

"Favorite boy."

"Thurston Kohler."

A murmur of disappointment.

"Who's he?"

"A boy in the East."

This was manifestly an evasion.

"Who's your favorite boy here?"

Gladys hesitated. "Basil," she said at length.

The faces turned up to the balustrade this time were less teasing, less jocular. Basil depreciated the matter with "Oh, yes-s! Sure! Oh, yes-s!" But he had a pleasant feeling of recognition, a familiar delight.

Imogene Bissel, a dark little beauty and the most popular girl in their crowd, took Gladys' place. The interlocutors were tired of gastronomic preferences—the first question went straight to the point.

"Imogene, have you ever kissed a boy?"

"No." A cry of wild unbelief. "I have not!" she declared indignantly.

"Well, have you ever been kissed?"

Pink but tranquil, she nodded, adding, "I couldn't help it."

"Who by?"

"I won't tell."

"Oh-h-h! How about Hubert Blair?"

"What's your favorite book, Imogene?"

"Beverly of Graustark."

"Favorite girl?"

"Passion Johnson."

"Who's she?"

"Oh, just a girl at school."

Mrs. Bissel had fortunately left the window.

"Who's your favorite boy?"

Imogene answered steadily, "Basil Lee."

This time an impressed silence fell. Basil was not surprised—we are never surprised at our own popularity—but he knew that these were not those ineffable girls, made up out of books and faces momentarily encountered, whose voices he had heard for a moment in Joe Gorman's song. And when, presently, the first telephone rang inside, calling a daughter home, and the girls, chattering like birds, piled all together into Gladys Van Schellinger's limousine, he lingered back in the shadow so as not to seem to be showing off. Then, perhaps because he nourished a vague idea that if he got to know Joe Gorman very well he would get to sing like him, he approached him and asked him to go to Lambert's for a soda.

Joe Gorman was a tall boy with white eyebrows and a stolid face who had only recently become one of their "crowd." He did not like Basil, who, he considered, had been "stuck up" with him last year, but he was acquisitive of useful knowledge and he was momentarily overwhelmed by Basil's success with girls.

It was cheerful in Lambert's, with great moths batting against the screen door and languid couples in white dresses and light suits spread about the little tables. Over their sodas, Joe proposed that Basil come home with him to spend the night; Basil's permission was obtained over the telephone.

Passing from the gleaming store into the darkness, Basil was submerged in an unreality in which he seemed to see himself from the outside, and the pleasant events of the evening began to take on fresh importance.

Disarmed by Joe's hospitality, he began to discuss the matter.

"That was a funny thing that happened tonight," he said, with a disparaging little laugh.

"What was?"

"Why, all those girls saying I was their favorite boy." The remark jarred on Joe. "It's a funny thing," went on Basil. "I was sort of unpopular at school for a while, because I was fresh, I guess. But the thing must be that some boys are popular with boys and some are popular with girls."

He had put himself in Joe's hands, but he was unconscious of it; even Joe was only aware of a certain desire to change the subject.

"When I get my car," suggested Joe, up in his room, "we could take Imogene and Margaret and go for rides."

"All right."

"You could have Imogene and I'd take Margaret, or anybody I wanted. Of course I know they don't like me as well as they do you."

"Sure they do. It's just because you haven't been in our crowd very long yet."

Joe was sensitive on that point and the remark did not please him. But Basil continued: "You ought to be more polite to the older people if you want to be popular. You didn't say how do you do to Mrs. Bissel tonight."

"I'm hungry," said Joe quickly. "Let's go down to the pantry and get something to eat."

Clad only in their pajamas, they went downstairs. Principally to dissuade Basil from pursuing the subject, Joe began to sing in a low voice:

> "Oh, you beautiful doll,
> You great—big——"

But the evening, coming after the month of enforced humility at school, had been too much for Basil. He got a little awful. In the kitchen, under the impression that his advice had been asked, he broke out again:

"For instance, you oughtn't to wear those white ties. Nobody does that that goes East to school." Joe, a little red, turned around from the ice box and Basil felt a slight misgiving. But he pursued with: "For instance, you ought to get your family to send you East to school. It'd be a great thing for you. Especially if you want to go East to college, you ought to first go East to school. They take it out of you."

Feeling that he had nothing special to be taken out of him, Joe found the implication distasteful. Nor did Basil appear to him at that moment to have been perfected by the process.

"Do you want cold chicken or cold ham?" They drew up chairs to the kitchen table. "Have some milk?"

"Thanks."

Intoxicated by the three full meals he had had since supper, Basil warmed to his subject. He built up Joe's life for him little by little, transformed him radiantly from what was little more than a Midwestern bumpkin to an Easterner bursting with *savoir-faire* and irresistible to girls. Going into the pantry to put away the milk, Joe paused by the open window for a breath of quiet air; Basil followed. "The thing is if a boy doesn't get it taken out of him at school, he gets it taken out of him at college," he was saying.

Moved by some desperate instinct, Joe opened the door and stepped out onto the back porch. Basil followed. The house abutted on the edge of the bluff occupied by the residential section, and the two boys stood silent for a moment, gazing at the scattered lights of the lower city. Before the mystery of the unknown human life coursing through the streets below, Basil felt the purport of his words grow thin and pale.

He wondered suddenly what he had said and why it had seemed important to him, and when Joe began to sing again softly, the quiet mood of the early evening, the side of him that was best, wisest and most enduring, stole over him once more. The flattery, the vanity, the fatuousness of the last hour moved off, and when he spoke it was almost in a whisper:

"Let's walk around the block."

The sidewalk was warm to their bare feet. It was only midnight, but the square was deserted save for their whitish figures, inconspicuous against the starry darkness. They snorted with glee at their daring. Once a shadow, with loud human shoes, crossed the street far ahead, but the sound served only to increase their own unsubstantiality. Slipping quickly through the clearings made by gas lamps among the trees, they rounded the block, hurrying when they neared the Gorman house as though they had been really lost in a midsummer night's dream.

Up in Joe's room, they lay awake in the darkness.

"I talked too much," Basil thought. "I probably sounded pretty bossy and maybe I made him sort of mad. But probably when we walked around the block he forgot everything I said."

Alas, Joe had forgotten nothing—except the advice by which Basil had intended him to profit.

"I never saw anybody as stuck up," he said to himself wrathfully. "He thinks he's wonderful. He thinks he's so darn popular with girls."

III

An element of vast importance had made its appearance with the summer; suddenly the great thing in Basil's crowd was to own an automobile. Fun no longer seemed available save at great distances, at suburban lakes or remote country clubs. Walking downtown ceased to be a legitimate pastime. On the contrary, a single block from one youth's house to another's must be navigated in a car. Dependent groups formed around owners and they began to wield what was, to Basil at least, a disconcerting power.

On the morning of a dance at the lake he called up Riply Buckner.

"Hey, Rip, how you going out to Connie's tonight?"

"With Elwood Leaming."

"Has he got a lot of room?"

Riply seemed somewhat embarrassed. "Why, I don't think he has. You see, he's taking Margaret Torrence and I'm taking Imogene Bissel."

"Oh!"

Basil frowned. He should have arranged all this a week ago. After a moment he called up Joe Gorman.

"Going to the Davies' tonight, Joe?"

"Why, yes."

"Have you got room in your car—I mean, could I go with you?"

"Why, yes, I suppose so."

There was a perceptible lack of warmth in his voice.

"Sure you got plenty of room?"

"Sure. We'll call for you quarter to eight."

Basil began preparations at five. For the second time in his life he shaved, completing the operation by cutting a short straight line under his nose. It bled profusely, but on the advice of Hilda, the maid, he finally stanched the flow with little pieces of toilet paper. Quite a number of pieces were necessary; so, in order to facilitate breathing, he trimmed it down with a scissors, and with this somewhat awkward mustache of paper and gore clinging to his upper lip, wandered impatiently around the house.

At six he began working on it again, soaking off the tissue paper and dabbing at the persistently freshening crimson line. It dried at length, but when he rashly hailed his mother it opened once more and the tissue paper was called back into play.

At quarter to eight, dressed in blue coat and white flannels, he drew one last bar of powder across the blemish, dusted it carefully with his handkerchief and hurried out to Joe Gorman's car. Joe was driving in person, and in front with him were Lewis Crum and Hubert Blair. Basil got in the big rear seat alone and they drove without stopping out of the city onto the Black Bear Road, keeping their backs to him and talking in low voices together. He thought at first that they were going to pick up other boys; now he was shocked, and for a moment he considered getting out of the car, but this would imply that he was hurt. His spirit, and with it his face, hardened a little and he sat without speaking or being spoken to for the rest of the ride.

After half an hour the Davies' house, a huge rambling bungalow occupying a small peninsula in the lake, floated into sight. Lanterns outlined its shape and wavered in gleaming lines on the gold-and-rose colored water, and as they came near, the low notes of bass horns and drums were blown toward them from the lawn.

Inside Basil looked about for Imogene. There was a crowd around her seeking dances, but she saw Basil; his heart bounded at her quick intimate smile.

"You can have the fourth, Basil, and the eleventh and the second extra. . . . How did you hurt your lip?"

"Cut it shaving," he said hurriedly. "How about supper?"

"Well, I have to have supper with Riply because he brought me."

"No, you don't," Basil assured her.

"Yes, she does," insisted Riply, standing close at hand. "Why don't you get your own girl for supper?"

—but Basil had no girl, though he was as yet unaware of the fact.

After the fourth dance, Basil led Imogene down to the end of the pier, where they found seats in a motorboat.

"Now what?" she said.

He did not know. If he had really cared for her he would have known. When her hand rested on his knee for a moment he did not notice it. Instead, he talked. He told her how he had pitched on the second baseball team at school and had once beaten the first in a five-inning game. He told her that the thing was that some boys were popular with boys and some boys were popular with girls—he, for instance, was popular with girls. In short, he unloaded himself.

At length, feeling that he had perhaps dwelt disproportionately on himself, he told her suddenly that she was his favorite girl.

Imogene sat there, sighing a little in the moonlight. In another

boat, lost in the darkness beyond the pier, sat a party of four. Joe
Gorman was singing:

> "My little love—
>   —in honey man,
> He sure has won my——"

"I thought you might want to know," said Basil to Imogene. "I
thought maybe you thought I liked somebody else. The truth game
didn't get around to me the other night."

"What?" asked Imogene vaguely. She had forgotten the other
night, all nights except this, and she was thinking of the magic in
Joe Gorman's voice. She had the next dance with him; he was going
to teach her the words of a new song. Basil was sort of peculiar,
telling her all this stuff. He was good-looking and attractive and all
that, but—she wanted the dance to be over. She wasn't having any
fun.

The music began inside—"Everybody's Doing It," played with
many little nervous jerks on the violins.

"Oh, listen!" she cried, sitting up and snapping her fingers. "Do
you know how to rag?"

"Listen, Imogene"—He half realized that something had slipped
away—"let's sit out this dance—you can tell Joe you forgot."

She rose quickly. "Oh, no, I can't!"

Unwillingly Basil followed her inside. It had not gone well—he
had talked too much again. He waited moodily for the eleventh
dance so that he could behave differently. He believed now that he
was in love with Imogene. His self-deception created a tightness in
his throat, a counterfeit of longing and desire.

Before the eleventh dance he was aware that some party was being
organized from which he was purposely excluded. There were whis-
perings and arguings among some of the boys, and unnatural silences
when he came near. He heard Joe Gorman say to Riply Buckner,
"We'll just be gone three days. If Gladys can't go, why don't you
ask Connie? The chaperons'll—" he changed his sentence as he saw
Basil—"and we'll all go to Smith's for ice-cream soda."

Later, Basil took Riply Buckner aside but failed to elicit any information: Riply had not forgotten Basil's attempt to rob him of Imogene tonight.

"It wasn't about anything," he insisted. "We're going to Smith's, honest. . . . How'd you cut your lip?"

"Cut it shaving."

When his dance with Imogene came she was even vaguer than before, exchanging mysterious communications with various girls as they moved around the room, locked in the convulsive grip of the Grizzly Bear. He led her out to the boat again, but it was occupied, and they walked up and down the pier while he tried to talk to her and she hummed:

"My little lov-in honey man——"

"Imogene, listen. What I wanted to ask you when we were on the boat before was about the night we played Truth. Did you really mean what you said?"

"Oh, what do you want to talk about that silly game for?"

It had reached her ears, not once but several times, that Basil thought he was wonderful—news that was flying about with as much volatility as the rumor of his graces two weeks before. Imogene liked to agree with everyone—and she had agreed with several impassioned boys that Basil was terrible. And it was difficult not to dislike him for her own disloyalty.

But Basil thought that only ill luck ended the intermission before he could accomplish his purpose; though what he had wanted he had not known.

Finally, during the intermission, Margaret Torrence, whom he had neglected, told him the truth.

"Are you going on the touring party up to the St. Croix River?" she asked. She knew he was not.

"What party?"

"Joe Gorman got it up. I'm going with Elwood Leaming."

"No, I'm not going," he said gruffly. "I couldn't go."

"Oh!"

"I don't like Joe Gorman."

"I guess he doesn't like you much either."

"Why? What did he say?"

"Oh, nothing."

"But what? Tell me what he said."

After a minute she told him, as if reluctantly: "Well, he and Hubert Blair said you thought—you thought you were wonderful." Her heart misgave her.

But she remembered he had asked her for only one dance. "Joe said you told him that all the girls thought you were wonderful."

"I never said anything like that," said Basil indignantly, "never!"

He understood—Joe Gorman had done it all, taken advantage of Basil's talking too much—an affliction which his real friends had always allowed for—in order to ruin him. The world was suddenly compact of villainy. He decided to go home.

In the coat room he was accosted by Bill Kampf: "Hello, Basil, how did you hurt your lip?"

"Cut it shaving."

"Say, are you going to this party they're getting up next week?"

"No."

"Well, look, I've got a cousin from Chicago coming to stay with us and mother said I could have a boy out for the week-end. Her name is Minnie Bibble."

"Minnie Bibble?" repeated Basil, vaguely revolted.

"I thought maybe you were going to that party, too, but Riply Buckner said to ask you and I thought——"

"I've got to stay home," said Basil quickly.

"Oh, come on, Basil," he pursued. "It's only for two days, and she's a nice girl. You'd like her."

"I don't know," Basil considered. "I'll tell you what I'll do, Bill. I've got to get the street car home. I'll come out for the week-end if you'll take me over to Wildwood now in your car."

"Sure I will."

Basil walked out on the veranda and approached Connie Davies.

"Good-by," he said. Try as he might, his voice was stiff and proud. "I had an awfully good time."

"I'm sorry you're leaving so early, Basil." But she said to herself: "He's too stuck up to have a good time. He thinks he's wonderful."

From the veranda he could hear Imogene's laughter down at the

end of the pier. Silently he went down the steps and along the
walk to meet Bill Kampf, giving strollers a wide berth as though he
felt the sight of him would diminish their pleasure.

It had been an awful night.

Ten minutes later Bill dropped him beside the waiting trolley. A
few last picnickers sauntered aboard and the car bobbed and clanged
through the night toward St. Paul.

Presently two young girls sitting opposite Basil began looking
over at him and nudging each other, but he took no notice—he was
thinking how sorry they would all be—Imogene and Margaret, Joe
and Hubert and Riply.

"Look at him now!" they would say to themselves sorrowfully.
"President of the United States at twenty-five! Oh, if we only hadn't
been so bad to him that night!"

He thought he was wonderful!

IV

Ermine Gilberte Labouisse Bibble was in exile. Her parents had
brought her from New Orleans to Southampton in May, hoping that
the active outdoor life proper to a girl of fifteen would take her
thoughts from love. But North or South, a storm of sappling arrows
flew about her. She was "engaged" before the first of June.

Let it not be gathered from the foregoing that the somewhat
hard outlines of Miss Bibble at twenty had already begun to appear.
She was of a radiant freshness; her head had reminded otherwise
not illiterate young men of damp blue violets, pierced with blue
windows that looked into a bright soul, with today's new roses showing through.

She was in exile. She was going to Glacier National Park to
forget. It was written that in passage she would come to Basil as a
sort of initiation, turning his eyes out from himself and giving him
a first dazzling glimpse into the world of love.

She saw him first as a quiet handsome boy with an air of consideration in his face, which was the mark of his recent re-discovery
that others had wills as strong as his, and more power. It appeared to

Minnie—as a few months back it had appeared to Margaret Torrence, like a charming sadness. At dinner he was polite to Mrs.
Kampf in a courteous way that he had from his father, and he
listened to Mr. Bibble's discussion of the word "Creole" with such
evident interest and appreciation that Mr. Bibble thought, "Now
here's a young boy with something *to* him."

After dinner, Minnie, Basil and Bill rode into Black Bear village
to the movies, and the slow diffusion of Minnie's charm and personality presently became the charm and personality of the affair itself.

It was thus that all Minnie's affairs for many years had a family
likeness. She looked at Basil, a childish open look; then opened her
eyes wider as if she had some sort of comic misgivings, and smiled
—she smiled—

For all the candor of this smile, the effect—because of the special
contours of Minnie's face and independent of her mood—was sparkling invitation. Whenever it appeared Basil seemed to be suddenly
inflated and borne upward, a little farther each time, only to be set
down when the smile had reached a point where it must become a
grin, and chose instead to melt away. It was like a drug. In a little
while he wanted nothing except to watch it with a vast buoyant
delight.

Then he wanted to see how close he could get to it.

There is a certain stage of an affair between young people when
the presence of a third party is a stimulant. Before the second day
had well begun, before Minnie and Basil had progressed beyond the
point of great gross compliments about each other's surpassing beauty
and charm, both of them had begun to think about the time when
they could get rid of their host, Bill Kampf.

In the late afternoon, when the first cool of the evening had
come down and they were fresh and thin-feeling from swimming,
they sat in a cushioned swing, piled high with pillows and shaded
by the thick veranda vines; Basil put his arm around her and leaned
toward her cheek and Minnie managed it that he touched her fresh
lips instead. And he had always learned things quickly.

They sat there for an hour, while Bill's voice reached them, now
from the pier, now from the hall above, now from the pagoda at
the end of the garden, and three saddled horses chafed their bits
in the stable and all around them the bees worked faithfully among

the flowers. Then Minnie reached up to reality, and they allowed themselves to be found—

"Why, we were looking for you too."

And Basil, by simply waving his arms and wishing, floated miraculously upstairs to brush his hair for dinner.

"She certainly is a wonderful girl. Oh, gosh, she certainly is a wonderful girl!"

He mustn't lose his head. At dinner and afterward he listened with unwavering deferential attention while Mr. Bibble talked of the boll weevil.

"But I'm boring you. You children want to go off by yourselves."

"Not at all, Mr. Bibble. I was very interested—honestly."

"Well, you all go on and amuse yourselves. I didn't realize time was getting on. Nowadays it's so seldom you meet a young man with good manners and good common sense in his head, that an old man like me is likely to go along forever."

Bill walked down with Basil and Minnie to the end of the pier. "Hope we'll have a good sailing tomorrow. Say, I've got to drive over to the village and get somebody for my crew. Do you want to come along?"

"I reckon I'll sit here for a while and then go to bed," said Minnie.

"All right. You want to come, Basil?"

"Why—why, sure, if you want me, Bill."

"You'll have to sit on a sail I'm taking over to be mended."

"I don't want to crowd you."

"You won't crowd me. I'll go get the car."

When he had gone they looked at each other in despair. But he did not come back for an hour—something happened about the sail or the car that took a long time. There was only the threat, making everything more poignant and breathless, that at any minute he *would* be coming.

By and by they got into the motorboat and sat close together murmuring: "This fall—" "When you come to New Orleans—" "When I go to Yale year after next—" "When I come North to school—" "When I get back from Glacier Park—" "Kiss me once more." . . . "You're terrible. Do you know you're terrible? . . . You're absolutely terrible——"

The water lapped against the posts; sometimes the boat bumped gently on the pier; Basil undid one rope and pushed, so that they swung off and way from the pier, and became a little island in the night. . .

. . . next morning, while he packed his bag, she opened the door of his room and stood beside him. Her face shone with excitement; her dress was starched and white.

"Basil, listen! I have to tell you: Father was talking after breakfast and he told Uncle George that he'd never met such a nice, quiet, level-headed boy as you, and Cousin Bill's got to tutor this month, so father asked Uncle George if he thought your family would let you go to Glacier Park with us for two weeks so I'd have some company." They took hands and danced excitedly around the room. "Don't say anything about it, because I reckon he'll have to write your mother and everything. Basil, isn't it wonderful?"

So when Basil left at eleven, there was no misery in their parting. Mr. Bibble, going into the village for a paper, was going to escort Basil to his train, and till the motor-car moved away the eyes of the two young people shone and there was a secret in their waving hands.

Basil sank back in the seat, replete with happiness. He relaxed—to have made a success of the visit was so nice. He loved her—he loved even her father sitting beside him, her father who was privileged to be so close to her, to fuddle himself at that smile.

Mr. Bibble lit a cigar. "Nice weather," he said. "Nice climate up to the end of October."

"Wonderful," agreed Basil. "I miss October now that I go East to school."

"Getting ready for college?"

"Yes, sir; getting ready for Yale." A new pleasurable thought occurred to him. He hesitated, but he knew that Mr. Bibble, who liked him, would share his joy. "I took my preliminaries this spring and I just heard from them—I passed six out of seven."

"Good for you!"

Again Basil hesitated, then he continued: "I got A in ancient history and B in English history and English A. And I got C in algebra A and Latin A and B. I failed French A."

"Good!" said Mr. Bibble.

"I should have passed them all," went on Basil, "but I didn't study hard at first. I was the youngest boy in my class and I had a sort of swelled head about it."

It was well that Mr. Bibble should know he was taking no dullard to Glacier National Park. Mr. Bibble took a long puff of his cigar.

On second thought, Basil decided that his last remark didn't have the right ring and he amended it a little.

"It wasn't exactly a swelled head, but I never had to study very much, because in English I'd usually read most of the books before, and in history I'd read a lot too." He broke off and tried again: "I mean, when you say swelled head you think of a boy just going around with his head swelled, sort of, saying, 'Oh, look how much I know!' Well, I wasn't like that. I mean, I didn't think I knew everything, but I was sort of——"

As he searched for the elusive word, Mr. Bibble said, "H'm!" and pointed with his cigar at a spot in the lake.

"There's a boat," he said.

"Yes," agreed Basil. "I don't know much about sailing. I never cared for it. Of course I've been out a lot, just tending boards and all that, but most of the time you have to sit with nothing to do. I like football."

"H'm!" said Mr. Bibble. "When I was your age I was out in the Gulf in a catboat every day."

"I guess it's fun if you like it," conceded Basil.

"Happiest days of my life."

The station was in sight. It occurred to Basil that he should make one final friendly gesture.

"Your daughter certainly is an attractive girl, Mr. Bibble," he said. "I usually get along with girls all right, but I don't usually like them very much. But I think your daughter is the most attractive girl I ever met." Then, as the car stopped, a faint misgiving overtook him and he was impelled to add with a disparaging little laugh. "Good-by. I hope I didn't talk too much."

"Not at all," said Mr. Bibble. "Good luck to you. Goo'-by."

A few minutes later, when Basil's train had pulled out, Mr. Bibble stood at the newsstand buying a paper and already drying his forehead against the hot July day.

"Yes, sir! That was a lesson not to do anything in a hurry," he was saying to himself vehemently. "Imagine listening to that fresh kid gabbling about himself all through Glacier Park! Thank the good Lord for that little ride!"

On his arrival home, Basil literally sat down and waited. Under no pretext would he leave the house save for short trips to the drug store for refreshments, whence he returned on a full run. The sound of the telephone or the door-bell galvanized him into the rigidity of the electric chair.

That afternoon he composed a wondrous geographical poem, which he mailed to Minnie:

> Of all the fair flowers of Paris,
>   Of all the red roses of Rome,
> Of all the deep tears of Vienna
>   The sadness wherever you roam,
> I think of that night by the lakeside,
>   The beam of the moon and stars,
> And the smell of an aching like perfume,
>   The tune of the Spanish guitars.

But Monday passed and most of Tuesday and no word came. Then, late in the afternoon of the second day, as he moved vaguely from room to room looking out of different windows into a barren lifeless street, Minnie called him on the phone.

"Yes?" His heart was beating wildly.

"Basil, we're going this afternoon."

"Going!" he repeated blankly.

"Oh, Basil, I'm so sorry. Father changed his mind about taking anybody West with us."

"Oh!"

"I'm so sorry, Basil."

"I probably couldn't have gone."

There was a moment's silence. Feeling her presence over the wire, he could scarcely breathe, much less speak.

"Basil, can you hear me?"

"Yes."

"We may come back this way. Anyhow, remember we're going to meet this winter in New York."

"Yes," he said, and he added suddenly: "Perhaps we won't ever meet again."

"Of course we will. They're calling me, Basil. I've got to go. Good-by."

He sat down beside the telephone, wild with grief. The maid found him half an hour later bowed over the kitchen table. He knew what had happened as well as if Minnie had told him. He had made the same old error, undone the behavior of three days in half an hour. It would have been no consolation if it had occurred to him that it was just as well. Somewhere on the trip he would have let go and things might have been worse—though perhaps not so sad. His only thought now was that she was gone.

He lay on his bed, baffled, mistaken, miserable but not beaten. Time after time, the same vitality that had led his spirit to a scourging made him able to shake off the blood like water not to forget, but to carry his wounds with him to new disasters and new atonements—toward his unknown destiny.

Two days later his mother told him that on condition of his keeping the batteries on charge, and washing it once a week, his grandfather had consented to let him use the electric whenever it was idle in the afternoon. Two hours later he was out in it, gliding along Crest Avenue at the maximum speed permitted by the gears and trying to lean back as if it were a Stutz Bearcat. Imogene Bissel waved at him from in front of her house and he came to an uncertain stop.

"You've got a car!"

"It's grandfather's," he said modestly. "I thought you were up on that party at the St. Croix."

She shook her head. "Mother wouldn't let me go—only a few girls went. There was a big accident over in Minneapolis and mother won't even let me ride in a car unless there's someone over eighteen driving."

"Listen, Imogene, do you suppose your mother meant electrics?"

"Why, I never thought—I don't know. I could go and see."

"Tell your mother it won't go over twelve miles an hour," he called after her.

A minute later she ran joyfully down the walk. "I can go, Basil," she cried. "Mother never heard of any wrecks in an electric. What'll we do?"

"Anything," he said in a reckless voice. "I didn't mean that about this bus making only twelve miles an hour—it'll make fifteen. Listen, let's go down to Smith's and have a claret lemonade."

"Why, Basil Lee!"

THE CAPTURED SHADOW

BASIL DUKE LEE shut the front door behind him and turned on the dining-room light. His mother's voice drifted sleepily downstairs:

"Basil, is that you?"

"No, mother, it's a burglar."

"It seems to me twelve o'clock is pretty late for a fifteen-year-old boy."

"We went to Smith's and had a soda."

Whenever a new responsibility devolved upon Basil he was "a boy almost sixteen," but when a privilege was in question, he was "a fifteen-year-old boy."

There were footsteps above, and Mrs. Lee, in kimono, descended to the first landing.

"Did you and Riply enjoy the play?"

"Yes, very much."

"What was it about?"

"Oh, it was just about this man. Just an ordinary play."

"Didn't it have a name?"

" 'Are You a Mason?' "

"Oh." She hesitated, covetously watching his alert and eager face, holding him there. "Aren't you coming to bed?"

"I'm going to get something to eat."

"Something more?"

For a moment he didn't answer. He stood in front of a glassed-in bookcase in the living room, examining its contents with an equally glazed eye.

"We're going to get up a play," he said suddenly. "I'm going to write it."

"Well—that'll be very nice. Please come to bed soon. You were up late last night, too, and you've got dark circles under your eyes."

From the bookcase Basil presently extracted "Van Bibber and Others," from which he read while he ate a large plate of strawberries softened with half a pint of cream. Back in the living room he sat for a few minutes at the piano, digesting, and meanwhile staring at the colored cover of a song from "The Midnight Sons." It showed three men in evening clothes and opera hats sauntering jovially along Broadway against the blazing background of Times Square.

Basil would have denied incredulously the suggestion that that was currently his favorite work of art. But it was.

He went upstairs. From a drawer of his desk he took out a composition book and opened it.

BASIL DUKE LEE

St. Regis School
Eastchester, Conn.
Fifth Form French

and on the next page, under Irregular Verbs:

Present

je connais   nous con
tu connais
il connaît

He turned over another page.

MR. WASHINGTON SQUARE

A Musical Comedy by
Basil Duke Lee
Music by Victor Herbert

ACT I

[*The porch of the Millionaires' Club, near New York. Opening Chorus,*
Leilia *and* Debutantes:

> We sing not soft, we sing not loud
>   For no one ever heard an opening chorus.
> We are a very merry crowd
>   But no one ever heard an opening chorus.

We're just a crowd of debutantes
  As merry as can be
  And nothing that there is could ever bore us
We're the wittiest ones, the prettiest ones.
  In all society
  But no one ever heard an opening chorus.

LEILIA (*stepping forward*): Well, girls, has Mr. Washington Square been around here today?

Basil turned over a page. There was no answer to Leilia's question. Instead in capitals was a brand-new heading:

HIC! HIC! HIC!

A Hilarious Farce in One Act

by

BASIL DUKE LEE

SCENE

[*A fashionable apartment near Broadway, New York City. It is almost midnight. As the curtain goes up there is a knocking at the door and a few minutes later it opens to admit a handsome man in a full evening dress and a companion. He has evidently been imbibing, for his words are thick, his nose is red, and he can hardly stand up. He turns up the light and comes down centre.*

STUYVESANT: Hic! Hic! Hic!
O'HARA (*his companion*): Begorra, you been sayin' nothing else all this evening.

Basil turned over a page and then another, reading hurriedly, but not without interest.

PROFESSOR PUMPKIN: Now, if you are an educated man, as you claim, perhaps you can tell me the Latin word for "this."
STUYVESANT: Hic! Hic! Hic!
PROFESSOR PUMPKIN: Correct. Very good indeed. I——

At this point Hic! Hic! Hic! came to an end in midsentence. On the following page, in just as determined a hand as if the last two works had not faltered by the way, was the heavily underlined beginning of another:

THE CAPTURED SHADOW

A Melodramatic Farce in Three Acts

by

BASIL DUKE LEE

SCENE

[*All three acts take place in the library of the* VAN BAKERS' *house in New York. It is well furnished with a red lamp on one side and some crossed spears and helmets and so on and a divan and a general air of an oriental den.*

When the curtain rises MISS SAUNDERS, LEILIA VAN BAKER *and* ESTELLA CARRAGE *are sitting at a table.* MISS SAUNDERS *and* ESTELLA CARRAGE *are sitting at a table.* MISS SAUNDERS *is an old maid about forty very kittenish.* LEILIA *is pretty with dark hair.* ESTELLA *has light hair. They are a strikeing combination.*

"The Captured Shadow" filled the rest of the book and ran over into several loose sheets at the end. When it broke off Basil sat for a while in thought. This had been a season of "crook comedies" in New York, and the feel, the swing, the exact and vivid image of the two he had seen, were in the foreground of his mind. At the time they had been enormously suggestive, opening out into a world much larger and more brilliant than themselves that existed outside their windows and beyond their doors, and it was this suggested world rather than any conscious desire to imitate "Officer 666," that had inspired the effort before him. Presently he printed ACT II at the head of a new tablet and began to write.

An hour passed. Several times he had recourse to a collection of joke books and to an old Treasury of Wit and Humor which embalmed the faded Victorian cracks of Bishop Wilberforce and Sydney Smith. At the moment when, in his story, a door moved slowly open, he heard a heavy creak upon the stairs. He jumped to his feet, aghast and trembling, but nothing stirred; only a white moth bounced against the screen, a clock struck the half-hour far across the city, a bird whacked its wings in a tree outside.

Voyaging to the bathroom at half-past four, he saw with a shock that morning was already blue at the window. He had stayed up all night. He remembered that people who stayed up all night went crazy, and transfixed in the hall, he tried agonizingly to listen to himself, to feel whether or not he was going crazy. The things around him seemed preternaturally unreal, and rushing frantically back into his bedroom, he began tearing off his clothes, racing after the vanishing night. Undressed, he threw a final regretful glance at his pile of manuscript—he had the whole next scene in his head. As a compromise with incipient madness he got into bed and wrote for an hour more.

Late next morning he was startled awake by one of the ruthless Scandinavian sisters who, in theory, were the Lees' servants. "Eleven o'clock!" she shouted. "Five after!"

"Let me alone," Basil mumbled. "What do you come and wake me up for?"

"Somebody downstairs." He opened his eyes. "You ate all the cream last night," Hilda continued. "Your mother didn't have any for her coffee."

"All the cream!" he cried. "Why, I saw some more."

"It was sour."

"That's terrible," he exclaimed, sitting up. "Terrible!"

For a moment she enjoyed his dismay. Then she said, "Riply Buckner's downstairs," and went out, closing the door.

"Send him up!" he called after her. "Hilda, why don't you ever listen for a minute? Did I get any mail?"

There was no answer. A moment later Riply came in.

"My gosh, are you still in bed?"

"I wrote on the play all night. I almost finished Act Two." He pointed to his desk.

"That's what I want to talk to you about," said Riply. "Mother thinks we ought to get Miss Halliburton."

"What for?"

"Just to sort of be there."

Though Miss Halliburton was a pleasant person who combined the occupations of French teacher and bridge teacher, unofficial chaperon and children's friend, Basil felt that her superintendence would give the project an unprofessional ring.

"She wouldn't interfere," went on Riply, obviously quoting his mother. "I'll be the business manager and you'll direct the play, just like we said, but it would be good to have her there for prompter and to keep order at rehearsals. The girls' mothers'll like it."

"All right," Basil agreed reluctantly. "Now look, let's see who we'll have in the cast. First, there's the leading man—this gentleman burglar that's called The Shadow. Only it turns out at the end that he's really a young man about town doing it on a bet, and not really a burglar at all."

"That's you."

"No, that's you."

"Come on! You're the best actor," protested Riply.

"No, I'm going to take a smaller part, so I can coach."

"Well, haven't I got to be business manager?"

Selecting the actresses, presumably all eager, proved to be a difficult matter. They settled finally on Imogene Bissel for leading lady; Margaret Torrence for her friend, and Connie Davies for "Miss Saunders, an old maid very kittenish."

On Riply's suggestion that several other girls wouldn't be pleased at being left out, Basil introduced a maid and a cook, "who could just sort of look in from the kitchen." He rejected firmly Riply's further proposal that there should be two or three maids, "a sort of sewing woman," and a trained nurse. In a house so clogged with femininity even the most umbrageous of gentleman burglars would have difficulty in moving about.

"I'll tell you two people we won't have," Basil said meditatively— "that's Joe Gorman and Hubert Blair."

"I wouldn't be in it if we had Hubert Blair," asserted Riply.

"Neither would I."

Hubert Blair's almost miraculous successes with girls had caused Basil and Riply much jealous pain.

They began calling up the prospective cast and immediately the enterprise received its first blow. Imogene Bissel was going to Rochester, Minnesota, to have her appendix removed, and wouldn't be back for three weeks.

They considered.

"How about Margaret Torrence?"

Basil shook his head. He had vision of Leilia Van Baker as some-one rarer and more spirited than Margaret Torrence. Not that Leilia had much being, even to Basil—less than the Harrison Fisher girls pinned around his wall at school. But she was not Margaret Torrence. She was no one you could inevitably see by calling up half an hour before on the phone.

He discarded candidate after candidate. Finally a face began to flash before his eyes, as if in another connection, but so insistently that at length he spoke the name.

"Evelyn Beebe."

"Who?"

Though Evelyn Beebe was only sixteen, her precocious charms had elevated her to an older crowd and to Basil she seemed of the very generation of his heroine, Leilia Van Baker. It was a little like asking Sarah Bernhardt for her services, but once her name had occurred to him, other possibilities seemed pale.

At noon they rang the Beebe's door-bell, stricken by a paralysis of embarrassment when Evelyn opened the door herself and, with politeness that concealed a certain surprise, asked them in.

Suddenly, through the portière of the living room, Basil saw and recognized a young man in golf knickerbockers.

"I guess we better not come in," he said quickly.

"We'll come some other time," Riply added.

Together they started precipitately for the door, but she barred their way.

"Don't be silly," she insisted. "It's just Andy Lockheart."

Just Andy Lockheart—winner of the Western Golf Championship at eighteen, captain of his freshman baseball team, handsome, suc-cessful at everything he tried, a living symbol of the splendid, glamorous world of Yale. For a year Basil had walked like him and tried unsuccessfully to play the piano by ear as Andy Lockheart was able to do.

Through sheer ineptitude at escaping, they were edged into the room. Their plan suddenly seemed presumptuous and absurd.

Perceiving their condition Evelyn tried to soothe them with pleas-ant banter.

"Well it's about time you came to see me," she told Basil. "Here

I've been sitting at home every night waiting for you—ever since the Davies dance. Why haven't you been here before?"

He stared at her blankly, unable even to smile, and muttered: "Yes, you have."

"I have though. Sit down and tell me why you've been neglecting me! I suppose you've both been rushing the beautiful Imogene Bissel."

"Why, I understand—" said Basil. "Why, I heard from somewhere that she's gone up to have some kind of an appendicitis—that is—" He ran down to a pitch of inaudibility as Andy Lockheart at the piano began playing a succession of thoughtful chords, which resolved itself into the maxixe, an eccentric stepchild of the tango. Kicking back a rug and lifting her skirts a little, Evelyn fluently tapped on a circle with her heels around the floor.

They sat inanimate as cushions on the sofa watching her. She was almost beautiful, with rather large features and bright fresh color behind which her heart seemed to be trembling a little with laughter. Her voice and her lithe body were always mimicking, ceaselessly caricaturing every sound and movement near by, until even those who disliked her admitted that "Evelyn could always make you laugh." She finished her dance now with a false stumble and an awed expression as she clutched at the piano, and Basil and Riply chuckled. Seeing their embarrassment lighten, she came and sat down beside them, and they laughed again when she said: "Excuse my lack of self-control."

"Do you want to be the leading lady in a play we're going to give?" demanded Basil with sudden desperation. "We're going to have it at the Martindale School, for the benefit of the Baby Welfare."

"Basil, this is so sudden."

Andy Lockheart turned around from the piano.

"What're you going to give—a minstrel show?"

"No, it's a crook play named The Captured Shadow. Miss Halliburton is going to coach it." He suddenly realized the convenience of that name to shelter himself behind.

"Why don't you give something like The Private Secretary?" interrupted Andy. "There's a good play for you. We gave it my last year at school."

"Oh, no, it's all settled," said Basil quickly. "We're going to put on this play that I wrote."

"You wrote it yourself?" exclaimed Evelyn.

"Yes."

"My-y gosh!" said Andy. He began to play again.

"Look, Evelyn," said Basil. "It's only for three weeks, and you'd be the leading lady."

She laughed. "Oh, no. I couldn't. Why don't you get Imogene?"

"She's sick, I tell you. Listen——"

"Or Margaret Torrence?"

"I don't want anybody but you."

The directness of this appeal touched her and momentarily she hesitated. But the hero of the Western Golf Championship turned around from the piano with a teasing smile and she shook her head.

"I can't do it, Basil. I may have to go East with the family."

Reluctantly Basil and Riply got up.

"Gosh, I wish you'd be in it, Evelyn."

"I wish I could."

Basil lingered, thinking fast, wanting her more than ever; indeed, without her, it scarcely seemed worth while to go on with the play. Suddenly a desperate expedient took shape on his lips:

"You certainly would be wonderful. You see, the leading man is going to be Hubert Blair."

Breathlessly he watched her, saw her hesitate.

"Good-by," he said.

She came with them to the door and then out on the veranda, frowning a little.

"How long did you say the rehearsals would take?" she asked thoughtfully.

II

On an August evening three days later Basil read the play to the cast on Miss Halliburton's porch. He was nervous and at first there were interruptions of "Louder" and "Not so fast." Just as his audience was beginning to be amused by the repartee of the two comic crooks—repartee that had seen service with Weber and Fields—he was interrupted by the late arrival of Hubert Blair.

Hubert was fifteen, a somewhat shallow boy save for two or three felicities which he possessed to an extraordinary degree. But one excellence suggests the presence of others, and young ladies never failed to respond to his most casual fancy, enduring his fickleness of heart and never convinced that his fundamental indifference might not be overcome. They were dazzled by his flashing self-confidence, by his cherubic ingenuousness, which concealed a shrewd talent for getting around people, and by his extraordinary physical grace. Long-legged, beautifully proportioned, he had that tumbler's balance usually characteristic only of men "built near the ground." He was in constant motion that was a delight to watch, and Evelyn Beebe was not the only older girl who had found in him a mysterious promise and watched him for a long time with something more than curiosity.

He stood in the doorway now with an expression of bogus reverence on his round pert face.

"Excuse me," he said. "Is this the First Methodist Episcopal Church?" Everybody laughed—even Basil. "I didn't know. I thought maybe I was in the right church, but in the wrong pew."

They laughed again, somewhat discouraged. Basil waited until Hubert had seated himself beside Evelyn Beebe. Then he began to read once more, while the others, fascinated, watched Hubert's efforts to balance a chair on its hind legs. This squeaky experiment continued as an undertone to the reading. Not until Basil's desperate "Now, here's where you come in, Hube," did attention swing back to the play.

Basil read for more than an hour. When, at the end, he closed the composition book and looked up shyly, there was a burst of spontaneous applause. He had followed his models closely, and for all its grotesqueries, the result was actually interesting—it was a play. Afterward he lingered, talking to Miss Halliburton, and he walked home glowing with excitement and rehearsing a little by himself into the August night.

The first week of rehearsal was a matter of Basil climbing back and forth from auditorium to stage, crying, "No! Look here, Connie;

you come in more like this." Then things began to happen. Mrs. Van Schellinger came to rehearsal one day, and lingering afterward, announced that she couldn't let Gladys be in "a play about criminals." Her theory was that this element could be removed; for instance, the two comic crooks could be changed to "two funny farmers."

Basil listened with horror. When she had gone he assured Miss Halliburton that he would change nothing. Luckily Gladys played the cook, an interpolated part that could be summarily struck out, but her absence was felt in another way. She was tranquil and tractable, "the most carefully brought-up girl in town," and at her withdrawal rowdiness appeared during rehearsals. Those who had only such lines as "I'll ask Mrs. Van Baker, sir," in Act I and "No, ma'am," in Act III showed a certain tendency to grow restless in between. So now it was:

"Please keep that dog quiet or else send him home!" or:

"Where's that maid? Wake up, Margaret, for heaven's sake!" or:

"What is there to laugh at that's so darn funny?"

More and more the chief problem was the tactful management of Hubert Blair. Apart from his unwillingness to learn his lines, he was a satisfactory hero, but off the stage he became a nuisance. He gave an endless private performance for Evelyn Beebe, which took such forms as chasing her amorously around the hall or of flipping peanuts over his shoulder to land mysteriously on the stage. Called to order, he would mutter, "Aw, shut up yourself," just loud enough for Basil to guess, but not to hear.

But Evelyn Beebe was all that Basil had expected. Once on the stage, she compelled a breathless attention, and Basil recognized this by adding to her part. He envied the half-sentimental fun that she and Hubert derived from their scenes together and he felt a vague, impersonal jealousy that almost every night after rehearsal they drove around together in Hubert's car.

One afternoon when matters had progressed a fortnight, Hubert came in an hour late, loafed through the first act and then informed Miss Halliburton that he was going home.

"What for?" Basil demanded.

"I've got some things I got to do."

"Are they important?"

"What business is that of yours?"

"Of course it's my business," said Basil heatedly, whereupon Miss Halliburton interfered.

"There's no use of anybody getting angry. What Basil means, Hubert, is that if it's just some small thing—why, we're all giving up our pleasures to make this play a success."

Hubert listened with obvious boredom.

"I've got to drive downtown and get father."

He looked coolly at Basil, as if challenging him to deny the adequacy of this explanation.

"Then why did you come an hour late?" demanded Basil.

"Because I had to do something for mother."

A group had gathered and he glanced around triumphantly. It was one of those sacred excuses, and only Basil saw that it was disingenuous.

"Oh, tripe!" he said.

"Maybe you think so—Bossy."

Basil took a step toward him, his eyes blazing.

"What'd you say?"

"I said 'Bossy.' Isn't that what they call you at school?"

It was true. It had followed him home. Even as he went white with rage a vast impotence surged over him at the realization that the past was always lurking near. The faces of school were around him, sneering and watching. Hubert laughed.

"Get out!" said Basil in a strained voice. "Go on! Get right out!"

Hubert laughed again, but as Basil took a step toward him he retreated.

"I don't want to be in your play anyhow. I never did."

"Then go on out of this hall."

"Now, Basil!" Miss Halliburton hovered breathlessly beside them. Hubert laughed again and looked about for his cap.

"I wouldn't be in your crazy old show," he said. He turned slowly and jauntily, and sauntered out the door.

Riply Buckner read Hubert's part that afternoon, but there was a cloud upon the rehearsal. Miss Beebe's performance lacked its customary verve and the others clustered and whispered, falling silent when Basil came near. After the rehearsal, Miss Halliburton,

Riply and Basil held a conference. Upon Basil flatly refusing to take the leading part, it was decided to enlist a certain Mayall De Bec, known slightly to Riply, who had made a name for himself in theatricals at the Central High School.

But next day a blow fell that was irreparable. Evelyn, flushed and uncomfortable, told Basil and Miss Halliburton that her family's plans had changed—they were going East next week and she couldn't be in the play after all. Basil understood. Only Hubert had held her this long.

"Good-by," he said gloomily.

His manifest despair shamed her and she tried to justify herself. "Really, I can't help it. Oh, Basil, I'm so sorry!"

"Couldn't you stay over a week with me after your family goes?" Miss Halliburton asked innocently.

"Not possibly. Father wants us all to go together. That's the only reason. If it wasn't for that I'd stay."

"All right," Basil said. "Good-by."

"Basil, you're not mad, are you?" A gust of repentance swept over her. "I'll do anything to help. I'll come to rehearsals this week until you get someone else, and then I'll try to help her all I can. But father says we've got to go."

In vain Riply tried to raise Basil's morale after the rehearsal that afternoon, making suggestions which he waved contemptuously away. Margaret Torrence? Connie Davies? They could hardly play the parts they had. It seemed to Basil as if the undertaking was falling to pieces before his eyes.

It was still early when he got home. He sat dispiritedly by his bedroom window, watching the little Barnfield boy playing a lonesome game by himself in the yard next door.

His mother came in at five, and immediately sensed his depression.

"Teddy Barnfield has the mumps," she said, in an effort to distract him. "That's why he's playing there all alone."

"Has he?" he responded listlessly.

"It isn't at all dangerous, but it's very contagious. You had it when you were seven."

"H'm."

She hesitated.

"Are you worrying about your play? Has anything gone wrong?"

"No, mother. I just want to be alone."

After a while he got up and started after a malted milk at the soda fountain around the corner. It was half in his mind to see Mr. Beebe and ask him if he couldn't postpone his trip East. If he could only be sure that that was Evelyn's real reason.

The sight of Evelyn's nine-year-old brother coming along the street broke in on his thoughts.

"Hello, Ham. I hear you're going away."

Ham nodded.

"Going next week. To the seashore."

Basil looked at him speculatively, as if, through his proximity to Evelyn, he held the key to the power of moving her.

"Where are you going now?" he asked.

"I'm going to play with Teddy Barnfield."

"What!" Basil exclaimed. "Why, didn't you know—" He stopped. A wild, criminal idea broke over him; his mother's words floated through his mind: "It isn't at all dangerous, but it's very contagious." If little Ham Beebe got the mumps, and Evelyn *couldn't* go away—

He came to a decision quickly and coolly.

"Teddy's playing in his back yard," he said. "If you want to see him without going through his house, why don't you go down this street and turn up the alley?"

"All right. Thanks," said Ham trustingly.

Basil stood for a minute looking after him until he turned the corner into the alley, fully aware that it was the worst thing he had ever done in his life.

III

A week later Mrs. Lee had an early supper—all Basil's favorite things: chipped beef, french-fried potatoes, sliced peaches and cream, and devil's food.

Every few minutes Basil said, "Gosh! I wonder what time it is," and went out in the hall to look at the clock. "Does that clock work

right?" he demanded with sudden suspicion. It was the first time the matter had ever interested him.

"Perfectly all right. If you eat so fast you'll have indigestion and then you won't be able to act well."

"What do you think of the program?" he asked for the third time. "Riply Buckner, Jr., presents Basil Duke Lee's comedy, The Captured Shadow."

"I think it's very nice."

"He doesn't really present it."

"It sounds very well though."

"I wonder what time it is?" he inquired.

"You just said it was ten minutes after six."

"Well, I guess I better be starting."

"Eat your peaches, Basil. If you don't eat you won't be able to act."

"I don't have to act," he said patiently. "All I am is a small part, and it wouldn't matter—" It was too much trouble to explain.

"Please don't smile at me when I come on, mother," he requested. "Just act as if I was anybody else."

"Can't I even say how-do-you-do?"

"What?" Humor was lost on him. He said good-by. Trying very hard to digest not his food but his heart, which had somehow slipped down into his stomach, he started off for the Martindale School.

As its yellow windows loomed out of the night his excitement became insupportable; it bore no resemblance to the building he had been entering so casually for three weeks. His footsteps echoed symbolically and portentously in its deserted hall; upstairs there was only the janitor setting out the chairs in rows, and Basil wandered about the vacant stage until someone came in.

It was Mayall De Bec, the tall, clever, not very likeable youth they had imported from Lower Crest Avenue to be the leading man. Mayall, far from being nervous, tried to engage Basil in casual conversation. He wanted to know if Basil thought Evelyn Beebe would mind if he went to see her sometime when the show was over. Basil supposed not. Mayall said he had a friend whose father owned a brewery who owned a twelve-cylinder car.

Basil said, "Gee!"

At quarter to seven the participants arrived in groups—Riply Buckner with the six boys he had gathered to serve as ticket takers and ushers; Miss Halliburton, trying to seem very calm and reliable; Evelyn Beebe, who came in as if she were yielding herself up to something and whose glance at Basil seemed to say: "Well, it looks as if I'm really going through with it after all."

Mayall De Bec was to make up the boys and Miss Halliburton the girls. Basil soon came to the conclusion that Miss Halliburton knew nothing about make-up, but he judged it diplomatic, in that lady's overwrought condition, to say nothing, but to take each girl to Mayall for corrections when Miss Halliburton had done.

An exclamation from Bill Kampf, standing at a crack in the curtain, brought Basil to his side. A tall bald-headed man in spectacles had come in and was shown to a seat in the middle of the house, where he examined the program. He was the public. Behind those waiting eyes, suddenly so mysterious and incalculable, was the secret of the play's failure or success. He finished the program, took off his glasses and looked around. Two old ladies and two little boys came in, followed immediately by a dozen more.

"Hey, Riply," Basil called softly. "Tell them to put the children down in front."

Riply, struggling into his policeman's uniform, looked up, and the long black mustache on his upper lip quivered indignantly.

"I thought of that long ago."

The hall, filling rapidly, was now alive with the buzz of conversation. The children in front were jumping up and down in their seats, and everyone was talking and calling back and forth save the several dozen cooks and housemaids who sat in stiff and quiet pairs about the room.

Then, suddenly, everything was ready. It was incredible. "Stop! Stop!" Basil wanted to say. "It can't be ready. There must be something—there always has been something," but the darkened auditorium and the piano and violin from Geyer's Orchestra playing "Meet Me in the Shadows" belied his words. Miss Saunders, Leilia Van Baker and Leilia's friend, Estella Carrage, were already seated on the stage, and Miss Halliburton stood in the wings with the prompt book. Suddenly the music ended and the chatter in front died away.

"Oh, gosh!" Basil thought. "Oh, my gosh!"

The curtain rose. A clear voice floated up from somewhere. Could it be from that unfamiliar group on the stage?

I will, Miss Saunders. I tell you I will!

But, Miss Leilia, I don't consider the newspapers proper for young ladies nowadays.

I don't care. I want to read about this wonderful gentleman burglar they call The Shadow.

It was actually going on. Almost before he realized it, a ripple of laughter passed over the audience as Evelyn gave her imitation of Miss Saunders behind her back.

"Get ready, Basil," breathed Miss Halliburton.

Basil and Bill Kampf, the crooks, each took an elbow of Victor Van Baker, the dissolute son of the house, and made ready to aid him through the front door.

It was strangely natural to be out on the stage with all those eyes looking up encouragingly. His mother's face floated past him, other faces that he recognized and remembered.

Bill Kampf stumbled on a line and Basil picked him up quickly and went on.

MISS SAUNDERS: So you are alderman from the Sixth Ward?

RABBIT SIMMONS: Yes, ma'am.

MISS SAUNDERS (*shaking her head kittenishly*): Just what is an alderman?

CHINAMAN RUDD: An alderman is halfway between a politician and a pirate.

This was one of Basil's lines that he was particularly proud of—but there was not a sound from the audience, not a smile. A moment later Bill Kampf absent-mindedly wiped his forehead with his handkerchief and then stared at it, startled by the red stains of make-up on it—and the audience roared. The theatre was like that.

MISS SAUNDERS: Then you believe in spirits, Mr. Rudd.

CHINAMAN RUDD: Yes, ma'am, I certainly do believe in spirits. Have you got any?

The first big scene came. On the darkened stage a window rose slowly and Mayall De Bec, "in a full evening dress," climbed over the sill. He was tiptoeing cautiously from one side of the stage to the other, when Leilia Van Baker came in. For a moment she was frightened, but he assured her that he was a friend of her brother Victor. They talked. She told him naïvely yet feelingly of her admiration for The Shadow, of whose exploits she had read. She hoped, though, that The Shadow would not come here tonight, as the family jewels were all in that safe at the right.

The stranger was hungry. He had been late for his dinner and so had not been able to get any that night. Would he have some crackers and milk? That would be fine. Scarcely had she left the room when he was on his knees by the safe, fumbling at the catch, undeterred by the unpromising word "Cake" stencilled on the safe's front. It swung open, but he heard footsteps outside and closed it just as Leilia came back with the crackers and milk.

They lingered, obviously attracted to each other. Miss Saunders came in, very kittenish, and was introduced. Again Evelyn mimicked her behind her back and the audience roared. Other members of the household appeared and were introduced to the stranger.

What's this? A banging at the door, and Mulligan, a policeman, rushes in.

We have just received word from the Central Office that the notorious Shadow has been seen climbing in the window! No one can leave this house tonight!

The curtain fell. The first rows of the audience—the younger brothers and sisters of the cast—were extravagant in their enthusiasm. The actors took a bow.

A moment later Basil found himself alone with Evelyn Beebe on the stage. A weary doll in her make-up she was leaning against a table.

"Heigh-ho, Basil," she said.

She had not quite forgiven him for holding her to her promise after her little brother's mumps had postponed their trip East and

Basil had tactfully avoided her, but now they met in the genial glow of excitement and success.

He lingered a moment. He could never please her, for she wanted someone like herself, someone who could reach her through her senses, like Hubert Blair. Her intuition told her that Basil was of a certain vague consequence; beyond that his incessant attempts to make people think and feel, bothered and wearied her. But suddenly, in the glow of the evening, they leaned forward and kissed peacefully, and from that moment, because they had no common ground even to quarrel on, they were friends for life.

When the curtain rose upon the second act Basil slipped down a flight of stairs and up to another to the back of the hall, where he stood watching in the darkness. He laughed silently when the audience laughed, enjoying it as if it were a play he had never seen before.

There was a second and a third act scene that were very similar. In each of them The Shadow, alone on the stage, was interrupted by Miss Saunders. Mayall De Bec, having had but ten days of rehearsal, was inclined to confuse the two, but Basil was totally unprepared for what happened. Upon Connie's entrance Mayall spoke his third-act line and involuntarily Connie answered in kind.

Others coming on the stage were swept up in the nervousness and confusion, and suddenly they were playing the third act in the middle of the second. It happened so quickly that for a moment Basil had only a vague sense that something was wrong. Then he dashed down one stairs and up another and into the wings, crying:

"Let down the curtain! Let down the curtain!"

The boys who stood there aghast sprang to the rope. In a minute Basil, breathless, was facing the audience.

"Ladies and gentlemen," he said, "there's been changes in the cast and what just happened was a mistake. If you'll excuse us we'd like to do that scene over."

He stepped back in the wings to a flutter of laughter and applause.

"All right, Mayall!" he called excitedly. "On the stage alone. Your line is: 'I just want to see that the jewels are all right,' and Connie's is: 'Go ahead, don't mind me.' All right! Curtain up!"

In a moment things righted themselves. Someone brought water for Miss Halliburton, who was in a state of collapse, and as the act ended they all took a curtain call once more. Twenty minutes later it was over. The hero clasped Leilia Van Baker to his breast, confessing that he was The Shadow, "and a captured Shadow at that"; the curtain went up and down, up and down; Miss Halliburton was dragged unwillingly on the stage and the ushers came up the aisles laden with flowers. Then everything became informal and the actors mingled happily with the audience, laughing and important, congratulated from all sides. An old man whom Basil didn't know came up to him and shook his hand, saying, "You're a young man that's going to be heard from some day," and a reporter from the paper asked him if he was really only fifteen. It might all have been very bad and demoralizing for Basil, but it was already behind him. Even as the crowd melted away and the last few people spoke to him and went out, he felt a great vacancy come into his heart. It was over, it was done and gone—all that work, and interest and absorption. It was a hollowness like fear.

"Good night, Miss Halliburton. Good night, Evelyn."

"Good night, Basil. Congratulations, Basil. Good night."

"Where's my coat? Good night, Basil."

"Leave your costumes on the stage, please. They've got to go back tomorrow."

He was almost the last to leave, mounting to the stage for a moment and looking around the deserted hall. His mother was waiting and they strolled home together through the first cool night of the year.

"Well, I thought it went very well indeed. Were you satisfied?" He didn't answer for a moment. "Weren't you satisfied with the way it went?"

"Yes." He turned his head away.

"What's the matter?"

"Nothing," and then. "Nobody really cares, do they?"

"About what?"

"About anything."

"Everybody cares about different things. I care about you, for instance."

Instinctively he ducked away from a hand extended caressingly toward him: "Oh, don't. I don't mean like that."

"You're just overwrought, dear."

"I am not overwrought. I just feel sort of sad."

"You shouldn't feel sad. Why, people told me after the play——"

"Oh, that's all over. Don't talk about that—don't ever talk to me about that any more."

"Then what are you sad about?"

"Oh, about a little boy."

"What little boy?"

"Oh, little Ham—you wouldn't understand."

"When we get home I want you to take a real hot bath and quiet your nerves."

"All right."

But when he got home he fell immediately into deep sleep on the sofa. She hesitated. Then covering him with a blanket and a comforter, she pushed a pillow under his protesting head and went upstairs.

She knelt for a long time beside her bed.

"God, help him! help him," she prayed, "because he needs help that I can't give him any more."

THE PERFECT LIFE

I

WHEN he came into the dining room, a little tired, but with his clothes hanging cool and free on him after his shower, the whole school stood up and clapped and cheered until he slunk down into his seat. From one end of the table to the other, people leaned forward and smiled at him.

"Nice work, Lee. Not your fault we didn't win."

Basil knew that he had been good. Up to the last whistle he could feel his expended energy miraculously replacing itself after each surpassing effort. But he couldn't realize his success all at once, and only little episodes lingered with him, such as when that shaggy Exeter tackle stood up big in the line and said, "Let's get that quarter! He's yellow." Basil shouted back, "Yellow your gra'mother!" and the linesman grinned good-naturedly, knowing it wasn't true. During that gorgeous hour bodies had no weight or force; Basil lay under piles of them, tossed himself in front of them without feeling the impact, impatient only to be on his feet dominating those two green acres once more. At the end of the first half he got loose for sixty yards and a touchdown, but the whistle had blown and it was not allowed. That was the high point of the game for St. Regis. Outweighed ten pounds to the man, they wilted down suddenly in the fourth quarter and Exeter put over two touchdowns, glad to win over a school whose membership was only one hundred and thirty-five.

When lunch was over and the school was trooping out of the dining hall, the Exeter coach came over to Basil and said:

"Lee, that was about the best game I've ever seen played by a prep-school back, and I've seen a lot of them."

Doctor Bacon beckoned to him. He was standing with two old St. Regis boys, up from Princeton for the day.

"It was a very exciting game, Basil. We are all very proud of the team and—ah—especially of you." And, as if this praise had been an indiscretion, he hastened to add: "And of all the others."

He presented him to the two alumni. One of them, John Granby, Basil knew by reputation. He was said to be a "big man" at Princeton—serious, upright, handsome, with a kindly smile and large, earnest blue eyes. He had graduated from St. Regis before Basil entered.

"That was pretty work, Lee!" Basil made the proper deprecatory noises. "I wonder if you've got a moment this afternoon when we could have a little talk."

"Why, yes, sir." Basil was flattered. "Any time you say."

"Suppose we take a walk about three o'clock. My train goes at five."

"I'd like to very much."

He walked on air to his room in the Sixth Form House. One short year ago he had been perhaps the most unpopular boy at St. Regis —"Bossy" Lee. Only occasionally did people forget and call him "Bossy" now, and then they corrected themselves immediately.

A youngster leaned out of the window of Mitchell House as he passed and cried, "Good work!" The negro gardener, trimming a hedge, chuckled and called, "You almost beatum by y' own self!" Mr. Hicks the housemaster cried, "They ought to have given you that touchdown! That was a crime!" as Basil passed his door. It was a frosty gold October day, tinged with the blue smoke of Indian summer, weather that set him dreaming of future splendors, triumphant descents upon cities, romantic contacts with mysterious and scarcely mortal girls. In his room he floated off into an ambulatory dream in which he walked up and down repeating to himself tag ends of phrases: "by a prep-school back, and I've seen a lot of them." . . . "Yellow your gra'mother!" . . . "You get off side again and I'll kick your fat bottom for you!"

Suddenly he rolled on his bed with laughter. The threatened one had actually apologized between quarters—it was Pork Corrigan who only last year had chased him up two flights of stairs.

At three he met John Granby and they set off along the Grunwald Pike, following a long, low red wall that on fair mornings always suggested to Basil an adventurous quest like in "The Broad High-way." John Granby talked awhile about Princeton, but when he realized that Yale was an abstract ideal deep in Basil's heart, he gave up. After a moment a far-away expression, a smile that seemed a re-flection of another and brighter world, spread over his handsome face.

"Lee, I love St. Regis School," he said suddenly. "I spent the happiest years of my life here. I owe it a debt I can never repay." Basil didn't answer and Granby turned to him suddenly. "I wonder if you realize what you could do here."

"What? Me?"

"I wonder if you know the effect on the whole school of that wonderful game you played this morning."

"It wasn't so good."

"It's like you to say that," declared Granby emphatically, "but it isn't the truth. However, I didn't come out here to sing your praises. Only I wonder if you realize your power for good. I mean your power of influencing all these boys to lead clean, upright, decent lives."

"I never thought about that," said Basil, somewhat startled; "I never thought about——"

Granby slapped him smartly on the shoulder.

"Since this morning a responsibility has come to you that you can't dodge. From this morning every boy in this school who goes around smoking cigarettes behind the gym and reeking with nicotine is a little bit your responsibility; every bit of cursing and swearing, or of learning to take the property of others by stealing milk and food supplies out of the pantry at night is a little bit your responsi-bility."

He broke off. Basil looked straight ahead, frowning.

"Gee!" he said.

"I mean it," continued Granby, his eyes shining. "You have the sort of opportunity very few boys have. I'm going to tell you a little story. Up at Princeton I knew two boys who were wrecking their lives with drink. I could have said, 'It's not my affair,' and let them go to pieces their own way, but when I looked deep into my own heart I found I couldn't. So I went to them frankly and put it up to them fairly and squarely, and those two boys haven't—at least one of them hasn't—touched a single drop of liquor from that day to this."

"But I don't think anybody in school drinks," objected Basil. "At least there was a fellow named Bates that got fired last year——"

"It doesn't matter," John Granby interrupted. "Smoking leads to drinking and drinking leads to—other things."

For an hour Granby talked and Basil listened; the red wall beside the road and the apple-heavy branches overhead seemed to become less vivid minute by minute as his thoughts turned inward. He was deeply affected by what he considered the fine unselfishness of this man who took the burdens of others upon his shoulders. Granby missed his train, but he said that didn't matter if he had succeeded in planting a sense of responsibility in Basil's mind.

Basil returned to his room awed, sobered and convinced. Up to this time he had always considered himself rather bad; in fact, the last hero character with which he had been able to identify himself was Hairbreadth Harry in the comic supplement, when he was ten. Though he often brooded, his brooding was dark and nameless and never concerned with moral questions. The real restraining influence on him was fear—the fear of being disqualified from achievement and power.

But this meeting with John Granby had come at a significant moment. After this morning's triumph, life at school scarcely seemed to hold anything more—and here was something new. To be perfect, wonderful inside and out—as Granby had put it, to try to lead the perfect life. Granby had outlined the perfect life to him, not without a certain stress upon its material rewards such as honor and influence at college, and Basil's imagination was already far in the future. When he was tapped last man for Skull and Bones at Yale and shook his head with a sad sweet smile, somewhat like John Granby's, pointing to another man who wanted it more, a burst of sobbing would break from the assembled crowd. Then, out into the world, where, at the age of twenty-five, he would face the nation from the inaugural platform on the Capitol steps, and all around him his people would lift up their faces in admiration and love. . . .

As he thought he absent-mindedly consumed half a dozen soda

crackers and a bottle of milk, left from a pantry raid the night before. Vaguely he realized that this was one of the things he was giving up, but he was very hungry. However, he reverently broke off the train of his reflections until he was through.

Outside his window the autumn dusk was split with shafts of lights from passing cars. In these cars were great football players and lovely débutantes, mysterious adventuresses and international spies—rich, gay, glamorous people moving toward brilliant encounters in New York, at fashionable dances and secret cafés, or on roof gardens under the autumn moon. He sighed; perhaps he could blend in these more romantic things later. To be of great wit and conversational powers, and simultaneously strong and serious and silent. To be generous and open and self-sacrificing, yet to be somewhat mysterious and sensitive and even a little bitter with melancholy. To be both light and dark. To harmonize this, to melt all this down into a single man—ah, there was something to be done. The very thought of such perfection crystallized his vitality into an ecstasy of ambition. For a moment longer his soul followed the speeding lights toward the metropolis; then resolutely he arose, put out his cigarette on the window sill, and turning on his reading lamp, began to note down a set of requirements for the perfect life.

II

One month later George Dorsey, engaged in the painful duty of leading his mother around the school grounds, reached the comparative seclusion of the tennis courts and suggested eagerly that she rest herself upon a bench.

Hitherto his conversation had confined itself to a few hoarse advices, such as "That's the gym." . . . "That's Cuckoo Conklin that teaches French. Everybody hates him." . . . "Please don't call me 'Brother' in front of boys." Now his face took on the preoccupied expression peculiar to adolescents in the presence of their parents. He relaxed. He waited to be asked things.

"Now, about Thanksgiving, George. Who is this boy you're bringing home?"

"His name is Basil Lee."

"Tell me something about him."

"There isn't anything to tell. He's just a boy in the Sixth Form, about sixteen."

"Is he a nice boy?"

"Yes. He lives in St. Paul, Minnesota. I asked him a long time ago."

A certain reticence in her son's voice interested Mrs. Dorsey.

"Do you mean you're sorry you asked him? Don't you like him any more?"

"Sure I like him."

"Because there's no use bringing anyone you don't like. You could just explain that your mother has made other plans."

"But I like him," George insisted, and then he added hesitantly: "It's just some funny way he's got to be lately."

"How?"

"Oh, just sort of queer."

"But how, George? I don't want you to bring anyone into the house that's queer."

"He isn't exactly queer. He just gets people aside and talks to them. Then he sort of smiles at them."

Mrs. Dorsey was mystified. "Smiles at them?"

"Yeah. He gets them off in a corner somewheres and talks to them as long as they can stand it, and then he smiles"—his own lips twisted into a peculiar grimace—"like that."

"What does he talk about?"

"Oh, about swearing and smoking and writing home and a lot of stuff like that. Nobody pays any attention except one boy he's got doing the same thing. He got stuck up or something because he was so good at football."

"Well, if you don't want him, don't let's have him."

"Oh, no," George cried in alarm. "I've got to have him. I asked him."

Naturally, Basil was unaware of this conversation when, one morning, a week later, the Dorseys' chauffeur relieved them of their bags in the Grand Central station. There was a slate-pink light over the city and people in the streets carried with them little balloons of frosted breath. About them the buildings broke up through many planes toward heaven, at their base the wintry color of an old man's smile, on through diagonals of diluted gold, edged with purple where the cornices floated past the stationary sky.

In a long, low, English town car—the first of the kind that Basil had ever seen—sat a girl of about his own age. As they came up she received her brother's kiss perfunctorily, nodded stiffly to Basil and murmured, "how-d'y'-do" without smiling. She said nothing further but seemed absorbed in meditations of her own. At first, perhaps because of her extreme reserve, Basil received no especial impression of her, but before they reached the Dorseys' house he began to realize that she was one of the prettiest girls he had ever seen in his life.

It was a puzzling face. Her long eyelashes lay softly against her pale cheeks, almost touching them, as if to conceal the infinite boredom in her eyes, but when she smiled, her expression was illumined by a fiery and lovely friendliness, as if she were saying, "Go on; I'm listening. I'm fascinated. I've been waiting—oh, ages—for just this moment with you." Then she remembered that she was shy or bored; the smile vanished, the gray eyes half closed again. Almost before it had begun, the moment was over, leaving a haunting and unsatisfied curiosity behind.

The Dorseys' house was on Fifty-third Street. Basil was astonished first at the narrowness of its white stone front and then at the full use to which the space was put inside. The formal chambers ran the width of the house, artificial sunlight bloomed in the dining-room windows, a small elevator navigated the five stories in deferential silence. For Basil there was a new world in its compact luxury. It was thrilling and romantic that a foothold on this island was more precious than the whole rambling sweep of the James J. Hill house at home. In his excitement the feel of school dropped momentarily away from him. He was possessed by the same longing for a new experience, that his previous glimpses of New York had aroused. In the hard bright glitter of Fifth Avenue, in this lovely girl with no words to waste beyond a mechanical "How-d'y'-do," in the perfectly organized house, he recognized nothing, and he knew that to recognize nothing in his surroundings was usually a guaranty of adventure.

But his mood of the last month was not to be thrown off so lightly. There was now an ideal that came first. A day mustn't pass when he wasn't, as John Granby put it, "straight with himself"—and that meant to help others. He could get in a good deal of work on George Dorsey in these five days; other opportunities might turn up, besides. Meanwhile, with the consciousness of making the best of both worlds, he unpacked his grip and got ready for luncheon.

He sat beside Mrs. Dorsey, who found him somewhat precipitately friendly in a Midwestern way, but polite, apparently not unbalanced. He told her he was going to be a minister and immediately he didn't believe it himself; but he saw that it interested Mrs. Dorsey and let it stand.

The afternoon was already planned; they were going dancing— for those were the great days: Maurice was tangoing in "Over the River," the Castles were doing a swift stiff-legged walk in the third act of "The Sunshine Girl"—a walk that gave the modern dance a social position and brought the nice girl into the café, thus beginning a profound revolution in American life. The great rich empire was feeling its oats and was out for some not too plebeian, yet not too artistic, fun.

By three o'clock seven young people were assembled, and they started in a limousine for Emil's. There were two stylish, anæmic girls of sixteen—one bore an impressive financial name—and two freshmen from Harvard who exchanged private jokes and were attentive only to Jobena Dorsey. Basil expected that presently everyone would begin asking each other such familiar questions as "Where do you go to school?" and "Oh, do you know So-and-So?" and the party would become more free and easy, but nothing of the sort happened. The atmosphere was impersonal; he doubted if the other four guests knew his name. "In fact," he thought, "it's just as if everyone's waiting for some one else to make a fool of himself." Here again was something new and unrecognizable; he guessed that it was a typical part of New York.

They reached Emil's. Only in certain Paris restaurants where the Argentines step untiringly through their native coils does anything survive of the dance craze as it existed just before the war. At that time it was not an accompaniment to drinking or love-making or hailing in the dawn—it was an end in itself. Sedentary stockbrokers, grandmothers of sixty, Confederate veterans, venerable statesmen and scientists, sufferers from locomotor ataxia, wanted not only to dance but to dance beautifully. Fantastic ambitions bloomed in hitherto sober breasts, violent exhibitionism cropped out in families modest for generations. Nonentities with long legs became famous overnight, and there were rendezvous where they could renew the dance, if they wished, next morning. Because of a neat glide or an awkward stumble careers were determined and engagements were made or broken, while the tall Englishman and the girl in the Dutch cap called the tune.

As they went into the cabaret sudden anxiety attacked Basil— modern dancing was one of the things upon which John Granby had been most severe.

He approached George Dorsey in the coat room.

"There's an extra man, so do you suppose I'd be all right if I only danced when there's a waltz? I'm no good at anything else."

"Sure. It's all right with me." He looked curiously at Basil. "Gosh, have you sworn off everything?"

"No, not everything," answered Basil uncomfortably.

The floor was already crowded. All ages and several classes of society shuffled around tensely to the nervous, disturbing beats of "Too Much Mustard." Automatically the other three couples were up and away, leaving Basil at the table. He watched, trying to pretend to himself that he disapproved of it all but was too polite to show it. However, with so much to see, it was difficult to preserve that attitude, and he was gazing with fascination at Jobena's active feet when a good-looking young man of about nineteen sat down beside him at the table.

"Excuse me," he said with exaggerated deference. "This Miss Jobena Dorsey's table?"

"Yes, it is."

"I'm expected. Name's De Vinci. Don't ask me if I'm any relation to the painter."

"My name's Lee."

"All right, Lee. What'll you have? What are you having?" The waiter arrived with a tray, and De Vinci looked at its contents with disgust. "Tea—all tea. . . . Waiter, bring me a double Bronx. . . . How about you, Lee? Another double Bronx?"

"Oh, no, thanks," said Basil quickly.

"One then, waiter."

De Vinci sighed; he had the unmistakable lush look of a man who has been drinking hard for several days.

"Nice dog under that table over there. They oughtn't to let people smoke if they're going to bring dogs in here."

"Why?"

"Hurts their eyes."

Confusedly Basil deliberated this piece of logic.

"But don't talk to me about dogs," said De Vinci with a profound sigh; "I'm trying to keep from thinking of dogs."

Basil obligingly changed the subject for him by asking him if he was in college.

"Two weeks." For emphasis De Vinci held up two fingers. "I passed quickly through Yale. First man fired out of '15 Sheff."

"That's too bad," said Basil earnestly. He took a deep breath and his lips twisted up in a kindly smile. "Your parents must have felt pretty badly about that."

De Vinci stared at him as if over a pair of spectacles, but before he could answer, the dance ended and the others came back to the table.

"Hello there, Skiddy."

"Well, well, Skiddy!"

They all knew him. One of the freshmen yielded him a place next to Jobena and they began to talk together in lowered voices.

"Skiddy De Vinci," George whispered to Basil. "He and Jobena were engaged last summer, but I think she's through." He shook his head. "They used to go off in his mother's electric up at Bar Harbor; it was disgusting."

Basil glowed suddenly with excitement as if he had been snapped on like an electric torch. He looked at Jobena—her face, infinitely reserved, lightened momentarily, but this time her smile had gone sad; there was the deep friendliness but not the delight. He wondered if Skiddy De Vinci cared about her being through with him. Perhaps, if he reformed and stopped drinking and went back to Yale, she would change her mind.

The music began again. Basil stared uncomfortably into his cup of tea.

"This is a tango," said George. "You can dance the tango, can't you? It's all right; it's Spanish."

Basil considered.

"Sure you can," insisted George. "It's Spanish, I tell you. There's nothing to stop your dancing if it's Spanish, is there?"

One of the freshmen looked at them curiously. Basil leaned over the table and asked Jobena to dance.

She made a last low-voiced remark to De Vinci before she rose; then, to atone for the slight rudeness, she smiled up at Basil. He was light-headed as they moved out on the floor.

Abruptly she made an outrageous remark and Basil started and nearly stumbled, doubtful that he had heard aright.

"I'll bet you've kissed about a thousand girls in your time," she said, "with that mouth."

"What!"

"Not so?"

"Oh, no," declared Basil. "Really, I——"

Her lids and lashes had drooped again indifferently; she was singing the band's tune:

> "Tango makes you warm inside;
> You bend and sway and glide;
> There's nothing far and wide——"

What was the implication—that kissing people was all right; was even admirable? He remembered what John Granby had said: "Every time you kiss a nice girl you may have started her on the road to the devil."

He thought of his own past—an afternoon on the Kampf's porch with Minnie Bibble, a ride home from Black Bear Lake with Imogene Bissel in the back seat of the car, a miscellany of encounters running back to games of post office and to childish kisses that were consummated upon an unwilling nose or ear.

That was over; he was never going to kiss another girl until he found the one who would become his wife. It worried him that this girl whom he found lovely should take the matter so lightly. The strange thrill he had felt when George spoke of her "behaving disgustingly" with Skiddy De Vinci in his electric, was transformed into indignation—steadily rising indignation. It was criminal—a girl not yet seventeen.

Suddenly it occurred to him that this was perhaps his responsibility, his opportunity. If he could implant in her mind the futility of it all, the misery she was laying up for herself, his visit to New York would not have been in vain. He could go back to school happy, knowing he had brought to one girl the sort of peace she had never known before.

In fact, the more he thought of Jobena and Skiddy De Vinci in the electric, the madder it made him.

At five they left Emil's to go to Castle House. There was a thin rain falling and the streets were gleaming. In the excitement of going out into the twilight Jobena slipped her arm quickly through Basil's.

"There's too many for the car. Let's take the hansom."

She gave the address to a septuagenarian in faded bottle green, and the slanting doors closed upon them, shutting them back away from the rain.

"I'm tired of them," she whispered. "Such empty faces, except Skiddy's, and in another hour he won't be able to even talk straight. He's beginning to get maudlin about his dog Eggshell that died last month, and that's always a sign. Do you ever feel the fascination of somebody that's doomed; who just goes on and on in the way he was born to go, never complaining, never hoping; just sort or resigned to it all?"

His fresh heart cried out against this.

"Nobody has to go to pieces," he assured her. "They can just turn over a new leaf."

"Not Skiddy."

"Anybody," he insisted. "You just make up your mind and resolve to live a better life, and you'd be surprised how easy it is and how much happier you are."

She didn't seem to hear him.

"Isn't it nice, rolling along in this hansom with the damp blowing in, and you and I back here"—she turned to him and smiled—"together."

"Yes," said Basil abstractedly. "The thing is that everybody should try to make their life perfect. They can't start young enough; in fact, they ought to start about eleven or twelve in order to make their life absolutely perfect."

"That's true," she said. "In a way Skiddy's life is perfect. He never worries, never regrets. You could put him back at the time of the—oh, the eighteenth century, or whenever it was they had the bucks and beaux—and he'd fit right in."

"I didn't mean that," said Basil in alarm. "That isn't at all what I mean by the perfect life."

"You mean something more masterful," she supplied. "I thought so, when I saw that chin of yours. I'll bet you just take everything you want."

Again she looked at him, swayed close to him.

"You don't understand—" he began.

She put her hand on his arm. "Wait a minute; we're almost there. Let's not go in yet. It's so nice with all the lights going on and it'll be so hot and crowded in there. Tell him to drive out a few blocks more. I noticed you only danced a few times; I like that. I hate men that pop up at the first sound of music as if their life depended on it. Is it true you're only sixteen?"

"Yes."

"You seem older. There's so much in your face."

"You don't understand—" Basil began again desperately.

She spoke through the trap to the cabby:

"Go up Broadway till we tell you to stop." Sitting back in the cab, she repeated dreamily, "The perfect life. I'd like my life to be perfect. I'd like to suffer, if I could find something worth suffering for, and I'd like to never do anything low or small or mean, but just have big sins."

"Oh, no!" said Basil, aghast. "That's no way to feel; that's morbid. Why, look, you oughtn't to talk like that—a girl sixteen years old. You ought to—to talk things over with yourself—you ought to think more of the after life." He stopped, half expecting to be interrupted, but Jobena was silent. "Why, up to a month ago I used to smoke as many as twelve or fifteen cigarettes a day, unless I was training for football. I used to curse and swear and only write home once in a while, so they had to telegraph sometimes to see if I was sick. I had no sense of responsibility. I never thought I could lead a perfect life until I tried."

He paused, overcome by his emotion.

"Didn't you?" said Jobena, in a small voice.

"Never. I was just like everybody else, only worse. I used to kiss girls and never think anything about it."

"What—what changed you?"

"A man I met." Suddenly he turned to her and, with an effort, caused to spread over his face a caricature of John Granby's sad sweet smile. "Jobena, you—you have the makings of a fine girl in you. It grieved me a lot this afternoon to see you smoking nicotine and dancing modern suggestive dances that are simply savagery. And the way you talk about kissing. What if you meet some man that has kept himself pure and never gone around kissing anybody except his family, and you have to tell him that you went around behaving disgustingly?"

She leaned back suddenly and spoke crisply through the panel.

"You can go back now—the address we gave you."

"You ought to cut it out." Again Basil smiled at her, straining and struggling to lift her up out of herself to a higher plane. "Promise me you'll try. It isn't so hard. And then some day when some upright and straightforward man comes along and says, 'Will you marry me?' you'll be able to say you never danced suggestive modern dances, except the Spanish tango and the Boston, and you never kissed anybody—that is, since you were sixteen, and maybe you wouldn't have to say that you ever kissed anybody at all."

"That wouldn't be the truth," she said in an odd voice. "Shouldn't I tell him the truth?"

"You could tell him you didn't know any better."

"Oh."

To Basil's regret the cab drew up at Castle House. Jobena hurried in, and to make up for her absence, devoted herself exclusively to Skiddy and the Harvard freshmen for the remainder of the afternoon. But doubtless she was thinking hard—as he had done a month before. With a little more time he could have clinched his argument by showing the influence that one leading a perfect life could exert on others. He must find an opportunity tomorrow.

But next day he scarcely saw her. She was out for luncheon and she did not appear at her rendezvous with Basil and George after the matinée; they waited in vain in the Biltmore grill for an hour. There was company at dinner and Basil began to feel a certain annoyance when she disappeared immediately afterwards. Was it possible that his seriousness had frightened her? In that case it was all the more necessary to see her, reassure her, bind her with the invisible cords of high purpose to himself. Perhaps—perhaps she was the ideal girl that he would some day marry. At the gorgeous idea his whole being was flooded with ecstasy. He planned out the years of waiting, each one helping the other to lead the perfect life, neither of them ever kissing anybody else—he would insist on that, absolutely insist on it; she must promise not even to see Skiddy De Vinci—and then marriage and a life of service, perfection, fame and love.

The two boys went to the theatre again that night. When they came home a little after eleven, George went upstairs to say good night to his mother, leaving Basil to make reconnaissance in the ice box. The intervening pantry was dark and as he fumbled unfamiliarly for the light he was startled by hearing a voice in the kitchen pronounce his name:

"—Mr. Basil Duke Lee."

"Seemed all right to me." Basil recognized the drawling tone of Skiddy De Vinci. "Just a kid."

"On the contrary, he's a nasty little prig," said Jobena decisively. "He gave me the old-fashioned moral lecture about nicotine and modern dancing and kissing, and about that upright, straightforward man that was going to come along some day—you know that upright straightforward man they're always talking about. I suppose he meant himself, because he told me he led a perfect life. Oh, it was all so oily and horrible, it made me positively sick. Skiddy. For the first time in my life I was tempted to take a cocktail."

"Oh, he's just a kid," said Skiddy moderately. "It's a phase. He'll get over it."

Basil listened in horror; his face burning, his mouth ajar. He wanted above all things to get away, but his dismay rooted him to the floor.

"What I think of righteous men couldn't be put on paper," said Jobena after a moment. "I suppose I'm just naturally bad, Skiddy; at least, all my contacts with upright young men have affected me like this."

"Then how about it, Jobena?"

There was a long silence.

"This has done something to me," she said finally. "Yesterday I thought I was through with you, Skiddy, but ever since this happened I've had a vision of a thousand Mr. Basil Duke Lees, all grown up and asking me to share their perfect lives. I refuse to— definitely. If you like, I'll marry you in Greenwich tomorrow."

III

At one Basil's light was still burning. Walking up and down his room, he made out case after case for himself, with Jobena in the rôle of villainness, but each case was wrecked upon the rock of his bitter humiliation. "A nasty little prig"—the words, uttered with conviction and scorn, had driven the high principles of John Granby from his head. He was a slave to his own admirations, and in the past twenty-four hours Jobena's personality had become the strongest force in his life; deep in his heart he believed that what she had said was true.

He woke up on Thanksgiving morning with dark circles rimming his eyes. His bag, packed for immediate departure, brought back the debacle of the night before, and as he lay staring at the ceiling, relaxed by sleep, giant tears welled up into his eyes. An older man might have taken refuge behind the virtue of his intentions, but Basil knew no such refuge. For sixteen years he had gone his own way without direction, due to his natural combativeness and to the fact that no older man save John Granby had yet captured his imagination. Now John Granby had vanished in the night, and it seemed the natural thing to Basil that he should struggle back to rehabilitation unguided and alone.

One thing he knew—Jobena must not marry Skiddy De Vinci. That was a responsibility she could not foist upon him. If necessary, he would go to her father and tell what he knew.

Emerging from his room half an hour later, he met her in the hall. She was dressed in a smart blue street suit with a hobble skirt and a ruff of linen at her throat. Her eyes opened a little and she wished him a polite good morning.

"I've got to talk to you," he said quickly.

"I'm terribly sorry." To his intense discomfort she flashed her smile at him, just as if nothing had happened. "I've only a minute now."

"It's something very important. I know you don't like me——"

"What nonsense!" She laughed cheerfully. "Of course I like you. How did you get such a silly idea in your head?"

Before he could answer, she waved her hand hastily and ran down the stairs.

George had gone to town and Basil spent the morning walking through large deliberate snowflakes in Central Park rehearsing what he should say to Mr. Dorsey.

"It's nothing to me, but I cannot see your only daughter throw away her life on a dissipated man. If I had a daughter of my own who was about to throw away her life, I would want somebody to tell me, and so I have come to tell you. Of course, after this I cannot stay in your house, and so I bid you good-by."

At quarter after twelve, waiting anxiously in the drawing-room, he heard Mr. Dorsey come in. He rushed downstairs, but Mr. Dorsey had already entered the lift and closed the door. Turning about, Basil raced against the machine to the third story and caught him in the hall.

"In regard to your daughter," he began excitedly—"in regard to your daughter——"

"Well," said Mr. Dorsey, "is something the matter with Jobena?"

"I want to talk to you about her."

Mr. Dorsey laughed. "Are you going to ask her hand in marriage?"

"Oh, no."

"Well, suppose we have a talk after dinner when we're full of turkey and stuffing, and feeling happy."

He clapped his hand on Basil's shoulder and went on into his room.

It was a large family dinner party, and under cover of the conversation Basil kept an attentive eye on Jobena, trying to determine her desperate intention from her clothes and the expression of her face. She was adept at concealing her real emotions, as he had discovered this morning, but once or twice he saw her eyes wander to her watch and a look of abstraction come into them.

There was coffee afterward in the library, and, it seemed to Basil, interminable chatter. When Jobena arose suddenly and left the room, he moved just as quickly to Mr. Dorsey's side.

"Well, young man, what can I do for you?"

"Why—" Basil hesistated.

"Now is the time to ask me—when I'm well fed and happy."

"Why—" Again Basil stopped.

"Don't be shy. It's something about my Jobena."

But a peculiar thing had happened to Basil. In sudden detachment he saw himself from the outside—saw himself sneaking to Mr. Dorsey, in a house in which he was a guest, to inform against a girl.

"Why—" he repeated blankly.

"The question is: Can you support her?" said Mr. Dorsey jovially. "And the second is: Can you control her?"

"I forgot what it was I wanted to say," Basil blurted out.

He hurried from the library, his brain in a turmoil. Dashing upstairs, he knocked at the door of Jobena's room. There was no answer and he opened the door and glanced inside. The room was empty, but a half-packed suitcase lay on the bed.

"Jobena," he called anxiously. There was no answer. A maid passing along the hall told him Miss Jobena was having a marcel wave in her mother's room.

He hurried downstairs and into his hat and coat, racking his brains for the address where they had dropped Skiddy De Vinci the other afternoon. Sure that he would recognize the building, he drove down Lexington Avenue in a taxi, tried three doors, and trembled with excitement as he found the name "Leonard Edward Davies De Vinci" on a card beside a bell. When he rang, a latch clicked on an inner door.

He had no plan. Failing argument, he had a vague melodramatic idea of knocking him down, tying him up and letting him lie there until it blew over. In view of the fact that Skiddy outweighed him by forty pounds, this was a large order.

Skiddy was packing—the overcoat he tossed hastily over his suitcase did not serve to hide this fact from Basil. There was an open bottle of whisky on his littered dresser, and beside it a half-full glass.

Concealing his surprise, he invited Basil to sit down.

"I had to come and see you"—Basil tried to make his voice calm—"about Jobena."

"Jobena?" Skiddy frowned. "What about her? Did she send you here?"

"Oh, no." Basil swallowed hard, stalling for time. "I thought—maybe you could advise me—you see, I don't think she likes me, and I don't know why."

Skiddy's face relaxed. "That's nonsense. Of course she likes you. Have a drink?"

"No. At least not now."

Skiddy finished his glass. After a slight hesitation he removed his overcoat from the suitcase.

"Excuse me if I go on packing, will you? I'm going out of town."

"Certainly."

"Better have a drink."

"No, I'm on the water wagon—just now."

"When you get worrying about nothing, the thing to do is to have a drink."

The phone rang and he answered it, squeezing the receiver close to his ear:

"Yes. . . . I can't talk now. . . . Yes. . . . At half-past five then. It's now about four. . . . I'll explain why when I see you. . . . Goodby." He hung up. "My office," he said with affected nonchalance . . . "Won't you have a little drink?"

"No, thanks."

"Never worry. Enjoy yourself."

"It's hard to be visiting in a house and know somebody doesn't like you."

"But she does like you. Told me so herself the other day."

While Skiddy packed they discussed the question. He was a little hazy and extremely nervous, and a single question asked in the proper serious tone would send him rambling along indefinitely. As yet Basil had evolved no plan save to stay with Skiddy and wait for the best opportunity of coming into the open.

But staying with Skiddy was going to be difficult; he was becoming worried at Basil's tenacity. Finally he closed his suitcase with one of those definite snaps, took down a large drink quickly and said:

"Well, guess I ought to get started."

They went out together and Skiddy hailed a taxi.

"Which way are you going?" Basil asked.

"Uptown—I mean downtown."

"I'll ride with you," volunteered Basil. "We might—we might have a drink in the—Biltmore."

Skiddy hesitated. "I'll drop you there," he said.

When they reached the Biltmore, Basil made no move to get out.

"You're coming in with me, aren't you?" he asked in a surprised voice.

Frowning, Skiddy looked at his watch. "I haven't got much time."

Basil's face fell; he sat back in the car.

"Well, there's no use my going in alone, because I look sort of young and they wouldn't give me anything unless I was with an older man."

The appeal succeeded. Skiddy got out, saying, "I'll have to hurry," and they went into the bar.

"What'll it be?"

"Something strong," Basil said, lighting his first cigarette in a month.

"Two stingers," ordered Skiddy.

"Let's have something really strong."

"Two double stingers then."

Out of the corner of his eye Basil looked at the clock. It was twenty after five. Waiting until Skiddy was in the act of taking down his drink he signalled to the waiter to repeat the order.

"Oh, no!" cried Skiddy.

"You'll have to have one on me."

"You haven't touched yours."

Basil sipped his drink, hating it. He saw that with the new alcohol Skiddy had relaxed a little.

"Got to be going," he said automatically. "Important engagement."

Basil had an inspiration.

"I'm thinking of buying a dog," he announced.

"Don't talk about dogs," said Skiddy mournfully. "I had an awful experience about a dog. I've just got over it."

"Tell me about it."

"I don't even like to talk about it; it was awful."

"I think a dog is the best friend a man has," Basil said.

"Do you?" Skiddy slapped the table emphatically with his open hand. "So do I, Lee. So do I."

"Nobody ever loves him like a dog," went on Basil, staring off sentimentally into the distance.

The second round of double stingers arrived.

"Let me tell you about my dog that I lost," said Skiddy. He looked at his watch. "I'm late, but a minute won't make any difference, if you like dogs."

"I like them better than anything in the world." Basil raised his first glass, still half full. "Here's to man's best friend—a dog."

They drank. There were tears in Skiddy's eyes.

"Let me tell you. I raised this dog Eggshell from a pup. He was a beauty—an Airedale, sired by McTavish VI."

"I bet he was a beauty."

"He was! Let me tell you——"

As Skiddy warmed to his subject, Basil pushed his new drink toward Skiddy, whose hand presently closed upon the stem. Catching the bartender's attention, he ordered two more. The clock stood at five minutes of six.

Skiddy rambled on. Ever afterward the sight of a dog story in a magazine caused Basil an attack of acute nausea. At half-past six Skiddy rose uncertainly.

"I've gotta go. Got important date. Be mad."

"All right. We'll stop by the bar and have one more."

The bartender knew Skiddy and they talked for a few minutes, for time seemed of no account now. Skiddy had a drink with his old friend to wish him luck on a very important occasion. Then he had another.

At a quarter before eight o'clock Basil piloted Leonard Edward Davies De Vinci from the hotel bar, leaving his suitcase in care of the bartender.

"Important engagement," Skiddy mumbled as they hailed a taxi.

"Very important," Basil agreed. "I'm going to see that you get there."

When the car rolled up, Skiddy tumbled in and Basil gave the address to the driver.

"Good-by and thanks!" Skiddy called fervently. "Ought to go in, maybe, and drink once more to best friend man ever had."

"Oh, no," said Basil, "it's too important."

"You're right. It's too important."

The car rolled off and Basil followed it with his eye as it turned the corner. Skiddy was going out on Long Island to visit Eggshell's grave.

IV

Basil had never had a drink before and, now with his jubilant relief, the three cocktails that he had been forced to down mounted swiftly to his head. On his way to the Dorseys' house he threw back his head and roared with laughter. The self-respect he had lost last night rushed back to him; he felt himself tingling with the confidence of power.

As the maid opened the door for him he was aware subconsciously that there was someone in the lower hall. He waited till the maid disappeared; then stepping to the door of the coat room, he pulled it open. Beside her suitcase stood Jobena, wearing a look of mingled impatience and fright. Was he deceived by his ebullience or, when she saw him, did her face lighten with relief?

"Hello." She took off her coat and hung it up as if that was her purpose there, and came out under the lights. Her face, pale and lovely, composed itself, as if she had sat down and folded her hands.

"George was looking for you," she said indifferently.

"Was he? I've been with a friend."

With an expression of surprise she sniffed the faint aroma of cocktails.

"But my friend went to visit his dog's tomb, so I came home."

She stiffened suddenly. "You've been with Skiddy?"

"He was telling me about his dog," said Basil gravely. "A man's best friend is his dog after all."

She sat down and stared at him, wide-eyed.

"Has Skiddy passed out?"

"He went to see a dog."

"Oh, the fool!" she cried.

"Were you expecting him? Is it possible that that's your suitcase?"

"It's none of your business."

Basil took it out of the closet and deposited it in the elevator.

"You won't need it tonight," he said.

Her eyes shone with big despairing tears.

"You oughtn't to drink," she said brokenly. "Can't you see what it's made of him?"

"A man's best friend is a stinger."

"You're just sixteen. I suppose all that you told me the other afternoon was a joke—I mean, about the perfect life."

"All a joke," he agreed.

"I thought you meant it. Doesn't anybody ever mean anything?"

"I like you better than any girl I ever knew," Basil said quietly. "I mean that."

"I liked you, too, until you said that about my kissing people."

He went and stood over her and took her hand.

"Let's take the bag upstairs before the maid comes in."

They stepped into the dark elevator and closed the door.

"There's a light switch somewhere," she said.

Still holding her hand, he drew her close and tightened his arm around her in the darkness.

"Just for this once we don't need the light."

Going back on the train, George Dorsey came to a sudden resolution. His mouth tightened.

"I don't want to say anything, Basil—" He hesitated. "But look —Did you have something to drink Thanksgiving Day?"

Basil frowned and nodded.

"Sometimes I've got to," he said soberly. "I don't know what it is. All my family died of liquor."

"Gee!" exclaimed George.

"But I'm through. I promised Jobena I wouldn't touch anything more till I'm twenty-one. She feels that if I go on with this constant dissipation it'll ruin my life."

George was silent for a moment.

"What were you and she talking about those last few days? Gosh, I thought you were supposed to be visiting *me*."

"It's—it's sort of sacred," Basil said placidly. . . . "Look here; if we don't have anything fit to eat for dinner, let's get Sam to leave the pantry window unlocked tonight."

JOSEPHINE

FIRST BLOOD

"I REMEMBER your coming to me in despair when Josephine was about three!" cried Mrs. Bray. "George was furious because he couldn't decide what to go to work at, so he used to spank little Josephine."

"I remember," said Josephine's mother.

"And so this is Josephine."

This was, indeed, Josephine. She looked at Mrs. Bray and smiled, and Mrs. Bray's eyes hardened imperceptibly. Josephine kept on smiling.

"How old are you, Josephine?"

"Just sixteen."

"Oh-h. I would have said you were older."

At the first opportunity Josephine asked Mrs. Perry, "Can I go to the movies with Lillian this afternoon?"

"No, dear; you have to study." She turned to Mrs. Bray as if the matter were dismissed—but: "You darn fool," muttered Josephine audibly.

Mrs. Bray said some words quickly to cover the situation, but, of course, Mrs. Perry could not let it pass unreproved.

"What did you call mother, Josephine?"

"I don't see why I can't go to the movies with Lillian."

Her mother was content to let it go at this.

"Because you've got to study. You go somewhere every day, and you father wants it to stop."

"How crazy!" said Josephine, and she added vehemently, "How utterly insane! Father's got to be a maniac I think. Next thing he'll start tearing his hair and think he's Napoleon or something."

"No," interposed Mrs. Bray jovially as Mrs. Perry grew rosy. "Perhaps she's right. Maybe George *is* crazy—I'm sure my husband's crazy. It's this war."

But she was not really amused; she thought Josephine ought to be beaten with sticks.

They were talking about Anthony Harker, a contemporary of Josephine's older sister.

"He's divine," Josephine interposed—not rudely, for, despite the foregoing, she was not rude; it was seldom even that she appeared to talk too much, though she lost her temper, and swore sometimes when people were unreasonable. "He's perfectly——"

"He's very popular. Personally, I don't see very much to him. He seems rather superficial."

"Oh, no, mother," said Josephine. "He's far from it. Everybody says he has a great deal of personality—which is more than you can say of most of these jakes. Any girl would be glad to get their hands on him. I'd marry him in a minute."

She had never thought of this before; in fact, the phrase had been invented to express her feeling for Travis de Coppet. When, presently, tea was served, she excused herself and went to her room.

It was a new house, but the Perrys were far from being new people. They were Chicago Society, and almost very rich, and not uncultured as things went thereabouts in 1914. But Josephine was an unconscious pioneer of the generation that was destined to "get out of hand."

In her room she dressed herself for going to Lillian's house, thinking meanwhile of Travis de Coppet and of riding home from the Davidsons' dance last night. Over his tuxedo, Travis had worn a loose blue cape inherited from an old-fashioned uncle. He was tall and thin, an exquisite dancer, and his eyes had often been described by female contemporaries as "very dark"—to an adult it appeared that he had two black eyes in the collisional sense, and that probably they were justifiably renewed every night; the area surrounding them was so purple, or brown, or crimson, that they were the first thing you noticed about his face, and, save for his white teeth, the last. Like Josephine, he was also something new. There were a lot of new things in Chicago then, but lest the interest of this narrative be divided, it should be remarked that Josephine was the newest thing of all.

Dressed, she went down the stairs and through a softly opening side door, out into the street. It was October and a harsh breeze blew her along under trees without leaves, past houses with cold corners, past caves of the wind that were the mouths of residential streets. From that time until April, Chicago is an indoor city, where entering by a door is like going into another world, for the cold of the lake is unfriendly and not like real northern cold—it serves only to accentuate the things that go on inside. There is no music outdoors, or love-making, and even in prosperous times the wealth that rolls by in limousines is less glamorous than embittering to those on the sidewalk. But in the houses there is a deep, warm quiet, or else an excited, singing noise, as if those within were inventing things like new dances. That is part of what people mean when they say they love Chicago.

Josephine was going to meet her friend Lillian Hammell, but their plan did not include attending the movies. In comparison to it, their mothers would have preferred the most objectionable, the most lurid movie. It was no less than to go for a long auto ride with Travis de Coppet and Howard Page, in the course of which they would kiss not once but a lot. The four of them had been planning this since the previous Saturday, when unkind circumstances had combined to prevent its fulfillment.

Travis and Howard were already there—not sitting down, but still in their overcoats, like symbols of action, hurrying the girls breathlessly into the future. Travis wore a fur collar on his overcoat and carried a gold-headed cane; he kissed Josephine's hand facetiously yet seriously, and she said, "Hello, Travis!" with the warm affection of a politician greeting a prospective vote. But for a minute the two girls exchanged news aside.

"I saw him," Lillian whispered, "just now."

"Did you?"

Their eyes blazed and fused together.

"Isn't he di*vine*?" said Josephine.

They were referring to Mr. Anthony Harker, who was twenty-two, and unconscious of their existence, save that in the Perry house he occasionally recognized Josephine as Constance's younger sister.

"He has the most beautiful nose," cried Lillian, suddenly laughing. "It's—" She drew it on the air with her finger and they both became hilarious. But Josephine's face composed itself as Travis' black eyes, conspicuous as if they had been freshly made the previous night, peered in from the hall.

"Well!" he said tensely.

The four young people went out, passed through fifty bitter feet of wind and entered Page's car. They were all very confident and knew exactly what they wanted. Both girls were expressly disobeying their parents, but they had no more sense of guilt about it than a soldier escaping from an enemy prison camp. In the black seat, Josephine and Travis looked at each other; she wailed as he burned darkly.

"Look," he said to his hand; it was trembling. "Up till five this morning. Girls from the Follies."

"Oh, Travis!" she cried automatically, but for the first time a communication such as this failed to thrill her. She took his hand, wondering what the matter was inside herself.

It was quite dark, and he bent over her suddenly, but as suddenly she turned her face away. Annoyed, he made cynical nods with his head and lay back in the corner of the car. He became engaged in cherishing his dark secret—the secret that always made her yearn toward him. She could see it come into his eyes and fill them, down to the cheek bones and up to the brows, but she could not concentrate on him. The romantic mystery of the world had moved into another man.

Travis waited ten minutes for her capitulation; then he tried again, and with this second approach she saw him plain for the first time. It was enough. Josephine's imagination and her desires were easily exploited up to a certain point, but after that her very impulsiveness protected her. Now, suddenly, she found something real against Travis, and her voice was modulated with lowly sorrow.

"I heard what you did last night. I heard very well."

"What's the matter?"

"You told Ed Bement you were in for a big time because you were going to take me home in your car."

"Who told you that?" he demanded, guilty but belittling.

"Ed Bement did, and he told me he almost hit you in the face when you said it. He could hardly keep restraining himself."

Once more Travis retired to his corner of the seat. He accepted this as the reason for her coolness, as in a measure it was. In view of Doctor Jung's theory that innumerable male voices argue in the subconscious of a woman, and even speak through her lips, then the absent Ed Bement, was probably speaking through Josephine at that moment.

"I've decided not to kiss any more boys, because I won't have anything left to give the man I really love."

"Bull!" replied Travis.

"It's true. There's been too much talk around Chicago about me. A man certainly doesn't respect a girl he can kiss whenever he wants to, and I want to be respected by the man I'm going to marry some day."

Ed Bement would have been overwhelmed had he realized the extent of his dominance over her that afternoon.

Walking from the corner, where the youths discreetly left her, to her house, Josephine felt that agreeable lightness which comes with the end of a piece of work. She would be a good girl now forever, see less of boys, as her parents wished, try to be what Miss Benbower's school denominated An Ideal Benbower Girl. Then next year, at Brearley, she could be an Ideal Brearley Girl. But the first stars were out over Lake Shore Drive, and all about her could feel Chicago swinging around its circle at a hundred miles an hour, and Josephine knew that she only wanted to want such wants for her soul's sake. Actually, she had no desire for achievement. Her grandfather had had that, her parents had had the consciousness of it, but Josephine accepted the proud world into which she was born. This was easy in Chicago, which, unlike New York, was a city state, where the old families formed a caste—intellect was represented by the university professors, and there were no ramifications, save that even the Perrys had to be nice to half a dozen families even richer and more important than themselves. Josephine loved to dance, but the field of feminine glory, the ballroom floor, was something you slipped away from with a man.

As Josephine came to the iron gate of her house, she saw her sister shivering on the top steps with a departing young man; then the front door closed and the man came down the walk. She knew who he was.

He was abstracted, but he recognized her for just a moment in passing.

"Oh, hello," he said.

She turned all the way round so that he could see her face by the street lamp; she lifted her face full out of her fur collar and toward him, and then smiled.

"Hello," she said modestly.

They passed. She drew in her head like a turtle.

"Well, now he knows what I look like, anyhow," she told herself excitedly as she went on into the house.

II

Several days later Constance Perry spoke to her mother in a serious tone:

"Josephine is so conceited that I really think she's a little crazy."

"She's very conceited," admitted Mrs. Perry. "Father and I were talking and we decided that after the first of the year she should go East to school. But you don't say a word about it until we know more definitely."

"Heavens, mother, it's none too soon! She and that terrible Travis de Coppet running around with his cloak, as if they were about a thousand years old. They came into the Blackstone last week and my *spine* crawled. They looked just like two maniacs—Travis slinking along, and Josephine twisting her mouth around as if she had St. Vitus dance. *Honestly*——"

"What did you begin to say about Anthony Harker?" interrupted Mrs. Perry.

"That she's got a crush on him, and he's about old enough to be her grandfather."

"Not quite."

"Mother, he's twenty-two and she's sixteen. Every time Jo and Lillian go by him, they giggle and stare——"

"Come here, Josephine," said Mrs. Perry.

Josephine came into the room slowly and leaned her backbone against the edge of the opened door, teetering upon it calmly.

"What, mother?"

"Dear, you don't want to be laughed at, do you?"

Josephine turned sulkily to her sister. "Who laughs at me? You do, I guess. You're the only one that does."

"You're so conceited that you don't see it. When you and Travis de Coppet came into the Blackstone that afternoon, my *spine* crawled. Everybody at our table and most of the other tables laughed —the ones that weren't shocked."

"I guess they were more shocked," guessed Josephine complacently.

"You'll have a fine reputation by the time you come out."

"Oh, shut your mouth!" said Josephine.

There was a moment's silence. Then Mrs. Perry whispered solemnly, "I'll have to tell your father about this as soon as he comes home."

"Go on, tell him." Suddenly Josephine began to cry. "Oh, why can't anybody ever leave me alone? I wish I was dead."

Her mother stood with her arm around her, saying, "Josephine— now, Josephine"; but Josephine went on with deep, broken sobs that seemed to come from the bottom of her heart.

"Just a lot—of—of ugly and jealous girls who get mad when anybody looks at m-me, and make up all sorts of stories that are absolutely untrue, just because I can get anybody I want. I suppose that Constance is mad about it because I went in and sat for *five* minutes with Anthony Harker while he was waiting last night."

"Yes, I was *ter*ribly jealous! I sat up and cried all night about it. Especially because he comes to talk to me about Marice Whaley. Why!—you got him so crazy about you in that five minutes that he couldn't stop laughing all the way to the Warrens."

Josephine drew in her breath in one last gasp, and stopped crying. "If you want to know, I've decided to give him up."

"Ha-ha!" Constance exploded. "Listen to *that*, mother! She's going to give him up—as if he ever looked at her or knew she was al*ive*! Of all the conceited——"

But Mrs. Perry could stand no more. She put her arm around Josephine and hurried her to her room down the hall.

"All your sister meant was that she didn't like to see you laughed at," she explained.

"Well, I've given him up," said Josephine gloomily.

She had given him up, renouncing a thousand kisses she had never had, a hundred long, thrilling dances in his arms, a hundred evenings not to be recaptured. She did not mention the letter she had written him last night—and had not sent, and now would never send.

"You musn't think about such things at your age," said Mrs. Perry. "You're just a child."

Josephine got up and went to the mirror.

"I promised Lillian to come over to her house. I'm late now."

Back in her room, Mrs. Perry thought: "Two months to February." She was a pretty woman who wanted to be loved by everyone around her; there was no power of governing in her. She tied up her mind like a neat package and put it in the post office, with Josephine inside it safely addressed to the Brearley School.

An hour later, in the tea room at the Blackstone Hotel, Anthony Harker and another young man lingered at table. Anthony was a happy fellow, lazy, rich enough, pleased with his current popularity. After a brief career in an Eastern university, he had gone to a famous college in Virginia and in its less exigent shadow completed his education; at least, he had absorbed certain courtesies and mannerisms that Chicago girls found charming.

"There's that guy Travis de Coppet," his companion had just remarked. "What's he think he is, anyhow?"

Anthony looked remotely at the young people across the room, recognizing the little Perry girl and other young females whom he seemed to have encountered frequently in the street of late. Although obviously much at home, they seemed silly and loud; presently his eyes left them and searched the room for the party he was due to join for dancing, but he was still sitting there when the room—it had a twilight quality, in spite of the lights within and the full dark outside—woke up to confident and exciting music. A thickening parade drifted past him. The men in sack suits, as though they had just come from protentous affairs, and the women in hats that seemed about to take flight, gave a special impermanence to the scene. This implication that this gathering, a little more than uncalculated, a little less than clandestine, would shortly be broken into formal series, made him anxious to seize its last minutes, and he looked more and more intently into the crowd for the face of anyone he knew.

One face emerged suddenly around a man's upper arm not five feet away, and for a moment Anthony was the object of the saddest and most tragic regard that had ever been directed upon him. It was a smile and not a smile—two big gray eyes with bright triangles of color underneath, and a mouth twisted into a universal sympathy that seemed to include both him and herself—yet withal, the expression not of a victim, but rather of the very *de*mon of tender melancholy—and for the first time Anthony really saw Josephine.

His immediate instinct was to see with whom she was dancing. It was a young man he knew, and with this assurance he was on his feet giving a quick tug to his coat, and then out upon the floor.

"May I cut in, please?"

Josephine came close to him as they started, looked up into his eyes for an instant, and then down and away. She said nothing. Realizing that she could not possibly be more than sixteen, Anthony hoped that the party he was to join would not arrive in the middle of the dance.

When that was over, she raised eyes to him again; a sense of having been mistaken, of her being older than he had thought, possessed him. Just before he left her at her table, he was moved to say:

"Couldn't I have another later?"

"Oh, sure."

She united her eyes with his, every glint a spike—perhaps from the railroads on which their family fortunes were founded, and upon which they depended. Anthony was disconcerted as he went back to his table.

One hour later, they left the Blackstone together in her car.

This had simply happened—Josephine's statement, at the end of their second dance, that she must leave, then her request, and his own extreme self-consciousness as he walked beside her across the empty floor. It was a favor to her sister to take her home—but he had that unmistakable feeling of expectation.

Nevertheless, once outside and shocked into reconsideration by the bitter cold, he tried again to allocate his responsibilities in the matter. This was hard going with Josephine's insistent dark and ivory youth pressed up against him. As they got in the car he tried to dominate the situation with a masculine stare, but her eyes, shining as if with fever, melted down his bogus austerity in a whittled second.

Idly he patted her hand—then suddenly he was inside the radius of her perfume and kissing her breathlessly.

"So that's that," she whispered after a moment. Startled, he wondered if he had forgotten something—something he had said to her before.

"What a cruel remark," he said, "just when I was getting interested."

"I only meant that any minute with you may be the last one," she said miserably. "The family are going to send me away to school —they think I haven't found that out yet."

"Too bad."

"—and today they got together—and tried to tell me that you didn't know I was al*ive*!"

After a long pause, Anthony contributed feebly. "I hope you didn't let them convince you."

She laughed shortly. "I just laughed and came down here."

Her hand burrowed its way into his; when he pressed it, her eyes, bright now, not dark, rose until they were as high as his, and came toward him. A minute later he thought to himself: "This is a rotten trick I'm doing."

He was sure he was doing it.

"You're so sweet," she said.

"You're a dear child."

"I hate jealousy worse than anything in the world," Josephine broke forth, "and *I* have to suffer from it. And my own sister worse than all the rest."

"Oh, no," he protested.

"I couldn't help it if I fell in love with you. I tried to help it. I used to go out of the house when I knew you were coming."

The force of her lies came from her sincerity and from her simple and superb confidence that whomsoever she loved must love her in return. Josephine was never either ashamed nor plaintive. She was in the world of being alone with a male, a world through which she had moved surely since she was eight years old. She did not plan; she merely let herself go, and the overwhelming life in her did the rest. It is only when youth is gone and experience has given us a sort of cheap courage that most of us realize how simple such things are.

"But you couldn't be in love with me," Anthony wanted to say, and couldn't. He fought with a desire to kiss her again, even tenderly, and began to tell her that she was being unwise, but before he got really started at this handsome project, she was in his arms again, and whispering something that he had to accept, since it was wrapped up in a kiss. Then he was alone, driving away from her door.

What had he agreed to? All they had said rang and beat in his ear like an unexpected temperature—tomorrow at four o'clock on that corner.

"Good God!" he thought uneasily. "All that stuff about giving me up. She's a crazy kid, she'll get into trouble if somebody looking for trouble comes along. *Big* chance of my meeting her tomorrow!"

But neither at dinner or dance that he went to that night could Anthony get the episode out of his mind; he kept looking around the ballroom regretfully, as if he missed someone who should be there.

III

Two weeks later, waiting for Marice Whaley in a meagre, indefinable down-stairs "sitting room," Anthony reached in his pocket for some half-forgotten mail. Three letters he replaced; the other—after a moment of listening—he opened quickly and read with his back to the door. It was the third of a series—for one had followed each of his meetings with Josephine—and it was exactly like the others—the letter of a child. Whatever maturity of emotion could accumulate in her expression, when once she set pen to paper was snowed under by ineptitude. There was much about "your feeling for me" and "my feeling for you," and sentences began, "Yes, I know I am sentimental," or more gawkily, "I have always been sort of pash, and I can't help that," and inevitably much quoting of lines from current popular songs, as if they expressed the writer's state of mind more fully than verbal struggles of her own.

The letter disturbed Anthony. As he reached the postcript, which coolly made a rendezvous for five o'clock this afternoon, he heard Marice coming down-stairs, and put it back in his pocket.

Marice hummed and moved about the room. Anthony smoked.

"I saw you Tuesday afternoon," she said suddenly. "You seemed to be having a fine time."

"Tuesday," he repeated, as if thinking. "Oh, yeah. I ran into some kids and we went to a tea dance. It was amusing."

"You were *al*most alone when I saw you."

"What are you getting at?"

Marice hummed again. "Let's go out. Let's go to a matinée."

On the way Anthony explained how he had happened to be with Connie's little sister; the necessity of the explanation somehow angered him. When he had done, Marice said crisply:

"If you wanted to rob the cradle, why did you have to pick out that little devil? Her reputation's so bad already that Mrs. McRae didn't want to invite her to dancing class this year—she only did it on account of Constance."

"Why is she so awful?" asked Anthony, disturbed.

"I'd rather not discuss it."

His five o'clock engagement was on his mind throughout the matinée. Though Marice's remarks served only to make him dangerously sorry for Josephine, he was nevertheless determined that this meeting should be the last. It was embarassing to have been remarked in her company, even though he had tried honestly to avoid it. The matter could very easily develop into a rather dangerous little mess, with no benefit either to Josephine or to himself. About Marice's indignation he did not care; she had been his for the asking all autumn, but Anthony did not want to get married; did not want to get involved with anybody at all.

It was dark when he was free at 5:30, and turned his car toward the new Philanthrophilogical Building in the maze of reconstruction in Grant Park. The bleakness of place and time depressed him, gave a further painfulness to the affair. Getting out of his car, he walked past a young man in a waiting roadster—a young man whom he seemed to recognize—and found Josephine in the half darkness of the little chamber that the storm doors formed.

With an indefinable sound of greeting, she walked determinedly into his arms, putting up her face.

"I can only stay for a sec," she protested, just as if he had begged her to come. "I'm supposed to go to a wedding with sister, but I had to see you."

When Anthony spoke, his voice froze into a white mist, obvious in the darkness. He said things he had said to her before but this time firmly and finally. It was easier, because he could scarcely see her face and because somewhere in the middle she irritated him by starting to cry.

"I knew you were supposed to be fickle," she whispered, "but I didn't expect this. Anyhow, I've got enough pride not to bother you any further." She hesitated. "But I wish we could meet just once more to try and arrive at a more different settlement."

"No."

"Some jealous girl has been talking to you about me."

"No." Then, in despair, he struck at her heart. "I'm *not* fickle. I've never loved you and I *never* told you I did."

Guessing at the forlorn expression that would come into her face, Anthony turned away and took a purposeless step; when we wheeled nervously about, the storm door had just shut—she was gone.

"Josephine!" he shouted in helpless pity, but there was no answer. He waited, heart in his boots, until presently he heard a car drive away.

At home, Josephine thanked Ed Bement, whom she had used, with a tartlet of hope, went in by a side door and up to her room. The window was open and, as she dressed hurriedly for the wedding she stood close to it so that she would catch cold and die.

Seeing her face in the bathroom mirror, she broke down and sat on the edge of the tub, making a small choking sound like a struggle with a cough, and cleaning her finger nails. Later she could cry all night in bed when everyone else was asleep, but now it was still afternoon.

The two sisters and their mother stood side by side at the wedding of Mary Jackson and Jackson Dillon. It was a sad and sentimental wedding—an end to the fine, glamorous youth of a girl who was universally admired and loved. Perhaps to no onlooker there were its details symbolical of the end of a period, yet from the vantage point of a decade, certain things that happened are already powdered with yesterday's ridiculousness, and even tinted with the lavender of the day before. The bride raised her veil, smiling that grave sweet smile that made her "adored," but with tears pouring down her cheeks, and faced dozens of friends hands outheld as if embracing all of them for the last time. Then she turned to a husband as serious and immaculate as herself, at him as if to say, "That's done. All this that I am is yours forever and ever."

In her pew, Constance, who had been at school with Mary Jackson, was frankly weeping, from a heart that was a ringing vault. But the face of Josephine beside her was a more intricate study watched intently. Once or twice, though her eyes lost none of their level straight intensity, an isolated tear escaped, and, as if startled by the feel of it, the face hardened slightly and the mouth remained in defiant immobility, like a child well warned against making a disturbance. Only once did she move; hearing a voice behind her say: "That's the little Perry girl. Isn't she lovely looking?" she turned presently and gazed at a stained-glass window lest her unknown admirers miss the sight of the side face.

Josephine's family went on to the reception, so she dined alone— or rather with her little brother and his nurse, which was the same thing.

She felt all empty. Tonight Anthony Harker, "so deeply lovable— so sweetly lovable—so deeply, sweetly lovable" was making love to someone new, kissing her ugly, jealous face; soon he would have disappeared forever, together with all the men of his generation, into a loveless matrimony, leaving only a world of Travis de Coppets and

Ed Bements—people so easy as to scarcely be worth the effort of a smile.

Up in her room, she was excited again by the sight of herself in the bathroom mirror. Oh, what if she should die in her sleep tonight?

"Oh, what a shame," she whispered.

She opened the window, and holding her only souvenir of Anthony, a big initialed linen handkerchief, crept desolately into bed. While the sheets were still cold, there was a knock at the door.

"Special delivery letter," said the maid.

Putting on the light, Josephine opened it, turned to the signature, then back again, her breast rising and falling quickly under her nightgown.

DARLING LITTLE JOSEPHINE: It's no use. I can't help it, I can't lie about it. I'm desperately, terribly in love with you. When you went away this afternoon, it all rushed over me, and I knew I couldn't give you up. I drove home, and I couldn't eat or sit still, but only walk up and down thinking of your darling face and your darling tears, there in that vestibule. And now I sit writing this letter——

It was four pages long. Somewhere it disposed of their disparate ages as unimportant, and the last words were:

I know how miserable you must be, and I would give ten years of my life to be there to kiss your sweet lips good night.

When she had read it through, Josephine sat motionless for some minutes; grief was suddenly gone, and for a moment she was so overwhelmed that she supposed joy had come in its stead. On her face was a twinkling frown.

"Gosh!" she said to herself. She read over the letter once more.

Her first instinct was to call up Lillian, but she thought better of it. The image of the bride at the wedding popped out at her—the reproachless bride, unsullied, beloved and holy with a sweet glow. An adolescence of uprightness, a host of friends, then the appearance of the perfect lover, the Ideal. With an effort, she recalled her drifting mind to the present occasion. Certainly Mary Jackson would never have kept such a letter. Getting out of bed, Josephine tore it into little pieces and, with some difficulty, caused by an unexpected amount of smoke, burned it on a glass-topped table. No well-brought up girl would have answered such a letter; the proper thing was to simply ignore it.

She wiped up the table top with the man's linen handkerchief she held in her hand, threw it absently into a laundry basket and crept into bed. She suddenly was very sleepy.

IV

For what ensued, no one, not even Constance, blamed Josephine. If a man of twenty-two should so debase himself as to pay frantic court to a girl of sixteen against the wishes of her parents and herself, there was only one answer—he was a person who shouldn't be received by decent people. When Travis de Coppet made a controversial remark on the affair at a dance, Ed Bement beat him into what was described as "a pulp," down in the washroom, and Josephine's reputation rose to normal and stayed there. Accounts of how Anthony had called time and time again at the house, each time denied admittance, how he had threatened Mr. Perry, how he had tried to bribe a maid to deliver letters, how he had attempted to waylay Josephine on her way back from school—these things pointed to the fact that he was a little mad. It was Anthony Harkers' own family who insisted that he should go West.

All this was a trying time for Josephine. She saw how close she had come to disaster, and by constant consideration and implicit obedience, tried to make up to her parents for the trouble she had unwittingly caused. At first she decided she didn't want to go to any Christmas dances, but she was persuaded by her mother, who hoped she would be distracted by boys and girls home from school for the holidays. Mrs. Perry was taking her East to the Brearley School early in January, and in the buying of clothes and uniforms, mother and daughter were much together, and Mrs. Perry was delighted at Josephine's new feeling of responsibility and maturity.

As a matter of fact, it was sincere, and only once did Josephine do anything that she could not have told the world. The day after New

Year's she put on her new travelling suit and her new fur coat and
went out by her familiar egress, the side door, and walked down the
block to the waiting car of Ed Bement. Downtown she left Ed waiting at a corner and entered a drug store opposite the old Union
Station on LaSalle Street. A man with an unhappy mouth and
desperate, baffled eyes was waiting for her there.

"Thank you for coming," he said miserably.

She didn't answer. Her face was grave and polite.

"Here's what I want—just one thing," he said quickly: "Why did
you change? What did I do that made you change so suddenly?
Was it something that happened, something I did? Was it what I
said in the vestibule that night?"

Still looking at him, she tried to think, but she could only think
how unattractive and rather terrible she found him now, and try not
to let him see it. There would have been no use saying the simple
truth—that she could not help what she had done, that great beauty
has a need, almost an obligation, of trying itself, that her ample cup
of emotion had spilled over on its own accord, and it was an accident
that it had destroyed him and not her. The eyes of pity might follow
Anthony Harker in his journey West, but most certainly the eyes
of destiny followed Josephine as she crossed the street through the
falling snow to Ed Brement's car.

She sat quiet for a minute as they drove away, relieved and yet
full of awe. Anthony Harker was twenty-two, handsome, popular and
sought after—and how he had loved her—so much that he had to
go away. She was as impressed as if they had been two other people.

Taking her silence for depression, Ed Bement said:

"Well, it did one thing anyhow—it stopped that other story they
had around about you."

She turned to him quickly. "What story?"

"Oh, just some crazy story."

"What was it?" she demanded.

"Oh, nothing much," he said hesitantly, "but there was a story
around last August that you and Travis de Coppet were married."

"Why, how perfectly terrible!" she exclaimed. "Why, I never heard
of such a lie. It—" She stopped herself short of saying the truth—
that though she and Travis had adventurously driven twenty miles

to New Ulm, they had been unable to find a minister willing to marry them. It all seemed ages behind her, childish, forgotten.

"Oh, how perfectly terrible!" she repeated. "That's the kind of story that gets started by jealous girls."

"I know," agreed Ed. "I'd just like to hear any boy try to repeat it to me. Nobody believed it anyhow."

It was the work of ugly and jealous girls. Ed Bement, aware of her body next to him, and of her face shining like fire through the half darkness, knew that nobody so beautiful could ever do anything really wrong.

A NICE QUIET PLACE

I

ALL THAT week she couldn't decide whether she was a lollipop or a roman candle—through her dreams, dreams that promised uninterrupted sleep through many vacation mornings, drove a series of long, incalculable murmuring in tune with the put-put-put of their cut-outs, "I love you—I love you," over and over. She wrote in the evening:

DEAR RIDGE: When I think of not being able to come to the freshman dance with you this June, I could lie down and *die,* but mother is sort of narrow-minded in some ways, and she feels that sixteen is too young to go to a prom; and Lil Hammel's mother feels the same way. When I think of you dancing around with *some other girl* and hear you handing her a line, like you do to everybody, I could lie down and *scream.* Oh, I *know*—because a girl here at school met you after I left Hot Springs at Easter. Anyhow, if you start rushing some other kid when you come out to Ed Bement's house party this summer, I intend to *cut her throat,* or my own, or something desperate. And probably no one will even be sorry I'm dead. Ha-ha——

Summer, summer, summer—bland inland sun and friendly rain. Lake Forest, with its thousand enchanted verandas, the dancing on the outdoor platform at the club, and always the boys, centaurs, in new cars. Her mother came East to meet her, and as they walked together out of the Grand Central Station, the symphony of promise became so loud that Josephine's face was puckered and distorted, as with the pressure of strong sunshine.

"We've got the best plans," her mother said.

"Oh, what? What, mother?"

"A real change. I'll tell you all about it when we get to the hotel."

There was a sudden discord; a shadow fell upon Josephine's heart.

"What do you mean? Aren't we going to Lake Forest?"

"Some place much better"—her mother's voice was alarmingly cheerful. "I'm saving it till we get to the hotel."

Before Mrs. Perry had left Chicago, she and Josephine's father had decided, from observations of their own and some revelations on the part of their elder daughter, Constance, that Josephine knew her way around Lake Forest all too well. The place had changed in the twenty years that it had been the summer rendezvous of fashionable Chicago; less circumscribed children of new families were resoundingly in evidence and, like most parents, Mrs. Perry thought of her daughter as one easily led into mischief by others. The more impartial eyes of other members of the colony had long regarded Josephine herself as the principal agent of corruption. But, preventive or penalty, the appalling thing to Josephine was that the Perrys were going to a "nice quiet place" this summer.

"Mother, I simply can't go to Island Farms. I simply——"

"Father feels——"

"Why don't you take me to a reform school if I'm so awful? Or to state's penitentiary? I simply can't go to a horrible old farm with a lot of country jakes and no fun and no friends except a lot of hicks."

"But, dear, it's not like that at all. They just call it Island Farms. In fact, your aunt's place isn't a farm; it's really a nice little resort up in Michigan where lots of people spend the summer. Tennis and swimming and—and fishing."

"Fishing?" repeated Josephine incredulously. "Do you call *that* something to do?" She shook her head in mute incomprehension. "I'll just be forgotten, that's all. When it's my year to come out nobody will know who I am. They'll just say, 'Who in heck is this Josephine Perry? I never saw her around here.' 'Oh, she's just some hick from a horrible old farm up in Michigan. Let's not invite her.' Just when everybody else is having a wonderful time——"

"Nobody'll forget you in one summer, dear."

"Yes, they will. Everybody'll have new friends and know new dances, and I'll be up there in the backwoods, full of hayseed, forgetting everything I know. If it's so wonderful why isn't Constance coming?"

Lying awake in their drawing-room on the Twentieth Century, Josephine brooded upon the terrible injustice of it all. She knew that her mother was going on her account, and mostly because of the gossip of a few ugly and jealous girls. These ugly and jealous girls, her relentless enemies, were not entirely creatures of Josephine's imagination. There was something in the frank sensuousness of her beauty that plain women found absolutely intolerable; they stared at her in a frightened, guarded way.

It was only recently that gossip had begun to worry Josephine. Her own theory was that, though at thirteen or fourteen she had been "speedy"—a convenient word that lacked the vulgar implication of "fast"—she was now trying to do her best, and a difficult enough business it was, without the past being held against her; for the only thing she cared about in the world was being in love and being with the person she currently loved.

Toward midnight her mother spoke to her softly and found that she was asleep. Turning on the berth light, she looked for a moment at the flushed young face, smoothed now of all its disappointment by a faint, peculiar smile. She leaned over and kissed Josephine's brow, behind which, doubtless, were passing in review those tender and eagerly awaited orgies of which she was to be deprived this summer.

II

Into Chicago, resonant with shrill June clamor; out to Lake Forest, where her friends moved already in an aura of new boys, new tunes, parties and house parties yet to be. One concession was granted her—she was to come back from Island Farms in time for Ed Bement's house party—which is to say, for Ridgeway Saunders' visit, the first of September.

Then northward, leaving all gayety behind, to the nice quiet place, implicit in its very station, which breathed no atmosphere of hectic arrivals or feverish partings: there was her aunt, her fifteen-year-old cousin, Dick, with the blank resentful stare of youth in spectacles, there were the dozen or so estates with tired people asleep inside them and the drab village three miles away. It was worse, even, than Josephine had imagined; to her the vicinity was literally unpopulated, for, as a representative of her generation, she stood alone. In despair, she buried herself in ceaseless correspondence with the outer world or, as a variant, played tennis with Dick and carried on a slow indifferent quarrel at his deliberately spiteful immaturity.

"Are you going to be this way always?" she demanded, breaking down at his stupidity one day. "Can't you do anything about it? Does it hurt?"

"What way?" Dick shambled around the tennis net in the way that so offended her.

"Oh, such a pill! You ought to be sent away to some good school."

"I am going to be."

"Why, at your age most of the boys in Chicago have cars of their own."

"Too many," he responded.

"How do you mean?" Josephine flared up.

"I heard my aunt say there was too much of that there. That's why they made you come up here. You're too much for that sort of thing."

Josephine flushed. "Couldn't you *help* being such a pill, if you honestly tried?"

"I don't know," admitted Dick. "I don't even think that maybe I *am* one."

"Oh, yes, you are. I can assure you of that."

It occurred to her, not very hopefully, that under proper supervision something might be made of him. Perhaps she could teach him to dance or have him learn to drive his mother's car. She went to the extent of trying to smarten him up, to make him wash his hands bidiurnally and to soak his hair and cleave it down the middle. She suggested that he would be more beautiful without his spectacles, and he obediently bumped around without them for several afternoons. But when he developed a feverish headache one night and confessed to his mother why he had been "so utterly insane," Josephine gave him up without a pang.

But she could have cared for almost anyone. She wanted to hear the mystical terminology of love, to feel the lift and pull inside herself that each one of a dozen affairs had given her. She had written, of course, to Ridgeway Saunders. He answered. She wrote again. He answered—but after two weeks. On the first of August, with one month gone and one to go, came a letter from Lillian Hammel, her best friend in Lake Forest.

DEAREST Jo: You said to write you every single thing, and I will, but some of it will be sort of a fatal blow to you—about Ridgeway Saunders. Ed Bement visited him in Philadelphia, and he says he is so crazy about a girl there that he wants to leave Yale and get married. Her name is Evangeline Ticknor and she was fired from Foxcroft last year for smoking; quite a speed and said to be beautiful and something like you, from what I hear. Ed said that Ridgeway was so crazy about her that he wouldn't even come out here in September unless Ed invited her, too; so Ed did. Probably a lot you care! You've probably had lots of crushes up there where you are, or aren't there any attractive boys——

Josephine walked slowly up and down her room. Her parents had what they wanted now; the plot against her was complete. For the first time in her life she had been thrown over, and by the most attractive, the most desirable boy she had ever known, cut out by a girl "very much like herself." Josephine wished passionately that she had been fired from school—then the family might have given up and let her alone.

She was not so much humiliated as full of angry despair, but for the sake of her pride, she had a letter to write immediately. Her eyes were bright with tears as she began:

DEAREST LIL: I was not surprised when I heard that about R. S. I knew he was fickle and never gave him a second *thought* after school closed in June. As a matter of fact, you know how fickle I am myself, darling, and you can imagine that I haven't had time to let it worry *me*. Everybody has a right to do what they want, say I. Live and let live is my motto. I wish you could have been here this summer. More *wonderful* parties——

She paused, knowing that she should invent more circumstantial evidence of gayety. Pen in air, she gazed out into the deep, still mass of northern trees. Inventing was delicate work, and having dealt always in realities, her imagination was ill-adapted to the task. Nevertheless, after several minutes a vague, synthetic figure began to take shape in her mind. She dipped the pen and wrote: "One of the darlingest—" hesitated and turned again for inspiration to the window.

Suddenly she started and bent forward, the tears drying in her eyes. Striding down the road, not fifty feet from her window, was the handsomest, the most fascinating boy she had ever seen in her life.

III

He was about nineteen and tall, with a blond viking head; the fresh color in his slender, almost gaunt cheeks was baked warm and dry by the sun. She had a glimpse of his eyes—enough to know that they were "sad" and of an extraordinary glistening blue. His model legs were in riding breeches, above which he wore a soft sweater jacket of blue chamois, and as he walked he swung a crop acrimoniously at the overhanging leaves.

For a moment the vision endured; then the path turned into a clump of trees and he was gone, save for the small crunch of his boots on the pine needles.

Josephine did not move. The dark green trees that had seemed so lacking in promise were suddenly like a magic wall that had opened and revealed a short cut to possible delight; the trees gave forth a great trembling rustle. For another instant she waited; then she threw herself at the unfinished letter:

—he usually wears the best-looking riding clothes. He has the *most* beautiful eyes. On top he usually wears a blue chamois thing that is simply *divine*.

IV

When her mother came in, half an hour later, she found Josephine getting into her best afternoon dress with an expression that was at once animated and far away.

"I thought—" she said. "I don't suppose you'd want to come with me and pay a few calls?"

"I'd adore to," said Josephine unexpectedly.

Her mother hesitated. "I'm afraid it's been a rather stupid month for you. I didn't realize that there wouldn't be anyone your age. But something nice has happened that I can't tell you about yet, and perhaps I'll soon have some news for you."

Josephine did not appear to hear.

"Who shall we call on?" she demanded eagerly. "Let's just call on everybody, even if it takes until ten o'clock tonight. Let's start at the nearest house and just keep going until we've killed everybody off."

"I don't know whether we can do that."

"Come on." Josephine was putting on her hat. "Let's get going, mother."

Perhaps, Mrs. Perry thought, the summer was really making a difference in her daughter; perhaps it was developing in her a more gently social vein. At each house they visited she positively radiated animation, and displayed sincere disappointment when they found no one home. When her mother called it a day, the light in her eyes went out.

"We can try again tomorrow," she said impatiently. "We'll kill the rest of them off. We'll go back to those houses where there was no one home."

It was almost seven—a nostalgic hour, for it had been the loveliest of all at Lake Forest a year ago. Bathed and positively shining, one had intruded then for a last minute into the departing day, and, sitting alone on the veranda, turned over the romantic prospects of the night, while lighted windows sprang out on the blurring shapes of houses, and cars flew past with people late home from tea.

But tonight the murmurous Indian twilight of the lake country had a promise of its own, and strolling out into the lane that passed the house, Josephine broke suddenly into a certain walk, rather an externallized state of mind, that had been hitherto reserved for more sophisticated localities. It implied, through a skimming lift of the feet, through an impatience of the moving hips, through an abstracted smile, lastly through a glance that fell twenty feet ahead, that this girl was about to cross some material threshold where she was eagerly awaited; that, in fact, she had already crossed it in her imagination and left her surroundings behind. It was just at that moment she heard a strong clear whistle in front of her and the sound as of a stick swishing through leaves:

> "Hel-lo,
> Fris-co,
> Hello!
>
> How do you do, my dear?
> I only wish that you were here."

Her heart beat a familiar tattoo; she realized that they would pass each other just where a last rift of sunset came down through the pines.

> "Hel-lo,
> Fris-co,
> Hel-lo!"

There he was, a fine shape against the foreground. His gallant face, drawn in a single dashing line, his chamois vest, so blue—she was near enough that she could have touched it. Then she realized with a shock that he had passed without noticing her proximity by a single flicker of his unhappy eyes.

"The conceited pill!" she thought indignantly. "Of all the conceited——"

She was silent during dinner; at the end she said to her aunt, with small preliminary:

"I passed the most conceited-looking young man today. I wonder who he could have been."

"Maybe it was the nephew of old Dorrance," offered Dick, "or the fellow staying at old Dorrance's. Somebody said it was his nephew or some sort of relation."

His mother said pointedly to Josephine: "We don't see the Dorrances. Mr. Charles Dorrance considered that my husband was unjust to him about our boundary some years ago. Old Mr. Dorrance was a very stubborn man indeed."

Josephine wondered if that was why he had failed to respond this afternoon. It was a silly reason.

But next day, at the same place, at the same hour, he literally jumped at her soft "Good evening"; he stared at her with unmistakable signs of dismay. Then his hand went up as if to remove a hat, found none, and he bowed instead and went on by.

But Josephine turned swiftly and walked at his side, smiling.

"You might be more sociable. You really shouldn't be so exclusive, since we're the only two people in this place. I do think it's silly to let older people influence young people."

He was walking so fast that she could scarcely keep up with him.

"Honestly, I'm a nice girl," she persisted, still smiling. "Quite a few people rush me at dances and I once had a blind man in love with me."

They were almost at her aunt's gate, still walking furiously.

"Here's where I live," she said.

"Then I'll say good-by."

"What *is* the matter?" she demanded. "How *can* you be so rude?"

His lips formed the words, "I'm sorry."

"I suppose you've got to hurry home so you can stare at yourself at the mirror."

She knew this was untrue. He wore his good looks in almost an apologetic way. But it reached him, for he came to a precipitate halt, immediately moving off a little.

"Excuse my rudeness," he exploded. "But I'm not used to girls."

She was too winded to answer. But as her shaken composure gradually returned, she became aware of an odd weariness in his face.

"At least you might talk to me for a minute, if I don't come any nearer."

After a moment's hesitation he hoisted himself tentatively onto a fence rail.

"If you're so frightened of females, isn't it time something was done about it?" she inquired.

"It's too late."

"Never," she said positively. "Why, you're missing half of life. Don't you want to marry and have children and make some woman a fine wife—I mean, a fine husband?"

In answer he only shivered.

"I used to be terribly timid myself," she lied kindly. "But I saw that I was missing half of life."

"It isn't a question of will power. It's just that I'm a little crazy on the subject. A minute ago I had an instinct to throw a stone at you. I know it's terrible, so if you'll excuse me——"

He jumped down off the fence, but she cried quickly: "Wait! Let's talk it all over."

He lingered reluctantly.

"Why, in Chicago," she said, "any man as good-looking as you could have any girl he wanted. Everyone would simply pursue him."

The idea seemed to distress him still further; his face grew so sad that impulsively she moved nearer, but he swung one leg over the fence.

"All right. We'll talk about something else," she conceded. "Isn't this the most dismal place you ever saw? I was supposed to be a speed in Lake Forest, so the family sentenced me to this, and I've had the most *kill*ing month, just sitting and twirling my thumbs. Then yesterday I looked out the window and saw you."

"What do you mean you were a speed?" he inquired.

"Just sort of speedy—you know, sort of pash."

He got up—this time with an air of finality.

"You really must excuse me. I know I'm an idiot on this woman question, but there's nothing to do about it."

"Will you meet me here tomorrow?"

"Heavens, no!"

Josephine was suddenly angry; she had humbled herself enough for one afternoon. With a cold nod, she started homeward down the lane.

"Wait!"

Now that there was thirty feet between them, his timidity had left him. She was tempted to go back, resisted the impulse with difficulty.

"I'll be here tomorrow," she said coolly.

Walking slowly home, she saw, by instinct rather than logic, that there was something here she failed to understand. In general, a lack of self-confidence was enough to disqualify any boy from her approval; it was the unforgivable sin, the white flag, the refusal of battle. Yet now that this young man was out of sight, she saw him as he had appeared the previous afternoon—unself-conscious, prob-

ably arrogant, utterly debonair. Again she wondered if the unpleasantness between the families could be responsible for his attitude.

In spite of their unsatisfactory conversation, she was happy. In
the soft glow of the sunset it seemed certain that it would all come
right tomorrow. Already the oppressive sense of being wasted had
deserted her. The boy who had passed her window yesterday afternoon was capable of anything—love, drama, or even that desperate
recklessness that she loved best of all.

Her mother was waiting on the veranda.

"I wanted to see you alone," she said, "because I thought Aunt
Gladys would be offended if you looked too delighted. We're going
back to Lake Forest tomorrow."

"Mother!"

"Constance is announcing her engagement tomorrow and getting
married in ten days. Malcolm Libby is in the State Department and
he's ordered abroad. Isn't it wonderful? Your sister's opening up the
Lake Forest house today."

"It'll be marvellous." After a moment Josephine repeated, with
more conviction: "Perfectly marvellous."

Lake Forest—she could feel the fast-beating excitement of it
already. Yet there was something missing, as if the note of an
essential trumpet had become separated from the band. For five
weeks she had passionately hated Island Farms, but glancing around
her in the gathering dusk, she felt rather sorry for it, a little ashamed
of her desertion.

Throughout dinner the odd feeling persisted. She would be deep
in exciting thoughts that began, "Won't it be fun to—" then the
imminent brilliance would fade and there would be a stillness
inside her like the stillness of these Michigan nights. That was what
was lacking in Lake Forest—a stillness for things to happen in, for
people to walk into.

"We'll be terribly busy," her mother said. "Next week there'll
be bridesmaids in the house, and parties, and the wedding itself.
We should have left tonight."

Josephine went up to her room immediately and sat looking out
into the darkness. Too bad; a wasted summer after all. If yesterday
had happened sooner she might have gone away with some sense of

having lived after all. Too late. "But there'll be lots of boys," she told herself—Ridgeway Saunders.

She could hear their confident lines, and somehow they rang silly on her ears. Suddenly she realized that what she was regretting was not the lost past but the lost future, no what had not been but what would never be. She stood up, breathing quickly.

A few minutes later she left the house by a side door and crossed the lawn to the gardener's gate. She heard Dick call after her uncertainly, but she did not answer. It was dark and cool, and the feeling that the summer was rushing away from her. As if to overtake it, she walked faster, and in ten minutes turned in at the gate of the Dorrance house, set behind the jagged silhouettes of many trees. Someone on the veranda hailed her as she came near:

"Good evening. I can't see who it is."

"It's the girl who was so fresh this afternoon."

She heard him catch his breath suddenly.

"May I sit here on the steps for a moment? See? Quite safe and far away. I came to say good-by, because we're going home tomorrow."

"Are you really?" She could not tell whether his tone showed concern or relief. "It'll be very quiet."

"I want to explain about this afternoon, because I don't want you to think I was just being fresh. Usually I like boys with more experience, but I just thought that since we were the only ones here, we might manage to have a good time, and there weren't any days to waste."

"I see." After a moment he asked, "What will you do in Lake Forest? Be a—a speed?"

"I don't much care what I do. I've wasted the whole six weeks."

She heard him laugh.

"I gather from your tone that someone is going to have to pay for it," he said.

"I hope so," she answered rather grimly. She felt tears rise in her eyes. Everything was wrong. Everything seemed to be fixed against her.

"Please let me come up there on the settee," she asked suddenly.

There was a creak as it stopped swinging.

"Please don't. I hate to ask you, but really I'll have to go if you do. Let's talk about— Do you like horses?"

She got up swiftly, mounted the steps and walked toward the corner where he sat.

"No," she said, "I think that what I'd like would be to be liked by you."

In the light of the moon just lifting over the woods his face was positively haggard. He jumped to his feet; then his hands were on her arms and he was drawing her slowly toward him.

"You simply want to be kissed," he was saying through scarcely opened lips. "I knew it the first time I saw that mouth of yours— that perfectly selfish, self-sufficient look that——"

Suddenly he dropped his arms and stepped away from her with a gesture of horror.

"Don't stop!" she cried. "Do anything, tell me anything, even if it isn't complimentary. I don't care."

But he had vaulted swiftly over the railing and, with his hands clasping the back of his head, was walking across the lawn. In a minute she overtook him and stood beseechingly in his path, her small bosom rising and falling.

"Why do you suppose I'm here?" he demanded suddenly. "Do you think I'm alone?"

"What——"

"My wife is with me."

Josephine shivered.

"Oh—oh—then why doesn't anybody know?"

"Because my wife is—my wife is colored."

If it had not been so dark Josephine would have seen that for an instant he was laughing silently and uncontrollably.

"Oh," she repeated.

"I didn't know," he continued.

In spite of a subconscious scepticism, an uncanny feeling stole over Josephine.

"What dealings could I have with a girl like you?"

She began to weep softly.

"Oh, I'm sorry. If I could only help you."

"You can't help me." He turned gruffly away.

"You want me to go."

He nodded.

"All right. I'll go."

Still sobbing, she half walked, half backed away from him, intimidated now, yet still hoping he would call to her. When she saw him for the last time from the gate, he was standing where she had left him, his fine thin face clear and handsome in the suddenly streaming light of an emergent moon.

She had gone a quarter of a mile down the road when she became conscious of running footsteps behind her. Before she could do more than start and turn anxiously, a figure sprang out at her. It was her cousin, Dick.

"Oh!" she cried. "You frightened me!"

"I followed you here. You had no business going out at night like this."

"What a sneaky thing!" she said contemptuously.

They walked along side by side.

"I heard you with that fellow. You had a crush on him, didn't you?"

"Will you be quiet! What does a horrible little pill like you know about anything?"

"I know a lot," said Dick glumly. "I know there's too much of that sort of thing at Lake Forest."

She scorned to answer; they reached her aunt's gate in silence.

"I tell you one thing," he said uncertainly. "I'll bet you wouldn't want your mother to know about this."

"You mean you're going to my mother?"

"Just hold your horses. I was going to say I wouldn't say anything about it——"

"I should hope not."

"——on one condition."

"Well?"

"The condition is——" He fidgeted uncomfortably. "You told me once that a lot of girls at Lake Forest had kissed boys and never thought anything about it."

"Yes." Suddenly she guessed what was coming, and an astonished laugh rose to her lips.

"Well, will you, then—kiss me?"

A vision of her mother arose—of a return to Lake Forest in chains. Deciding quickly, she bent toward him. Less than a minute later she was in her room, almost hysterical with tears and laughter. That, then, was the kiss with which destiny had seen fit to crown the summer.

V

Josephine's sensational return to Lake Forest that August marked a revision of opinion about her; it can be compared to the moment when the robber bandit evolved through sheer power into the feudal seignior.

To the three months of nervous energy conserved since Easter beneath the uniform of her school were added six weeks of resentment—added, that is, as the match might be said to be added to the powder. For Josephine exploded with an audible, visible bang; for weeks thereafter pieces of her were gathered up from Lake Forest's immaculate lawns.

It began quietly; it began with the long-awaited house party, on the first evening of which she was placed next to the unfaithful Ridgeway Saunders at dinner.

"I certainly felt pretty badly when you threw me over," Josephine said indifferently—to rid him of any lingering idea that he had thrown her over. Once she had chilled him into wondering if, after all, he had come off best in the affair, she turned to the man on the other side. By the time the salad was served, Ridgeway was explaining himself to her. And his girl from the East, Miss Ticknor, was becoming increasingly aware of what an obnoxious person Josephine Perry was. She made the mistake of saying so to Ridgeway. Josephine made no such mistake; toward the end of dinner she merely asked him the innocent question as to who was his friend with the high button shoes.

By ten o'clock Josephine and Ridgeway were out in somebody's car—far out where the colony becomes a prairie. As minute by minute she grew wearier of his softness, his anguish increased. She let him kiss her, just to be sure; and it was a desperate young man who returned to his host's that night.

All next day his eyes followed her about miserably; Miss Ticknor was unexpectedly called East the following afternoon. This was pathetic, but certainly someone had to pay for Josephine's summer. That score settled, she returned her attention to her sister's wedding.

Immediately on her return she had demanded a trousseau in keeping with the splendor of a maid of honor, and under cover of the family rush had so managed to equip herself as to add a charming year to her age. Doubtless this contributed to the change of attitude toward her, for though her emotional maturity, cropping out of a schoolgirl dress, had seemed not quite proper, in more sophisticated clothes she was an incontestable little beauty; and as such she was accepted by at least the male half of the wedding party.

Constance was openly hostile. On the morning of the wedding itself, she unburdened herself to her mother.

"I do hope you'll take her in hand after I'm gone, mother. It's really unendurable the way she's behaving. None of the bridesmaids have had a good time."

"Let's not worry," Mrs. Perry urged. "After all, she's had a very quiet summer."

"I'm not worrying about *her*," said Constance indignantly.

The wedding party were lunching at the club, and Josephine found herself next to a jovial usher who had arrived inebriated and remained in that condition ever since. However, it was early enough in the day for him to be coherent.

"The belle of Chicago, the golden girl of the golden West. Oh, why didn't I come out here this summer?"

"I wasn't here. I was up in a place called Island Farms."

"Ah!" he exclaimed. "Ah-ha! That accounts for a lot of things— that accounts for the sudden pilgrimage of Sonny Dorrance."

"Of who?"

"The famous Sonny Dorrance, the shame of Harvard, but the maiden's prayer. Now don't tell me you didn't exchange a few warm glances with Sonny Dorrance."

"But isn't he," she demanded faintly—"isn't he supposed to be— married?"

He roared with laughter.

"Married—sure, married to a mulatto! You didn't fall for *that* old line. He always pulls it when he's reacting from some violent affair—that's to protect himself while he recovers. You see, his whole life has been cursed by that fatal beauty."

In a few minutes she had the story. Apart from everything else, Sonny Dorrance was fabulously rich—women had pursued him since he was fifteen—married women, débutantes, chorus girls. It was legendary.

There actually had been plots to entangle him into marriage, to entangle him into anything. There was the girl who tried to kill herself, there was the one who tried to kill him. Then, this spring, there was the annulled marriage business that had cost him an election to Porcellian at Harvard, and was rumored to have cost his father fifty thousand dollars.

"And now," Josephine asked tensely, "you say he doesn't like women?"

"Sonny? I tell you he's the most susceptible man in America. This last thing shook him, and so he keeps off admirers by telling them anything. But by this time next month he'll be involved again."

As he talked, the dining room faded out like a scene in a moving picture, and Josephine was back at Island Farms, staring out the window, as a young man appeared between the pine trees.

"He was afraid of me," she thought to herself, her heart tapping like a machine gun. "He thought I was like the others."

Half an hour later she interrupted her mother in the midst of the wedding's last and most violent confusion.

"Mother, I want to go back to Island Farms for the rest of the summer," she said at once.

Mrs. Perry looked at her in a daze, and Josephine repeated her statement.

"Why, in less than a month you'll be starting back to school."

"I want to go anyhow."

"I simply can't understand you. In the first place, you haven't been invited, and in the second place, I think a little gayety is good for you before you go back to school, and in the third place, I want you here with me."

"Mother," Josephine wailed, "don't you understand? I want to go! You take me up there all summer when I don't want to go, and just when I *do* want to, you make me stay in this ghastly place. Let me tell you this isn't any place for a sixteen-year-old girl, if you knew everything."

"What nonsense to be bothering me with just at this time!"

Josephine threw up her hands in despair; the tears were streaming down her cheeks.

"It's ruining me here!" she cried. "Nobody thinks of anything but boys and dances from morning till night. They go out in their cars and kiss them from morning till night."

"Well, I know my little girl doesn't do anything like that."

Josephine hesitated, taken a little aback.

"Well, I will," she announced. "I'm weak. You told me I was. I always do what anybody tells me to do, and all these boys are just simply immoral, that's all. The first thing you know I'll be entirely ruined, and then you'll be sorry you didn't let me go to Island Farms. You'll be sorry——"

She was working herself into hysteria. Her distracted mother took her by the shoulders and forced her down into a chair.

"I've never heard such silly talk. If you weren't so old I'd spank you. If you keep this up you'll be punished."

Suddenly dry-eyed, Josephine got up and stalked out of the room. Punished! They had been punishing her all summer, and now they refused to punish her, refused to send her away. Oh, she was tired of trying. If she could think of something really awful to do, so that they would send her away forever——

Mr. Malcolm Libby, the prospective bridegroom, happened upon her fifteen minutes later, in an obscure corner of the garden. He was pacing restlessly about, steadying himself for the rehearsal at four o'clock and for the ceremony two hours later.

"Why, hello!" he cried. "Why, what's the matter? You've been crying."

He sat down on the bench, full of sympathy for Constance's little sister.

"I'm not crying," she sobbed. "I'm just angry."

"About Constance going away? Don't you think I'll take good care of her?"

Leaning over, he patted her hand. If he had seen the look that flashed suddenly across her face it would have alarmed him, for it was curiously like the expression associated with a prominent character in Faust.

When she spoke, her voice was calm, almost cool, and yet tenderly sad:

"No, that wasn't it. It was something else."

"Tell me about it. Maybe I can help."

"I was crying"—she hesitated delicately—"I was crying because Constance has all the luck."

Half an hour later when, with the rehearsal twenty minutes late, the frantic bride-to-be came searching through the garden and happened upon them suddenly, Malcolm Libby's arm was around Josephine, who seemed dissolved in uncontrollable grief, and on his face was a wildly harassed expression she had never seen there before. Constance gave a little gasping cry and sank down upon the pebbled path.

The next hour passed in an uproar. There was a doctor; there were shut doors; there was Mr. Malcolm Libby in an agonized condition, the sweat pouring off his brow, explaining to Mrs. Perry over and over that he could explain if he could only see Constance. There was Josephine, tight-lipped, in a room, being talked to coldly by various members of the family. There was the clamor of arriving guests; then frantic last minutes' patching up of things, with Constance and Malcolm in each other's arms and Josephine, unforgiven, being bundled into her dress.

Then a solemn silence fell and, moving to music, the maid of honor, her head demurely bowed, followed her sister up the two aisles of people that crowded the drawing-room. It was a lovely, sad wedding; the two sisters, light and dark, were a lovely contrast; there was as much interest in one as in the other. Josephine had become a great beauty and the prophets were busy; she stood for the radiant future, there at her sister's side.

The crush was so great at the reception that not until it was over was Josephine missed. And long before nine o'clock, before Mrs.

Perry had time to be uneasy, a note from the station had been handed in at the door:

My DEAREST MOTHER: Ed Bement brought me here in his car, and I am catching the train to Island Farms at seven. I have wired the house-keeper to meet me, so don't worry. I feel I have behaved *terribly* and am ashamed to *face* anyone, and I am punishing myself as I deserve by going back to the *simple* life. It is, after all, better for a girl of sixteen, I feel, and when you think it over you will agree. With dearest love.

JOSEPHINE.

After all, thought Mrs. Perry, perhaps it was just as well. Her husband was really angry, and she herself was exhausted and didn't feel up to another problem at the moment. Perhaps a nice quiet place was best.

A WOMAN WITH A PAST

I

Driving slowly through New Haven, two of the young girls became alert. Josephine and Lillian darted soft frank glances into strolling groups of three or four undergraduates, into larger groups on corners, which swung about as one man to stare at their receding heads. Believing that they recognized an acquaintance in a solitary loiterer, they waved wildly, whereupon the youth's mouth fell open, and as they turned the next corner he made a dazed dilatory gesture with his hand. They laughed, "We'll send him a post card when we get back to school tonight, to see if it really was him."

Adele Craw, sitting on one of the little seats, kept on talking to Miss Chambers, the chaperone. Glancing sideways at her, Lillian winked at Josephine without batting an eye, but Josephine had gone into a reverie.

This was New Haven—city of her adolescent dreams, of glittering proms where she would move on air among men as intangible as the tunes they danced to. City sacred as Mecca, shining as Paris, hidden as Timbuctoo. Twice a year the lifeblood of Chicago, her home, flowed into it, and twice a year flowed back, bringing Christmas or bringing summer. Bingo, bingo, bingo, that's the lingo; love of mine, I pine for one of your glances; the darling boy on the left there; underneath the stars I wait.

Seeing it for the first time, she found herself surprisingly unmoved —the men they passed seemed young and rather bored with the possibilities of the day, glad of anything to stare at; seemed undynamic and purposeless against the background of bare elms, lakes of dirty snow and buildings crowded together under the February sky. A wisp of hope, a well-turned-out derby-crowned man, hurrying with stick and suitcase toward the station, caught her attention, but his reciprocal glance was too startled, too ingenuous. Josephine wondered at the extent of her own disillusionment.

She was exactly seventeen and she was blasé. Already she had been a sensation and a scandal; she had driven mature men to a state of disequilibrium; she had, it was said, killed her grandfather, but as he was over eighty at the time perhaps he just died. Here and there in the Middle West were discouraged little spots which upon inspection turned out to be the youths who had once looked full into her green and wistful eyes. But her love affair of last summer had ruined her faith in the all-sufficiency of men. She had grown bored with the waning September days—and it seemed as though it had happened once too often. Christmas with its provocative short-ness, its travelling glee clubs, had brought no one new. There remained to her only a persistent, a physical hope; hope in her stomach that there was someone whom she would love more than he loved her.

They stopped at a sporting-goods store and Adele Craw, a pretty girl with clear honorable eyes and piano legs, purchased the sporting equipment which was the reason for their trip—they were the spring hockey committee for the school. Adele was in addition the president of the senior class and the school's ideal girl. She had lately seen a change for the better in Josephine Perry—rather as an honest citizen might guilelessly approve a peculator retired on his profits. On the other hand, Adele was simply incomprehensible to Josephine—admirable, without doubt, but a member of another species. Yet with the charming adaptability that she had hitherto reserved for men, Josephine was trying hard not to disillusion her, trying to be honestly interested in the small, neat, organized politics of the school.

Two men who had stood with their backs to them at another counter turned to leave the store, when they caught sight of Miss Chambers and Adele. Immediately they came forward. The one who spoke to Miss Chambers was thin and rigid of face. Josephine recognized him as Miss Brereton's nephew, a student at New Haven, who had spent several weekends with his aunt at the school. The other man Josephine had never seen before. He was tall and broad, with blond curly hair and an open expression in which strength of purpose and a nice consideration were pleasantly mingled. It was not the sort of face that generally appealed to Josephine. The eyes were obviously

without a secret, without a sidewise gambol, without a desperate
flicker to show that they had a life of their own apart from the
mouth's speech. The mouth itself was large and masculine; its smile
was an act of kindness and control. It was rather with curiosity as to
the sort of man who would be attentive to Adele Craw that Josephine
continued to look at him, for his voice that obviously couldn't lie
greeted Adele as if this meeting was the pleasant surprise of his
day.

In a moment Josephine and Lillian were called over and
introduced.

"This is Mr. Waterbury"—that was Miss Brereton's nephew—
"and Mr. Dudley Knowleton."

Glancing at Adele, Josephine saw on her face an expression of
tranquil pride, even of possession. Mr. Knowleton spoke politely,
but it was obvious that though he looked at the younger girls he did
not quite see them. But since they were friends of Adele's he made
suitable remarks, eliciting the fact that they were both coming down
to New Haven to their first prom the following week. Who were
their hosts? Sophomores; he knew them slightly. Josephine thought
that was unnecessarily superior. Why, they were the charter members
of the Loving Brothers' Association—Ridgeway Saunders and George
Davey—and on the glee-club trip the girls they picked out to rush
in each city considered themselves a sort of élite, second only to the
girls they asked to New Haven.

"And oh, I've got some bad news for you," Knowleton said to
Adele. "You may be leading the prom. Jack Coe went to the infirmary
with appendicitis, and against my better judgment I'm the provisional
chairman." He looked apologetic. "Being one of these stone-age
dancers, the two-step king, I don't see how I ever got on the committee at all."

When the car was on its way back to Miss Brereton's school,
Josephine and Lillian bombarded Adele with questions.

"He's an old friend from Cincinnati," she explained demurely.
"He's captain of the baseball team and he was last man for Skull
and Bones."

"You're going to the prom with him?"

"Yes. You see, I've known him all my life."

Was there a faint implication in this remark that only those who had known Adele all her life knew her at her true worth?

"Are you engaged?" Lillian demanded.

Adele laughed. "Mercy, I don't think of such matters. It doesn't seem to be time for that sort of thing yet, does it?" ["Yes," interpolated Josephine silently.] "We're just good friends. I think there can be a perfectly healthy friendship between a man and a girl without a lot of——"

"Mush," supplied Lillian helpfully.

"Well, yes, but I dont' like that word. I was going to say without a lot of sentimental romantic things that ought to come later."

"Bravo, Adele!" said Miss Chambers somewhat perfunctorily.

But Josephine's curiosity was unappeased.

"Doesn't he say he's in love with you, and all that sort of thing?"

"Mercy, no! Dud doesn't believe in such stuff any more than I do. He's got enough to do at New Haven serving on the committees and the team."

"Oh!" said Josephine.

She was oddly interested. That two people who were attracted to each other should never even say anything about it but be content to "not believe in such stuff," was something new in her experience. She had known girls who had no beaus, others who seemed to have no emotions, and still others who lied about what they thought and did; but here was a girl who spoke of the attentions of the last man tapped for Skull and Bones as if they were two of the limestone gargoyles that Miss Chambers had pointed out on the just completed Harkness Hall. Yet Adele seemed happy—happier than Josephine, who had always believed that boys and girls were made for nothing but each other, and as soon as possible.

In the light of his popularity and achievements, Knowleton seemed more attractive. Josephine wondered if he would remember her and dance with her at the prom, or if that depended on how well she knew her escort, Ridgeway Saunders. She tried to remember whether she had smiled at him when he was looking at her. If she had really smiled he would remember her and dance with her. She was still trying to be sure of that over her two French irregular verbs and her ten stanzas of the Ancient Mariner that night; but she was still uncertain when she fell asleep.

II

Three gay young sophomores, the founders of the Loving Brothers' Association, took a house together for Josephine, Lillian and a girl from Farmington and their three mothers. For the girls it was a first prom, and they arrived at New Haven with all the nervousness of the condemned; but a Sheffield fraternity tea in the afternoon yielded up such a plethora of boys from home, and boys who had visited there, and friends of those boys, and new boys with unknown possibilities but obvious eagerness, that they were glowing with self-confidence as they poured into the glittering crowd that thronged the armory at ten.

It was impressive; for the first time Josephine was at a function run by men upon men's standards—an outward projection of the New Haven world from which women were excluded and which went on mysteriously behind the scenes. She perceived that their three escorts, who had once seemed the very embodiments of world-liness, were modest fry in this relentless microcosm of accomplishment and success. A man's world! Looking around her at the glee-club concert, Josephine had felt a grudging admiration for the good fellowship, the good feeling. She envied Adele Craw, barely glimpsed in the dressing-room, for the position she automatically occupied by being Dudley Knowleton's girl tonight. She envied her more stepping off under the draped bunting through a gateway of hydrangeas at the head of the grand march, very demure and faintly unpowdered in a plain white dress. She was temporarily the centre of all attention, and at the sight something that had long lain dormant in Josephine awakened—her sense of a problem, a scarcely defined possibility.

"Josephine," Ridgeway Saunders began, "you can't realize how happy I am now that it's come true. I've looked forward to this so long, and dreamed about it——"

She smiled up at him automatically, but her mind was elsewhere, and as the dance progressed the idea continued to obsess her. She was rushed from the beginning; to the men from the tea were added a dozen new faces, a dozen confident or timid voices, until, like all the more popular girls, she had her own queue trailing her about the room. Yet all this had happened to her before, and there was something missing. One might have ten men to Adele's two, but Josephine was abruptly aware that here a girl took on the importance of the man who had brought her.

She was discomforted by the unfairness of it. A girl earned her popularity by being beautiful and charming. The more beautiful and charming she was, the more she could afford to disregard public opinion. It seemed absurd that simply because Adele had managed to attach a baseball captain, who mightn't know anything about girls at all, or be able to judge their attractions, she should be thus elevated in spite of her thick ankles, her rather too pinkish face.

Josephine was dancing with Ed Bement from Chicago. He was her earliest beau, a flame of pigtail days in dancing school when one wore white cotton stockings, lace drawers with a waist attached and ruffled dresses with the inevitable sash.

"What's the matter with me?" she asked Ed, thinking aloud. "For months I've felt as if I were a hundred years old, and I'm just seventeen and that party was only seven years ago."

"You've been in love a lot since then," Ed said.

"I haven't," she protested indignantly. "I've had a lot of silly stories started about me, without any foundation, usually by girls who were jealous."

"Jealous of what?"

"Don't get fresh," she said tartly. "Dance me near Lillian."

Dudley Knowleton had just cut in on Lillian. Josephine spoke to her friend; then waiting until their turns would bring them face to face over a space of seconds, she smiled at Knowleton. This time she made sure that smile intersected as well as met glance, that he passed beside the circumference of her fragrant charm. If this had been named like French perfume of a later day it might have been called "Please." He bowed and smiled back; a minute later he cut in on her.

It was in an eddy in a corner of the room and she danced slower so that he adapted himself, and for a moment they went around in a slow circle.

"You looked so sweet leading the march with Adele," she told him. "You seemed so serious and kind, as if the others were all a lot of children. Adele looked sweet too." And she added on an inspiration, "At school I've taken her for a model."

"You have!" She saw him conceal his sharp surprise as he said, "I'll have to tell her that."

He was handsomer than she had thought, and behind his cordial good manners there was a sort of authority. Correctly attentive to her, she saw his eyes search the room quickly to see if all went well; he spoke quietly, in passing, to the orchestra leader, who came down deferentially to the edge of his dais. Last man for Bones. Josephine knew what that meant—her father had been Bones. Ridgeway Saunders and the rest of the Loving Brothers' Association would certainly not be Bones. She wondered, if there had been a Bones for girls, whether she would be tapped—or Adele Craw with her ankles, symbol of solidity.

> Come on o-ver here,
> Want to have you near;
> Come on join the part-y,
> Get a wel-come heart-y.

"I wonder how many boys here have taken you for a model," she said. "If I were a boy you'd be exactly what I'd like to be. Except I'd be terribly bothered having girls falling in love with me all the time."

"They don't," he said simply. "They never have."

"Oh, yes—but they hide it because they're so impressed with you, and they're afraid of Adele."

"Adele wouldn't object." And he added hastily, "—if it ever happened. Adele doesn't believe in being serious about such things."

"Are you engaged to her?"

He stiffened a little. "I don't believe in being engaged till the right time comes."

"Neither do I," agreed Josephine readily. "I'd rather have one good friend than a hundred people hanging around being mushy all the time."

"Is that what that crowd does that keep following you around tonight?"

"What crowd?" she asked innocently.

"The 50 per cent of the sophomore class that's rushing you."

"A lot of parlor snakes," she said ungratefully.

Josephine was radiantly happy now as she turned beautifully through the newly enchanted hall in the arms of the chairman of the prom committee. Even this extra time with him she owed to the awe which he inspired in her entourage; but a man cut in eventually and there was a sharp fall in her elation. The man was impressed that Dudley Knowleton had danced with her; he was more respectful, and his modulated admiration bored her. In a little while, she hoped, Dudley Knowleton would cut back, but as midnight passed, dragging on another hour with it, she wondered if after all it had only been a courtesy to a girl from Adele's school. Since then Adele had probably painted him a neat little landscape of Josephine's past. When finally he approached her she grew tense and watchful, a state which made her exteriorly pliant and tender and quiet. But instead of dancing he drew her into the edge of a row of boxes.

"Adele had an accident on the cloakroom steps. She turned her ankle a little and tore her stocking on a nail. She'd like to borrow a pair from you because you're staying near here and we're way out at the Lawn Club."

"Of course."

"I'll run over with you—I have a car outside."

"But you're busy, you mustn't bother."

"Of course I'll go with you."

There was thaw in the air; a hint of thin and lucid spring hovered delicately around the elms and cornices of buildings whose bareness and coldness had so depressed her the week before. The night had a quality of asceticism, as if the essence of masculine struggle were seeping everywhere through the little city where men of three centuries had brought their energies and aspirations for winnowing. And Dudley Knowleton sitting beside her, dynamic and capable, was symbolic of it all. It seemed that she had never met a man before.

"Come in, please," she said as he went up the steps of the house with her. "They've made it very comfortable."

There was an open fire burning in the dark parlor. When she came downstairs with the stockings she went in and stood beside him, very still for a moment, watching it with him. Then she looked up, still silent, looked down, looked at him again.

"Did you get the stockings?" he asked, moving a little.

"Yes," she said breathlessly. "Kiss me for being so quick."

He laughed as if she had said something witty and moved toward the door. She was smiling and her disappointment was deeply hidden as they got into the car.

"It's been wonderful meeting you," she told him. "I can't tell you how many ideas I've gotten from what you said."

"But I haven't any ideas."

"You have. All that about not getting engaged till the proper time comes. I haven't had much opportunity to talk to a man like you. Otherwise my ideas would be different, I guess. I've just realized that I've been wrong about a lot of things. I used to want to be exciting. Now I want to help people."

"Yes," he agreed, "that's very nice."

He seemed about to say more when they arrived at the armory. In their absence supper had begun; and crossing the great floor by his side, conscious of many eyes regarding them, Josephine wondered if people thought that they had been up to something.

"We're late," said Knowleton when Adele went off to put on the stockings. "The man you're with has probably given you up long ago. You'd better let me get you something here."

"That would be too divine."

Afterward, back on the floor again, she moved in a sweet aura of abstraction. The followers of several departed belles merged with hers until now no girl on the floor was cut in on with such frequency. Even Miss Brereton's nephew, Ernest Waterbury, danced with her in stiff approval. Danced? With a tentative change of pace she simply swung from man to man in a sort of hands-right-and-left around the floor. She felt a sudden need to relax, and as if in answer to her mood a new man was presented, a tall, sleek Southerner with a persuasive note:

"You lovely creacha. I been strainin my eyes watchin your cameo face floatin round. You stand out above all these othuz like an Amehken Beauty Rose over a lot of field daisies."

Dancing with him the second time, Josephine hearkened to his pleadings.

"All right. Let's go outside."

"It wasn't outdaws I was considerin," he explained as they left the floor. "I happen to have a mortgage on a nook right hee in the building."

"All right."

Book Chaffee, of Alabama, led the way through the cloakroom, through a passage to an inconspicuous door.

"This is the private apartment of my friend Sergeant Boone, instructa of the battery. He wanted to be particularly sure it'd be used as a nook tonight and not a readin room or anything like that."

Opening the door he turned on a dim light; she came in and he shut it behind her, and they faced each other.

"Mighty sweet," he murmured. His tall face came down, his long arms wrapped around her tenderly, and very slowly, so that their eyes met for quite a long time, he drew her up to him. Josephine kept thinking that she had never kissed a Southern boy before.

They started apart at the sudden sound of a key turning in the lock outside. Then there as a muffled snicker followed by retreating footsteps, and Book sprang for the door and wrenched at the handle, just as Josephine noticed that this was not only Sergeant Boone's parlor, it was his bedroom as well.

"Who was it?" she demanded. "Why did they lock us in?"

"Some funny boy. I'd like to get my hands on him."

"Will he come back?"

Book sat down on the bed to think. "I couldn't say. Don't even know who it was. But if somebody on the committee came along it wouldn't look too good, would it?"

Seeing her expression change, he came over and put his arm around her. "Don't you worry, honey. We'll fix it."

She returned his kiss, briefly but without distraction. Then she broke away and went into the next apartment, which was hung with boots, uniform coats and various military equipment.

"There's a window up here," she said. It was high in the wall and had not been opened for a long time. Book mounted on a chair and forced it ajar.

"About ten feet down," he reported, after a moment, "but there's a big pile of snow just underneath. You might get a nasty fall and you'll sure soak your shoes and stockin's."

"We've got to get out," Josephine said sharply.

"We'd better wait and give this funny man a chance——"

"I won't wait. I want to get out. Look—throw out all the blankets from the bed and I'll jump on that; or you jump first and spread them over the pile of snow."

After that it was merely exciting. Carefully Book Chaffee wiped the dust from the window to protect her dress; then they were struck silent by a footstep that approached—and passed the outer door. Book jumped, and she heard him kicking profanely as he waded out of the soft drift below. He spread the blankets. At the moment when Josephine swung her legs out the window, there was the sound of voices outside the door and the key turned again in the lock. She landed softly, reaching for his hand, and convulsed with laughter they ran and skidded down the half block toward the corner, and reaching the entrance to the armory, they stood panting for a moment, breathing in the fresh night. Book was reluctant to go inside.

"Why don't you let me conduct you where you're stayin? We can sit around and sort of recuperate."

She hesitated, drawn toward him by the community of their late predicament; but something was calling her inside, as if the fulfillment of her elation awaited her there.

"No," she decided.

As they went in she collided with a man in a great hurry, and looked up to recognize Dudley Knowleton.

"So sorry," he said. "Oh, hello——"

"Won't you dance me over to my box?" she begged him impulsively. "I've torn my dress."

As they started off he said abstractedly: "The fact is, a little mischief has come up and the buck has been passed to me. I was going along to see about it."

Her heart raced wildly and she felt the need of being another sort of person immediately.

"I can't tell you how much it's meant meeting you. It would be wonderful to have one friend I could be serious with without being all mushy and sentimental. Would you mind if I wrote you a letter —I mean, would Adele mind?"

"Lord, no." His smile had become utterly unfathomable to her. As they reached the box she thought of one more thing:

"Is it true that the baseball team is training at Hot Springs during Easter?"

"Yes. You going there?"

"Yes. Good night, Mr. Knowleton."

But she was destined to see him once more. It was outside the men's coat room, where she waited among a crowd of other pale survivors and their paler mothers, whose wrinkles had doubled and tripled with the passing night. He was explaining something to Adele, and Josephine heard the phrase. "The door was locked, and the window open——"

Suddenly it occurred to Josephine that, meeting her coming in damp and breathless, he must have guessed at the truth—and Adele would doubtless confirm his suspicion. Once again the spectre of her old enemy, the plain and jealous girl, arose before her. Shutting her mouth tight together she turned away.

But they had seen her, and Adele called to her in her cheerful ringing voice:

"Come say good night. You were *so* sweet about the stockings. Here's a girl you won't find doing shoddy, silly things, Dudley." Impulsively she leaned and kissed Josephine on the cheek. "You'll see I'm right, Dudley—next year she'll be the most respected girl in school."

III

As things go in the interminable days of early March, what happened next happened quickly. The annual senior dance at Miss Brereton's school came on a night soaked through with spring, and all the junior girls lay awake listening to the sighing tunes from the gymnasium. Between the numbers, when boys up from New Haven and Princeton wandered about the grounds, cloistered glances looked down from dark open windows upon the vague figures.

Not Josephine, though she lay awake like the others. Such vicarious diversions had no place in the sober pattern she was spinning now from day to day; yet she might as well have been in the forefront of those who called down to the men and threw notes and entered into conversations, for destiny had suddenly turned against her and was spinning a dark web of its own.

> Lit-tle lady, don't be depressed and blue,
> After all we're both in the same can-noo——

Dudley Knowleton was over in the gymnasium fifty yards away, but proximity to a man did not thrill her as it would have done a year ago—not, at least, in the same way. Life, she saw now, was a serious matter, and in the modest darkness a line of a novel cease-lessly recurred to her: "He is a man fit to be the father of my children." What were the seductive graces, the fast lines of a hundred parlor snakes compared to such realities. One couldn't go on forever kissing comparative strangers behind half-closed doors.

Under her pillow now were two letters, answers to her letters. They spoke in a bold round hand of the beginning of baseball prac-tice; they were glad Josephine felt as she did about things; and the writer certainly looked forward to seeing her at Easter. Of all the letters she had ever received they were the most difficult from which to squeeze a single drop of heart's blood—one couldn't even read the "Yours" of the subscription as "Your"—but Josephine knew them by heart. They were precious because he had taken the time to write them; they were eloquent in the very postage stamp because he used so few.

She was restless in her bed—the music had begun again in the gymnasium:

> Oh, my love, I've waited so long for you,
> Oh, my love, I'm singing this song for you——
> Oh-h-h-h——

From the next room there was light laughter, and then from below a male voice, and a long interchange of comic whispers. Josephine recognized Lillian's laugh and the voices of two other girls. She could imagine them as they lay across the window in their nightgowns, their heads just showing from the open window. "Come right down," one boy kept saying. "Don't be formal—come just as you are."

There was a sudden silence, then a quick crunching of footsteps on gravel, a suppressed snicker and a scurry, and the sharp, protesting groan of several beds in the next room and the banging of a door down the hall. Trouble for somebody, maybe. A few minutes later Josephine's door half opened, she caught a glimpse of Miss Kwain against the dim corridor light, and then the door closed.

The next afternoon Josephine and four other girls, all of whom denied having breathed so much as a word into the night, were placed on probation. There was absolutely nothing to do about it. Miss Kwain had recognized their faces in the window and they were all from two rooms. It was an injustice, but it was nothing compared to what happened next. One week before Easter vacation the school motored off on a one-day trip to inspect a milk farm—all save the ones on probation. Miss Chambers, who sympathized with Josephine's misfortune, enlisted her services in entertaining Mr. Ernest Waterbury, who was spending a week-end with his aunt. This was only vaguely better than nothing, for Mr. Waterbury was a very dull, very priggish young man. He was so dull and so priggish that the following morning Josephine was expelled from school.

It had happened like this: They had strolled in the grounds, they had sat down at a garden table and had tea. Ernest Waterbury had expressed a desire to see something in the chapel, just a few minutes before his aunt's car rolled up the drive. The chapel was reached by descending winding mock-medieval stairs; and, her shoes still wet from the garden, Josephine had slipped on the top step and fallen five feet directly into Mr. Waterbury's unwilling arms, where she lay helpless, convulsed with irresistible laughter. It was in this position that Miss Brereton and the visiting trustee had found them.

"But I had nothing to do with it!" declared the ungallant Mr. Waterbury. Flustered and outraged, he was packed back to New

Haven, and Miss Brereton, connecting this with last week's sin, proceeded to lose her head. Josephine, humiliated and furious, lost hers, and Mr. Perry, who happened to be in New York, arrived at the school the same night. At his passionate indignation, Miss Brereton collapsed and retracted, but the damage was done, and Josephine packed her trunk. Unexpectedly, monstrously, just as it had begun to mean something, her school life was over.

For the moment all her feelings were directed against Miss Brereton, and the only tears she shed at leaving were of anger and resentment. Riding with her father up to New York, she saw that while at first he had instinctively and whole-heartedly taken her part, he felt also a certain annoyance with her misfortune.

"We'll all survive," he said. "Unfortunately, even that old idiot Miss Brereton will survive. She ought to be running a reform school." He brooded for a moment. "Anyhow, your mother arrives tomorrow and you and she can go down to Hot Springs as you planned."

"Hot Springs!" Josephine cried, in a choked voice. "Oh, no!"

"Why not?" he demanded in surprise. "It seems the best thing to do. Give it a chance to blow over before you go back to Chicago."

"I'd rather go to Chicago," said Josephine breathlessly. "Daddy, I'd much rather go to Chicago."

"That's absurd. Your mother's started East and the arrangements are all made. At Hot Springs you can get out and ride and play golf and forget that old she-devil——"

"Isn't there another place in the East we could go? There's people I know going to Hot Springs who'll know all about this, people that I don't want to meet—girls from school."

"Now, Jo, you keep your chin up—this is one of those times. Sorry I said that about letting it blow over in Chicago; if we hadn't made other plans we'd go back and face every old shrew and gossip in town right away. When anybody slinks off in a corner they think you've been up to something bad. If anybody says anything to you, you tell them the truth—what I said to Miss Brereton. You tell them she said you could come back and I damn well wouldn't let you go back."

"They won't believe it."

There would be, at all events, four days of respite at Hot Springs before the vacations of the schools. Josephine passed this time taking golf lessons from a professional so newly arrived from Scotland that he surely knew nothing of her misadventure; she even went riding with a young man one afternoon, feeling almost at home with him after his admission that he had flunked out of Princeton in February —a confidence, however, which she did not reciprocate in kind. But in the evenings, despite the young man's importunity, she stayed with her mother, feeling nearer to her than she ever had before.

But one afternoon in the lobby Josephine saw by the desk two dozen good-looking young men waiting by a stack of bat cases and bags, and knew that what she dreaded was at hand. She ran upstairs and with an invented headache dined there that night, but after dinner she walked restlessly around their apartment. She was ashamed not only of her situation but of her reaction to it. She had never felt any pity for the unpopular girls who skulked in dressing-rooms because they could attract no partners on the floor, or for girls who were outsiders at Lake Forest, and now she was like them— hiding miserably out of life. Alarmed lest already the change was written in her face, she paused in front of the mirror, fascinated as ever by what she found there.

"The darn fools," she said aloud. And as she said it her chin went up and the faint cloud about her eyes lifted. The phrases of the myriad love letters she had received passed before her eyes; behind her, after all, was the reassurance of a hundred lost and pleading faces, of innumerable tender and pleading voices. Her pride flooded back into her till she could see the warm blood rushing up into her cheeks.

There was a knock at the door—it was the Princeton boy.

"How about slipping downstairs?" he proposed. "There's a dance. It's full of Ee-lies, the whole Yale baseball team. I'll pick up one of them and introduce you and you'll have a big time. How about it?"

"All right, but I don't want to meet anybody. You'll just have to dance with me all evening."

"You know that suits *me*."

She hurried into a new spring evening dress of the frailest fairy blue. In the excitement of seeing herself in it, it seemed as if she

had shed the old skin of winter and emerged a shining chrysalis with
no stain; and going downstairs her feet fell softly just off the beat of
the music from below. It was a tune from a play she had seen a
week ago in New York, a tune with a future—ready for gayeties as
yet unthought of, lovers not yet met. Dancing off, she was certain
that life had innumerable beginnings. She had hardly gone ten steps
when she was cut in upon by Dudley Knowleton.

"Why, Josephine!" He had never used her first name before—he
stood holding her hand. "Why, I'm glad to see you. I've been hoping
you'd be here."

She soared skyward on a rocket of surprise and delight. He was
actually glad to see her—the expression on his face was obviously
sincere. Could it be possible that he hadn't heard?

"Adele wrote me you might be here. She wasn't sure."

—Then he knew and didn't care; he liked her anyhow.

"I'm in sackcloth and ashes," she said.

"Well, they're very becoming to you."

"You know what happened—" she ventured.

"I do. I wasn't going to say anything, but it's generally agreed
that Waterbury behaved like a fool—and it's not going to be much
help to him in the elections next month. Look—I want you to dance
with some men who are just starving for a touch of beauty."

Presently she was dancing with, it seemed to her, the entire team
at once. Intermittently Dudley Knowleton cut back in, as well as the
Princeton man, who was somewhat indignant at this unexpected
competition. There were many girls from many schools in the room,
but with an admirable team spirit the Yale men displayed a sharp
prejudice in Josephine's favor; already she was pointed out from the
chairs along the wall.

But interiorly she was waiting for what was coming, for the
moment when she would walk with Dudley Knowleton into the
warm, Southern night. It came naturally, just at the end of a number, and they strolled along an avenue of early-blooming lilacs and
turned a corner and another corner . . .

"You were glad to see me, weren't you!" Josephine said.

"Of course."

"I was afraid at first. I was sorriest about what happened at school because of you. I'd been trying so hard to be different—because of you."

"You mustn't think of that school business any more. Everybody that matters knows you got a bad deal. Forget it and start over."

"Yes," she agreed tranquilly. She was happy. The breeze and the scent of lilacs—that was she, lovely and intangible; the rustic bench where they sat and the trees—that was he, rugged and strong beside her, protecting her.

"I'd thought so much of meeting you here," she said after a minute. "You'd been so good for me, that I thought maybe in a different way I could be good for you—I mean I know ways of having a good time that you don't know. For instance, we've certainly got to go horseback riding by moonlight some night. That'll be fun."

He didn't answer.

"I can really be very nice when I like somebody—that's really not often," she interpolated hastily, "not seriously. But I mean when I do feel seriously that a boy and I are really friends I don't believe in having a whole mob of other boys hanging around taking up time. I like to be with him all the time, all day and all evening, don't you?"

He stirred a little on the bench; he leaned forward with his elbows on his knees, looking at his strong hands. Her gently modulated voice sank a note lower.

"When I like anyone I don't even like dancing. It's sweeter to be alone."

Silence for a moment.

"Well, you know"—he hesitated, frowning—"as a matter of fact, I'm mixed up in a lot of engagements made some time ago with some people." He floundered about unhappily. "In fact, I won't even be at the hotel after tomorrow. I'll be at the house of some people down the valley—a sort of house party. As a matter of fact, Adele's getting here tomorrow."

Absorbed in her own thoughts, she hardly heard him at first, but at the name she caught her breath sharply.

"We're both to be at this house party while we're here, and I imagine it's more or less arranged what we're going to do. Of course, in the daytime I'll be here for baseball practice."

"I see." Her lips were quivering. "You won't be—you'll be with Adele."

"I think that—more or less—I will. She'll—want to see you, of course."

Another silence while he twisted his big fingers and she helplessly imitated the gesture.

"You were just sorry for me," she said. "You like Adele—much better."

"Adele and I understand each other. She's been more or less my ideal since we were children together."

"And I'm not your kind of girl." Josephine's voice trembled with a sort of fright. "I suppose because I've kissed a lot of boys and got a reputation for a speed and raised the deuce."

"It isn't that."

"Yes, it is," she declared passionately. "I'm just paying for things." She stood up. "You better take me back inside so I can dance with the kind of boys that like me."

She walked quickly down the path, tears of misery streaming from her eyes. He overtook her by the steps, but she only shook her head and said, "Excuse me for being so fresh. I'll grow up—I got what was coming to me—it's all right."

A little later when she looked around the floor for him he had gone—and Josephine realized with a shock that for the first time in her life she had tried for a man and failed. But, save in the very young, only love begets love, and from the moment Josephine had perceived that his interest in her was merely kindness she realized the wound was not in her heart but in her pride. She would forget him quickly, but she would never forget what she had learned from him. There were two kinds of men, those you played with and those you might marry. And as this passed through her mind, her restless eyes wandered casually over the group of stags, resting very lightly on Mr. Gordon Tinsley, the current catch of Chicago, reputedly the richest young man in the Middle West. He had never paid any attention to young Josephine until tonight. Ten minutes ago he had asked her to go driving with him tomorrow.

But he did not attract her—and she decided to refuse. One mustn't run through people, and, for the sake of a romantic half-hour, trade a possibility that might develop—quite seriously—later, at the proper time. She did not know that this was the first mature thought that she had ever had in her life, but it was.

The orchestra were packing their instruments and the Princeton man was still at her ear, still imploring her to walk out with him into the night. Josephine knew without cogitation which sort of man he was—and the moon was bright even on the windows. So with a certain sense of relaxation she took his arm and they strolled out to the pleasant bower she had so lately quitted, and their faces turned toward each other, like little moons under the great white one which hovered high over the Blue Ridge; his arm dropped softly about her yielding shoulder.

"Well?" he whispered.

"Well?"

CRAZY SUNDAY

I

It was Sunday—not a day, but rather a gap between two other days.
Behind, for all of them, lay sets and sequences, the long waits under
the crane that swung the microphone, the hundred miles a day by
automobiles to and fro across a county, the struggles of rival ingenu-
ities in the conference rooms, the ceaseless compromise, the clash
and strain of many personalities fighting for their lives. And now
Sunday, with individual life starting up again, with a glow kindling
in eyes that had been glazed with monotony the afternoon before.
Slowly as the hours waned they came awake like "Puppenfeen" in a
toy shop: an intense colloquy in a corner, lovers disappearing to neck
in a hall. And the feeling of "Hurry, it's not too late, but for God's
sake hurry before the blessed forty hours of leisure are over."

Joel Coles was writing continuity. He was twenty-eight and not
yet broken by Hollywood. He had had what were considered nice
assignments since his arrival six months before and he submitted his
scenes and sequences with enthusiasm. He referred to himself modestly as a hack but really did not think of it that way. His mother
had been a successful actress; Joel had spent his childhood between
London and New York trying to separate the real from the unreal,
or at least to keep one guess ahead. He was a handsome man with
the pleasant cow-brown eyes that in 1913 had gazed out at Broadway
audiences from his mother's face.

When the invitation came it made him sure that he was getting
somewhere. Ordinarily he did not go out on Sundays but stayed
sober and took work home with him. Recently they had given him
a Eugene O'Neill play destined for a very important lady indeed.
Everything he had done so far had pleased Miles Calman, and Miles
Calman was the only director on the lot who did not work under
a supervisor and was responsible to the money men alone. Everything
was clicking into place in Joel's career. ("This is Mr. Calman's

172

secretary. Will you come to tea from four to six Sunday—he lives in Beverly Hills, number——.")

Joel was flattered. It would be a party out of the top-drawer. It was a tribute to himself as a young man of promise. The Marion Davies' crowd, the high-hats, the big currency numbers, perhaps even Dietrich and Garbo and the Marquise, people who were not seen everywhere, would probably be at Calman's.

"I won't take anything to drink," he assured himself. Calman was audibly tired of rummies, and thought it was a pity the industry could not get along without them.

Joel agreed that writers drank too much—he did himself, but he wouldn't this afternoon. He wished Miles would be within hearing when the cocktails were passed to hear his succinct, unobtrusive, "No, thank you."

Miles Calman's house was built for great emotional moments— there was an air of listening, as if the far silences of its vistas hid an audience, but this afternoon it was thronged, as though people had been bidden rather than asked. Joel noted with pride that only two other writers from the studio were in the crowd, an ennobled limey and, somewhat to his surprise, Nat Keogh, who had evoked Calman's impatient comment on drunks.

Stella Calman (Stella Walker, of course) did not move on to her other guests after she spoke to Joel. She lingered—she looked at him with the sort of beautiful look that demands some sort of acknowledgment and Joe drew quickly on the dramatic adequacy inherited from his mother:

"Well, you look about sixteen! Where's your kiddy car?"

She was visibly pleased; she lingered. He felt that he should say something more, something confident and easy—he had first met her when she was struggling for bits in New York. At the moment a tray slid up and Stella put a cocktail glass into his hand.

"Everybody's afraid, aren't they?" he said, looking at it absently. "Everybody watches for everybody else's blunders, or tries to make sure they're with people that'll do them credit. Of course that's not true in your house," he covered himself hastily. "I just meant generally in Hollywood."

Stella agreed. She presented several people to Joel as if he were important. Reassuring himself that Miles was at the other side of the room, Joel drank the cocktail.

"So you have a baby?" he said. "That's the time to look out. After a pretty woman has had her first child, she's very vulnerable, because she wants to be reassured about her own charm. She's got to have some new man's unqualified devotion to prove to herself she hasn't lost anything."

"I never get anybody's unqualified devotion," Stella said rather resentfully.

"They're afraid of your husband."

"You think that's it?" She wrinkled her brow over the idea; then the conversation was interrupted at the exact moment Joel would have chosen.

Her attentions had given him confidence. Not for him to join safe groups, to slink to refuge under the wings of such acquaintances as he saw about the room. He walked to the window and looked out toward the Pacific, colorless under its sluggish sunset. It was good here—the American Riviera and all that, if there were ever time to enjoy it. The handsome, well-dressed people in the room, the lovely girls, and the—well, the lovely girls. You couldn't have everything.

He saw Stella's fresh boyish face, with the tired eyelid that always drooped a little over one eye, moving about among her guests and he wanted to sit with her and talk a long time as if she were a girl instead of a name; he followed her to see if she paid anyone as much attention as she had paid him. He took another cocktail—not because he needed confidence but because she had given him so much of it. Then he sat down beside the director's mother.

"Your son's gotten to be a legend, Mrs. Calman—Oracle and a Man of Destiny and all that. Personally, I'm against him but I'm in a minority. What do you think of him? Are you impressed? Are you surprised how far he's gone?"

"No, I'm not surprised," she said calmly. "We always expected a lot from Miles."

"Well now, that's unusual," remarked Joel. "I always think all mothers are like Napoleon's mother. My mother didn't want me to have anything to do with the entertainment business. She wanted me to go to West Point and be safe."

"We always had every confidence in Miles." . . .

He stood by the built-in bar of the dining room with the good-humored, heavy-drinking, highly paid Nat Keogh.

"—I made a hundred grand during the year and lost forty grand gambling, so now I've hired a manager."

"You mean an agent," suggested Joel.

"No, I've got that too. I mean a manager. I make over everything to my wife and then he and my wife get together and hand me out the money. I pay him five thousand a year to hand me out my money."

"You mean your agent."

"No, I mean my manager, and I'm not the only one—a lot of other irresponsible people have him."

"Well, if you're irresponsible why are you responsible enough to hire a manager?"

"I'm just irresponsible about gambling. Look here——"

A singer performed; Joel and Nat went forward with the others to listen.

II

The singing reached Joel vaguely; he felt happy and friendly toward all the people gathered there, people of bravery and industry, superior to a bourgeoisie that outdid them in ignorance and loose living, risen to a position of the highest prominence in a nation that for a decade had wanted only to be entertained. He liked them—he loved them. Great waves of good feeling flowed through him.

As the singer finished his number and there was a drift toward the hostess to say good-by, Joel had an idea. He would give them "Building It Up," his own composition. It was his only parlor trick, it had amused several parties and it might please Stella Walker. Possessed by the hunch, his blood throbbing with the scarlet corpuscles of exhibitionism, he sought her.

"Of course," she cried. "Please! Do you need anything?"

"Someone has to be the secretary that I'm supposed to be dictating to."

"I'll be her."

As the word spread the guests in the hall, already putting on their coats to leave, drifted back and Joel faced the eyes of many strangers. He had a dim foreboding, realizing that the man who had just performed was a famous radio entertainer. Then someone said "Sh!" and he was alone with Stella, the center of a sinister Indian-like half-circle. Stella smiled up at him expectantly—he began.

His burlesque was based upon the cultural limitations of Mr. Dave Silverstein, an independent producer; Silverstein was presumed to be dictating a letter outlining a treatment of a story he had bought.

"—a story of divorce, the younger generators and the Foreign Legion," he heard his voice saying, with intonations of Mr. Silverstein. "But we got to build it up, see?"

A sharp pang of doubt struck through him. The faces surrounding him in the gently molded light were intent and curious, but there was no ghost of a smile anywhere; directly in front the Great Lover of the screen glared at him with an eye as keen as the eye of a potato. Only Stella Walker looked up at him with a radiant, never faltering smile.

"If we make him a Menjou type, then we get a sort of Michael Arlen only with a Honolulu atmosphere."

Still not a ripple in front, but in the rear a rustling, a perceptible shift toward the left, toward the front door.

"—then she says she feels the sex appil for him and he burns out and says 'Oh go on destroy yourself'—"

At some point he heard Nat Keogh snicker and here and there were a few encouraging faces, but as he finished he had the sickening realization that he had made a fool of himself in view of an important section of the picture world, upon whose favor depended his career.

For a moment he existed in the midst of a confused silence, broken by a general trek for the door. He felt the undercurrent of derision that rolled through the gossip; then—all this was in the space of ten seconds—the Great Lover, his eye hard and empty as the eye of of a needle, shouted "Boo! Boo!" voicing in an overtone what he felt was the mood of the crowd. It was the resentment of the professional toward the amateur, of the community toward the stranger, the thumbs-down of the clan.

Only Stella Walker was still standing near and thanking him as if he had been an unparalleled success, as if it hadn't occurred to her that anyone hadn't liked it. As Nat Keogh helped him into his overcoat, a great wave of self-disgust swept over him and he clung desperately to his rule of never betraying an inferior emotion until he no longer felt it.

"I was a flop," he said lightly, to Stella. "Never mind, it's a good number when appreciated. Thanks for your cooperation."

The smile did not leave her face—he bowed rather drunkenly and Nat drew him toward the door. . . .

The arrival of his breakfast awakened him into a broken and ruined world. Yesterday he was himself, a point of fire against an industry, today he felt that he was pitted under an enormous disadvantage, against those faces, against individual contempt and collective sneer. Worse than that, to Miles Calman he was become one of those rummies, stripped of dignity, whom Calman regretted he was compelled to use. To Stella Walker, on whom he had forced to martyrdom to preserve the courtesy of her house—her opinion he did not dare to guess. His gastric juices ceased to flow and he set his poached eggs back on the telephone table. He wrote:

DEAR MILES: You can imagine my profound self-disgust. I confess to a taint of exhibitionism, but at six o'clock in the afternoon, in broad daylight! Good God! My apologies to your wife.
                                    Yours ever,
                                                JOEL COLES.

Joel emerged from his office on the lot only to slink like a malefactor to the tobacco store. So suspicious was his manner that one of the studio police asked to see his admission card. He had decided to eat lunch when Nat Keogh, confident and cheerful, overtook him.

"What do you mean you're in permanent retirement? What if that Three Piece Suit did boo you?

"Why, listen," he continued, drawing Joel into the studio restaurant. "The night of one of his premiers at Grauman's, Joe Squires kicked his tail while he was bowing to the crowd. The ham said Joe'd hear from him later but when Joe called him up at eight o'clock next day and said, 'I thought I was going to hear from you,' he hung up the phone."

The preposterous story cheered Joel, and he found a gloomy consolation in staring at the group at the next table, the sad, lovely Siamese twins, the mean dwarfs, the proud giant from the circus picture. But looking beyond at the yellow-stained faces of pretty women, their eyes all melancholy and startling with mascara, their ball gowns garish in full day, he saw a group who had been at Calman's and winced.

"Never again," he exclaimed aloud, "absolutely my last social appearance in Hollywood!"

The following morning a telegram was waiting for him at his office:

You were one of the most agreeable people at our party. Expect you at my sister June's buffet supper next Sunday.

STELLA WALKER CALMAN.

The blood rushed fast through his veins for a feverish minute. Incredulously he read the telegram over.

"Well, that's the sweetest thing I ever heard of in my life!"

III

Crazy Sunday again. Joel slept until eleven, then he read a newspaper to catch up with the past week. He lunched in his room on trout, avocado salad and a pint of California wine. Dressing for the tea, he selected a pin-check suit, a blue shirt, a burnt orange tie. There were dark circles of fatigue under his eyes. In his second-hand car he drove to the Riviera apartments. As he was introducing himself to Stella's sister, Miles and Stella arrived in riding clothes— they had been quarrelling fiercely most of the afternoon on all the dirt roads back of Beverly Hills.

Miles Calman, tall, nervous, with a desperate humor and the unhappiest eyes Joel ever saw, was an artist from the top of his curiously shaped head to his niggerish feet. Upon these last he stood firmly—he had never made a cheap picture though he had sometimes paid heavily for the luxury of making experimental flops. In spite of his excellent company, one could not be with him long without realizing that he was not a well man.

From the moment of their entrance Joel's day bound itself up inextricably with theirs. As he joined the group around them Stella turned away from it with an impatient little tongue click—and Miles Calman said to the man who happened to be next to him:

"Go easy on Eva Goebel. There's hell to pay about her at home." Miles turned to Joel, "I'm sorry I missed you at the office yesterday. I spent the afternoon at the analyst's."

"You being psychoanalyzed?"

"I have been for months. First I went for claustrophobia, now I'm trying to get my whole life cleared up. They say it'll take over a year."

"There's nothing the matter with your wife," Joel assured him.

"Oh, no? Well, Stella seems to think so. Ask anybody—they can all tell you about it," he said bitterly.

A girl perched herself on the arm of Miles' chair; Joel crossed to Stella, who stood disconsolately by the fire.

"Thank you for your telegram," he said. "It was darn sweet. I can't imagine anybody as good-looking as you are being so good-humored."

She was a little lovelier than he had ever seen her and perhaps the unstinted admiration in his eyes prompted her to unload on him —it did not take long, for she was obviously at the emotional bursting point.

"—and Miles has been carrying on this thing for two years, and I never knew. Why, she was one of my best friends, always in the house. Finally when people began to come to me, Miles had to admit it."

She sat down vehemently on the arm of Joel's chair. Her riding breeches were the color of the chair and Joel saw that the mass of her hair was made up of some strands of red gold and some of pale gold, so that it could not be dyed, and that she had on no make-up. She was that good-looking——

Still quivering with the shock of her discovery, Stella found unbearable the spectacle of a new girl hovering over Miles; she led Joel into a bedroom, and seated at either end of a big bed they went on talking. People on their way to the washroom glanced in and made wisecracks, but Stella, emptying out her story, paid no attention. After a while Miles stuck his head in the door and said, "There's no use trying to explain something to Joel in half an hour that I don't understand myself and the psychoanalyst says will take a whole year to understand."

She talked on as if Miles were not there. She loved Miles, she said—under considerable difficulties she had always been faithful to him.

"The psychoanalyst told Miles that he had a mother complex. In his first marriage he transferred his mother complex to his wife, you see—and then his sex turned to me. But when we married the thing repeated itself—he transferred his mother complex to me and all his libido turned toward this other woman."

Joel knew that this probably wasn't gibberish—yet it sounded like gibberish. He knew Eva Goebel; she was a motherly person, older and probably wiser than Stella, who was a golden child.

Miles now suggested impatiently that Joel come back with them since Stella had so much to say, so they drove out to the mansion in Beverly Hills. Under the high ceilings the situation seemed more dignified and tragic. It was an eerie bright night with the dark very clear outside of all the windows and Stella all rose-gold raging and crying around the room. Joel did not quite believe in picture actresses' grief. They have other preoccupations—they are beautiful rose-gold figures blown full of life by writers and directors, and after hours they sit around and talk in whispers and giggle innuendoes, and the ends of many adventures flow through them.

Sometimes he pretended to listen and instead thought how well she was got up—sleek breeches with a matched set of legs in them, an Italian-colored sweater with a little high neck, and a short brown chamois coat. He couldn't decide whether she was an imitation of an English lady or an English lady was an imitation of her. She hovered somewhere between the realest of realities and the most blatant of impersonations.

"Miles is so jealous of me that he questions everything I do," she cried scornfully. "When I was in New York I wrote him that I'd been to the theatre with Eddie Baker. Miles was so jealous he phoned me ten times in one day."

"I was wild," Miles snuffled sharply, a habit he had in times of stress. "The analyst couldn't get any results for a week."

Stella shook her head despairingly. "Did you expect me just to sit in the hotel for three weeks?"

"I don't expect anything. I admit that I'm jealous. I try not to be. I worked on that with Dr. Bridgebane, but it didn't do any good. I was jealous of Joel this afternoon when you sat on the arm of his chair."

"You were?" She started up. "You were! Wasn't there somebody on the arm of your chair? And did you speak to me for two hours?"

"You were telling your troubles to Joel in the bedroom."

"When I think that that woman"—she seemed to believe that to omit Eva Goebel's name would be to lessen her reality—"used to come here——"

"All right—all right," said Miles wearily. "I've admitted everything and I feel as bad about it as you do." Turning to Joel he began talking about pictures, while Stella moved restlessly along the far walls, her hands in her breeches pockets.

"They've treated Miles terribly," she said, coming suddenly back into the conversation as if they'd never discussed her personal affairs. "Dear, tell him about old Beltzer trying to change your picture."

As she stood hovering protectively over Miles, her eyes flashing with indignation in his behalf, Joel realized that he was in love with her. Stifled with excitement he got up to say good night.

With Monday the week resumed its workaday rhythm, in sharp contrast to the theoretical discussions, the gossip and scandal of Sunday; there was the endless detail of script revision—"Instead of a lousy dissolve, we can leave her voice on the sound track and cut to a medium shot of the taxi from Bell's angle or we can simply pull the camera back to include the station, hold it a minute and then pan to the row of taxis"—by Monday afternoon Joel had again forgotten that people whose business was to provide entertainment were ever privileged to be entertained. In the evening he phoned Miles' house. He asked for Miles but Stella came to the phone.

"Do things seem better?"

"Not particularly. What are you doing next Saturday evening?"

"Nothing."

"The Perrys are giving a dinner and theatre party and Miles won't be here—he's flying to South Bend to see the Notre Dame-California game, I thought you might go with me in his place."

After a long moment Joel said, "Why—surely. If there's a conference I can't make dinner but I can get to the theatre."

"Then I'll say we can come."

Joel walked his office. In view of the strained relations of the Calmans, would Miles be pleased, or did she intend that Miles shouldn't know of it? That would be out of the question—if Miles didn't mention it Joel would. But it was an hour or more before he could get down to work again.

Wednesday there was a four-hour wrangle in a conference room crowded with planets and nebulae of cigarette smoke. Three men and a woman paced the carpet in turn, suggesting or condemning, speaking sharply or persuasively, confidently or despairingly. At the end Joel lingered to talk to Miles.

The man was tired—not with the exaltation of fatigue but life-tired, with his lids sagging and his beard prominent over the blue shadows near his mouth.

"I hear you're flying to the Notre Dame game."

Miles looked beyond him and shook his head.

"I've given up the idea."

"Why?"

"On account of you." Still he did not look at Joel.

"What the hell, Miles?"

"That's why I've given it up." He broke into a perfunctory laugh at himself. "I can't tell what Stella might do just out of spite—she's invited you to take her to the Perrys', hasn't she? I wouldn't enjoy the game."

The fine instinct that moved swiftly and confidently on the set, muddled so weakly and helplessly through his personal life.

"Look, Miles," Joel said frowning. "I've never made any passes whatsoever at Stella. If you're really seriously canceling your trip on account of me, I won't go to the Perrys' with her. I won't see her. You can trust me absolutely."

Miles looked at him, carefully now.

"Maybe." He shrugged his shoulders. "Anyhow there'd just be somebody else. I wouldn't have any fun."

"You don't seem to have much confidence in Stella. She told me she'd always been true to you."

"Maybe she has." In the last few minutes several more muscles had sagged around Miles' mouth, "But how can I ask anything of her after what's happened? How can I expect her—" He broke off and his face grew harder as he said, "I'll tell you one thing, right or wrong and no matter what I've done, if I ever had anything on her I'd divorce her. I can't have my pride hurt—that would be the last straw."

His tone annoyed Joel, but he said:

"Hasn't she calmed down about the Eva Goebel thing?"

"No." Miles snuffled pessimistically. "I can't get over it either."

"I thought it was finished."

"I'm trying not to see Eva again, but you know it isn't easy just to drop something like that—it isn't some girl I kissed last night in a taxi! The psychoanalyst says——"

"I know," Joel interrupted. "Stella told me." This was depressing. "Well, as far as I'm concerned if you go to the game I won't see Stella. And I'm sure Stella has nothing on her conscience about anybody."

"Maybe not," Miles repeated listlessly. "Anyhow I'll stay and take her to the party. Say," he said suddenly, "I wish you'd come too. I've got to have somebody sympathetic to talk to. That's the trouble— I've influenced Stella in everything. Especially I've influenced her so that she likes all the men I like—it's very difficult."

"It must be," Joel agreed.

IV

Joel could not get to the dinner. Self-conscious in his silk hat against the unemployment, he waited for the others in front of the Hollywood Theatre and watched the evening parade: obscure replicas of bright, particular picture stars, spavined men in polo coats, a stomping dervish with the beard and staff of an apostle, a pair of chic Filipinos in collegiate clothes, reminder that this corner of the Republic opened to the seven seas, a long fantastic carnival of young shouts which proved to be a fraternity initiation. The line split to pass two smart limousines that stopped at the curb.

There she was, in a dress like ice-water, made in a thousand pale-blue pieces, with icicles trickling at the throat. He started forward.

"So you like my dress?"

"Where's Miles?"

"He flew to the game after all. He left yesterday morning—at least I think—" She broke off. "I just got a telegram from South Bend saying that he's starting back. I forgot—you know all these people?"

The party of eight moved into the theatre.

Miles had gone after all and Joel wondered if he should have come. But during the performance, with Stella a profile under the pure grain of light hair, he thought no more about Miles. Once he turned and looked at her and she looked back at him, smiling and meeting his eyes for as long as he wanted. Between the acts they smoked in the lobby and she whispered:

"They're all going to the opening of Jack Johnson's night club— I don't want to go, do you?"

"Do we have to?"

"I suppose not." She hesitated. "I'd like to talk to you. I suppose we could go to our house—if I were only sure——"

Again she hesitated and Joel asked:

"Sure of what?"

"Sure that—oh, I'm haywire I know, but how can I be sure Miles went to the game?"

"You mean you think he's with Eva Goebel?"

"No, not so much that—but supposing he was here watching everything I do. You know Miles does odd things sometimes. Once he wanted a man with a long beard to drink tea with him and he sent down to the casting agency for one, and drank tea with him all afternoon."

"That's different. He sent you a wire from South Bend—that proves he's at the game."

After the play they said good night to the others at the curb and were answered by looks of amusement. They slid off along the golden garish thoroughfare through the crowd that had gathered around Stella.

"You see he could arrange the telegrams," Stella said, "very easily."

That was true. And with the idea that perhaps her uneasiness was justified, Joel grew angry: if Miles had trained a camera on them he felt no obligations toward Miles. Aloud he said:

"That's nonsense."

There were Christmas trees already in the shop windows and the full moon over the boulevard was only a prop, as scenic as the giant boudoir lamps of the corners. On into the dark foliage of Beverly Hills that flamed as eucalyptus by day, Joel saw only the flash of a white face under his own, the arc of her shoulder. She pulled away suddenly and looked up at him.

"Your eyes are like your mother's," she said. "I used to have a scrap book full of pictures of her."

"Your eyes are like your own and not a bit like any other eyes," he answered.

Something made Joel look out into the grounds as they went into the house, as if Miles were lurking in the shrubbery. A telegram waited on the hall table. She read aloud:

CHICAGO.

Home tomorrow night. Thinking of you. Love.

MILES.

"You see," she said, throwing the slip back on the table, "he could easily have faked that." She asked the butler for drinks and sandwiches and ran upstairs, while Joel walked into the empty reception rooms. Strolling about he wandered to the piano where he had stood in disgrace two Sundays before.

"Then we could put over," he said aloud, "a story of divorce, the younger generators and the Foreign Legion."

His thoughts jumped to another telegram.

"You were one of the most agreeable people at our party——"

An idea occurred to him. If Stella's telegram had been purely a gesture of courtesy then it was likely that Miles had inspired it, for it was Miles who had invited him. Probably Miles had said:

"Send him a wire—he's miserable—he thinks he's queered himself."

It fitted in with "I've influenced Stella in everything. Especially I've influenced her so that she likes all the men I like." A woman would do a thing like that because she felt sympathetic—only a man would do it because he felt responsible.

When Stella came back into the room he took both her hands.

"I have a strange feeling that I'm a sort of pawn in a spite game you're playing against Miles," he said.

"Help yourself to a drink."

"And the odd thing is that I'm in love with you anyhow."

The telephone rang and she freed herself to answer it.

"Another wire from Miles," she announced. "He dropped it, or it says he dropped it, from the airplane at Kansas City."

"I suppose he asked to be remembered to me."

"No, he just said he loved me. I believe he does. He's so very weak."

"Come sit beside me," Joel urged her.

It was early. And it was still a few minutes short of midnight a half-hour later, when Joel walked to the cold hearth, and said tersely:

"Meaning that you haven't any curiosity about me?"

"Not at all. You attract me a lot and you know it. The point is that I suppose I really do love Miles."

"Obviously."

"And tonight I feel uneasy about everything."

He wasn't angry—he was even faintly relieved that a possible entanglement was avoided. Still as he looked at her, the warmth and softness of her body thawing her cold blue costume, he knew she was one of the things he would always regret.

"I've got to go," he said. "I'll phone a taxi."

"Nonsense—there's a chauffeur on duty."

He winced at her readiness to have him go, and seeing this she kissed him lightly and said, "You're sweet, Joel." Then suddenly three things happened: he took down his drink at a gulp, the phone rang loud through the house and a clock in the hall struck in trumpet notes.

Nine—ten—eleven—twelve——

V

It was Sunday again. Joel realized that he had come to the theatre this evening with the work of the week still hanging about him like cerements. He had made love to Stella as he might attack some matter to be cleaned up hurriedly before the day's end. But this was Sunday—the lovely, lazy perspective of the next twenty-four hours unrolled before him—every minute was something to be approached with lulling indirection, every moment held the germ of innumerable possibilities. Nothing was impossible—everything was just beginning. He poured himself another drink.

With a sharp moan, Stella slipped forward inertly by the telephone. Joel picked her up and laid her on the sofa. He squirted soda-water on a handkerchief and slapped it over her face. The telephone mouthpiece was still grinding and he put it to his ear.

"—the plane fell just this side of Kansas City. The body of Miles Calman has been identified and——"

He hung up the receiver.

"Lie still," he said, stalling, as Stella opened her eyes.

"Oh, what's happened?" she whispered. "Call them back. Oh, what's happened?"

"I'll call them right away. What's your doctor's name?"

"Did they say Miles was dead?"

"Lie quiet—is there a servant still up?"

"Hold me—I'm frightened."

He put his arm around her.

"I want the name of your doctor," he said sternly. "It may be a mistake but I want someone here."

"It's Doctor—Oh, God, is Miles dead?"

Joel ran upstairs and searched through strange medicine cabinets for spirits of ammonia. When he came down Stella cried:

"He isn't dead—I know he isn't. This is part of his scheme. He's torturing me. I know he's alive. I can feel he's alive."

"I want to get hold of some close friend of yours, Stella. You can't stay here alone tonight."

"Oh, no," she cried. "I can't see anybody. You stay. I haven't got any friend." She got up, tears streaming down her face. "Oh, Miles is my only friend. He's not dead—he can't be dead. I'm going there right away and see. Get a train. You'll have to come with me."

"You can't. There's nothing to do tonight. I want you to tell me the name of some woman I can call: Lois? Joan? Carmel? Isn't there somebody?"

Stella stared at him blindly.

"Eva Goebel was my best friend," she said.

Joel thought of Miles, his sad and desperate face in the office two days before. In the awful silence of his death all was clear about him. He was the only American-born director with both an interesting temperament and an artistic conscience. Meshed in an industry, he had paid with his ruined nerves for having no resilience, no healthy cynicism, no refuge—only a pitiful and precarious escape.

There was a sound at the outer door—it opened suddenly, and there were footsteps in the hall.

"Miles!" Stella screamed. "Is it you, Miles? Oh, it's Miles."

A telegraph boy appeared in the doorway.

"I couldn't find the bell. I heard you talking inside."

The telegram was a duplicate of the one that had been phoned. While Stella read it over and over, as though it were a black lie, Joel telephoned. It was still early and he had difficulty getting anyone; when finally he succeeded in finding some friends he made Stella take a stiff drink.

"You'll stay here, Joel," she whispered, as though she were half-asleep. "You won't go away. Miles liked you—he said you—" She shivered violently, "Oh, my God, you don't know how alone I feel." Her eyes closed, "Put your arms around me. Miles had a suit like that." She started bolt upright. "Think of what he must have felt. He was afraid of almost everything, anyhow."

She shook her head dazedly. Suddenly she siezed Joel's face and held it close to hers.

"You won't go. You like me—you love me, don't you? Don't call up anybody. Tomorrow's time enough. You stay here with me tonight."

He stared at her, at first incredulously, and then with shocked understanding. In her dark groping Stella was trying to keep Miles alive by sustaining a situation in which he had figured—as if Miles' mind could not die so long as the possibilities that had worried him still existed. It was a distraught and tortured effort to stave off the realization that he was dead.

Resolutely Joel went to the phone and called a doctor.

"Don't, oh, don't call anybody!" Stella cried. "Come back here and put your arms around me."

"Is Doctor Bales in?"

"Joel," Stella cried. "I thought I could count on you. Miles liked you. He was jealous of you—Joel, come here."

Ah then—if he betrayed Miles she would be keeping him alive— for if he were really dead how could he be betrayed?

"—has just had a very severe shock. Can you come at once, and get hold of a nurse?"

"Joel!"

Now the door-bell and the telephone began to ring intermittently, and automobiles were stopping in front of the door.

"But you're not going," Stella begged him. "You're going to stay, aren't you?"

"No," he answered. "But I'll be back, if you need me."

Standing on the steps of the house which now hummed and palpitated with the life that flutters around death like protective leaves, he began to sob a little in his throat.

"Everything he touched he did something magical to," he thought. "He even brought that little gamin alive and made her a sort of masterpiece."

And then:

"What a hell of a hole he leaves in this damn wilderness— already!"

And then with a certain bitterness, "Oh, yes, I'll be back—I'll be back!"

TWO WRONGS

I

Look at those shoes," said Bill—"twenty-eight dollars." Mr. Brancusi looked. "Purty."

"Made to order."

"I knew you were a great swell. You didn't get me up here to show me those shoes, did you?"

"I am not a great swell. Who said I was a great swell?" demanded Bill. "Just because I've got more education than most people in show business."

"And then, you know, you're a handsome young fellow," said Brancusi dryly.

"Sure I am—compared to you anyhow. The girls think I must be an actor, till they find out. . . . Got a cigarette? What's more, I look like a man—which is more than most of these pretty boys round Times Square do."

"Good-looking. Gentleman. Good shoes. Shot with luck."

"You're wrong there," objected Bill. "Brains. Three years—nine shows—four big hits—only one flop. Where do you see any luck in that?"

A little bored, Brancusi just gazed. What he would have seen—had he not made his eyes opaque and taken to thinking about something else—was a fresh-faced young Irishman exuding aggressiveness and self-confidence until the air of his office was thick with it. Presently, Brancusi knew, Bill would hear the sound of his own voice and be ashamed and retire into his other humor—the quietly superior, sensitive one, the patron of the arts, modeled on the intellectuals of the Theatre Guild. Bill McChesney had not quite decided between the two, such blends are seldom complete before thirty.

"Take Ames, take Hopkins, take Harris—take any of them," Bill insisted. "What have they got on me? What's the matter? Do you

190

want a drink?"—seeing Brancusi's glance wander toward the cabinet on the opposite wall.

"I never drink in the morning. I just wondered who was it keeps on knocking. You ought to make it stop it. I get a nervous fidgets, kind of half crazy, with that kind of thing."

Bill went quickly to the door and threw it open.

"Nobody," he said . . . "Hello! What do you want?"

"Oh, I'm so sorry," a voice answered; "I'm terribly sorry. I got so excited and I didn't realize I had this pencil in my hand."

"What is it you want?"

"I want to see you, and the clerk said you were busy. I have a letter for you from Alan Rogers, the playwright—and I wanted to give it to you personally."

"I'm busy," said Bill. "See Mr. Cadorna."

"I did, but he wasn't very encouraging, and Mr. Rogers said——"

Brancusi, edging over restlessly, took a quick look at her. She was very young, with beautiful red hair, and more character in her face than her chatter would indicate; it did not occur to Mr. Brancusi that this was due to her origin in Delaney, South Carolina.

"What shall I do?" she inquired, quietly laying her future in Bill's hands. "I had a letter to Mr. Rogers, and he just gave me this one to you."

"Well, what do you want me to do—marry you?" exploded Bill.

"I'd like to get a part in one of your plays."

"Then sit down and wait. I'm busy. . . . Where's Miss Cohalan?" He rang a bell, looked once more, crossly, at the girl and closed the door of his office. But during the interruption his other mood had come over him, and he resumed his conversation with Brancusi in the key of one who was hand in glove with Reinhardt for the artistic future of the theatre.

By 12:30 he had forgotten everything except that he was going to be the greatest producer in the world and that he had an engagement to tell Sol Lincoln about it at lunch. Emerging from his office, he looked expectantly at Miss Cohalan.

"Mr. Lincoln won't be able to meet you," she said. "He jus' 'is minute called."

"Just this minute," repeated Bill, shocked. "All right. Just cross him off that list for Thursday night."

Miss Cohalan drew a line on a sheet of paper before her.

"Mr. McChesney, now you haven't forgotten me, have you?"

He turned to the red-headed girl.

"No," he said vaguely, and then to Miss Cohalan: "That's all right; ask him for Thursday anyhow. To hell with him."

He did not want to lunch alone. He did not like to do anything alone now, because contacts were too much fun when one had prominence and power.

"If you would just let me talk to you two minutes—" she began.

"Afraid I can't now." Suddenly he realized that she was the most beautiful person he had ever seen in his life.

He stared at her.

"Mr. Rogers told me——"

"Come and have a spot of lunch with me," he said, and then, with an air of great hurry, he gave Miss Cohalan some quick and contradictory instructions and held open the door.

They stood on Forty-second Street and he breathed his preempted air—there is only enough air there for a few people at a time. It was November and the first exhilarating rush of the season was over, but he could look east and see the electric sign of one of his plays, and west and see another. Around the corner was the one he had put on with Brancusi—the last time he would produce anything except alone.

They went to the Bedford, where there was a to-do of waiters and captains as he came in.

"This is ver' tractive restaurant," she said, impressed and on company behavior.

"This is hams' paradise." He nodded to several people. "Hello, Jimmy—Bill. . . . Hello there, Jack. . . . That's Jack Dempsey. . . . I don't eat here much. I usually eat up at the Harvard Club."

"Oh, did you go to Harvard? I used to know——"

"Yes." He hesitated; there were two versions about Harvard, and he decided suddenly on the true one. "Yes, and they had me down

for a hick there, but not any more. About a week ago I was out on
Long Island at the Gouverneer Haights—very fashionable people—
and a couple of Gold Coast boys that never knew I was alive up in
Cambridge began pulling this 'Hello, Bill, old boy' on me."

He hesitated and suddenly decided to leave the story there.

"What do you want—a job?" he demanded. He remembered suddenly that she had holes in her stockings. Holes in stockings always
moved him, softened him.

"Yes, or else I've got to go home," she said. "I want to be a dancer
—you know, Russian ballet. But the lessons cost so much, so I've got
to get a job. I thought it'd give me stage presence anyhow."

"Hoofer, eh?"

"Oh, no, serious."

"Well, Pavlova's a hoofer, isn't she?"

"Oh, no." She was shocked at this profanity, but after a moment
she continued: "I took with Miss Campbell—Georgia Berriman
Campbell—back home—maybe you know her. She took from Ned
Wayburn, and she's really wonderful. She——"

"Yeah?" he said abstractedly. "Well, it's a tough business—casting
agencies bursting with people that can all do anything, till I give
them a try. How old are you?"

"Eighteen."

"I'm twenty-six. Came here four years ago without a cent."

"My!"

"I could quit now and be comfortable the rest of my life."

"My!"

"Going to take a year off next year—get married. . . . Ever hear
of Irene Rikker?"

"I should say! She's about my favorite of all."

"We're engaged."

"My!"

When they went out into Times Square after a while he said
carelessly, "What are you doing now?"

"Why, I'm trying to get a job."

"I mean right this minute."

"Why, nothing."

"Do you want to come up to my apartment on Forty-sixth Street and have some coffee?"

Their eyes met, and Emmy Pinkard made up her mind she could take care of herself.

It was a great bright studio apartment with a ten-foot divan, and after she had coffee and he a highball, his arm dropped round her shoulder.

"Why should I kiss you?" she demanded. "I hardly know you, and besides, you're engaged to somebody else."

"Oh, that! She doesn't care."

"No, really!"

"You're a good girl."

"Well, I'm certainly not an idiot."

"All right, go on being a good girl."

She stood up, but lingered a minute, very fresh and cool, and not upset at all.

"I suppose this means you won't give me a job?" she asked pleasantly.

He was already thinking about something else—about an interview and a rehearsal—but now he looked at her again and saw she still had holes in her stockings. He telephoned:

"Joe, this is the Fresh Boy. . . . You didn't think I knew you called me that, did you? . . . It's all right. . . . Say, have you got those three girls for the party scene? Well, listen; save one for a Southern kid I'm sending around today."

He looked at her jauntily, conscious of being such a good fellow.

"Well, I don't know how to thank you. And Mr. Rogers," she added audaciously. "Good-by, Mr. McChesney."

He disdained to answer.

II

During rehearsal he used to come around a great deal and stand watching with a wise expression, as if he knew everything in people's minds; but actually he was in a haze about his own good fortune and didn't see much and didn't for the moment care. He spent most of his week-ends on Long Island with the fashionable people who had "taken him up." When Brancusi referred to him as the "big social butterfly," he would answer, "Well, what about it? Didn't I go to Harvard? You think they found me in a Grand Street apple cart, like you?" He was well liked among his new friends for his good looks and good nature, as well as his success.

His engagement to Irene Rikker was the most unsatisfactory thing in his life; they were tired of each other but unwilling to put an end to it. Just as, often, the two richest young people in a town are drawn together by the fact, so Bill McChesney and Irene Rikker, borne side by side on waves of triumph, could not spare each other's nice appreciation of what was due such success. Nevertheless, they indulged in fiercer and more frequent quarrels, and the end was approaching. It was embodied in one Frank Llewellen, a big, fine-looking actor playing opposite Irene. Seeing the situation at once, Bill became bitterly humorous about it; from the second week of rehearsals there was tension in the air.

Meanwhile Emmy Pinkard, with enough money for crackers and milk, and a friend who took her out to dinner, was being happy. Her friend, Easton Hughes from Delaney, was studying at Columbia to be a dentist. He sometimes brought along other lonesome young men studying to be dentists, and at the price, if it can be called that, of a few casual kisses in taxicabs, Emmy dined when hungry. One afternoon she introduced Easton to Bill McChesney at the stage door, and afterward Bill made his facetious jealousy the basis of their relationship.

"I see that dental number has been slipping it over on me again. Well, don't let him give you any laughing gas is my advice."

Though their encounters were few, they always looked at each other. When Bill looked at her he stared for an instant as if he had not seen her before, and then remembered suddenly that she was to be teased. When she looked at him she saw many things—a bright day outside, with great crowds of people hurrying through the streets; a very good new limousine that waited at the curb for two people with very good new clothes, who got in and went somewhere that was just like New York, only away, and more fun there. Many times she had wished she had kissed him, but just as many times she was glad she hadn't; since, as the weeks passed, he grew less romantic, tied up, like the rest of them, to the play's laborious evolution.

They were opening in Atlantic City. A sudden moodiness apparent to everyone, came over Bill. He was short with the director and sarcastic with the actors. This, it was rumored, was because Irene Rikker had come down with Frank Llewellen on a different train. Sitting beside the author on the night of the dress rehearsal, he was an almost sinister figure in the twilight of the auditorium; but he said nothing until the end of the second act, when, with Llewellen and Irene Rikker on the stage alone, he suddenly called:

"We'll go over that again—and cut out the mush!"

Llewellen came down to the footlights.

"What do you mean—cut out the mush?" he inquired. "Those are the lines, aren't they?"

"You know what I mean—stick to business."

"I don't know what you mean."

Bill stood up. "I mean all that damn whispering."

"There wasn't any whispering. I simply asked——"

"That'll do—take it over."

Llewellen turned away furiously and was about to proceed, when Bill added audibly: "Even a ham has got to do his stuff."

Llewellen whipped about. "I don't have to stand that kind of talk, Mr. McChesney."

"Why not? You're a ham, aren't you? When did you get ashamed of being a ham? I'm putting on this play and I want you to stick to your stuff." Bill got up and walked down the aisle. "And when you don't do it, I'm going to call you just like anybody else."

"Well, you watch out for your tone of voice——"

"What'll you do about it?"

Llewellen jumped down into the orchestra pit.

"I'm not taking anything from you!" he shouted.

Irene Rikker called to them from the stage, "For heaven's sake, are you two crazy?" And then Llewellen swung at him, one short, mighty blow. Bill pitched back across a row of seats, fell through one, splintering it, and lay wedged there. There was a moment's wild confusion, then people holding Llewellen, then the author, with a white face, pulling Bill up, and the stage manager crying: "Shall I kill him, chief? Shall I break his fat face?" and Llewellen panting and Irene Rikker frightened.

"Get back there!" Bill cried, holding a handkerchief to his face and teetering in the author's supporting arms. "Everybody get back! Take that scene again, and no talk! Get back, Llewellen!"

Before they realized it they were all back on the stage, Irene pulling Llewellen's arm and talking to him fast. Someone put on the auditorium lights full and then dimmed them again hurriedly. When Emmy came out presently for her scene, she saw in a quick glance that Bill was sitting with a whole mask of handkerchiefs over his bleeding face. She hated Llewellen and was afraid that presently they would break up and go back to New York. But Bill had saved the show from his own folly, since for Llewellen to take the further initiative of quitting would hurt his professional standing. The act ended and the next one began without an interval. When it was over, Bill was gone.

Next night, during the performance, he sat on a chair in the wings in view of everyone coming on or off. His face was swollen and bruised, but he neglected to seem conscious of the fact and there were no comments. Once he went around in front, and when he returned, word leaked out that two of the New York agencies were making big buys. He had a hit—they all had a hit.

At the sight of him to whom Emmy felt they all owed so much, a great wave of gratitude swept over her. She went up and thanked him.

"I'm a good picker, red-head," he agreed grimly.

"Thank you for picking me."

And suddenly Emmy was moved to a rash remark.

"You've hurt your face so badly!" she exclaimed. "Oh, I think it was so brave of you not to let everything go to pieces last night."

He looked at her hard for a moment and then an ironic smile tried unsuccessfully to settle on his swollen face.

"Do you admire me, baby?"

"Yes."

"Even when I fell in the seats, did you admire me?"

"You got control of everything so quick."

"That's loyalty for you. You found something to admire in that fool mess."

And her happiness bubbled up into, "Anyhow, you behaved just wonderfully." She looked so fresh and young that Bill, who had had a wretched day, wanted to rest his swollen cheek against her cheek.

He took both the bruise and the desire with him to New York next morning; the bruise faded, but the desire remained. And when they opened in the city, no sooner did he see other men begin to crowd around her beauty than she became this play for him, this success, the thing that he came to see when he came to the theatre. After a good run it closed just as he was drinking too much and needed someone on the gray days of reaction. They were married suddenly in Connecticut, early in June.

III

Two men sat in the Savoy Grill in London, waiting for the Fourth of July. It was already late in May.

"Is he a nice guy?" asked Hubbel.

"Very nice," answered Brancusi; "very nice, very handsome, very popular." After a moment, he added: "I want to get him to come home."

"That's what I don't get about him," said Hubbel. "Show business over here is nothing compared to home. What does he want to stay here for?"

"He goes around with a lot of dukes and ladies."

"Oh?"

"Last week when I met him he was with three ladies—Lady this, Lady that, Lady the other thing."

"I thought he was married."

"Married three years," said Brancusi, "got a fine child, going to have another."

He broke off as McChesney came in, his very American face staring about boldly over the collar of a box-shouldered topcoat.

"Hello, Mac; meet my friend Mr. Hubbel."

"J'doo," said Bill. He sat down, continuing to stare around the bar to see who was present. After a few minutes Hubbel left, and Bill asked:

"Who's that bird?"

"He's only been here a month. He ain't got a title yet. You been here six months, remember."

Bill grinned.

"You think I'm high-hat, don't you? Well, I'm not kidding myself anyhow. I like it; it gets me. I'd like to be the Marquis of McChesney."

"Maybe you can drink yourself into it," suggested Brancusi.

"Shut your trap. Who said I was drinking? Is that what they say now? Look here; if you can tell me any American manager in the history of the theatre who's had the success that I've had in London in less than eight months, I'll go back to America with you tomorrow. If you'll just tell me——"

"It was with your old shows. You had two flops in New York."

Bill stood up, his face hardening.

"Who do you think you are?" he demanded. "Did you come over here to talk to me like that?"

"Don't get sore now, Bill. I just want you to come back. I'd say anything for that. Put over three seasons like you had in '22 and '23, and you're fixed for life."

"New York makes me sick," said Bill moodily. "One minute you're a king; then you have two flops, they go around saying you're on the toboggan."

Brancusi shook his head.

"That wasn't why they said it. It was because you had that quarrel with Aronstael, your best friend."

"Friend hell!"

"Your best friend in business anyhow. Then——"

"I don't want to talk about it." He looked at his watch. "Look here; Emmy's feeling bad so I'm afraid I can't have dinner with you tonight. Come around to the office before you sail."

Five minutes later, standing by the cigar counter, Brancusi saw Bill enter the Savoy again and descend the steps that led to the tea room.

"Grown to be a great diplomat," thought Brancusi; "he used to just say when he had a date. Going with these dukes and ladies is polishing him up even more."

Perhaps he was a little hurt, though it was not typical of him to be hurt. At any rate he made a decision, then and there, that McChesney was on the down grade; it was quite typical of him that at that point he erased him from his mind forever.

There was no outward indication that Bill was on the down grade; a hit at the New Strand, a hit at the Prince of Wales, and the weekly grosses pouring in almost as well as they had two or three years before in New York. Certainly a man of action was justified in changing his base. And the man who, an hour later, turned into his Hyde Park house for dinner had all the vitality of the late twenties. Emmy, very tired and clumsy, lay on a couch in the upstairs sitting room. He held her for a moment in his arms.

"Almost over now," he said. "You're beautiful."

"Don't be ridiculous."

"It's true. You're always beautiful. I don't know why. Perhaps because you've got character, and that's always in your face, even when you're like this."

She was pleased; she ran her hand through his hair.

"Character is the greatest thing in the world," he declared, "and you've got more than anybody I know."

"Did you see Brancusi?"

"I did, the little louse! I decided not to bring him home to dinner."

"What was the matter?"

"Oh, just snooty—talking about my row with Aronstael, as if it was my fault."

She hesitated, closed her mouth tight, and then said quietly, "You got into that fight with Aronstael because you were drinking."

He rose impatiently.

"Are you going to start——"

"No, Bill, but you're drinking too much now. You know you are."

Aware that she was right, he evaded the matter and they went in to dinner. On the glow of a bottle of claret he decided he would go on the wagon tomorrow till after the baby was born.

"I always stop when I want, don't I? I always do what I say. You never saw me quit yet."

"Never yet."

They had coffee together, and afterward he got up.

"Come back early," said Emmy.

"Oh, sure. . . . What's the matter, baby?"

"I'm just crying. Don't mind me. Oh, go on; don't just stand there like a big idiot."

"But I'm worried, naturally. I don't like to see you cry."

"Oh, I don't know where you go in the evenings; I don't know who you're with. And that Lady Sybil Combrinck who kept phoning. It's all right, I suppose, but I wake up in the night and I feel so alone, Bill. Because we've always been together, haven't we, until recently?"

"But we're together still. . . . What's happened to you, Emmy?"

"I know—I'm just crazy. We'd never let each other down, would we? We never have——"

"Of course not."

"Come back early, or when you can."

He looked in for a minute at the Prince of Wales Theatre; then he went into the hotel next door and called a number.

"I'd like to speak to her Ladyship. Mr. McChesney calling."

It was some time before Lady Sybil answered:

"This is rather a surprise. It's been several weeks since I've been lucky enough to hear from you."

Her voice was flip as a whip and cold as automatic refrigeration, in the mode grown familiar since British ladies took to piecing themselves together out of literature. It had fascinated Bill for a while, but just for a while. He had kept his head.

"I haven't had a minute," he explained easily. "You're not sore, are you?"

"I should scarcely say 'sore.'"

"I was afraid you might be; you didn't send me an invitation to your party tonight. My idea was that after we talked it all over we agreed——"

"You talked a great deal," she said; "possibly a little too much."

Suddenly, to Bill's astonishment, she hung up.

"Going British on me," he thought. "A little skit entitled The Daughter of a Thousand Earls."

The snub roused him, the indifference revived his warning interest. Usually women forgave his changes of heart because of his obvious devotion to Emmy, and he was remembered by various ladies with a not unpleasant sigh. But he had detected no such sigh upon the phone.

"I'd like to clear up this mess," he thought. Had he been wearing evening clothes, he might have dropped in at the dance and talked it over with her, still he didn't want to go home. Upon consideration it seemed important that the misunderstanding should be fixed up at once, and presently he began to entertain the idea of going as he was; Americans were excused unconventionalities of dress. In any case, it was not nearly time, and, in the company of several highballs, he considered the matter for an hour.

At midnight he walked up the steps of her Mayfair house. The coat-room attendants scrutinized his tweeds disapprovingly and a footman peered in vain for his name on the list of guests. Fortunately his friend Sir Humphrey Dunn arrived at the same time and convinced the footman it must be a mistake.

Inside, Bill immediately looked about for his hostess.

She was a very tall young woman, half American and all the more intensely English. In a sense, she had discovered Bill McChesney, vouched for his savage charms; his retirement was one of her most humiliating experiences since she had begun being bad.

She stood with her husband at the head of the receiving line— Bill had never seen them together before. He decided to choose a less formal moment for presenting himself.

As the receiving went on interminably, he became increasingly uncomfortable. He saw a few people he knew, but not many, and he was conscious that his clothes were attracting a certain attention; he was aware also that Lady Sybil saw him and could have relieved his embarrassment with a wave of her hand, but she made no sign. He was sorry he had come, but to withdraw now would be absurd, and going to a buffet table, he took a glass of champagne.

When he turned around she was along at last, and he was about to approach her when the butler spoke to him:

"Pardon me, sir. Have you a card?"

"I'm a friend of Lady Sybil's," said Bill impatiently. He turned away, but the butler followed.

"I'm sorry, sir, but I'll have to ask you to step aside with me and straighten this up."

"There's no need. I'm just about to speak to Lady Sybil now."

"My orders are different, sir," said the butler firmly.

Then, before Bill realized what was happening, his arms were pressed quietly to his sides and he was propelled into a little anteroom back of the buffet.

There he faced a man in a pince-nez in whom he recognized the Combrinck's private secretary.

The secretary nodded to the butler, saying, "This is the man"; whereupon Bill was released.

"Mr. McChesney," said the secretary, "you have seen fit to force your way here without a card, and His Lordship requests that you leave his house at once. Will you kindly give me the check for your coat?"

Then Bill understood, and the single word that he found applicable to Lady Sybil sprang to his lips; whereupon the secretary gave a sign to two footmen, and in a furious struggle Bill was carried through a pantry where busy bus boys stared at the scene, down a long hall, and pushed out a door into the night. The door closed; a moment later it was opened again to let his coat billow forth and his cane clatter down the steps.

As he stood there, overwhelmed, stricken aghast, a taxicab stopped beside him and the driver called:

"Feeling ill, gov'nor?"

"What?"

"I know where you can get a good pick-me-up, gov'nor. Never too late." The door of the taxi opened on a nightmare. There was a cabaret that broke the closing hours; there was being with strangers he had picked up somewhere; then there were arguments, and trying to cash a check, and suddenly proclaiming over and over that he was William McChesney, the producer, and convincing no one of the fact, not even himself. It seemed important to see Lady Sybil right away and call her to account; but presently nothing was important at all. He was in a taxicab whose driver had just shaken him awake in front of his own home.

The telephone was ringing as he went in, but he walked stonily past the maid and only heard her voice when his foot was on the stair.

"Mr. McChesney, it's the hospital calling again. Mrs. McChesney's there and they've been phoning every hour."

Still in a daze, he held the receiver up to his ear.

"We're calling from the Midland Hospital, for your wife. She was delivered of a still-born child at nine this morning."

"Wait a minute." His voice was dry and cracking. "I don't understand."

After a while he understood that Emmy's child was dead and she wanted him. His knees sagged groggily as he walked down the street, looking for a taxi.

The room was dark; Emmy looked up and saw him from a rumpled bed.

"It's you!" she cried. "I thought you were dead! Where did you go?"

He threw himself down on his knees beside the bed, but she turned away.

"Oh, you smell awful," she said. "It makes me sick."

But she kept her hand in his hair, and he knelt there motionless for a long time.

"I'm done with you," she muttered, "but it was awful when I thought you were dead. Everybody's dead. I wish I was dead."

A curtain parted with the wind, and as he rose to arrange it, she saw him in the full morning light, pale and terrible, with rumpled clothes and bruises on his face. This time she hated him instead of those who had hurt him. She could feel him slipping out of her heart, feel the space he left, and all at once he was gone, and she could even forgive him and be sorry for him. All this in a minute.

She had fallen down at the door of the hospital, trying to get out of the taxicab alone.

IV

When Emmy was well, physically and mentally, her incessant idea was to learn to dance; the old dream inculcated by Miss Georgia

Berriman Campbell of South Carolina persisted as a bright avenue leading back to first youth and days of hope in New York. To her, dancing meant that elaborate blend of tortuous attitudes and formal pirouettes that evolved out of Italy several hundred years ago and reached is apogee in Russia at the beginning of this century. She wanted to use herself on something she could believe in, and it seemed to her that the dance was woman's interpretation of music; instead of strong fingers, one had limbs with which to render Tschaikowsky and Stravinski; and feet could be as eloquent in Chopiniana as voices in "The Ring." At the bottom, it was something sandwiched in between the acrobats and the trained seals; at the top it was Pavlova and art.

Once they were settled in an apartment back in New York, she plunged into her work like a girl of sixteen—four hours a day at barre exercises, attitudes, *sauts*, arabesques and pirouettes. It became the realest part of her life, and her only worry was whether or not she was too old. At twenty-six she had ten years to make up, but she was a natural dancer with a fine body—and that lovely face.

Bill encouraged it; when she was ready he was going to build the first real American ballet around her. There were even times when he envied her her absorption; for affairs in his own line were more difficult since they had come home. For one thing, he had made many enemies in those early days of self-confidence; there were exaggerated stories of his drinking and of his being hard on actors and difficult to work with.

It was against him that he had always been unable to save money and must beg a backing for each play. Then, too, in a curious way, he was intelligent, as he was brave enough to prove in several uncommercial ventures, but he had no Theatre Guild behind him, and what money he lost was charged against him.

There were successes, too, but he worked harder for them, or it seemed so, for he had begun to pay a price for his irregular life. He always intended to take a rest or give up his incessant cigarettes, but there was so much competition now—new men coming up, with new reputations for infallibility—and besides, he wasn't used to regularity. He liked to do his work in those great spurts, inspired by black coffee, that seem so inevitable in show business, but which took so much out of a man after thirty. He had come to lean, in a way, on Emmy's fine health and vitality. They were always together, and if he felt a vague dissatisfaction that he had grown to need her more than she needed him, there was always the hope that things would break better for him next month, next season.

Coming home from ballet school one November evening, Emmy swung her little gray bag, pulled her hat far down over her still damp hair, and gave herself up to pleasant speculation. For a month she had been aware of people who had come to the studio especially to watch her—she was ready to dance. Once she had worked just as hard for as long a time on something else—her relations with Bill— only to reach a climax of misery and despair, but here there was nothing to fail her except herself. Yet even now she felt a little rash in thinking: "Now it's come. I'm going to be happy."

She hurried, for something had come up today that she must talk over with Bill.

Finding him in the living room, she called him to come back while she dressed. She began to talk without looking around:

"Listen what happened!" Her voice was loud, to compete with the water running in the tub. "Paul Makova wants me to dance with him at the Metropolitan this season; only it's not sure, so it's a secret —even I'm not supposed to know."

"That's great."

"The only thing is whether it wouldn't be better for me to make a début abroad? Anyhow Donilof says I'm ready to appear. What do you think?"

"I don't know."

"You don't sound very enthusiastic."

"I've got something on my mind. I'll tell you about it later. Go on."

"That's all, dear. If you still feel like going to Germany for a month, like you said, Donilof would arrange a début for me in Berlin, but I'd rather open here and dance with Paul Makova. Just imagine—" She broke off, feeling suddenly through the thick skin of her elation how abstracted he was. "Tell me what you've got on your mind."

"I went to Doctor Kearns this afternoon."

"What did he say?" Her mind was still singing with her own

happiness. Bill's intermittent attacks of hypochondria had long ceased to worry her.

"I told him about that blood this morning, and he said what he said last year—it was probably a little broken vein in my throat. But since I'd been coughing and was worried, perhaps it was safer to take an X-ray and clear the matter up. Well, we cleared it up all right. My left lung is practically gone."

"Bill!"

"Luckily there are no spots on the other."

She waited, horribly afraid.

"It's come at a bad time for me," he went on steadily, "but it's got to be faced. He thinks I ought to go to the Adirondacks or to Denver for the winter, and his idea is Denver. That way it'll probably clear up in five or six months."

"Of course we'll have to—" she stopped suddenly.

"I wouldn't expect you to go—especially if you have this opportunity."

"Of course I'll go," she said quickly. "Your health comes first. We've always gone everywhere together."

"Oh, no."

"Why, of course." She made her voice strong and decisive. "We've always been together. I couldn't stay here without you. When do you have to go?"

"As soon as possible. I went in to see Brancusi to find out if he wanted to take over the Richmond piece, but he didn't seem enthusiastic." His face hardened. "Of course there won't be anything else for the present, but I'll have enough, with what's owing——"

"Oh, if I was only making some money!" Emmy cried. "You work so hard, and here I've been spending two hundred dollars a week for just my dancing lessons alone—more than I'll be able to earn for years."

"Of course in six months I'll be as well as ever—he says."

"Sure, dearest; we'll get you well. We'll start as soon as we can."

She put an arm around him and kissed his cheek.

"I'm just an old parasite," she said. "I should have known my darling wasn't well."

He reached automatically for a cigarette, and then stopped.

"I forgot—I've got to start cutting down smoking." He rose to the occasion suddenly: "No, baby, I've decided to go alone. You'd go crazy with boredom out there, and I'd just be thinking I was keeping you away from your dancing."

"Don't think about that. The thing is to get you well."

They discussed the matter hour after hour for the next week, each of them saying everything except the truth—that he wanted her to go with him and that she wanted passionately to stay in New York. She talked it over guardedly with Donilof, her ballet master, and found that he thought any postponement would be a terrible mistake. Seeing other girls in the ballet school making plans for the winter, she wanted to die rather than go, and Bill saw all the involuntary indications of her misery. For a while they talked of compromising on the Adirondacks, whither she would commute by aeroplane for the week-ends, but he was running a little fever now and he was definitely ordered West.

Bill settled it all one gloomy Sunday night, with that rough, generous justice that had first made her admire him, that made him rather tragic in his adversity, as he had always been bearable in his overweening success:

"It's just up to me, baby. I got into this mess because I didn't have any self-control—you seem to have all of that in this family—and now it's only me that can get me out. You've worked hard at your stuff for three years and you deserve your chance—and if you came out there now you'd have it on me the rest of my life." He grinned. "And I couldn't stand that. Besides, it wouldn't be good for the kid."

Eventually she gave in, ashamed of herself, miserable—and glad. For the world of her work, where she existed without Bill, was bigger to her now than the world in which they existed together. There was more room to be glad in one than to be sorry in the other.

Two days later, with his ticket bought for that afternoon at five, they passed the last hours together, talking of everyhing hopeful. She protested still, and sincerely; had he weakened for a moment she would have gone. But the shock had done something to him, and he showed more character under it than he had for years. Perhaps it would be good for him to work it out alone.

"In the spring!" they said.

Then in the station with little Billy, and Bill saying: "I hate these grave-side partings. You leave me here. I've got to make a phone call from the train before it goes."

They had never spent more than a night apart in six years, save when Emmy was in the hospital; save for the time in England they had a good record of faithfulness and of tenderness toward each other, even though she had been alarmed and often unhappy at this insecure bravado from the first. After he went through the gate alone, Emmy was glad he had a phone call to make and tried to picture him making it.

She was a good woman; she had loved him with all her heart. When she went out into Thirty-third Street, it was just as dead as dead for a while, and the apartment he paid for would be empty of him, and she was here, about to do something that would make her happy.

She stopped after a few blocks, thinking: "Why, this is terrible— what I'm doing! I'm letting him down like the worst person I ever heard of. I'm leaving him flat and going off to dinner with Donilof and Paul Makova, whom I like for being beautiful and for having the same color eyes and hair. Bill's on the train alone."

She swung little Billy around suddenly as if to go back to the station. She could see him sitting in the train, with his face so pale and tired, and no Emmy.

"I can't let him down," she cried to herself as wave after wave of sentiment washed over her. But only sentiment—hadn't he let her down—hadn't he done what he wanted in London?

"Oh, poor Bill!"

She stood irresolute, realizing for one last honest moment how quickly she would forget this and find excuses for what she was doing. She had to think hard of London, and her conscience cleared. But with Bill all alone in the train it seemed terrible to think that way. Even now she could turn and go back to the station and tell him that she was coming, but still she waited, with life very strong in her, fighting for her. The sidewalk was narrow where she stood; presently a great wave of people, pouring out of the theatre, came flooding along it, and she and little Billy were swept along with the crowd.

In the train, Bill telephoned up to the last minute, postponed going back to his stateroom, because he knew it was almost certain that he would not find her there. After the train started he went back and, of course, there was nothing but his bags in the rack and some magazines on the seat.

He knew then that he had lost her. He saw the set-up without any illusions—this Paul Makova, and months of proximity, and loneliness—afterward nothing would ever be the same. When he had thought about it all a long time, reading *Variety* and *Zit's* in between, it began to seem, each time he came back to it, as if Emmy somehow were dead.

"She was a fine girl—one of the best. She had character." He realized perfectly that he had brought all this on himself and that there was some law of compensation involved. He saw, too, that by going away he had again become as good as she was; it was all evened up at last.

He felt beyond everything, even beyond his grief, an almost comfortable sensation of being in the hands of something bigger than himself; and grown a little tired and unconfident—two qualities he could never for a moment tolerate—it did not seem so terrible if he were going West for a definite finish. He was sure that Emmy would come at the end, no matter what she was doing or how good an engagement she had.

THE NIGHT AT CHANCELLORSVILLE

I TELL you I didn't have any notion what I was getting into or I wouldn't of gone down there. They can have their army—it seems to me they were all a bunch of yella-bellies. But my friend Nell said to me: "Nora, Philly, is as dead as Baltimore and we've got to eat this summer." She just got a letter from a girl that said they were living fine down there in "Ole Virginia." The soldiers were getting big pay-offs and figuring maybe they'd stay there all summer, at least till the Johnny Rebs gave up. They got their pay regular too, and a good clean-looking girl could ask—well, I forget now, because, after what happened to us, I guess you can't expect me to remember anything.

I've always been used to decent treatment—somehow when I meet a man, no matter how fresh he is in the beginning, he comes to respect me in the end, and I've never had things done to me like some girls—getting left in a strange town or had my purse stolen.

Well, I started to tell you how I went down to the army in "Ole Virginia." Never again! Wait'll you hear.

I was used to traveling nice—once when I was a little girl my daddy took me on the cars to Baltimore—we lived in York, Pa. And we couldn't have been more comfortable; we had pillows and the men came through with baskets of oranges and apples. You know, singing out: "Want to buy some oranges or apples—or beer?"

You know what they sell—but I never took any beer because——

Oh I know, I'll go on— You only want to talk about the war, like all you men. But if this is your idea what a war is——

Well, they stuck us all in one car and a fresh fella took our tickets, and winked and said:

"Oh you're going down to Hooker's army."

The lights were terrible in the car, smoky and full of bugs, so everything looked sort of yella. And say, that car was so old it was falling to pieces.

There must of been forty gay girls in it, a lot of them from Baltimore and Philly. Only there were three or four that weren't gay—I mean they were more, oh, you know, rich people, and sat up front. Every once an awhile an officer would pop in from the next car and ask them if they wanted anything. I was in the seat behind with Nell and we heard him whisper: "You're in terrible company, but we'll be there in a few hours. And we'll go right to headquarters, and I guarantee you some solid comfort."

I never will forget that night. None of us had any food except some girls behind us had some sausages and bread, and they gave us what they had left. There was a spigot you turned but no water came out. After about two hours—stopping every two minutes it seemed to me—a couple of lieutenants, drunk as monkeys, came in from the next car and offered Nell and me some whiskey out of a bottle. Nell took some and I pretended to, and they set on the side of our seats. One of them started to make up to Nell, but just then the officer that had spoken to the women, pretty high up I guess, a major or a general, came back again and asked:

"You all right? Anything I can do?"

One of the ladies kind of whispered to him, and he turned to the one that was talking to Nell and made him go back in the other car. After that there was only one officer with us; he wasn't really so drunk, just feeling sick.

"This certainly is a happy looking gang," he said. "It's good you can hardly see them in this light. They look as if their best friend just died."

"What if they do," Nell answered back quick. "How would you look yourself if you come all the way from Philly and then got in a buggy like this?"

"I come all the way from The Seven Days, sister," he answered. "Maybe I'd be more pretty for you if I hadn't lost an eye at Gaines' Mill."

Then we noticed he *had* lost an eye. He kept it sort of closed so we hadn't remarked it before. Pretty soon he left and said he'd try and get us some water or coffee, that was what we wanted most.

The car kept rocking and it made us both feel funny. Some of the girls was sick and some was asleep on each other's shoulders.

"Hey, where *is* this army?" Nell said. "Down in Mexico?"

I was kind of half asleep myself by that time and didn't answer. The next thing I knew I was woke up by a storm, the car was stopped again, and I said, "It's raining."

"Raining!" said Nell. "That's cannons—they're having a battle."

"Oh!" I got awake. "Well, after *this* ride I don't care who wins."

It seemed to get louder all the time, but out the windows you couldn't see anything on account of the mist.

In about half an hour another officer came in the car—he looked pretty messy as if he'd just crawled out of bed: his coat was still unbuttoned and he kept hitching up his trousers as if he didn't have any suspenders on.

"All you ladies outside," he said. "We need this car for wounded."

"Hey!"

"We paid for our tickets, didn't we?"

"We need all the cars for the wounded and the other cars are filled up."

"Hey! We didn't come down to fight in any battle!"

"It doesn't matter what you came down for—you're in a hell of a battle."

I was scared, I can tell *you*. I thought maybe the Rebs would capture us and send us down to one of those prisons you hear about, where they starve you to death unless you sing Dixie all the time and kiss niggers.

"Hurry up!"

But another officer had come in who looked more nice.

"Stay where you are, ladies," he said. And then he said to the officer, "What do you want to do? leave them standing on the siding! If Sedgewick's Corps is broken, like they say, the Rebs may come up in this direction!"

Some of the girls began crying out loud.

"These are northern women after all," he said.

"These are——"

"Shut up and go back to your command! I'm detailed to this transportation job—I'm taking these girls back to Washington with us."

I thought they were going to hit each other, but they both walked off together. And we girls sat wondering what we were going to do.

What happened next I don't remember exact. The cannons were sometimes very loud and then sometimes more far away, but there was firing of shots right near us—and a girl down the car had her window smashed like a hole in the center, sort of, all smashed you know, not like when you break a glass, more like ice in cold weather, just a hole and streaks around—you know. I heard a whole bunch of horses gallop by our windows, but I still couldn't see anything.

That went on half an hour—galloping and more shots. We couldn't tell how far away but they sounded like up by the engine.

Then it got quiet—and two men came into our car—we all knew right away they were Rebels, not officers, just plain Private ones, with muskets. One had on a old brown blouse sort of thing and one had on a blue thing—all spotted—I know I could never of let *that* man make love to me. It had spots—it was too short—anyway, it was out of style. Oh it was disgusting. I was surprised because I thought they always wore grey. They were disgusting looking and very dirty; one had a big pot of jam smeared all over his face and the other one had a big box of crackers.

"Hi ladies."

"What you gals doin' down here?"

"Kain't you see, Steve, this is old Joe Hooker's staff."

"Reckin we ought to take em back to the General?"

They talked outlandish like that—I could hardly understand, they talked so funny.

One of the girls got historical she was so scared, and that made them kind of shy. They were just kids under those beards, and one of them tipped his hat or cap or whatever the old thing was.

"We're not fixin' to hurt you."

At that moment there was a whole bunch more shooting down by the engine and the Rebs turned and ran.

We were glad, I can tell you.

Then, about fifteen minutes later, in came one of our officers. This was another new one.

"You better duck down!" he shouted to us. "They may fire on

this train. We're starting you off as soon as we unload two more ambulances."

Half of us was on the floor already. The rich women sitting ahead of Nell and me had gone up into the car ahead where the wounded were—to see if they could do anything. Nell thought she'd look in too, but she came back holding her nose. She said it smelled awful in there.

It was lucky she didn't go in, because two of the girls did from our car. People that is sick can never seem to get much consideration for other people who happen to be well. The nurses sent them right back—as if they was dirt under their feet.

After I don't know how long the train began to move. A soldier come in and poured oil out of all our lights except one, and took it into the wounded car. So now we could hardly see at all.

If the trip down was slow the trip back was slower—The wounded began making so much noise, grunting and all, that we could hear it and couldn't get a decent sleep.

We stopped everywhere.

When we got in Washington at last there was a lot of people in the station and they were all anxious about what had happened to the army, but I said You can search me. All I wanted was my little old room and my little old bed. I never been treated like that in my life.

One of the girls said she was going to write to President Lincoln about it.

And in the papers next day they never said anything about how our train got attacked, or about us girls at all! Can you beat it?

THE LAST OF THE BELLES

I

AFTER Atlanta's elaborate and theatrical rendition of Southern charm, we all underestimated Tarleton. It was a little hotter than anywhere we'd been—a dozen rookies collapsed the first day in that Georgia sun—and when you saw herds of cows drifting through the business streets, hi-yaed by colored drovers, a trance stole down over you out of the hot light; you wanted to move a hand or foot to be sure you were alive.

So I stayed out at camp and let Lieutenant Warren tell me about the girls. This was fifteen years ago, and I've forgotten how I felt, except that the days went along, one after another, better than they do now, and I was empty hearted, because up North she whose legend I had loved for three years was getting married. I saw the clippings and newspaper photographs. It was "a romantic wartime wedding," all very rich and sad. I felt vividly the dark radiance of the sky under which it took place, and, as a young snob, was more envious than sorry.

A day came when I went into Tarleton for a haircut and ran into a nice fellow named Bill Knowles, who was in my time at Harvard. He'd been in the National Guard division that preceded us in camp; at the last moment he had transferred to aviation and been left behind.

"I'm glad I met you, Andy," he said with undue seriousness. "I'll hand you on all my information before I start for Texas. You see, there're really only three girls here——"

I was interested; there was something mystical about there being three girls.

"——and here's one of them now."

We were in front of a drug store and he marched me in and introduced me to a lady I promptly detested.

"The other two are Ailie Calhoun and Sally Carrol Happer."

I guessed from the way he pronounced her name, that he was interested in Ailie Calhoun. It was on his mind what she would be doing while he was gone; he wanted her to have a quiet, uninteresting time.

At my age I don't even hesitate to confess that entirely unchivalrous images of Ailie Calhoun—that lovely name—rushed into my mind. At twenty-three there is no such thing as a pre-empted beauty; though, had Bill asked me, I would doubtless have sworn in all sincerity to care for her like a sister. He didn't; he was just fretting out loud at having to go. Three days later he telephoned me that he was leaving next morning and he'd take me to her house that night.

We met at the hotel and walked uptown through the flowery, hot twilight. The four white pillars of the Calhoun house faced the street, and behind them the veranda was dark as a cave with hanging, weaving, climbing vines.

When we came up the walk a girl in a white dress tumbled out of the front door, crying, "I'm so sorry I'm late!" and seeing us, added: "Why, I thought I heard you come ten minutes——"

She broke off as a chair creaked and another man, an aviator from Camp Harry Lee, emerged from the obscurity of the veranda.

"Why, Canby!" she cried. "How are you?"

He and Bill Knowles waited with the tenseness of open litigants.

"Canby, I want to whisper to you, honey," she said, after just a second. "You'll excuse us, Bill."

They went aside. Presently Lieutenant Canby, immensely displeased, said in a grim voice, "Then we'll make it Thursday, but that means sure." Scarcely nodding to us, he went down the walk, the spurs with which he presumably urged on his aeroplane gleaming in the lamplight.

"Come in—I don't just know your name——"

There she was—the Southern type in all its purity. I would have recognized Ailie Calhoun if I'd never heard Ruth Draper or read Marse Chan. She had the adroitness sugarcoated with sweet, voluble simplicity, the suggested background of devoted fathers, brothers and admirers stretching back into the South's heroic age, the unfailing coolness acquired in the endless struggle with the heat. There were notes in her voice that order slaves around, that withered up Yankee captains, and then soft, wheedling notes that mingled in unfamiliar loveliness with the night.

I could scarcely see her in the darkness, but when I rose to go— it was plain that I was not to linger—she stood in the orange light from the doorway. She was small and very blond; there was too much fever-colored rouge on her face, accentuated by a nose dabbed clownish white, but she shone through that like a star.

"After Bill goes I'll be sitting here all alone night after night. Maybe you'll take me to the country club dances." The pathetic prophecy brought a laugh from Bill. "Wait a minute," Ailie murmured. "Your guns are all crooked."

She straightened my collar pin, looking up at me for a second with something more than curiosity. It was a seeking look, as if she asked, "Could it be you?" Like Lieutenant Canby, I marched off unwillingly into the suddenly insufficient night.

Two weeks later I sat with her on the same veranda, or rather she half lay in my arms and yet scarcely touched me—how she managed that I don't remember. I was trying unsuccessfully to kiss her, and had been trying for the best part of an hour. We had a sort of joke about my not being sincere. My theory was that if she'd let me kiss her I'd fall in love with her. Her argument was that I was obviously insincere.

In a lull between two of these struggles she told me about her brother who had died in his senior year at Yale. She showed me his picture—it was a handsome, earnest face with a Leyendecker fore-lock—and told me that when she met someone who measured up to him she'd marry. I found this family idealism discouraging; even my brash confidence couldn't compete with the dead.

The evening and other evenings passed like that, and ended with my going back to camp with the remembered smell of magnolia flowers and a mood of vague dissatisfaction. I never kissed her. We went to the vaudeville and to the country club on Saturday nights, where she seldom took ten consecutive steps with one man, and she took me to barbecues and rowdy watermelon parties, and never thought it was worth while to change what I felt for her into love.

I see now that it wouldn't have been hard, but she was a wise nineteen and she must have seen that we were emotionally incompatible. So I became her confidant instead.

We talked about Bill Knowles. She was considering Bill; for, though she wouldn't admit it, a winter at school in New York and a prom at Yale had turned her eyes North. She said she didn't think she'd marry a Southern man. And by degrees I saw that she was consciously and voluntarily different from these other girls who sang nigger songs and shot craps in the country club bar. That's why Bill and I and others were drawn to her. We recognized her.

June and July, while the rumors reached us faintly, ineffectually, of battle and terror overseas, Ailie's eyes roved here and there about the country club floor, seeking for something among the tall young officers. She attached several, choosing them with unfailing perspicacity—save in the case of Lieutenant Canby, whom she claimed to despise, but, nevertheless, gave dates to "because he was so sincere"—and we apportioned her evenings among us all summer.

One day she broke all her dates—Bill Knowles had leave and was coming. We talked of the event with scientific impersonality—would he move her to a decision? Lieutenant Canby, on the contrary, wasn't impersonal at all; made a nuisance of himself. He told her that if she married Knowles he was going to climb up six thousand feet in his aeroplane, shut off the motor and let go. He frightened her— I had to yield him my last date before Bill came.

On Saturday night she and Bill Knowles came to the country club. They were very handsome together and once more I felt envious and sad. As they danced out on the floor the three-piece orchestra was playing After You've Gone, in a poignant incomplete way that I can hear yet, as if each bar were trickling off a precious minute of that time. I knew then that I had grown to love Tarleton, and I glanced about half in panic to see if some face wouldn't come in for me out of that warm, singing, outer darkness that yielded up couple after couple in organdie and olive drab. It was a time of youth and war, and there was never so much love around.

When I danced with Ailie she suddenly suggested that we go outside to a car. She wanted to know why didn't people cut in on her tonight? Did they think she was already married?

"Are you going to be?"

"I don't know, Andy. Sometimes, when he treats me as if I were sacred, it thrills me." Her voice was hushed and far away. "And then——"

She laughed. Her body, so frail and tender, was touching mine, her face was turned up to me, and there, suddenly, with Bill Knowles ten yards off, I could have kissed her at last. Our lips just touched experimentally; then an aviation officer turned a corner of the veranda near us, peered into our darkness and hesitated.

"Ailie."

"Yes."

"You heard about this afternoon?"

"What?" She leaned forward, tenseness already in her voice.

"Horace Canby crashed. He was instantly killed."

She got up slowly and stepped out of the car.

"You mean he was killed?" she said.

"Yes. They don't know what the trouble was. His motor——"

"Oh-h-h!" Her rasping whisper came through the hands suddenly covering her face. We watched her helplessly as she put her head on the side of the car, gagging dry tears. After a minute I went for Bill, who was standing in the stag line, searching anxiously about for her, and told him she wanted to go home.

I sat on the steps outside. I had disliked Canby, but his terrible, pointless death was more real to me then than the day's toll of thousands in France. In a few minutes Ailie and Bill came out. Ailie was whimpering a little, but when she saw me her eyes flexed and she came over swiftly.

"Andy"—she spoke in a quick, low voice—"of course you must never tell anybody what I told you about Canby yesterday. What he said, I mean."

"Of course not."

She looked at me a second longer as if to be quite sure. Finally she was sure. Then she sighed in such a quaint little way that I could hardly believe my ears, and her brow went up in what can only be described as mock despair.

"An-dy!"

I looked uncomfortably at the ground, aware that she was calling my attention to her involuntarily disastrous effect on men.

"Good night, Andy!" called Bill as they got into a taxi.

"Good night," I said, and almost added: "You poor fool."

II

Of course I should have made one of those fine moral decisions that people make in books, and despised her. On the contrary, I don't doubt that she could still have had me by raising her hand.

A few days later she made it all right by saying wistfully, "I know you think it was terrible of me to think of myself at a time like that, but it was such a shocking coincidence."

At twenty-three I was entirely unconvinced about anything, except that some people were strong and attractive and could do what they wanted, and others were caught and disgraced. I hoped I was of the former. I was sure Ailie was.

I had to revise other ideas about her. In the course of a long discussion with some girl about kissing—in those days people still talked about kissing more than they kissed—I mentioned the fact that Ailie had only kissed two or three men, and only when she thought she was in love. To my considerable disconcertion the girl figuratively just lay on the floor and howled.

"But it's true," I assured her, suddenly knowing it wasn't. "She told me herself."

"Ailie Calhoun! Oh, my heavens! Why, last year at the Tech spring house party——"

This was in September. We were going overseas any week now, and to bring us up to full strength a last batch of officers from the fourth training camp arrived. The fourth camp wasn't like the first three—the candidates were from the ranks; even from the drafted divisions. They had queer names without vowels in them, and save for a few young militiamen, you couldn't take it for granted that they came out of any background at all. The addition to our company was Lieutenant Earl Schoen from New Bedford, Massachusetts; as fine a physical specimen as I have ever seen. He was six-foot-three, with black hair, high color and glossy dark brown eyes. He wasn't very smart and he was definitely illiterate, yet he was a good officer, high-tempered and commanding, and with that becoming touch of vanity that sits well on the military. I had an idea that New Bedford was a country town, and set down his bumptious qualities to that.

We were doubled up in living quarters and he came into my hut. Inside of a week there was a cabinet photograph of some Tarleton girl nailed brutally to the shack wall.

"She's no jane or anything like that. She's a society girl; goes with all the best people here."

The following Sunday afternoon I met the lady at a semi-private swimming pool in the country. When Ailie and I arrived, there was Schoen's muscular body rippling out of a bathing suit at the far end of the pool.

"Hey, lieutenant!"

When I waved back at him he grinned and winked, jerking his head toward the girl at his side. Then, digging her in the ribs, he jerked his head at me. It was a form of introduction."

"Who's that with Kitty Preston?" Ailie asked, and when I told her she said he looked like a street-car conductor, and pretended to look for her transfer.

A moment later he crawled powerfully and gracefully down the pool and pulled himself up at our side. I introduced him to Ailie.

"How do you like my girl, lieutenant?" he demanded. "I told you she was all right, didn't I?" He jerked his head toward Ailie; this time to indicate that his girl and Ailie moved in the same circles. "How about us all having dinner together down at the hotel some night?"

I left them in a moment, amused as I saw Ailie visibly making up her mind that here, anyhow, was not the ideal. But Lieutenant Earl Schoen was not to be dismissed so lightly. He ran his eyes cheerfully and inoffensively over her cute, slight figure, and decided that she would do even better than the other. Then minutes later I saw them in the water together, Ailie swimming away with a grim little stroke she had, and Schoen wallowing riotously around her and ahead of her, sometimes pausing and staring at her, fascinated, as a boy might look at a nautical doll.

While the afternoon passed he remained at her side. Finally Ailie came over to me and whispered, with a laugh: "He's following me around. He thinks I haven't paid my carfare."

She turned quickly. Miss Kitty Preston, her face curiously flustered, stood facing us.

"Ailie Calhoun, I didn't think it of you to go out and delib'ately try to take a man away from another girl."—An expression of distress at the impending scene flitted over Ailie's face.—"I thought you considered yourself above anything like that."

Miss Preston's voice was low, but it held that tensity that can be felt farther than it can be heard, and I saw Ailie's clear lovely eyes glance about in panic. Luckily, Earl himself was ambling cheerfully and innocently toward us.

"If you care for him you certainly oughtn't to belittle yourself in front of him," said Ailie in a flash, her head high.

It was her acquaintance with the traditional way of behaving against Kitty Preston's naïve and fierce possessiveness, or if you prefer it, Ailie's "breeding" against the other's "commonness." She turned away.

"Wait a minute, kid!" cried Earl Schoen. "How about your address? Maybe I'd like to give you a ring on the phone."

She looked at him in a way that should have indicated to Kitty her entire lack of interest.

"I'm very busy at the Red Cross this month," she said, her voice as cool as her slicked-back blond hair. "Good-by."

On the way home she laughed. Her air of having been unwittingly involved in a contemptible business vanished.

"She'll never hold that young man," she said. "He wants somebody new."

"Apparently he wants Ailie Calhoun."

The idea amused her.

"He could give me his ticket punch to wear, like a fraternity pin. What fun! If mother ever saw anybody like that come in the house, she'd just lie down and die."

And to give Ailie credit, it was fully a fortnight before he did come in her house, although he rushed her until she pretended to be annoyed at the next country club dance.

"He's the biggest tough, Andy," she whispered to me. "But he's so sincere."

She used the word "tough" without the conviction it would have carried had he been a Southern boy. She only knew it with her mind; her ear couldn't distinguish between one Yankee voice and another. And somehow Mrs. Calhoun didn't expire at his appearance on the threshold. The supposedly ineradicable prejudices of Ailie's parents were a convenient phenomenon that disappeared at her wish. It was her friends who were astonished. Ailie, always a little above Tarleton, whose beaux had been very carefully the "nicest" men of the camp—Ailie and Lieutenant Schoen! I grew tired of assuring people that she was merely distracting herself—and indeed every week or so there was someone new—an ensign from Pensacola, an old friend from New Orleans—but always, in between times, there was Earl Schoen.

Orders arrived for an advance party of officers and sergeants to proceed to the port of embarkation and take ship to France. My name was on the list. I had been on the range for a week and when I got back to camp, Earl Schoen buttonholed me immediately.

"We're giving a little farewell party in the mess. Just you and I and Captain Craker and three girls."

Earl and I were to call for the girls. We picked up Sally Carrol Happer and Nancy Lamar, and went on to Ailie's house; to be met at the door by the butler with the announcement that she wasn't home.

"Isn't home?" Earl repeated blankly. "Where is she?"

"Didn't leave no information about that; just said she wasn't home."

"But this is a darn funny thing!" he exclaimed. He walked around the familiar dusky veranda while the butler waited at the door. Something occurred to him. "Say," he informed me—"say, I think she's sore."

I waited. He said sternly to the butler, "You tell her I've got to speak to her a minute."

"How'm I goin' tell her that when she ain't home?"

Again Earl walked musingly around the porch. Then he nodded several times and said:

"She's sore at something that happened downtown."

In a few words he sketched out the matter to me.

"Look here; you wait in the car," I said. "Maybe I can fix this." And when he reluctantly retreated: "Oliver, you tell Miss Ailie I want to see her alone."

After some argument he bore this message and in a moment returned with a reply:

"Miss Ailie say she don't want to see that other gentleman about nothing never. She say come in if you like."

She was in the library. I had expected to see a picture of cool, outraged dignity, but her face was distraught, tumultuous, despairing. Her eyes were red-rimmed, as though she had been crying slowly and painfully, for hours.

"Oh, hello, Andy," she said brokenly. "I haven't seen you for so long. Has he gone?"

"Now, Ailie——"

"Now, Ailie!" she cried. "Now, Ailie! He spoke to me, you see. He lifted his hat. He stood there ten feet from me with that horrible —that horrible woman—holding her arm and talking to her, and then when he saw me he raised his hat. Andy, I didn't know what to do. I had to go in the drug store and ask for a glass of water, and I was so afraid he'd follow in after me that I asked Mr. Rich to let me go out the back way. I never want to see him or hear of him again."

I talked. I said what one says in such cases. I said it for half an hour. I could not move her. Several times she answered by murmuring something about his not being "sincere," and for the fourth time I wondered what the word meant to her. Certainly not constancy; it was, I half suspected, some special way she wanted to be regarded.

I got up to go. And then, unbelievably, the automobile horn sounded three times impatiently outside. It was stupefying. It said as plainly as if Earl were in the room, "All right; go to the devil then! I'm not going to wait here all night."

Ailie looked at me aghast. And suddenly a peculiar look came into her face, spread, flickered, broke into a teary, hysterical smile.

"Isn't he awful?" she cried in helpless despair. "Isn't he terrible?"

"Hurry up," I said quickly. "Get your cape. This is our last night."

And I can still feel that last night vividly, the candlelight that flickered over the rough boards of the mess shack, over the frayed paper decorations left from the supply company's party, the sad mandolin down a company street that kept picking My Indiana Home out of the universal nostalgia of the departing summer. The three girls lost in this mysterious men's city felt something, too—a bewitched impermanence as though they were on a magic carpet that had lighted on the Southern countryside, and any moment the wind would life it and waft it away. We toasted ourselves and the South. Then we left our napkins and empty glasses and a little of the past on the table, and hand in hand went out into the moonlight itself. Taps had been played; there was no sound but the far-away whinny of a horse, and a loud persistent snore at which we laughed, and the leathery snap of a sentry coming to port over by the guard-house. Craker was on duty; we others got into a waiting car, motored into Tarleton and left Craker's girl.

Then Ailie and Earl, Sally and I, two and two in the wide back seat, each couple turned from the other, absorbed and whispering, drove away into the wide, flat darkness.

We drove through pine woods heavy with lichen and Spanish moss, and between the fallow cotton fields along a road white as the rim of the world. We parked under the broken shadow of a mill where there was the sound of running water and restive squawky birds and over everything a brightness that tried to filter in anywhere—into the lost nigger cabins, the automobile, the fastnesses of the heart. The South sang to us—I wonder if they remember. I remember—the cool pale faces, the somnolent amorous eyes and the voices:

"Are you comfortable?"

"Yes; are you?"

"Are you sure you are?"

"Yes."

Suddenly we knew it was late and there was nothing more. We turned home.

Our detachment started for Camp Mills next day, but I didn't go to France after all. We passed a cold month on Long Island, marched aboard a transport with steel helmets slung at our sides and then marched off again. There wasn't any more war. I had missed the war. When I came back to Tarleton I tried to get out of the Army, but I had a regular commission and it took most of the winter. But Earl Schoen was one of the first to be demobilized. He wanted to find a good job "while the picking was good." Ailie was non-committal, but there was an understanding between them that he'd be back.

By January the camps, which for two years had dominated the little city, were already fading. There was only the persistent inciner-ator smell to remind one of all that activity and bustle. What life remained centred bitterly about divisional headquarters building, with the disguntled regular officers who had also missed the war.

And now the young men of Tarleton began drifting back from the ends of the earth—some with Canadian uniforms, some with crutches or empty sleeves. A returned battalion of the National Guard paraded through the streets with open ranks for their dead, and then stepped down out of romance forever and sold you things over the counters of local stores. Only a few uniforms mingled with the dinner coats at the country club dance.

Just before Christmas, Bill Knowles arrived unexpectedly one day and left the next—either he gave Ailie an ultimatum or she had made up her mind at last. I saw her sometimes when she wasn't busy with returned heroes from Savannah and Augusta, but I felt like an outmoded survival—and I was. She was waiting for Earl Schoen with such a vast uncertainty that she didn't like to talk about it. Three days before I got my final discharge he came.

I first happened upon them walking down Market Street together, and I don't think I've ever been so sorry for a couple in my life; though I suppose the same situation was repeating itself in every city where there had been camps. Exteriorly Earl had about every-thing wrong with him that could be imagined. His hat was green, with a radical feather; his suit was slashed and braided in a grotesque fashion that national advertising and the movies have put an end to. Evidently he had been to his old barber, for his hair bloused neatly on his pink, shaved neck. It wasn't as though he had been shiny and poor, but the background of mill-town dance halls and outing clubs flamed out at you—or rather flamed out at Ailie. For she had never quite imagined the reality; in these clothes even the natural grace of that magnificent body had departed. At first he boasted of his fine job; it would get them along all right until he could "see some easy money." But from the moment he came back into her world on its own terms he must have known it was hopeless. I don't know what Ailie said or how much her grief weighed against her stupefaction. She acted quickly—three days after his arrival, Earl and I went North together on the train.

"Well, that's the end of that," he said moodily. "She's a wonderful girl, but too much of a highbrow for me. I guess she's got to marry some rich guy that'll give her a great social position. I can't see that stuck-up sort of thing." And then, later: "She said to come back and see her in a year, but I'll never go back. This aristocat stuff is all right if you got the money for it, but——"

"But it wasn't real," he meant to finish. The provincial society in which he had moved with so much satisfaction for six months already appeared to him as affected, "dudish" and artificial.

"Say, did you see what I saw getting on the train?" he asked me after a while. "Two wonderful janes, all alone. What do you say we mosey into the next car and ask them to lunch? I'll take the one in blue." Halfway down the car he turned around suddenly. "Say, Andy," he demanded, frowning; "one thing—how do you suppose she knew I used to command a street car? I never told her that."

"Search me."

III

This narrative arrives now at one of the big gaps that stared me in the face when I began. For six years, while I finished at Harvard Law and built commercial aeroplanes and backed a pavement block that went gritty under trucks, Ailie Calhoun was scarcely more than a name on a Christmas card; something that blew a little in my mind on warm nights when I remembered the magnolia flowers. Occasionally an acquaintance of Army days would ask me, "What became of that blond girl who was so popular?" but I didn't know. I ran into Nancy Lamar at the Montmartre in New York one evening and learned that Ailie had become engaged to a man in Cincinnati, had gone North to visit his family and then broken it off. She was lovely as ever and there was always a heavy beau or two. But neither Bill Knowles nor Earl Schoen had ever come back.

And somewhere about that time I heard that Bill Knowles had married a girl he met on a boat. There you are—not much of a patch to mend six years with.

Oddly enough, a girl seen at twilight in a small Indiana station started me thinking about going South. The girl, in stiff pink organdie, threw her arms about a man who got off our train and hurried him to a waiting car, and I felt a sort of pang. It seemed to me that she was bearing him off into the lost midsummer world of my early twenties, where time had stood still and charming girls, dimly seen like the past itself, still loitered along the dusky streets. I suppose that poetry is a Northern man's dream of the South. But it was months later that I sent off a wire to Ailie, and immediately followed it to Tarleton.

It was July. The Jefferson Hotel seemed strangely shabby and stuffy—a boosters' club burst into intermittent song in the dining room that my memory had long dedicated to officers and girls. I recognized the taxi driver who took me up to Ailie's house, but his "Sure, I do, lieutenant," was unconvincing. I was only one of twenty thousand.

It was a curious three days. I suppose some of Ailie's first young lustre must have gone the way of such mortal shining, but I can't bear witness to it. She was still so physically appealing that you wanted to touch the personality that trembled on her lips. No—the change was more profound than that.

At once I saw she had a different line. The modulations of pride, the vocal hints that she knew the secrets of a brighter, finer ante-bellum day, were gone from her voice; there was no time for them now as it rambled on in the half-laughing, half-desperate banter of the newer South. And everything was swept into this banter in order to make it go on and leave no time for thinking—the present, the future, herself, me. We went to a rowdy party at the house of some young married people, and she was the nervous, glowing centre of it. After all, she wasn't eighteen, and she was as attractive in her rôle of reckless clown as she had ever been in her life.

"Have you heard anything from Earl Schoen?" I asked her the second night, on our way to the country club dance.

"No." She was serious for a moment. "I often think of him. He was the——" She hesitated.

"Go on."

"I was going to say the man I loved most, but that wouldn't be true. I never exactly loved him, or I'd have married him any old how, wouldn't I?" She looked at me questioningly. "At least I wouldn't have treated him like that."

"It was impossible."

"Of course," she agreed uncertainly. Her mood changed; she became flippant: "How the Yankees did deceive us poor little Southern girls. Ah, me!"

When we reached the country club she melted like a chameleon into the—to me—unfamiliar crowd. There was a new generation upon the floor, with less dignity than the ones I had known, but none of them were more a part of its lazy, feverish essence than Ailie. Possibly she had perceived that in her initial longing to escape from Tarleton's provincialism she had been walking alone, following a generation which was doomed to have no successors. Just where she lost the battle, waged behind the white pillars of her veranda, I don't know. But she had guessed wrong, missed out somewhere. Her wild animation, which even now called enough men around her to rival the entourage of the youngest and freshest, was an admission of defeat.

I left her house, as I had so often left it that vanished June, in a mood of vague dissatisfaction. It was hours later, tossing about my bed in the hotel, that I realized what was the matter, what had always been the matter—I was deeply and incurably in love with her. In spite of every incompatibility, she was still, she would always be to me, the most attractive girl I had ever known. I told her so next afternoon. It was one of those hot days I knew so well, and Ailie sat beside me on a couch in the darkened library.

"Oh, no, I couldn't marry you," she said, almost frightened; "I don't love you that way at all. . . . I never did. And you don't love me. I didn't mean to tell you now, but next month I'm going to marry another man. We're not even announcing it, because I've done that twice before." Suddenly it occurred to her that I might be hurt: "Andy, you just had a silly idea, didn't you? You know I couldn't ever marry a Northern man."

"Who is he?" I demanded.

"A man from Savannah."

"Are you in love with him?"

"Of course I am." We both smiled. "Of course I am! What are you trying to make me say?"

There were no doubts, as there had been with other men. She couldn't afford to let herself have doubts. I knew this because she had long ago stopped making any pretensions with me. This very naturalness, I realized, was because she didn't consider me as a suitor. Beneath her mask of an instinctive thoroughbred she had always been on to herself, and she couldn't believe that anyone not taken in to the point of uncritical worship could really love her. That was what she called being "sincere"; she felt most security with men like Canby and Earl Schoen, who were incapable of passing judgments on the ostensibly aristocratic heart.

"All right," I said, as if she had asked my permission to marry. "Now, would you do something for me?"

"Anything."

"Ride out to camp."

"But there's nothing left there, honey."

"I don't care."

We walked downtown. The taxi driver in front of the hotel repeated her objection: "Nothing there now, cap."

"Never mind. Go there anyhow."

Twenty minutes later he stopped on a wide unfamiliar plain powdered with new cotton fields and marked with isolated clumps of pine.

"Like to drive over yonder where you see the smoke?" asked the driver. "That's the new state prison."

"No. Just drive along this road. I want to find where I used to live."

An old race course, inconspicuous in the camp's day of glory, had reared its dilapidated grandstand in the desolation. I tried in vain to orient myself.

"Go along this road past that clump of trees, and then turn right—no, turn left."

He obeyed, with professional disgust.

"You won't find a single thing, darling," said Ailie. "The contractors took it all down."

"We rode slowly along the margin of the fields. It might have been here——

"All right. I want to get out," I said suddenly.

I left Ailie sitting in the car, looking very beautiful with the warm breeze stirring her long, curly bob.

It might have been here. That would make the company streets down there and the mess shack, where we dined that night, just over the way.

The taxi driver regarded me indulgently while I stumbled here and there in the knee-deep underbrush, looking for my youth in a clapboard or a strip of roofing or a rusty tomato can. I tried to sight on a vaguely familiar clump of trees, but it was growing darker now and I couldn't be quite sure they were the right trees.

"They're going to fix up the old race course," Ailie called from the car. "Tarleton's getting quite doggy in its old age."

No. Upon consideration they didn't look like the right trees. All I could be sure of was this place that had once been so full of life and effort was gone, as if it had never existed, and that in another month Ailie would be gone, and the South would be empty for me forever.

MAJESTY

THE extraordinary thing is not that people in a lifetime turn out worse or better than we had prophesied; particularly in America that is to be expected. The extraordinary thing is how people keep their levels, fulfill their promises, seem actually buoyed up by an inevitable destiny.

One of my conceits is that no one has ever disappointed me since I turned eighteen and could tell a real quality from a gift for sleight of hand, and even many of the merely showy people in my past seem to go on being blatantly and successfully showy to the end.

Emily Castleton was born in Harrisburg in a medium-sized house, moved to New York at sixteen to a big house, went to the Brearley School, moved to an enormous house, moved to a mansion at Tuxedo Park, moved abroad, where she did various fashionable things and was in all the papers. Back in her débutante year one of those French artists who are so dogmatic about American beauties, included her with eleven other public and semipublic celebrities as one of America's perfect types. At the time numerous men agreed with him.

She was just faintly tall, with fine, rather large features, eyes with such an expanse of blue in them that you were really aware of it whenever you looked at her, and a good deal of thick blond hair—arresting and bright. Her mother and father did not know very much about the new world they had commandeered so Emily had to learn everything for herself, and she became involved in various situations and some of the first bloom wore off. However, there was bloom to spare. There were engagements and semi-engagements, short passionate attractions, and then a big affair at twenty-two that embittered her and sent her wandering the continents looking for happiness. She became "artistic" as most wealthy unmarried girls do at that age, because artistic people seem to have some secret, some inner refuge, some escape. But most of her friends were married now, and her life was a great disappointment to her father; so, at twenty-four, with marriage in her head if not in her heart, Emily came home.

This was a low point in her career and Emily was aware of it. She had not done well. She was one of the most popular, most beautiful girls of her generation with charm, money and a sort of fame, but her generation was moving into new fields. At the first note of condescension from a former schoolmate, now a young "matron," she went to Newport and was won by William Brevoort Blair. Immediately she was again the incomparable Emily Castleton. The ghost of the French artist walked once more in the newspapers; the most-talked-of leisure-class event of October was her wedding day.

Splendor to mark society nuptials. . . . Harold Castleton sets out a series of five-thousand-dollar pavilions arranged like the interconnecting tents of a circus, in which the reception, the wedding supper and the ball will be held. . . . Nearly a thousand guests, many of them leaders in business, will mingle with those who dominate the social world. . . . The wedding gifts are estimated to be worth a quarter of a million dollars.

An hour before the ceremony, which was to be solemnized at St. Bartholomew's, Emily sat before a dressing-table and gazed at her face in the glass. She was a little tired of her face at that moment and the depressing thought suddenly assailed her that it would require more and more looking after in the next fifty years.

"I ought to be happy," she said aloud, "but every thought that comes into my head is sad."

Her cousin, Olive Mercy, sitting on the side of the bed, nodded. "All brides are sad."

"It's such a waste," Emily said.

Olive frowned impatiently.

"Waste of what? Women are incomplete unless they're married and have children."

For a moment Emily didn't answer. Then she said slowly, "Yes, but whose children?"

For the first time in her life, Olive, who worshipped Emily, almost hated her. Not a girl in the wedding party but would have been glad of Brevoort Blair—Olive among the others.

"You're lucky," she said. "You're so lucky you don't even know it. You ought to be paddled for talking like that."

"I shall learn to love him," announced Emily facetiously. "Love will come with marriage. Now, isn't that a hell of a prospect?"

"Why so deliberately unromantic?"

"On the contrary, I'm the most romantic person I've ever met in my life. Do you know what I think when he puts his arms around me? I think that if I look up I'll see Garland Kane's eyes."

"But why, then——"

"Getting into his plane the other day I could only remember Captain Marchbanks and the little two-seater we flew over the Channel in, just breaking our hearts for each other and never saying a word about it because of his wife. I don't regret those men; I just regret the part of me that went into caring. There's only the sweepings to hand to Brevoort in a pink wastebasket. There should have been something more; I thought even when I was most carried away that I was saving something for the one. But apparently I wasn't." She broke off and then added: "And yet I wonder."

The situation was no less provoking to Olive for being comprehensible, and save for her position as a poor relation, she would have spoken her mind. Emily was well spoiled—eight years of men had assured her they were not good enough for her and she had accepted the fact as probably true.

"You're nervous." Olive tried to keep the annoyance out of her voice. "Why not lie down for an hour?"

"Yes," answered Emily absently.

Olive went out and downstairs. In the lower hall she ran into Brevoort Blair, attired in a nuptial cutaway even to the white carnation, and in a state of considerable agitation.

"Oh, excuse me," he blurted out. "I wanted to see Emily. It's about the rings—which ring, you know. I've got four rings and she never decided and I can't just hold them out in the church and have her take her pick."

"I happen to know she wants the plain platinum band. If you want to see her anyhow——"

"Oh, thanks very much. I don't want to disturb her."

They were standing close together, and even at this moment when he was gone, definitely preëmpted, Olive couldn't help thinking how alike she and Brevoort were. Hair, coloring, features—they might have been brother and sister—and they shared the same shy serious temperaments, the same simple straightforwardness. All this flashed through her mind in an instant, with the added thought that the blond, tempestuous Emily, with her vitality and amplitude of scale, was, after all, better for him in every way; and then, beyond this, a perfect wave of tenderness, of pure physical pity and yearning swept over her and it seemed that she must step forward only half a foot to find his arms wide to receive her.

She stepped backward instead, relinquishing him as though she still touched him with the tip of her fingers and then drew the tips away. Perhaps some vibration of her emotion fought its way into his consciousness, for he said suddenly:

"We're going to be good friends, aren't we? Please don't think I'm taking Emily away. I know I can't own her—nobody could—and I don't want to."

Silently, as he talked, she said good-by to him, the only man she had ever wanted in her life.

She loved the absorbed hesitancy with which he found his coat and hat and felt hopefully for the knob on the wrong side of the door.

When he had gone she went into the drawing-room, gorgeous and portentous; with its painted bacchanals and massive chandeliers and the eighteenth-century portraits that might have been Emily's ancesors, but weren't, and by that very fact belonged the more to her. There she rested, as always, in Emily's shadow.

Through the door that led out to the small, priceless patch of grass on Sixtieth Street now inclosed by the pavilions, came her uncle, Mr. Harold Castleton. He had been sampling his own champagne.

"Olive so sweet and fair." He cried emotionally, "Olive, baby, she's done it. She was all right inside, like I knew all the time. The good ones come through, don't they—the real thoroughbreds? I began to think that the Lord and me, between us, had given her too much, that she'd never be satisfied, but now she's come down to earth just like a"—he searched unsuccessfully for a metaphor—"like a thoroughbred, and she'll find it not such a bad place after all." He came closer. "You've been crying, little Olive."

"Not much."

"It doesn't matter," he said magnanimously. "If I wasn't so happy I'd cry too."

Later, as she embarked with two other bridesmaids for the church, the solemn throbbing of a big wedding seemed to begin with the vibration of the car. At the door the organ took it up, and later it would palpitate in the cellos and bass viols of the dance, to fade off finally with the sound of the car that bore bride and groom away.

The crowd was thick around the church, and ten feet out of it the air was heavy with perfume and faint clean humanity and the fabric smell of new clean clothes. Beyond the massed hats in the van of the church the two families sat in front rows on either side. The Blairs—they were assured a family resemblance by their expression of faint condescension, shared by their in-laws as well as by true Blairs—were represented by the Gardiner Blairs, senior and junior; Lady Mary Bowes Howard, née Blair; Mrs. Potter Blair; Mrs. Princess Potowki Parr Blair, née Inchbit; Miss Gloria Blair, Master Gardiner Blair III, and the kindred branches, rich and poor, of Smythe, Bickle, Diffendorfer and Hamn. Across the aisle the Castletons made a less impressive showing—Mr. Harold Castleton, Mr. and Mrs. Theodore Castleton and children, Harold Castleton Junior, and, from Harrisburg, Mr. Carl Mercy, and two little old aunts named O'Keefe hidden off in a corner. Somewhat to their surprise the two aunts had been bundled off in a limousine and dressed from head to foot by a fashionable couturière that morning.

In the vestry, where the bridesmaids fluttered about like birds in their big floppy hats, there was a last lip rouging and adjustment of pins before Emily should arrive. They represented several stages of Emily's life—a schoolmate at Brearley, a last unmarried friend of débutante year, a travelling companion of Europe, and the girl she had visited in Newport when she met Brevoort Blair.

"They've got Wakeman," this last one said, standing by the door listening to the music. "He played for my sister, but I shall never have Wakeman."

"Why not?"

"Why, he's playing the same thing over and over—'At Dawning.' He's played it half a dozen times."

At this moment another door opened and the solicitous head of a young man appeared around it. "Almost ready?" he demanded of the nearest bridesmaid. "Brevoort's having a quiet little fit. He just stands there wilting collar after collar——"

"Be calm," answered the young lady. "The bride is always a few minutes late."

"A few minutes!" protested the best man. "I don't call it a few minutes. They're beginning to rustle and wriggle like a circuit crowd out there, and the organist has been playing the same tune for half an hour. I'm going to get him to fill in with a little jazz."

"What time is it?" Olive demanded.

"Quarter of five—ten minutes of five."

"Maybe there's been a traffic tie-up." Olive paused as Mr. Harold Castleton, followed by an anxious curate, shouldered his way in, demanding a phone.

And now there began a curious dribbling back from the front of the church, one by one, then two by two, until the vestry was crowded with relatives and confusion.

"What's happened?"

"What on earth's the matter?"

A chauffeur came in and reported excitedly. Harold Castleton swore and, his face blazing, fought his way roughly toward the door. There was an attempt to clear the vestry, and then, as if to balance the dribbling, a ripple of conversation commenced at the rear of the church and began to drift up toward the altar, growing louder and faster and more excited, mounting always, bringing people to their feet, rising to a sort of subdued roar. The announcement from the altar that the marriage had been postponed was scarcely heard, for by that time everyone knew that they were participating in a front-page scandal, that Brevoort Blair had been left waiting at the altar and Emily Castleton had run away.

II

There were a dozen reporters outside the Castleton house on Sixteenth Street when Olive arrived, but in her absorption she failed even to hear their questions; she wanted desperately to go and comfort a certain man whom she must not approach, and as a sort of substitute she sought her Uncle Harold. She entered through the interconnecting five-thousand-dollar pavilions, where caterers and servants still stood about in a respectful funereal half-light, waiting for something to happen, amid trays of caviar and turkey's breast and pyramided wedding cake. Upstairs, Olive found her uncle sitting on a stool before Emily's dressing-table. The articles of make-up spread before him, the repertoire of feminine preparation in evidence about, made his singularly inappropriate presence a symbol of the mad catastrophe.

"Oh, it's you." His voice was listless; he had aged in two hours. Olive put her arm about his bowed shoulder.

"I'm so terribly sorry, Uncle Harold."

Suddenly a stream of profanity broke from him, died away, and a single large tear welled slowly from one eye.

"I want to get my massage man," he said. "Tell McGregor to get him." He drew a long broken sigh, like a child's breath after crying, and Olive saw that his sleeves were covered with a dust of powder from the dressing-table, as if he had been leaning forward on it, weeping, in the reaction from his proud champagne.

"There was a telegram," he muttered.

"It's somewhere."

And he added slowly,

"From now on *you're* my daughter."

"Oh, no, you mustn't say that!"

Unrolling the telegram, she read:

I can't make the grade I would feel like a fool either way but this will be over sooner so damn sorry for you

EMILY

When Olive had summoned the masseur and posted a servant outside her uncle's door, she went to the library, where a confused secretary was trying to say nothing over an inquisitive and persistent telephone.

"I'm so upset, Miss Mercy," he cried in a despairing treble. "I do declare I'm so upset I have a frightful headache. I've thought for half an hour I heard dance music from down below."

Then it occurred to Olive that she, too, was becoming hysterical; in the breaks of the street traffic a melody was drifting up, distinct and clear:

> "—Is she fair
> Is she sweet
> I don't care—cause
> I can't compete—
> Who's the——"

She ran quickly downstairs and through the drawing-room, the tune growing louder in her ears. At the entrance of the first pavilion she stopped in stupefaction.

To the music of a small but undoubtedly professional orchestra a dozen young couples were moving about the canvas floor. At the bar in the corner stood additional young men, and half a dozen of the caterer's assistants were busily shaking cocktails and opening champagne.

"Harold!" she called imperatively to one of the dancers. "Harold!"

A tall young man of eighteen handed his partner to another and came toward her.

"Hello, Olive. How did father take it?"

"Harold, what in the name of——"

"Emily's crazy," he said consolingly. "I always told you Emily was crazy. Crazy as a loon. Always was."

"What's the idea of this?"

"This?" He looked around innocently. "Oh, these are just some fellows that came down from Cambridge with me."

"But—*dancing!*"

"Well, nobody's dead, are they? I thought we might as well use up some of this——"

"Tell them to go home," said Olive.

"Why? What on earth's the harm? These fellows came all the way down from Cambridge——"

"It simply isn't dignified."

"But they don't care, Olive. One fellow's sister did the same thing—only she did it the day after instead of the day before. Lots of people do it nowadays."

"Send the music home, Harold," said Olive firmly, "or I'll go to your father."

Obviously he felt that no family could be disgraced by an episode on such a magnificent scale, but he reluctantly yielded. The abysmally depressed butler saw to the removal of the champagne, and the young people, somewhat insulted, moved nonchalantly out into the more tolerant night. Alone with the shadow—Emily's shadow—that hung over the house, Olive sat down in the drawing-room to think. Simultaneously the butler appeared in the doorway.

"It's Mrs. Blair, Miss Olive."

She jumped tensely to her feet.

"Who does he want to see?"

"He didn't say. He just walked in."

"Tell him I'm in here."

He entered with an air of abstraction rather than depression, nodded to Olive and sat down on a piano stool. She wanted to say, "Come here. Lay your head here, poor man. Never mind." But she wanted to cry, too, and so she said nothing.

"In three hours," he remarked quietly, "we'll be able to get the morning papers. There's a shop on Fifty-ninth Street."

"That's foolish——" she began.

"I am not a superficial man"—he interrupted her—"nevertheless, my chief feeling now is for the morning papers. Later there will be a politely silent gauntlet of relatives, friends and business acquaintances. About the actual affair I surprise myself by not caring at all."

"I shouldn't care about any of it."

"I'm rather grateful that she did it in time."

"Why don't you go away?" Olive leaned forward earnestly. "Go to Europe until it all blows over."

"Blows over." He laughed. "Things like this don't ever blow over. A little snicker is going to follow me around the rest of my life."

He groaned. "Uncle Hamilton started right for Park Row to make the rounds of the newspaper offices. He's a Virginian and he was unwise enough to use the old-fashioned word 'horsewhip' to one editor. I can hardly wait to see *that* paper." He broke off. "How is Mr. Castleton?"

"He'll appreciate your coming to inquire."

"I didn't come about that." He hesitated. "I came to ask you a question. I want to know if you'll marry me in Greenwich tomorrow morning."

For a minute Olive fell precipitately through space; she made a strange little sound; her mouth dropped ajar.

"I know you like me," he went on quickly. "In fact, I once imagined you loved me a little bit, if you'll excuse the presumption. Anyhow, you're very like a girl that once did love me, so maybe you would—" His face was pink with embarrassment, but he struggled grimly on; "anyhow, I like you enormously and whatever feeling I may have had for Emily has, I might say, flown."

The clangor and alarm inside her was so loud that it seemed he must hear it.

"The favor you'll be doing me will be very great," he continued. "My heavens, I know it sounds a little crazy, but what could be crazier than the whole afternoon? You see, if you married me the papers would carry quite a different story; they'd think that Emily went off to get out of our way, and the joke would be on her after all."

Tears of indignation came to Olive's eyes.

"I suppose I ought to allow for your wounded egotism, but do you realize you're making me an insulting proposition?"

His face fell.

"I'm sorry," he said after a moment. "I guess I was an awful fool even to think of it, but a man hates to lose the whole dignity of his life for a girl's whim. I see it would be impossible. I'm sorry."

He got up and picked up his cane.

Now he was moving toward the door, and Olive's heart came into her throat and a great, irresistible wave of self-preservation swept over her—swept over all her scruples and her pride. His steps sounded in the hall.

"Brevoort!" she called. She jumped to her feet and ran to the door. He turned. "Brevoort, what was the name of that paper—the one your uncle went to?"

"Why?"

"Because it's not too late for them to change their story if I telephone now! I'll say we were married tonight!"

III

There is a society in Paris which is merely a heterogeneous prolongation of American society. People moving in are connected by a hundred threads to the motherland, and their entertainments, eccentricities and ups and downs are an open book to friends and relatives at Southampton, Lake Forest or Back Bay. So during her previous European sojourn Emily's whereabouts, as she followed the shifting Continental season, were publicly advertised; but from the day, one month after the unsolemnized wedding, when she sailed from New York, she dropped completely from sight. There was an occasional letter from her father, an occasional rumor that she was in Cairo, Constantinople or the less frequented Riviera—that was all.

Once, after a year, Mr. Castleton saw her in Paris, but, as he told Olive, the meeting only served to make him uncomfortable.

"There was something about her," he said vaguely, "as if—well, as if she had a lot of things in the back of her mind I couldn't reach. She was nice enough, but it was all automatic and formal.—She asked about you."

Despite her solid background of a three-month-old baby and a beautiful apartment on Park Avenue, Olive felt her heart falter uncertainly.

"What did she say?"

"She was delighted about you and Brevoort." And he added to himself, with a disappointment he could not conceal: "Even though you picked up the best match in New York when she threw it away." . . .

. . . It was more than a year after this that his secretary's voice on the telephone asked Olive if Mr. Castleton could see them that night. They found the old man walking his library in a state of agitation.

"Well, it's come," he declared vehemently. "People won't stand still; nobody stands still. You go up or down in this world. Emily chose to go down. She seems to be somewhere near the bottom. Did you ever hear of a man described to me as a"—he referred to a letter in his hand—"dissipated ne'er-do-well named Petrocobesco? He calls himself Prince Gabriel Petrocobesco, apparently from—from nowhere. This letter is from Hallam, my European man, and it incloses a clipping from the Paris *Matin*. It seems that this gentleman was invited by the police to leave Paris, and among the small entourage who left with him was an American girl, Miss Castleton, 'rumored to be the daughter of a millionaire.' The party was escorted to the station by gendarmes." He handed clipping and letter to Brevoort Blair with trembling fingers. "What do you make of it? Emily come to that!"

"It's not so good," said Brevoort, frowning.

"It's the end. I though her drafts were big recently, but I never suspected that she was supporting——"

"It may be a mistake," Olive suggested. "Perhaps it's another Miss Castleton."

"It's Emily all right. Hallam looked up the matter. It's Emily, who was afraid ever to dive into the nice clean stream of life and ends up now by swimming around in the sewers."

Shocked, Olive had a sudden sharp taste of fate in its ultimate diversity. She with a mansion building in Westbury Hills, and Emily was mixed up with a deported adventurer in disgraceful scandal.

"I've got no right to ask you this," continued Mr. Castleton. "Certainly no right to ask Brevoort anything in connection with Emily. But I'm seventy-two and Fraser says if I put off the cure another fortnight he won't be responsible, and then Emily will be alone for good. I want you to set your trip abroad forward by two months and go over and bring her back."

"But do you think we'd have the necessary influence?" Brevoort asked. "I've no reason for thinking that she'd listen to me."

"There's no one else. If you can't go I'll have to."

"Oh, no," said Brevoort quickly. "We'll do what we can, won't we, Olive?"

"Of course."

"Bring her back—it doesn't matter how—but bring her back. Go before a court if necessary and swear she's crazy."

"Very well. We'll do what we can."

Just ten days after this interview the Brevoort Blairs called on Mr. Castleton's agent in Paris to glean what details were available. They were plentiful but unsatisfactory. Hallam had seen Petrocobesco in various restaurants—a fat little fellow with an attractive leer and a quenchless thirst. He was of some obscure nationality and had been moved around Europe for several years, living heaven knew how —probably on Americans, though Hallam understood that of late even the most outlying circles of international society were closed to him. About Emily, Hallam knew very little. They had been reported last week in Berlin and yesterday in Budapest. It was probable that such an undesirable as Petrocobesco was required to register with the police everywhere, and this was the line he recommended the Blairs to follow.

Forty-eight hours later, accompanied by the American vice consul, they called upon the prefect of police in Budapest. The officer talked in rapid Hungarian to the vice consul, who presently announced the gist of his remarks—the Blairs were too late.

"Where have they gone?"

"He doesn't know. He received orders to move them on and they left last night."

Suddenly the prefect wrote something on a piece of paper and handed it, with a terse remark, to the vice consul.

"He says try there."

Brevoort looked at the paper.

"Sturmdorp—where's that?"

Another rapid conversation in Hungarian.

"Five hours from here on a local train that leaves Tuesdays and Fridays. This is Saturday."

"We'll get a car at the hotel," said Brevoort.

They set out after dinner. It was a rough journey through the

night across the still Hungarian plain. Olive awoke once from a
worried doze to find Brevoort and the chauffeur changing a tire;
then again as they stopped at a muddy little river, beyond which
glowed the scattered lights of a town. Two soldiers in an unfamiliar
uniform glanced into the car; they crossed a bridge and followed a
narrow, warped main street to Sturmdorp's single inn; the roosters
were already crowing as they tumbled down on the mean beds.

Olive awoke with a sudden sure feeling that they had caught up
with Emily; and with it came that old sense of helplessness in the
face of Emily's moods; for a moment the long past and Emily dominant in it, swept back over her, and it seemed almost a presumption
to be here. But Brevoort's singleness of purpose reassured her and
confidence had returned when they went downstairs, to find a land-
lord who spoke fluent American, acquired in Chicago before the war.

"You are not in Hungary now," he explained. "You have crossed
the border into Czjeck-Hansa. But it is only a little country with
two towns, this one and the capital. We don't ask the visa from
Americans."

"That's probably why they came here," Olive thought.

"Perhaps you could give us some information about strangers?"
asked Brevoort. "We're looking for an American lady—" He described Emily, without mentioning her probable companion; as he
proceeded a curious change came over the innkeeper's face.

"Let me see your passports," he said; then: "And why you want
to see her?"

"This lady is her cousin."

The innkeeper hesitated momentarily.

"I think perhaps I be able to find her for you," he said.

He called the porter; there were rapid instructions in an unintelligible patois. Then:

"Follow this boy—he take you there."

They were conducted through filthy streets to a tumbledown
house on the edge of town. A man with a hunting rifle, lounging
outside, straightened up and spoke sharply to the porter, but after
an exchange of phrases they passed, mounted the stairs and knocked
at a door. When it opened a head peered around the corner; the
porter spoke again and they went in.

They were in a large dirty room which might have belonged to a poor boarding house in any quarter of the Western world—faded falls, split upholstery, a shapeless bed and an air, despite its bareness, of being overcrowded by the ghostly furniture, indicated by dust rings and worn spots, of the last decade. In the middle of the room stood a small stout man with hammock eyes and a peering nose over a sweet, spoiled little mouth, who stared intently at them as they opened the door, and then with a single disgusted "Chut!" turned impatiently away. There were several other people in the room, but Brevoort and Olive saw only Emily, who reclined in a chaise longue with half-closed eyes.

At the sight of them the eyes opened in mild astonishment; she made a move as though to jump up, but instead held out her hand, smiled and spoke their names in a clear polite voice, less as a greeting than as a sort of explanation to the others of their presence here. At their names a grudging amenity replaced the sullenness on the little man's face.

The girls kissed.

"Tutu!" said Emily, as if calling him to attention—"Prince Petrocobesco, let me present my cousin Mrs. Blair, and Mr. Blair."

"*Plaisir*," said Petrocobesco. He and Emily exchanged a quick glance, whereupon he said, "Won't you sit down?" and immediately seated himself in the only available chair, as if they were playing Going to Jerusalem.

"Plaisir," he repeated. Olive sat down on the foot of Emily's chaise longue and Brevoort took a stool from against the wall, meanwhile noting the other occupants of the room. There was a very fierce young man in a cape who stood, with arms folded and teeth gleaming, by the door, and two ragged, bearded men, one holding a revolver, the other with his head sunk dejectedly on his chest, who sat side by side in the corner.

"You come here long?" the prince asked.

"Just arrived this morning."

For a moment Olive could not resist comparing the two, the tall fair-featured American and the unprepossessing South European, scarcely a likely candidate for Ellis Island. Then she looked at Emily —the same thick bright hair with sunshine in it, the eyes with the hint of vivid seas. Her face was faintly drawn, there were slight new lines around her mouth, but she was the Emily of old—dominant, shining, large of scale. It seemed shameful for all that beauty and personality to have arrived in a cheap boarding house at the world's end.

The man in the cape answered a knock at the door and handed a note to Petrobesco, who read it, cried "*Chut!*" and passed it to Emily.

"You see, there are no carriages," he said tragically in French. "The carriages were destroyed—all except one, which is in a museum. Anyhow, I prefer a horse."

"No," said Emily.

"Yes, yes, yes!" he cried. "Whose business is it how I go?"

"Don't let's have a scene, Tutu."

"Scene!" He fumed. "Scene!"

Emily turned to Olive: "You came by automobile?"

"Yes."

"A big de luxe car? With a back that opens?"

"Yes."

"There," said Emily to the prince. "We can have the arms painted on the side of that."

"Hold on," said Brevoort. "This car belongs to a hotel in Budapest."

Apparently Emily didn't hear.

"Janierka could do it," she continued thoughtfully.

At this point there was another interruption. The dejected man in the corner suddenly sprang to his feet and made as though to run to the door, whereupon the other man raised his revolver and brought the butt down on his head. The man faltered and would have collapsed had not his assailant hauled him back to the chair, where he sat comatose, a slow stream of blood trickling over his forehead.

"Dirty townsman! Filthy, dirty spy!" shouted Petrocobesco between clenched teeth.

"Now that's just the kind of remark you're not to make!" said Emily sharply.

"Then why we don't hear?" he cried. "Are we going to sit here in this pigsty forever?"

Disregarding him, Emily turned to Olive and began to question her conventionally about New York. Was prohibition any more successful? What were the new plays? Olive tried to answer and simultaneously to catch Brevoort's eye. The sooner their purpose was broached, the sooner they could get Emily away.

"Can we see you alone, Emily?" demanded Brevoort abruptly.

"Why, for the moment we haven't got another room."

Petrocobesco had engaged the man with the cape in agitated conversation, and taking advantage of this, Brevoort spoke hurriedly to Emily in a lowered voice:

"Emily, your father's getting old; he needs you at home. He wants you to give up this crazy life and come back to America. He sent us because he couldn't come himself and no one else knew you well enough——"

She laughed. "You mean, knew the enormities I was capable of."

"No," put in Olive quickly. "Cared for you as we do. I can't tell you how awful it is to see you wandering over the face of the earth."

"But we're not wandering now," explained Emily. "This is Tutu's native country."

"Where's your pride, Emily?" said Olive impatiently. "Do you know that affair in Paris was in the papers? What do you suppose people think back home?"

"That affair in Paris was an outrage." Emily's blue eyes flashed around her. "Someone will pay for that affair in Paris."

"It'll be the same everywhere. Just sinking lower and lower, dragged in the mire, and one day deserted——"

"Stop, please!" Emily's voice was cold as ice. "I don't think you quite understand——"

Emily broke off as Petrocobesco came back, threw himself into his chair and buried his face in his hands.

"I can't stand it," he whispered. "Would you mind taking my pulse? I think it's bad. Have you got the thermometer in your purse?"

She held his wrist in silence for a moment.

"It's all right, Tutu." Her voice was soft now, almost crooning. "Sit up. Be a man."

"All right."

He crossed his legs as if nothing had happened and turned abruptly to Brevoort:

"How are financial conditions in New York?" he demanded.

But Brevoort was in no humor to prolong the absurd scene. The memory of a certain terrible hour three years before swept over him. He was no man to be made a fool of twice, and his jaw set as he rose to his feet.

"Emily, get your things together," he said tersely. "We're going home."

Emily did not move; an expression of astonishment, melting to amusement, spread over her face. Olive put her arm around her shoulder.

"Come, dear. Let's get out of this nightmare." Then:

"We're waiting," Brevoort said.

Petrocobesco spoke suddenly to the man in the cape, who approached and seized Brevoort's arm. Brevoort shook him off angrily, whereupon the man stepped back, his hand searching his belt.

"No!" cried Emily imperatively.

Once again there was an interruption. The door opened without a knock and two stout men in frock coats and silk hats rushed in and up to Petrocobesco. They grinned and patted him on the back chattering in a strange language, and presently he grinned and patted them on the back and they kissed all around; then, turning to Emily, Petrocobesco spoke to her in French.

"It's all right," he said excitedly. "They did not even argue the matter. I am to have the title of king."

With a long sigh Emily sank back in her chair and her lips parted in a relaxed, tranquil smile.

"Very well, Tutu. We'll get married."

"Oh, heavens, how happy!" He clasped his hands and gazed up ecstatically at the faded ceiling. "How extremely happy!" He fell on his knees beside her and kissed her inside arm.

"What's all this about kings?" Brevoort demanded. "Is this—is he a king?"

"He's a king. Aren't you, Tutu?" Emily's hand gently stroked his oiled hair and Olive saw that her eyes were unusually bright.

"I am your husband," cried Tutu weepily. "The most happy man alive."

"His uncle was Prince of Czjeck-Hansa before the war," explained Emily, her voice singing her content. "Since then there's been a republic, but the peasant party wanted a change and Tutu was next in line. Only I wouldn't marry him unless he insisted on being king instead of prince."

Brevoort passed his hand over his wet forehead.

"Do you mean that this is actually a fact?"

Emily nodded. "The assembly voted it this morning. And if you'll lend us this de luxe limousine of yours we'll make our official entrance into the capital this afternoon."

IV

Over two years later Mr. and Mrs. Brevoort Blair and their two children stood upon a balcony of the Carlton Hotel in London, a situation recommended by the management for watching royal processions pass. This one began with a fanfare of trumpets down by the Strand, and presently a scarlet line of horse guards came into sight.

"But, mummy," the little boy demanded, "is Aunt Emily Queen of England?"

"No, dear; she's queen of a little tiny country, but when she visits here she rides in the queen's carriage."

"Oh."

"Thanks to the magnesium deposits," said Brevoort dryly.

"Was she a princess before she got to be queen?" the little girl asked.

"No, dear; she was an American girl and then she got to be a queen."

"Why?"

"Because nothing else was good enough for her," said her father. "Just think, one time she could have married me. Which would you rather do, baby—marry me or be a queen?"

The little girl hesitated.

"Marry you," she said politely, but without conviction.

"That'll do, Brevoort," said her mother. "Here they come."

"I see them!" the little boy cried.

The cavalcade swept down the crowded street. There were more horse guards, a company of dragoons, outriders, then Olive found herself holding her breath and squeezing the balcony rail, as between a double line of beefeaters, a pair of great gilt-and-crimson coaches rolled past. In the first were the royal sovereigns, their uniforms gleaming with ribbons, crosses and stars, and in the second their two royal consorts, one old, the other young. There was about the scene the glamour shed always by the old empire of half the world, by her ships and ceremonies, her pomps and symbols; and the crowd felt it, and a slow murmur rolled along before the carriage, rising to a strong steady cheer. The two ladies bowed to left and right, and though few knew who the second queen was, she was cheered too. In a moment the gorgeous panoply had rolled below the balcony and on out of sight.

When Olive turned away from the window there were tears in her eyes.

"I wonder if she likes it, Brevoort. I wonder if she's really happy with that terrible little man."

"Well, she got what she wanted, didn't she? And that's something."

Olive drew a long breath.

"Oh, she's so wonderful," she cried—"so wonderful! She could always move me like that, even when I was angriest at her."

"It's all so silly," Brevoort said.

"I suppose so," answered Olive's lips. But her heart, winged with helpless adoration, was following her cousin through the palace gates half a mile away.

FAMILY IN THE WIND

THE two men drove up the hill toward the blood-red sun. The cotton fields bordering the road were thin and withered, and no breeze stirred in the pines.

"When I am totally sober," the doctor was saying—"I mean when I am totally sober—I don't see the same world that you do. I'm like a friend of mine who had one good eye and got glasses made to correct his bad eye; the result was that he kept seeing elliptical suns and falling off tilted curbs, until he had to throw the glasses away. Granted that I am thoroughly anaesthetized the greater part of the day—well, I only undertake work that I know I can do when I am in that condition."

"Yeah," agreed his brother Gene uncomfortably. The doctor was a little tight at the moment and Gene could find no opening for what he had to say. Like so many Southerners of the humbler classes, he had a deep-seated courtesy, characteristic of all violent and passionate lands—he could not change the subject until there was a moment's silence, and Forrest would not shut up.

"I'm very happy," he continued, "or very miserable. I chuckle or I weep alcoholically and, as I continue to slow up, life accommodatingly goes faster, so that the less there is of myself inside, the more diverting becomes the moving picture without. I have cut myself off from the respect of my fellow man, but I am aware of a compensatory cirrhosis of the emotions. And because my sensitivity, my pity, no longer has direction, but fixes itself on whatever is at hand, I have become an exceptionally good fellow—much more so than when I was a good doctor."

As the road straightened after the next bend and Gene saw his house in the distance, he remembered his wife's face as she had made him promise, and he could wait no longer: "Forrest, I got a thing——"

But at that moment the doctor brought his car to a sudden stop in front of a small house just beyond a grove of pines. On the front steps a girl of eight was playing with a gray cat.

"This is the sweetest little kid I ever saw," the doctor said to Gene, and then to the child, in a grave voice: "Helen, do you need any pills for kitty?"

The little girl laughed.

"Well, I don't know," she said doubtfully. She was playing another game with the cat now and this came as rather an interruption.

"Because kitty telephoned me this morning," the doctor continued, "and said her mother was neglecting her and couldn't I get her a trained nurse from Montgomery."

"She did not." The little girl grabbed the cat close indignantly; the doctor took a nickle from his pocket and tossed it to the steps.

"I recommend a good dose of milk," he said as he put the car into gear. "Good night, Helen."

"Good night, doctor."

As they drove off, Gene tried again: "Listen; stop," he said. "Stop here a little way down. . . . Here."

The doctor stopped the car and the brothers faced each other. They were alike as to robustness of figure and a certain asceticism of feature and they were both in their middle forties; they were unlike in that the doctor's glasses failed to conceal the veined, weeping eyes of a soak, and that he wore corrugated city wrinkles; Gene's wrinkles bounded fields, followed the lines of rooftrees, of poles propping up sheds. His eyes were a fine, furry blue. But the sharpest contrast lay in the fact that Gene Janney was a country man while Dr. Forrest Janney was obviously a man of education.

"Well?" the doctor asked.

"You know Pinky's at home," Gene said, looking down the road.

"So I hear," the doctor answered noncommittally.

"He got in a row in Birmingham and somebody shot him in the head." Gene hesitated. "We got Doc Behrer because we thought maybe you wouldn't—maybe you wouldn't——"

"I wouldn't," agreed Doctor Janney blandly.

"But look, Forrest; here's the thing," Gene insisted. "You know how it is—you often say Doc Behrer doesn't know nothing. Shucks,

I never thought he was much either. He says the bullet's pressing on the—pressing on the brain, and he can't take it out without causin' a hemmering, and he says he doesn't know whether we could get him to Birmingham or Montgomery, or not, he's so low. Doc wasn't no help. What we want——"

"No," said his brother, shaking his head. "No."

"I just want you to look at him and tell us what to do," Gene begged. "He's unconscious, Forrest. He wouldn't know you; you'd hardly know him. Thing is his mother's about crazy."

"She's in the grip of a purely animal instinct." The doctor took from his hip a flask containing half water and half Alabama corn, and drank. "You and I know that boy ought to been drowned the day he was born."

Gene flinched. "He's bad," he admitted, "but I don't know—You see him lying there——"

As the liquor spread over the doctor's insides he felt an instinct to do something, not to violate his prejudices but simply to make some gesture, to assert his own moribund but still struggling will to power.

"All right, I'll see him," he said. "I'll do nothing myself to help him, because he ought to be dead. And even his death wouldn't make up for what he did to Mary Decker."

Gene Janney pursed his lips. "Forrest, you sure about that?"

"Sure about it!" exclaimed the doctor. "Of course I'm sure. She died of starvation; she hadn't had more than a couple cups of coffee in a week. And if you looked at her shoes, you could see she'd walked for miles.

"Doc Behrer says——"

"What does he know? I performed the autopsy the day they found her on the Birmingham Highway. There was nothing the matter with her but starvation. That—that"—his voice shook with feeling—"that Pinky got tired of her and turned her out, and she was trying to get home. It suits me fine that he was invalided home himself a couple of weeks later."

As he talked, the doctor had plunged the car savagely into gear and let the clutch out with a jump; in a moment they drew up before Gene Janney's home.

It was a square frame house with a brick foundation and a well-kept lawn blocked off from the farm, a house rather superior to the buildings that composed the town of Bending and the surrounding agricultural area, yet not essentially different in type or in its interior economy. The last of the plantation houses in this section of Alabama had long disappeared, the proud pillars yielding to poverty, rot and rain.

Gene's wife, Rose, got up from her rocking-chair on the porch.

"Hello, doc." She greeted him a little nervously and without meeting his eyes. "You been a stranger here lately."

The doctor met her eyes for several seconds. "How do you do, Rose," he said. "Hi, Edith. . . . Hi, Eugene"—this to the little boy and girl who stood beside their mother; and then: "Hi, Butch!" to the stocky youth of nineteen who came around the corner of the house hugging a round stone.

"Goin to have a sort of low wall along the front here—kind of neater," Gene explained.

All of them had a lingering respect for the doctor. They felt reproachful toward him because they could no longer refer to him as their celebrated relative—"one of the bess surgeons up in Montgomery, yes, suh"—but there was his learning and the position he had once occupied in the larger world, before he had committed professional suicide by taking to cynicism and drink. He had come home to Bending and bought a half interest in the local drug store two years ago, keeping up his license, but practising only when sorely needed.

"Rose," said Gene, "doc says he'll take a look at Pinky."

Pinky Janney, his lips curved mean and white under a new beard, lay in bed in a darkened room. When the doctor removed the bandage from his head, his breath blew into a low groan, but his paunchy body did not move. After a few minutes, the doctor replaced the bandage and, with Gene and Rose, returned to the porch.

"Behrer wouldn't operate?" he asked.

"No."

"Why didn't they operate in Birmingham?"

"I don't know."

"H'm." The doctor put on his hat. "That bullet ought to come out, and soon. It's pressing against the carotid sheath. That's the—anyhow, you can't get him to Montgomery with that pulse."

"What'll we do?" Gene's question carried a little tail of silence as he sucked his breath back.

"Get Behrer to think it over. Or else get somebody in Montgomery. There's about a 25 per cent chance that the operation would save him; without the operation he hasn't any chance at all."

"Who'll we get in Montgomery?" asked Gene.

"Any good surgeon would do it. Eeven Behrer could do it if he had any nerve."

Suddenly Rose Janney came close to him, her eyes straining and burning with an animal maternalism. She seized his coat where it hung open.

"Doc, you do it! You can do it. You know you were as good a surgeon as any of em once. Please, doc, you go on do it."

He stepped back a little so that her hands fell from his coat, and held out his own hands in front of him.

"See how they tremble?" he said with elaborate irony. "Look close and you'll see. I wouldn't dare operate."

"You could do it all right," said Gene hastily, "with a drink to stiffen you up."

The doctor shook his head and said, looking at Rose: "No. You see, my decisions are not reliable, and if anything went wrong, it would seem to be my fault." He was acting a little now—he chose his words carefully. "I hear that when I found that Mary Decker died of starvation, my opinion was questioned on the ground that I was a drunkard."

"I didn't say that," lied Rose breathlessly.

"Certainly not. I just mention it to show how careful I've got to be." He moved down the steps. "Well, my advice is to see Behrer again, or, failing that, get somebody from the city. Good night."

But before he had reached the gate, Rose came tearing after him, her eyes white with fury.

"I did say you were a drunkard!" she cried. "When you said Mary Decker died of starvation, you made it out as if it was Pinky's fault —you, swilling yourself full of corn all day! How can anybody tell whether you know what you're doing or not? Why did you think

so much about Mary Decker, anyhow—a girl half your age? Everybody saw how she used to come in your drug store and talk
to you——"

Gene, who had followed, seized her arms. "Shut up now, Rose.
. . . Drive along, Forrest."

Forrest drove along, stopping at the next bend to drink from his
flask. Across the fallow cotton fields he could see the house where
Mary Decker had lived, and had it been six months before, he might
have detoured to ask her why she hadn't come into the store that day
for her free soda, or to delight her with a sample cosmetic left by a
salesman that morning. He had not told Mary Decker how he felt
about her; never intended to—she was seventeen, he was forty-five,
and he no longer dealt in futures—but only after she ran away to
Birmingham with Pinky Janney, did he realize how much his love
for her had counted in his lonely life.

His thoughts went back to his brother's house.

"Now, if I were a gentleman," he thought, "I wouldn't have done
like that. And another person might have been sacrificed to that
dirty dog, because if he died afterward Rose would say I killed him."

Yet he felt pretty bad as he put his car away; not that he could
have acted differently, but just that it was all so ugly.

He had been home scarcely ten minutes when a car creaked to
rest outside and Butch Janney came in. His mouth was sct tight
and his eyes were narrowed as though to permit of no escape to the
temper that possessed him until it should be unleashed upon its
proper objective.

"Hi, Butch."

"I want to tell you, Uncle Forrest, you can't talk to my mother
thataway. I'll kill you, you talk to my mother like that!"

"Now shut up, Butch, and sit down," said the doctor sharply.

"She's already bout sick on account of Pinky, and you come over
and talk to her like that."

"Your mother did all the insulting that was done, Butch. I just
took it."

"She doesn't know what she's saying and you ought to understand
that."

The doctor thought a minute. "Butch, what do you think of Pinky?"

Butch hesitated uncomfortably. "Well, I can't say I ever thought so much of him"—his tone changed defiantly—"but after all, he's my own brother——"

"Wait a minute, Butch. What do you think of the way he treated Mary Decker?"

But Butch had shaken himself free, and now he let go the artillery of his rage:

"That ant the point; the point is anybody that doesn't do right to my mother has me to answer to. It's only fair when you got all the education——"

"I got my education myself, Butch."

"I don't care. We're going to try again to get Doc Behrer to operate or get us some fellow from the city. But if we can't, I'm coming and get you, and you're going to take that bullet out if I have to hold a gun to you while you do it." He nodded, panting a little; then he turned and went out and drove away.

"Something tells me," said the doctor to himself, "that there's no more peace for me in Chilton County." He called to his colored boy to put supper on the table. Then he rolled himself a cigarette and went out on the back stoop.

The weather had changed. The sky was now overcast and the grass stirred restlessly and there was a sudden flurry of drops without a sequel. A minute ago it had been warm, but now the moisture on his forehead was suddenly cool, and he wiped it away with his handkerchief. There was a buzzing in his ears and he swallowed and shook his head. For a moment he thought he must be sick; then suddenly the buzzing detached itself from him, grew into a swelling sound, louder and ever nearer, that might have been the roar of an approaching train.

II

Butch Janney was halfway home when he saw it—a huge, black, approaching cloud whose lower edge bumped the ground. Even as he stared at it vaguely, it seemed to spread until it included the whole southern sky, and he saw pale electric fire in it had heard an increasing roar. He was in a strong wind now; blown débris, bits of broken branches, splinters, larger objects unidentifiable in the growing darkness, flew by him. Instinctively he got out of his car and, by now hardly able to stand against the wind, ran for a bank, or rather found himself thrown and pinned against a bank. Then for a minute, two minutes, he was in the black centre of pandemonium.

First there was the sound, and he was part of the sound, so engulfed in it and possessed by it that he had no existence apart from it. It was not a collection of sounds, it was just Sound itself; a great screeching bow drawn across the chords of the universe. The sound and force were inseparable. The sound as well as the force held him to what he felt was the bank like a man crucified. Somewhere in this first moment his face, pinned sideways, saw his automobile make a little jump, spin halfway around and then go bobbing off over a field in a series of great helpless leaps. Then began the bombardment, the sound dividing its sustained cannon note into the cracks of a gigantic machine gun. He was only half-conscious as he felt himself become part of one of those cracks, felt himself lifted away from the bank to tear through space, through a blinding, lacerating mass of twigs and branches, and then, for an incalculable time, he knew nothing at all.

His body hurt him. He was lying between two branches in the top of a tree; the air was full of dust and rain, and he could hear nothing; it was a long time before he realized that the tree he was in had been blown down and that his involuntary perch among the pine needles was only five feet from the ground.

"Say, man!" he cried aloud, outraged. "Say, man! Say, what a wind! Say, man!"

Made acute by pain and fear, he guessed that he had been standing on the tree's root and had been catapulted by the terrific wrench as the big pine was torn from the earth. Feeling over himself, he found that his left ear was caked full of dirt, as if someone had wanted to take an impression of the inside. His clothes were in rags, his coat had torn on the back seam, and he could feel where, as some stray gust tried to undress him, it had cut into him under the arms. Reaching the ground, he set off in the direction of his father's house, but it was a new and unfamiliar landscape he traversed. The Thing—he did not know it was a tornado—had cut a path a quarter of a mile wide, and he was confused, as the dust slowly settled, by vistas he had never seen before. It was unreal that Bending church tower should be visible from here; there had been groves of trees between.

But where was here? For he should be close to the Baldwin house; only as he tripped over great piles of boards, like a carelessly kept lumberyard, did Butch realize that there was no more Baldwin house, and then, looking around wildly, that there was no Necrawney house on the hill, no Peltzer house below it. There was not a light, not a sound, save the rain falling on the fallen trees.

He broke into a run. When he saw the bulk of his father's house in the distance, he gave a "Hey!" of relief, but coming closer, he realized that something was missing. There were no outhouses and the built-on wing that held Pinky's room had been sheared completely away.

"Mother!" he called. "Dad!" There was no answer; a dog bounded out of the yard and licked his hand. . . .

. . . It was full dark twenty minutes later when Doc Janney stopped his car in front of his own drug store in Bending. The electric lights had gone out, but there were men with lanterns in the street, and in a minute a small crowd had collected around him. He unlocked the door hurriedly.

"Somebody break open the old Wiggins Hospital." He pointed across the street. "I've got six badly injured in my car. I want some fellows to carry em in. Is Doc Behrer here?"

"Here he is," offered eager voices out of the darkness as the doctor, case in hand, came through the crowd. The two men stood face to face by lantern light, forgetting that they disliked each other.

"God knows how many more there's going to be," said Doc Janney. "I'm getting dressing and disinfectant. There'll be a lot of fractures—" He raised his voice, "Somebody bring me a barrel!"

"I'll get started over there," said Doc Behrer. "There's about half a dozen more crawled in."

"What's been done?" demanded Doc Janney of the men who

followed him into the drug store. "Have they called Birmingham and Montgomery?"

"The telephone wires are down, but the telegraph got through."

"Well, somebody get Doctor Cohen from Wettala, and tell any people who have automobiles to go up the Willard Pike and cut across toward Corsica and all through those roads there. There's not a house left at the crossroads by the nigger store. I passed a lot of folks walking in, all of them hurt, but I didn't have room for anybody else." As he talked he was throwing bandages, disinfectant and drugs into a blanket. "I thought I had a lot more stuff than this in stock! And wait!" he called. "Somebody drive out and look down in that hollow where the Wooleys live. Drive right across the fields— the road's blocked. . . . Now, you with the cap—Ed Jenks, ain't it?"

"Yes, doc."

"You see what I got here? You collect everything in the store that looks like this and bring it across the way, understand?"

"Yes, doc."

As the doctor went out into the street, the victims were streaming into town—a woman on foot wih a badly injured child, a buckboard full of groaning Negroes, frantic men gasping terrible stories. Everywhere confusion and hysteria mounted in the dimly illumined darkness. A mud-covered reporter from Birmingham drove up in a sidecar, the wheels crossing the fallen wires and brushwood that clogged the street, and there was the siren of a police car from Cooper, thirty miles away.

Already a crowd pressed around the doors of the hospital, closed these three months for lack of patients. The doctor squeezed past the mêlée of white faces and established himself in the nearest ward, grateful for the waiting row of old iron beds. Doctor Behrer was already at work across the hall.

"Get me half a dozen lanterns," he ordered.

"Doctors Behrer wants iodine and adhesive."

"All right, there it is. . . . Here, you, Shinkey, stand by the door and keep everybody out except cases that can't walk. Somebody run over and see if there ain't some candles in the grocery store."

The street outside was full of sound now—the cries of women, the contrary directions of volunteer gangs trying to clear the highway, the tense staccato of people rising to an emergency. A little before midnight arrived the first unit of the Red Cross. But the three doctors, presently joined by two others from near-by villages, had lost track of time long before that. The dead began to be brought in by ten o'clock; there were twenty, twenty-five, thirty, forty—the list grew. Having no more needs, these waited, as became simple husbandmen, in a garage behind, while the stream of injured— hundreds of them—flowed through the old hospital built to house only a score. The storm had dealt out fractures of the leg, collar bone, ribs and hip, lacerations of the back, elbows, ears, eyelids, nose; there were wounds from flying planks, and odd splinters in odd places, and a scalped man, who would recover to grow a new head of hair. Living or dead, Doc Janney knew every face, almost every name.

"Don't you fret now. Billy's all right. Hold still and let me tie this. People are drifting in every minute, but it's so consarned dark they can't find 'em— All right, Mrs. Oakey. That's nothing. Ev here'll touch it with iodine. . . . Now let's see this man."

Two o'clock. The old doctor from Wettala gave out, but now there were fresh men from Montgomery to take his place. Upon the air of the room, heavy with disinfectant, floated the ceaseless babble of human speech reaching the doctor dimly through layer after layer of increasing fatigue:

". . . Over and over—just rolled me over and over. Got hold of a bush and the bush came along too."

"Jeff! Where's Jeff?"

". . . I bet that pig sailed a hundred yards——"

"—just stopped the train in time. All the passengers got out and helped pull the poles——"

"Where's Jeff?"

"He says, 'Let's get down cellar,' and I says, 'We ain't got no cellar'——"

"—If there's no more stretchers, find some light doors."

". . . Five seconds? Say, it was more like five minutes!"

At some time he heard that Gene and Rose had been seen with their two youngest children. He had passed their house on the way in and, seeing it standing, hurried on. The Janney family had been lucky; the doctor's own house was outside the sweep of the storm.

Only as he saw the electric lights go on suddenly in the streets and glimpsed the crowd waiting for hot coffee in front of the Red Cross did the doctor realize how tired he was.

"You better go rest," a young man was saying. "I'll take this side of the room. I've got two nurses with me."

"All right—all right. I'll finish this row."

The injured were being evacuated to the cities by train as fast as their wounds were dressed, and their places taken by others. He had only two beds to go—in the first one he found Pinky Janney.

He put his stethoscope to the heart. It was beating feebly. That he, so weak, so nearly gone, had survived this storm at all was remarkable. How he had got there, who had found him and carried him, was a mystery in itself. The doctor went over the body; there were small contusions and lacerations, two broken fingers, the dirt-filled ears that marked every case—nothing else. For a moment the doctor hesitated, but even when he closed his eyes, the image of Mary Decker seemed to have receded, eluding him. Something purely professional that had nothing to do with human sensibilities had been set in motion inside him, and he was powerless to head it off. He held out his hands before him; they were trembling slightly.

"Hell's bells!" he muttered.

He went out of the room and around the corner of the hall, where he drew from his pocket the flask containing the last of the corn and water he had had in the afternoon. He emptied it. Returning to the ward, he disinfected two instruments and applied a local anaesthetic to a square section at the base of Pinky's skull where the wound had healed over the bullet. He called a nurse to his side and then, scalpel in hand, knelt on one knee beside his nephew's bed.

III

Two days later the doctor drove slowly around the mournful countryside. He had withdrawn from the emergency work after the first desperate night, feeling that his status as a pharmacist might embarrass his collaborators. But there was much to be done in bringing the damage to outlying sections under the aegis of the Red Cross, and he devoted himself to that.

The path of the demon was easy to follow. It had pursued an irregular course on its seven-league boots, cutting cross country, through woods, or even urbanely keeping to roads until they curved, when it went off on its own again. Sometimes the trail could be traced by cotton fields, apparently in full bloom, but this cotton came from the insides of hundreds of quilts and mattresses redistributed in the fields by the storm.

At a lumber pile that had lately been a Negro cabin, he stopped a moment to listen to a dialogue between two reporters and two shy pickaninnies. The old grandmother, her head bandaged, sat among the ruins, gnawing some vague meat and moving her rocker ceaselessly.

"But where is the river you were blown across?" one of the reporters demanded.

"There."

"Where?"

The pickaninnies looked to their grandmother for aid.

"Right there behind you-all," spoke up the old woman.

The newspapermen looked disgustedly at a muddy stream four yards wide.

"That's no river."

"That's a Menada River, we always calls it ever since I was a gull. Yes, suh, that's a Menada River. An them two boys was blowed right across it an set down on the othah side just as pretty, 'thout any hurt at all. Chimney fell on me," she concluded, feeling her head.

"Do you mean to say that's all it was?" demanded the younger reporter indignantly. "That's the river they were blow across! And one hundred and twenty million people have been led to believe——"

"That's all right, boys," interrupted Doc Janney. "That's a right good river for these parts. And it'll get bigger as those little fellahs get older."

He tossed a quarter to the old woman and drove on.

Passing a country church, he stopped and counted the new brown mounds that marred the graveyard. He was nearing the centre of the holocaust now. There was the Howden house where three had been killed; there remained a gaunt chimney, a rubbish heap and a scarecrow surviving ironically in the kitchen garden. In the ruins of the house across the way a rooster strutted on top of a piano, reigning vociferously over an estate of trunks, boots, cans, books, calendars, rugs, chairs and window frames, a twisted radio and a legless sewing machine. Everywhere there was bedding—blankets, mattresses, bent springs, shredded padding—he had not realized how much of people's lives was spent in bed. Here and there, cows and horses, often stained with disinfectant, were grazing again in the fields. At intervals there were Red Cross tents, and stitting by one of these, with the gray cat in her arms, the doctor came upon little Helen Kilrain. The usual lumber pile, like a child's building game knocked down in a fit of temper, told the story.

"Hello, dear," he greeted her, his heart sinking. "How did kitty like the tornado?"

"She didn't."

"What did she do?"

"She meowed."

"Oh."

"She wanted to get away, but I hanged on to her and she scratched me—see?"

He glanced at the Red Cross tent.

"Who's taking care of you?"

"The lady from the Red Cross and Mrs. Wells," she answered. "My father got hurt. He stood over me so it wouldn't fall on me, and I stood over kitty. He's in the hospital in Birmingham. When he comes back, I guess he'll build our house again."

The doctor winced. He knew that her father would build no more houses; he had died that morning. She was alone, and she did not know she was alone. Around her stretched the dark universe, impersonal, inconscient. Her lovely little face looked up at him confidently as he asked: "You got any kin anywhere, Helen?"

"I don't know."

"You've got kitty, anyhow, haven't you?"

"It's just a cat," she admitted calmly, but anguished by her own betrayal of her love, she hugged it closer.

"Taking care of a cat must be pretty hard."

"Oh, no," she said hurriedly. "It isn't any trouble at all. It doesn't eat hardly anything."

He put his hand in his pocket, and then changed his mind suddenly.

"Dear, I'm coming back and see you later—later today. You take good care of kitty now, won't you?"

"Oh, yes," she answered lightly.

The doctor drove on. He stopped next at a house that had escaped damaged. Walt Cupps, the owner, was cleaning a shotgun on his front porch.

"What's that, Walt? Going to shoot up the next tornado?"

"Ain't going to be a next tornado."

"You can't tell. Just take a look at that sky now. It's getting mighty dark."

Walt laughed and slapped his gun. "Not for a hundred years, anyhow. This here is for looters. There's a lot of 'em around, and not all black either. Wish when you go to town that you'd tell 'em to scatter some militia out here."

"I'll tell em now. You come out all right?"

"I did, thank God. With six of us in the house. It took off one hen, and probably it's still carrying it around somewhere."

The doctor drove on toward town, overcome by a feeling of uneasiness he could not define.

"It's the weather," he thought. "It's the same kind of feel in the air there was last Saturday."

For a month the doctor had felt an urge to go away permanently. Once this countryside had seemed to promise peace. When the impetus that had lifted him temporarily out of tired old stock was exhausted, he had come back here to rest, to watch the earth put forth, and live on simple, pleasant terms with his neighbors. Peace! He knew that the present family quarrel would never heal, nothing would ever be the same; it would all be bitter forever. And he had seen the placid countryside turned into a land of mourning. There was no peace here. Move on!

On the road he overtook Butch Janney walking to town.

"I was coming to see you," said Butch, frowning. "You operated on Pinky after all, didn't you?"

"Jump in. . . . Yes, I did. How did you know?"

"Doc Behrer told us." He shot a quick look at the doctor, who did not miss the quality of suspicion in it. "They don't think he'll last out the day."

"I'm sorry for your mother."

Butch laughed unpleasantly. "Yes, you are."

"I said I'm sorry for your mother," said the doctor sharply.

"I heard you."

They drove for a moment in silence.

"Did you find your automobile?"

"Did I?" Butch laughed ruefully. "I found something—I don't know whether you'd call it a car any more. And, you know, I could of had tornado insurance for twenty-five cents." His voice trembled indignantly: "Twenty-five cents—but who would ever of thought of getting tornado insurance?"

It was growing darker; there was a thin crackle of thunder far to the southward.

"Well, all I hope," said Butch with narrowed glance, "is that you hadn't been drinking anything when you operated on Pinky."

"You know, Butch," the doctor said slowly, "that was a pretty dirty trick of mine to bring that tornado here."

He had not expected the sarcasm to hit home, but he expected a retort—when suddenly he caught sight of Butch's face. It was fish-white, the mouth was open, the eyes fixed and staring, and from the throat came a mewling sound. Limply he raised one hand before him, and then the doctor saw.

Less than a mile away, an enormous, top-shaped black cloud filled the sky and bore toward them, dipping and swirling, and in front of it sailed already a heavy, singing wind.

"It's come back!" the doctor yelled.

Fifty yards ahead of them was the old iron bridge spanning Bilby Creek. He stepped hard on the accelerator and drove for it. The fields were full of running figures headed in the same direction. Reaching the bridge, he jumped out and yanked Butch's arm.

"Get out, you fool! Get out!"

A nerveless mass stumbled from the car; in a moment they were in a group of half a dozen, huddled in the triangular space that the bridge made with the shore.

"Is it coming here?"

"No, it's turning!"

"We had to leave grampa!"

"Oh, save me, save me! Jesus save me! Help me!"

"Jesus save my soul!"

There was a quick rush of wind outside, sending little tentacles under the bridge with a curious tension in them that made the doctor's skin crawl. Then immediately there was a vacuum, with no more wind, but a sudden thresh of rain. The doctor crawled to the edge of the bridge and put his head up cautiously.

"It's passed," he said. "We only felt the edge; the centre went way to the right of us."

He could see it plainly; for a second he could even distinguish objects in it—shrubbery and small trees, planks and loose earth. Crawling farther out, he produced his watch and tried to time it, but the thick curtain of rain blotted it from sight.

Soaked to the skin, he crawled back underneath. Butch lay shivering in the farthest corner, and the doctor shook him.

"It went in the direction of your house!" the doctor cried. "Pull yourself together! Who's there?"

"No one," Butch groaned. "They're all down with Pinky."

The rain had changed to hail now; first small pellets, then larger ones, and larger, until the sound of their fall upon the iron bridge was an ear-splitting tattoo.

The spared wretches under the bridge were slowly recovering, and in the relief there were titters of hysterical laughter. After a certain point of strain, the nervous system makes its transitions without dignity or reason. Even the doctor felt the contagion.

"This is worse than a calamity," he said dryly. "It's getting to be a nuisance."

IV

There were to be no more tornadoes in Alabama that spring. The second one—it was popularly thought to be the first one come back; for to the people of Chilton County it had become a personified force, definite as a pagan god—took a dozen houses, Gene Janney's among them, and injured about thirty people. But this time—perhaps because everyone had developed some scheme of self-protection—there were no fatalities. It made its last dramatic bow by sailing down the main street of Bending, prostrating the telephone poles and crushing in the fronts of three shops, including Doc Janney's drug store.

At the end of a week, houses were going up again, made of the old boards; and before the end of the long, lush Alabama summer the grass would be green again on all the graves. But it will be years before the people of the country cease to reckon events as happening "before the tornado" or "after the tornado,"—and for many families things will never be the same.

Doctor Janney decided that this was as good a time to leave as any. He sold the remains of his drug store, gutted alike by charity and catastrophe, and turned over his house to his brother until Gene could rebuild his own. He was going up to the city by train, for his car had been rammed against a tree and couldn't be counted on for much more than the trip to the station.

Several times on the way in he stopped by the roadside to say good-by—once it was to Walter Cupps.

"So it hit you, after all," he said, looking at the melancholy back house which alone marked the site.

"It's pretty bad," Walter answered. "But just think; they was six of us in or about the house and not one was injured. I'm content to give thanks to God for that."

"You were lucky there, Walt," the doctor agreed. "Do you happen to have heard whether the Red Cross took little Helen Kilrain to Montgomery or to Birmingham?"

"To Montgomery. Say, I was there when she came into town with that cat, tryin' to get somebody to bandage up its paw. She must of walked miles through that rain and hail, but all that mattered to her was her kitty. Bad as I felt, I couldn't help laughin' at how spunky she was."

The doctor was silent for a moment. "Do you happen to recollect if she has any people left?"

"I don't, suh," Walter replied, "but I think as not."

At his brother's place, the doctor made his last stop. They were all there, even the youngest, working among the ruins; already Butch had a shed erected to house the salvage of their goods. Save for this the most orderly thing surviving was the pattern of round white stone which was to have inclosed the garden.

The doctor took a hundred dollars in bills from his pocket and handed it to Gene.

"You can pay it back sometime, but don't strain yourself," he said. "It's money I got from the store." He cut off Gene's thanks: "Pack up my books carefully when I send for 'em."

"You reckon to practice medicine up there, Forrest?"

"I'll maybe try it."

The brothers held on to each other's hands for a moment; the two youngest children came up to say good-by. Rose stood in the background in an old blue dress—she had no money to wear black for her eldest son.

"Good-by, Rose," said the doctor.

"Good-by," she responded, and then added in a dead voice, "Good luck to you, Forrest."

For a moment he was tempted to say something conciliatory, but he saw it was no use. He was up against the maternal instinct, the same force that had sent little Helen through the storm with her injured cat.

At the station he bought a one-way ticket to Montgomery. The village was drab under the sky of a retarded spring, and as the train pulled out, it was odd to think that six months ago it had seemed to him as good a place as any other.

He was alone in the white section of the day coach; presently he felt for a bottle on his hip and drew it forth. "After all, a man of forty-five is entitled to more artificial courage when he starts over again." He began thinking of Helen. "She hasn't got any kin. I guess she's my little girl now."

He patted the bottle, then looked down at it as if in surprise.

"Well, we'll have to put you aside for a while, old friend. Any cat that's worth all that trouble and care is going to need a lot of grade-B milk."

He settled down in his seat, looking out the window. In his memory of that terrible week the winds still sailed about him, came in as draughts through the corridor of the car—winds of the world—cyclones, hurricane, tornadoes—grey and black, expected or unforeseen, some from the sky, some from the caves of hell.

But he would not let them touch Helen again—if he could help it.

He dozed momentarily, but a haunting dream woke him: *"Daddy stood over me and I stood over Kitty."*

"All right, Helen," he said aloud, for he often talked to himself, "I guess the old brig can keep afloat a little longer—in any wind."

A SHORT TRIP HOME*

I was near her, for I had lingered behind in order to get the short walk with her from the living room to the front door. That was a lot, for she had flowered suddenly and I, being a man and only a year older, hadn't flowered at all, had scarcely dared to come near her in the week we'd been home. Nor was I going to say anything in that walk of ten feet, or touch her; but I had a vague hope she'd do something, give a gay little performance of some sort, personal only in so far as we were alone together.

She had bewitchment suddenly in the twinkle of short hairs on her neck, in the sure, clear confidence that at about eighteen begins to deepen and sing in attractive American girls. The lamp light shopped in the yellow strands of her hair.

Already she was sliding into another world—the world of Joe Jelke and Jim Cathcart waiting for us now in the car. In another year she would pass beyond me forever.

As I waited, feeling the others outside in the snowy night, feeling the excitement of Christmas week and the excitement of Ellen here, blooming away, filling the room with "sex appeal"—a wretched phrase to express a quality that isn't like that at all—a maid came in from the dining room, spoke to Ellen quietly and handed her a note. Ellen read it and her eyes faded down, as when the current grows weak on rural circuits, and smouldered off into space. Then she gave me an odd look—in which I probably didn't show—and without a word, followed the maid into the dining room and beyond. I sat turning over the pages of a magazine for a quarter of an hour.

Joe Jelke came in, red-faced from the cold, his white silk muffler gleaming at the neck of his fur coat. He was a senior at New Haven,

* In a moment of hasty misjudgement a whole paragraph of description was lifted out of this tale where it originated, and properly belongs, and applied to quite a different character in a novel of mine. I have ventured none the less to leave it here, even at the risk of seeming to serve warmed-over fare.

I was a sophomore. He was prominent, a member of Scroll and Keys, and, in my eyes, very distinguished and handsome.

"Isn't Ellen coming?"

"I don't know," I answered discreetly. "She was all ready."

"Ellen!" he called. "Ellen!"

He had left the front door open behind him and a great cloud of frosty air rolled in from outside. He went halfway up the stairs—he was a familiar in the house—and called again, till Mrs. Baker came to the banister and said that Ellen was below. Then the maid, a little excited, appeared in the dining-room door.

"Mr. Jelke," she called in a low voice.

"Joe's face fell as he turned toward her, sensing bad news.

"Miss Ellen says for you to go to the party. She'll come later."

"What's the matter?"

"She can't come now. She'll come later."

He hesitated, confused. It was the last big dance of vacation, and he was mad about Ellen. He had tried to give her a ring for Christmas, and failing that, got her to accept a gold mesh bag that must have cost two hundred dollars. He wasn't the only one—there were three or four in the same wild condition, and all in the ten days she'd been home—but his chance came first, for he was rich and gracious and at that moment the "desirable" boy of St. Paul. To me it seemed impossible that she could prefer another, but the rumor was she'd described Joe as much too perfect. I suppose he lacked mystery for her, and when a man is up against that with a young girl who isn't thinking of the practical side of marriage yet—well——.

"No, she's not." The maid was defiant and a little scared.

"She is."

"She went out the back way, Mr. Jelke."

"I'm going to see."

I followed him. The Swedish servants washing dishes looked up sideways at our approach and an interested crashing of pans marked our passage through. The storm door, unbolted, was flapping in the wind and as we walked out into the snowy yard we saw the tail light of a car turn the corner at the end of the back alley.

"I'm going after her," Joe said slowly. "I don't understand this at all."

I was too awed by the calamity to argue. We hurried to his car and drove in a fruitless, despairing zigzag all over the residence section, peering into every machine on the streets. It was half an hour before the futility of the affair began to dawn upon him—St. Paul is a city of almost three hundred thousand people—and Jim Cathcart reminded him that we had another girl to stop for. Like a wounded animal he sank into a melancholy mass of fur in the corner, from which position he jerked upright every few minutes and waved himself backward and forward a little in protest and despair.

Jim's girl was ready and impatient, but after what had happened her impatience didn't seem important. She looked lovely though. That's one thing about Christmas vacation—the excitement of growth and change and adventure in foreign parts transforming the people you've known all your life. Joe Jelke was polite to her in a daze—he indulged in one burst of short, loud, harsh laughter by way of conversation—and we drove to the hotel.

The chauffeur approached it on the wrong side—the side on which the line of cars was not putting forth guests—and because of that we came suddenly upon Ellen Baker just getting out of a small coupé. Even before we came to a stop, Joe Jelke had jumped excitedly from the car.

Ellen turned toward us, a faintly distracted look—perhaps of surprise, but certainly not of alarm—in her face; in fact, she didn't seem very aware of us. Joe approached her with a stern, dignified, injured and, I thought, just exactly correct reproof in his expression. I followed.

Seated in the coupé—he had not dismounted to help Ellen out—was a hard thin-faced man of about thirty-five with an air of being scarred, and a slight sinister smile. His eyes were a sort of taunt to the whole human family—they were the eyes of an animal, sleepy and quiescent in the presence of another species. They were helpless yet brutal, uphopeful yet confident. It was as if they felt themselves powerless to originate activity, but infinitely capable of profiting by a single gesture of weakness in another.

Vaguely I placed him as one of the sort of men whom I had been conscious of from my earliest youth as "hanging around"—leaning with one elbow on the counters of tobacco stores, watching, through heaven knows what small chink of the mind, the people who hurried in and out. Intimate to garages, where he had vague business conducted in undertones, to barber shops and to the lobbies of theatres—in such places, anyhow, I placed the type, if type it was, that he reminded me of. Sometimes his face bobbed up in one of Tad's more savage cartoons, and I had always from earliest boyhood thrown a nervous glance toward the dim borderland where he stood, and seen him watching me and despising me. Once, in a dream, he had taken a few steps toward me, jerking his head back and muttering: "Say, kid" in what was intended to be a reassuring voice, and I had broken for the door in terror. This was that sort of man.

Joe and Ellen faced each other silently; she seemed, as I have said, to be in a daze. It was cold, but she didn't notice that her coat had blown open; Joe reached out and pulled it together, and automatically she clutched it with her hand.

Suddenly the man in the coupé, who had been watching them silently, laughed. It was a bare laugh, done with the breath—just a noisy jerk of the head—but it was an insult if I had ever heard one; definite and not to be passed over. I wasn't surprised when Joe, who was quick tempered, turned to him angrily and said:

"What's your trouble?"

The man waited a moment, his eyes shifting and yet staring, and always seeing. Then he laughed again in the same way. Ellen stirred uneasily.

"Who is this—this—" Joe's voice trembled with annoyance.

"Look out now," said the man slowly.

Joe turned to me.

"Eddie, take Ellen and Catherine in, will you?" he said quickly. . . . "Ellen, go with Eddie."

"Look out now," the man repeated.

Ellen made a little sound with her tongue and teeth, but she didn't resist when I took her arm and moved her toward the side door of the hotel. It struck me as odd that she should be so helpless, even to the point of acquiescing by her silence in this imminent trouble.

"Let it go, Joe!" I called back over my shoulder. "Come inside!"

Ellen, pulling against my arm, hurried us on. As we were caught up into the swinging doors I had the impression that the man was getting out of his coupé.

Ten minutes later, as I waited for the girls outside the women's dressing-room, Joe Jelke and Jim Cathcart stepped out of the elevator. Joe was very white, his eyes were heavy and glazed, there was a trickle of dark blood on his forehead and on his white muffler. Jim had both their hats in his hand.

"He hit Joe with brass knuckles," Jim said in a low voice. "Joe was out cold for a minute or so. I wish you'd send a bell boy for some witch-hazel and court-plaster."

It was late and the hall was deserted; brassy fragments of the dance below reached us as if heavy curtains were being blown aside and dropping back into place. When Ellen came out I took her directly downstairs. We avoided the receiving line and went into a dim room set with scraggly hotel palms where couples sometimes sat out during the dance; there I told her what had happened.

"It was Joe's own fault," she said, surprisingly. "I told him not to interfere."

This wasn't true. She had said nothing, only uttered one curious little click of impatience.

"You ran out the back door and disappeared for almost an hour," I protested. "Then you turned up with a hard-looking customer who laughed in Joe's face."

"A hard-looking customer," she repeated, as if tasting the sound of the words.

"Well, wasn't he? Where on earth did you get hold of him, Ellen?"

"On the train," she answered. Immediately she seemed to regret this admission. "You'd better stay out of things that aren't your business, Eddie. You see what happened to Joe."

Literally I gasped. To watch her, seated beside me, immaculately glowing, her body giving off wave after wave of freshness and delicacy—and to hear her talk like that.

"But that man's a thug!" I cried. "No girl could be safe with him. He used brass knuckles on Joe—brass knuckles!"

"Is that pretty bad?"

She asked this as she might have asked such a question a few years ago. She looked at me at last and really wanted an answer; for a moment it was as if she were trying to recapture an attitude that had almost departed; then she hardened again. I say "hardened," for I began to notice that when she was concerned with this man her eyelids fell a little, shutting other things—everything else—out of view.

That was a moment I might have said something, I suppose, but in spite of everything, I couldn't light into her. I was too much under the spell of her beauty and its success. I even began to find excuses for her—perhaps that man wasn't what he appeared to be; or perhaps—more romantically—she was involved with him against her will to shield some one else. At this point people began to drift into the room and come up to speak to us. We couldn't talk any more, so we went in and bowed to the chaperones. Then I gave her up to the bright restless sea of the dance, where she moved in an eddy of her own among the pleasant islands of colored favors set out on tables and the south winds from the brasses moaning across the hall. After a while I aw Joe Jelke sitting in a corner with a strip of court-plaster on his forehead watching Ellen as if she herself had struck him down, but I didn't go up to him. I felt queer myself—like I feel when I wake up after sleeping through an afternoon, strange and portentous, as if something had gone on in the interval that changed the values of everything and that I didn't see.

The night slipped on through successive phases of cardboard horns, amateur tableaux and flashlights for the morning papers. Then was the grand march and supper, and about two o'clock some of the committee dressed up as revenue agents pinched the party, and a facetious newspaper was distributed, burlesquing the events of the evening. And all the time out of the corner of my eye I watched the shining orchid on Ellen's shoulder as it moved like Stuart's plume about the room. I watched it with a definite foreboding until the last sleepy groups had crowded into the elevators, and then, bundled to the eyes in great shapeless fur coats, drifted out into the clear dry Minnesota night.

II

There is a sloping mid-section of our city which lies between the residence quarter on the hill and the business district on the level of the river. It is a vague part of town, broken by its climb into triangles and odd shapes—there are names like Seven Corners—and I don't believe a dozen people could draw an accurate map of it, though every one traversed it by trolley, auto or shoe leather twice a day. And though it was a busy section, it would be hard for me to name the business that comprised its activity. There were always long lines of trolley cars waiting to start somewhere; there was a big movie theatre and many small ones with posters of Hoot Gibson and Wonder Dogs and Wonder Horses outside; there were small stores with "Old King Brady" and "The Liberty Boys of '76" in the windows, and marbles, cigarettes and candy inside; and—one definite place at least—a fancy costumer whom we all visited at least once a year. Some time during boyhood I became aware that on one side of a certain obscure street there were bawdy houses, and all through the district were pawnshops, cheap jewellers, small athletic clubs and gymnasiums and somewhat too blatantly run-down saloons.

The morning after the Cotillion Club party, I woke up late and lazy, with the happy feeling that for a day or two more there was no chapel, no classes—nothing to do but wait for another party tonight. It was crisp and bright—one of those days when you forget how cold it is until your cheek freezes—and the events of the evening before seemed dim and far away. After luncheon I started downtown on foot through a light, pleasant snow of small flakes that would probably fall all afternoon, and I was about half through that halfway section of town—so far as I know, there's no inclusive name for it—when suddenly whatever idle thought was in my hand blew away like a hat and I began thinking hard of Ellen Baker. I began worrying about her as I'd never worried about anything outside myself before. I began to loiter, with an instinct to go upon the hill again and find her and talk to her; then I remembered that she was at a tea, and I went on again, but still thinking of her, and harder than ever. Right then the affair opened up again.

It was snowing, I said, and it was four o'clock on a December afternoon, when there is a promise of darkness in the air and the street lamps are just going on. I passed a combination pool parlor and restaurant, with a stove loaded with hot-dogs in the window, and a few loungers hanging around the door. The lights were on inside—not bright lights but just a few pale yellow high up on the ceiling—and the glow they threw out into the frosty dusk wasn't bright enough to tempt you to stare inside. As I went past, thinking hard of Ellen all this time, I took in the quartet of loafers out of the corner of my eye. I hadn't gone half a dozen steps down the street when one of them called to me, not by name but in a way clearly intended for my ear. I thought it was a tribute to my raccoon coat and paid no attention, but a moment later whoever it was called to me again in a peremptory voice. I was annoyed and turned around. There, standing in the group not ten feet away and looking at me with the half-sneer on his face with which he'd looked at Joe Jelke, was the scarred, thin-faced man of the night before.

He had on a black fancy-cut coat, buttoned up to his neck as if he were cold. His hands were deep in his pockets and he wore a derby and high button shoes. I was startled, and for a moment I hesitated, but I was most of all angry, and knowing that I was quicker with my hands than Joe Jelke, I took a tentative step back toward him. The other men weren't looking at me—I don't think they saw me at all—but I knew that this one recognized me; there was nothing casual about his look, no mistake.

"Here I am. What are you going to do about it?" his eyes seemed to say.

I took another step toward him and he laughed soundlessly, but with active contempt, and drew back into the group. I followed. I was going to speak to him—I wasn't sure what I was going to say—but when I came up he had either changed his mind and backed off, or else he wanted me to follow him inside, for he had slipped off and the three men watched my intent approach without curiosity. They were the same kind—sporty, but, unlike him, smooth rather than truculent; I didn't find any personal malice in their collective glance.

"Did he go inside?" I asked.

They looked at one another in that cagy way; a wink passed between them, and after a perceptible pause, one said:

"Who go inside?"

"I don't know his name."

There was another wink. Annoyed and determined, I walked past them and into the pool room. There were a few people at a lunch counter along one side and a few more playing billiards, but he was not among them.

Again I hesitated. If his idea was to lead me into any blind part of the establishment—there were some half-open doors farther back —I wanted more support. I went up to the man at the desk.

"What became of the fellow who just walked in here?"

Was he on his guard immediately, or was that my imagination? "What fellow?"

"Thin face—derby hat."

"How long ago?"

"Oh—a minute."

He shook his head again. "Didn't see him," he said.

I waited. The three men from outside had come in and were lined up beside me at the counter. I felt that all of them were looking at me in a peculiar way. Feeling helpless and increasingly uneasy, I turned suddenly and went out. A little way down the street I turned again and took a good look at the place, so I'd know it and could find it again. On the next corner I broke impulsively into a run, found a taxicab in front of the hotel and drove back up the hill.

Ellen wasn't home. Mrs. Baker came downstairs and talked to me. She seemed entirely cheerful and proud of Ellen's beauty, and ignorant of anything being amiss or of anything unusual having taken place the night before. She was glad that vacation was almost over— it was a strain and Ellen wasn't very strong. Then she said something that relieved my mind enormously. She was glad that I had come in, for of course Ellen would want to see me, and the time was so short. She was going back at half-past eight tonight.

"Tonight!" I exclaimed. "I thought it was the day after tomorrow."

"She's going to visit the Brokaws in Chicago," Mrs. Baker said.

"They want her for some party. We just decided it today. She's leaving with the Ingersoll girls tonight."

I was so glad I could barely restrain myself from shaking her hand. Ellen was safe. It had been nothing all along but a moment of the most casual adventure. I felt like an idiot, but I realized how much I cared about Ellen and how little I could endure anything terrible happening to her.

"She'll be in soon?"

"Any minute now. She just phoned from the University Club."

I said I'd be over later—I lived almost next door and I wanted to be alone. Outside I remembered I didn't have a key, so I started up the Baker's driveway to take the old cut we used in childhood through the intervening yard. It was still snowing, but the flakes were bigger now against the darkness, and trying to locate the buried walk I noticed that the Bakers' back door was ajar.

I scarcely know why I turned and walked into that kitchen. There was a time when I would have known the Bakers' servants by name. That wasn't true now, but they knew me, and I was aware of a sudden suspension as I came in—not only a suspension of talk but of some mood or expectation that had filled them. They began to go to work too quickly; they made unnecessary movements and clamor—those three. The parlor maid looked at me in a frightened way and I suddenly guessed she was waiting to deliver another message. I beckoned her into the pantry.

"I know all about this," I said. "It's a very serious business. Shall I go to Mrs. Baker now, or will you shut and lock that back door?"

"Don't tell Mrs. Baker, Mr. Stinson!"

"Then I don't want Miss Ellen disturbed. If she is—and if she is I'll know of it—" I delivered some outrageous threat about going to all the employment agencies and seeing she never got another job in the city. She was thoroughly intimidated when I went out; it wasn't a minute before the back door was locked and bolted behind me.

Simultaneously I heard a big car drive up in front, chains crunching on the soft snow; it was bringing Ellen home, and I went in to say good-by.

Joe Jelke and two other boys were along, and none of the three could manager to take their eyes off her, even to say hello to me. She had one of those exquisite rose skins frequent in our part of the country, and beautiful until the little veins begin to break at about forty; now, flushed with the cold, it was a riot of lovely delicate pinks like many carnations. She and Joe had reached some sort of reconciliation, or at least he was too far gone in love to remember last night; but I saw that though she laughed a lot she wasn't really paying any attention to him or any of them. She wanted them to go, so that there'd be a message from the kitchen, but I knew that the message wasn't coming—that she was safe. There was talk of the Pump and Slipper dance at New Haven and of the Princeton Prom, and then, in various moods, we four left and separated quickly outside. I walked home with a certain depression of spirit and lay for an hour in a hot bath thinking that vacation was all over for me now that she was gone; feeling, even more deeply than I had yesterday, that she was out of my life.

And something eluded me, some one more thing to do, something that I had lost amid the events of the afternoon, promising myself to go back and pick it up, only to find that it had escaped me. I associated it vaguely with Mrs. Baker, and now I seemed to recall that it had poked up its head somewhere in the stream of conversation with her. In my relief about Ellen I had forgotten to ask her a question regarding something she had said.

The Brokaws—that was it—where Ellen was to visit. I knew Bill Brokaw well; he was in my class at Yale. Then I remembered and sat bolt upright in the tub—the Brokaws weren't in Chicago this Christmas; they were at Palm Beach!

Dripping I sprang out of the tub, threw an insufficient union suit around my shoulders and sprang for the phone in my room. I got the connection quick, but Miss Ellen had already started for the train.

Luckily our car was in, and while I squirmed, still damp, into my clothes, the chauffeur brought it around to the door. The night was cold and dry, and we make good time to the station through the hard, crusty snow. I felt queer and insecure starting out this way, but somehow more confident as the station loomed up bright and new against the dark, cold air. For fifty years my family had owned the land on which it was built and that made my temerity seem all right somehow. There was always a possibility that I was rushing in where angels feared to tread, but that sense of having a solid foothold in the past made me willing to make a fool of myself. This business was all wrong—terribly wrong. Any idea I had entertained that it was harmless dropped away now; between Ellen and some vague overwhelming catastrophe there stood me, or else the police and a scandal. I'm no moralist—there was another element here, dark and frightening, and I didn't want Ellen to go through it alone.

There are three competing trains from St. Paul to Chicago that all leave within a few minutes of half-past eight. Hers was the Burlington, and as I ran across the station I saw the grating being pulled over and the light above it go out. I knew, though, that she had a drawing-room with the Ingersoll girls, because her mother had mentioned buying the ticket, so she was, literally speaking, tucked in until tomorrow.

The C., M. & St. P. gate was down at the other end and I raced for it and made it. I had forgotten one thing, though, and that was enough to keep me awake and worried half the night. This train got into Chicago ten minutes after the other. Ellen had that much time to disappear into one of the largest cities in the world.

I gave the porter a wire to my family to send from Milwaukee, and at eight o'clock next morning I pushed violently by a whole line of passengers, clamoring over their bags parked in the vestibule, and shot out of the door with a sort of scramble over the porter's back. For a moment the confusion of a great station, the voluminous sounds and echoes and cross-currents of bells and smoke struck me helpless. Then I dashed for the exit and toward the only chance I knew of finding her.

I had guessed right. She was standing at the telegraph counter, sending off heaven knows what black lie to her mother, and her expression when she saw me had a sort of terror mixed up with its surprise. There was cunning in it too. She was thinking quickly—she would have liked to walk away from me as if I weren't there, and go about her own business, but she couldn't. I was too matter-of-fact a thing in her life. So we stood silently watching each other and each thinking hard.

"The Brokaws are in Florida," I said after a minute.

"It was nice of you to take such a long trip to tell me that."

"Since you've found it out, don't you think you'd better go on to school?"

"Please let me alone, Eddie," she said.

"I'll go as far as New York with you. I've decided to go back early myself."

"You'd better let me alone." Her lovely eyes narrowed and her face took on a look of dumb-animal-like resistance. She made a visible effort, the cunning flickered back into it, then both were gone, and in their stead was a cheerful reassuring smile that all but convinced me.

"Eddie, you silly child, don't you think I'm old enough to take care of myself?" I didn't answer. "I'm going to meet a man, you understand. I just want to see him today. I've got my ticket East on the five o'clock train. If you don't believe it, here it is in my bag."

"I believe you."

"The man isn't anybody that you know and—frankly, I think you're being awfully fresh and impossible."

"I know who the man is."

Again she lost control of her face. That terrible expression came back into it and she spoke with almost a snarl:

"You'd better let me alone."

I took the blank out of her hand and wrote out an explanatory telegram to her mother. Then I turned to Ellen and said a little roughly:

"We'll take the five o'clock train East together. Meanwhile you're going to spend the day with me."

The mere sound of my own voice saying this so emphatically encouraged me, and I think it impressed her too; at any rate, she submitted—at least temporarily—and came along without protest while I bought my ticket.

When I start to piece together the fragments of that day a sort of confusion begins, as if my memory didn't want to yield up any of it, or my consciousness let any of it pass through. There was a bright, fierce morning during which we rode about in a taxicab and went to a department store where Ellen said she wanted to buy something and then tried to slip away from me by a back way. I had the feeling, for an hour, that someone was following us along Lake Shore Drive in a taxicab, and I would try to catch them by turning quickly or looking suddenly into the chauffeur's mirror; but I could find no one, and when I turned back I could see that Ellen's face was contorted with mirthless, unnatural laughter.

All morning there was a raw, bleak wind off the lake, but when we went to the Blackstone for lunch a light snow came down past the windows and we talked almost naturally about our friends, and about casual things. Suddenly her tone changed; she grew serious and looked me in the eye, straight and sincere.

"Eddie, you're the oldest friend I have," she said, "and you oughtn't to find it too hard to trust me. If I promise you faithfully on my word of honor to catch that five o'clock train, will you let me alone a few hours this afternoon?"

"Why?"

"Well"—she hesitated and hung her head a little—"I guess everybody has a right to say—good-by."

"You want to say good-by to that——"

"Yes, yes," she said hastily; "just a few hours, Eddie, and I promise faithfully that I'll be on that train."

"Well, I suppose no great harm could be done in two hours. If you really want to say good-by——"

I looked up suddenly, and surprised a look of such tense cunning in her face that I winced before it. Her lip was curled up and her eyes were slits again; there wasn't the faintest touch of fairness and sincerity in her whole face.

We argued. The argument was vague on her part and somewhat hard and reticent on mine. I wasn't going to be cajoled again into any weakness or be infected with any—and there was a contagion of evil in the air. She kept trying to imply, without any convincing evidence to bring forward, that everything was all right. Yet she was too full of the thing itself—whatever it was—to build up a real story, and she wanted to catch at any credulous and acquiescent train of thought that might start in my head, and work that for all it was worth. After every reassuring suggestion she threw out, she stared at me eagerly, as if she hoped I'd launch into a comfortable moral lecture with the customary sweet at the end—which in this case would be her liberty. But I was wearing her away a little. Two or three times it needed just a touch of pressure to bring her to the point of tears—which, of course, was what I wanted—but I couldn't seem to manage it. Almost I had her—almost possessed her interior attention—then she would slip away.

I bullied her remorselessly into a taxi about four o'clock and started for the station. The wind was raw again, with a sting of snow in it, and the people in the streets, waiting for busses and street cars too small to take them all in, looked cold and disturbed and unhappy. I tried to think how lucky we were to be comfortably off and taken care of, but all the warm, respectable world I had been part of yesterday had dropped away from me. There was something we carried with us now that was the enemy and the opposite of all that; it was in the cabs beside us, the streets we passed through. With a touch of panic, I wondered if I wasn't slipping almost imperceptibly into Ellen's attitude of mind. The column of passengers waiting to go aboard the train were as remote from me as people from another world, but it was I that was drifting away and leaving them behind.

My lower was in the same car with her compartment. It was an old-fashioned car, its lights somewhat dim, its carpets and upholstery full of the dust of another generation. There were half a dozen other travellers, but they made no special impression on me, except that they shared the unreality that I was beginning to feel everywhere around me. We went into Ellen's compartment, shut the door and sat down.

Suddenly I put my arms around her and drew her over to me, just as tenderly as I knew how—as if she were a little girl—as she was. She resisted a little, but after a moment she submitted and lay tense and rigid in my arms.

"Ellen," I said helplessly, "you asked me to trust you. You have much more reason to trust me. Wouldn't it help to get rid of all this, if you told me a little?"

"I can't," she said, very low—"I mean, there's nothing to tell."

"You met this man on the train coming home and you fell in love with him, isn't that true?"

"I don't know."

"Tell me, Ellen. You fell in love with him?"

"I don't know. Please let me alone."

"Call it anything you want," I went on, "he has some sort of hold over you. He's trying to use you; he's trying to get something from you. He's not in love with you."

"What does that matter?" she said in a weak voice.

"It does matter. Instead of trying to fight this—this thing—you're trying to fight me. And I love you, Ellen. Do you hear? I'm telling you all of a sudden, but it isn't new with me. I love you."

She looked at me with a sneer on her gentle face; it was an expression I had seen on men who were tight and didn't want to be taken home. But it was human. I was reaching her, faintly and from far away, but more than before.

"Ellen, I want you to answer me one question. Is he going to be on this train?"

She hesitated; then, an instant too late, she shook her head.

"Be careful, Ellen. Now I'm going to ask you one thing more, and I wish you'd try very hard to answer. Coming West, when did this man get on the train?"

"I don't know," she said with an effort.

Just at that moment I became aware, with the unquestionable knowledge reserved for facts, that he was just outside the door. She knew it, too; the blood left her face and that expression of low-animal perspicacity came creeping back. I lowered my face into my hands and tried to think.

We must have sat there, with scarcely a word, for well over an hour. I was conscious that the lights of Chicago, then of Englewood and of endless suburbs, were moving by, and then there were no more lights and we were out on the dark flatness of Illinois. The train seemed to draw in upon itself; it took on the air of being alone. The porter knocked at the door and asked if he could make up the berth, but I said no and he went away.

After a while I convinced myself that the struggle inevitably coming wasn't beyond what remained of my sanity, my faith in the essential all-rightness of things and people. That this person's purpose was what we call "criminal," I took for granted, but there was no need of ascribing to him an intelligence that belonged to a higher plane of human, or inhuman endeavor. It was still as a man that I considered him, and tried to get at his essence, his self-interest—

what took the place in him of a comprehensible heart—but I suppose I more than half knew what I would find when I opened the door.

When I stood up Ellen didn't seem to see me at all. She was hunched into the corner staring straight ahead with a sort of film over her eyes, as if she were in a state of suspended animation of body and mind. I lifted her and put two pillows under her head and threw my fur coat over her knees. Then I knelt beside her and kissed her two hands, opened the door and went out into the hall.

I closed the door behind me and stood with my back against it for a minute. The car was dark save for the corridor lights at each end. There was no sound except the groaning of the couplers, the even click-a-click of the rails and someone's loud sleeping breath farther down the car. I became aware after a moment that the figure of a man was standing by the water cooler just outside the men's smoking room, his derby hat on his head, his coat collar turned up around his neck as if he were cold, his hands in his coat pockets. When I saw him, he turned and went into the smoking room, and I followed. He was sitting in the far corner of the long leather bench; I took the single armchair beside the door.

As I went in I nodded to him and he acknowledged my presence with one of those terrible soundless laughs of his. But this time it was prolonged, it seemed to go on forever, and mostly to cut it short, I asked: "Where are you from?" in a voice I tried to make casual.

He stopped laughing and looked at me narrowly, wondering what my game was. When he decided to answer, his voice was muffled as though he were speaking through a silk scarf, and it seemed to come from a long way off.

"I'm from St. Paul, Jack."

"Been making a trip home?"

He nodded. Then he took a long breath and spoke in a hard, menacing voice:

"You better get off at Fort Wayne, Jack."

He was dead. He was dead as hell—he had been dead all along, but what force had flowed through him, like blood in his veins, out to St. Paul and back, was leaving him now. A new outline—the outline of him dead—was coming through the palpable figure that had knocked down Joe Jelke.

He spoke again, with a sort of jerking effort:

"You get off at Fort Wayne, Jack, or I'm going to wipe you out." He moved his hand in his coat pocket and showed me the outline of a revolver.

I shook my head. "You can't touch me," I answered. "You see, I know." His terrible eyes shifted over me quickly, trying to determine whether or not I did know. Then he gave a snarl and made as though he were going to jump to his feet.

"You climb off here or else I'm going to get you, Jack!" he cried hoarsely. The train was slowing up for Fort Wayne and his voice rang loud in the comparative quiet, but he didn't move from his chair—he was too weak, I think—and we sat staring at each other while workmen passed up and down outside the window banging the brakes and wheels, and the engine gave out loud mournful pants up ahead. No one got into our car. After a while the porter closed the vestibule door and passed back along the corridor, and we slid out of the murky yellow station light and into the long darkness.

What I remember next must have extended over a space of five or six hours, though it comes back to me as something without any existence in time—something that might have taken five minutes or a year. There began a slow, calculated assault on me, wordless and terrible. I felt what I can only call a strangeness stealing over me— akin to the strangeness I had felt all afternoon, but deeper and more intensified. It was like nothing so much as the sensation of drifting away, and I gripped the arms of the chair convulsively, as if to hang onto a piece in the living world. Sometimes I felt myself going out with a rush. There would be almost a warm relief about it, a sense of not caring; then, with a violent wrench of the will, I'd pull myself back into the room.

Suddenly I realized that from a while back I had stopped hating him, stopped feeling violently alien to him, and with the realization, I went cold and sweat broke out all over my head. He was getting around my abhorrence, as he had got around Ellen coming West on the train; and it was just that strength he drew from preying on people that had brought him up to the point of concrete violence in St. Paul, and that, fading and flickering out, still kept him fighting now.

He must have seen that faltering in my heart, for he spoke at once, in a low, even, almost gentle voice: "You better go now."

"Oh, I'm not going," I forced myself to say.

"Suit yourself, Jack."

He was my friend, he implied. He knew how it was with me and he wanted to help. He pitied me. I'd better go away before it was too late. The rhythm of his attack was soothing as a song: I'd better go away—*and let him get at Ellen.* With a little cry I sat bolt upright.

"What do you want of this girl?" I said, my voice shaking. "To make a sort of walking hell of her."

His glance held a quality of dumb surprise, as if I were punishing an animal for a fault of which he was not conscious. For an instant I faltered; then I went on blindly:

"You've lost her; she's put her trust in me."

His countenance went suddenly black with evil, and he cried: "You're a liar!" in a voice that was like cold hands.

"She trusts me," I said. "You can't touch her. She's safe!"

He controlled himself. His face grew bland, and I felt that curious weakness and indifference begin again inside me. What was the use of all this? What was the use?

"You haven't got much time left," I forced myself to say, and then, in a flash of intuition, I jumped at the truth. "You died, or you were killed, not far from here!"—Then I saw what I had not seen before— that his forehead was drilled with a small round hole like a larger picture nail leaves when it's pulled from a plaster wall. "And now you're sinking. You've only got a few hours. The trip home is over!"

His face contorted, lost all semblance of humanity, living or dead. Simultaneously the room was full of cold air and with a noise that was something between a paroxysm of coughing and a burst of horrible laughter, he was on his feet, reeking of shame and blasphemy.

"Come and look!" he cried. "I'll show you——"

He took a step toward me, then another and it was exactly as if a door stood open behind him, a door yawning out to an inconceivable abyss of darkness and corruption. There was a scream of mortal agony, from him or from somewhere behind, and abruptly the strength went out of him in a long husky sigh and he wilted to the floor. . . .

How long I sat there, dazed with terror and exhaustion, I don't know. The next thing I remember is the sleepy porter shining shoes across the room from me, and outside the window the steel fires of Pittsburgh breaking the flat perspective of the night. There was something extended on the bench also—something too faint for a man, too heavy for a shadow. Even as I perceived it it faded off and away.

Some minutes later I opened the door of Ellen's compartment. She was asleep where I had left her. Her lovely cheeks were white and wan, but she lay naturally—her hands relaxed and her breathing regular and clear. What had possessed her had gone out of her, leaving her exhausted but her own dear self again.

I made her a little more comfortable, tucked a blanket around her, extinguished the light and went out.

III

When I came home for Easter vacation, almost my first act was to go down to the billiard parlor near Seven Corners. The man at the cash register quite naturally didn't remember my hurried visit of three months before.

"I'm trying to locate a certain party who, I think, came here a lot some time ago."

I described the man rather accurately, and when I had finished, the cashier called to a little jockeylike fellow who was sitting near with an air of having something very important to do that he couldn't quite remember.

"Hey, Shorty, talk to this guy, will you? I think he's looking for Joe Varland."

The little man gave me a tribal look of suspicion. I went and sat near him.

"Joe Varland's dead, fella," he said grudgingly. "He died last winter."

I described him again—his overcoat, his laugh, the habitual expression of his eyes.

"That's Joe Varland you're looking for all right, but he's dead."

"I want to find out something about him."

"What you want to find out?"

"What did he do, for instance?"

"How should I know?"

"Look here! I'm not a policeman. I just want some kind of information about his habits. He's dead now and it can't hurt him. And it won't go beyond me."

"Well"—he hesitated, looking me over—"he was a great one for travelling. He got in a row in the station in Pittsburgh and a dick got him."

I nodded. Broken pieces of the puzzle began to assemble in my head.

"Why was he a lot on trains?"

"How should I know, fella?"

"If you can use ten dollars, I'd like to know anything you may have heard on the subject."

"Well," said Shorty reluctantly, "all I know is they used to say he worked the trains."

"Worked the trains?"

"He had some racket of his own he'd never loosen up about. He used to work the girls travelling alone on the trains. Nobody ever knew much about it—he was a pretty smooth guy—but sometimes he'd turn up here with a lot of dough and he let 'em know it was the janes he got it off of."

I thanked him and gave him the ten dollars and went out, very thoughtful, without mentioning that part of Joe Varland had made a last trip home.

Ellen wasn't West for Easter, and even if she had been I wouldn't have gone to her with the information, either—at least I've seen her almost every day this summer and we've managed to talk about everything else. Sometimes, though, she gets silent about nothing and wants to be very close to me, and I know what's in her mind.

Of course she's coming out this fall, and I have two more years at New Haven; still, things don't look so impossible as they did a few months ago. She belongs to me in a way—even if I lose her she belongs to me. Who knows? Anyhow, I'll always be there.

ONE INTERNE

Traditionally, the Coccidian Club show is given on the hottest night of spring, and that year was no exception. Two hundred doctors and students sweltered in the reception rooms of the old narrow house and another two hundred students pressed in at the doors, effectually sealing out any breezes from the Maryland night. The entertainment reached these latter clients only dimly, but refreshment was relayed back to them by a busy bucket brigade. Down cellar, the janitor made his annual guess that the sagging floors would hold up one more time.

Bill Tulliver was the coolest man in the hall. For no special reason he wore a light tunic and carried a crook during the only number in which he took part, the rendition of the witty, scurrilous and interminable song which described the failings and eccentricities of the medical faculty. He sat in comparative comfort on the platform and looked out over the hot sea of faces. The most important doctors were in front—Doctor Ruff, the ophthalmologist; Doctor Lane, the brain surgeon; Doctor Georgi, the stomach specialist; Doctor Barnett, the alchemist of internal medicine; and on the end of the row, with his saintlike face undisturbed by the rivulets of perspiration that poured down the long dome of his head, Doctor Norton, the diagnostician.

Like most young men who had sat under Norton, Bill Tulliver followed him with the intuition of the belly, but with a difference. He knelt to him selfishly as a sort of great giver of life. He wanted less to win his approval than to compel it. Engrossed in his own career, which would begin in earnest when he entered the hospital as an interne in July, his whole life was pointed toward the day when his own guess would be right and Doctor Norton's would be wrong. In that moment he would emancipate himself—he need not base himself on the adding machine-calculating machine-probability machine-St. Francis of Assisi machine any longer.

Bill Tulliver had not arrived unprovoked at this pitch of egotism. He was the fifth in an unbroken series of Dr. William Tullivers who had practised with distinction in the city. His father died last winter; it was not unnatural that even from the womb of school this last scion of a medical tradition should clamor for "self-expression."

The faculty song, immemorially popular, went on and on. There was a verse about the sanguinary Doctor Lane, about the new names Doctor Brune made up for the new diseases he invented, about the personal idiosyncrasies of Doctor Schwartze and the domestic embroilments of Doctor Gillespie. Doctor Norton, as one of the most popular men on the staff, got off easy. There were some new verses— several that Bill had written himself:

> "Herpes Zigler, sad and tired,
>   Will flunk you out or kill ya,
> If you forget Alfonso wired
>   For dope on hœmophilia.
> *Bum*tiddy-bum-bum,
> Tiddy-bum-bum.
> Three thousand years ago,
> Three thousand years ago."

He watched Doctor Zigler and saw the wince that puckered up under the laugh. Bill wondered how soon there would be a verse about him, Bill Tulliver, and he tentatively composed one as the chorus thundered on.

After the show the older men departed, the floors were sloshed with beer and the traditional roughhouse usurped the evening. But Bill had fallen solemn and, donning his linen suit, he watched for ten minutes and then left the hot hall. There was a group on the front steps, breathing the sparse air, and another group singing around the lamp-post at the corner. Across the street arose the great bulk of the hospital about which his life revolved. Between the Michael's Clinic and the Ward's Dispensary arose a round full moon.

The girl—she was hurrying—reached the loiterers at the lamp-post at the same moment as Bill. She wore a dark dress and a dark, flopping hat, but Bill got an impression that there was a gayety of cut, if not of color, about her clothes. The whole thing happened in less than a minute; the man turning about—Bill saw that he was not a member of the grand confraternity—and was simply hurling himself into her arms, like a child at its mother.

The girl staggered backward with a frightened cry; and everyone in the group acted at once.

"Are you sure you're all right?"

"Oh, yes," she gasped. "I think he just passed out and didn't realize he was grabbing at a girl."

"We'll take him over to the emergency ward and see if he can swallow a stomach pump."

Bill Tulliver found himself walking along beside the girl.

"Are you sure you're all right?"

"Oh, yes." She was still breathing hard; her bosom rose, putting out its eternal promises, as if the breath she had taken in were the last breather left in the world.

"Oh, catch it—oh, catch it and take it—oh, catch it," she sighed. "I realized right away that they were students. I shouldn't have gone by there tonight."

Her hair, dark and drawn back to her ears, brushed her shoulders. She laughed uncontrollably.

"He was so helpless," she said. "Lord knows I've seen men helpless —hundreds of them just helpless—but I'll never forget the expression in his face when he decided to—to lean on me."

Her dark eyes shone with mirth and Bill saw that she was really self-reliant. He stared at her, and the impression of her beauty grew until, uncommitted by a word, by even a formal introduction, he felt himself going out toward her, watching the turn of her lips and the shifting of her cheeks when she smiled . . .

All this was in the three or four minutes that he walked beside her; not till afterward did he realize how profound the impression had been.

As they passed the church-like bulk of the administration building, an open cabriolet slowed down beside them and a man of about thirty-five jumped out. The girl ran toward him.

"Howard!" she cried with excited gayety. "I was attacked. There were some students in front of the Coccidian Club building——"

The man swung sharply and menacingly toward Bill Tulliver.

"Is this one of them?" he demanded.

"No, no; he's all right."

Simultaneously Bill recognized him—it was Dr. Howard Durfee, brilliant among the younger surgeons, heartbreaker and swash-buckler of the staff.

"You haven't been bothering Miss——"

She stopped him, but not before Bill had answered angrily:

"I don't bother people."

Unappeased, as if Bill were in some way responsible, Doctor Durfee got into his car; the girl got in beside him.

"So long," she said. "And thanks." Her eyes shone at Bill with friendly interest, and then, just before the car shot away, she did something else with them—narrowed them a little and then widened them, recognizing by this sign the uniqueness of their relationship. "I see you," it seemed to say. "You registered. Everything's possible."

With the faint fanfare of a new motor, she vanished back into the spring night.

II

Bill was to enter the hospital in July with the first contingent of newly created doctors. He passed the intervening months at Martha's Vineyard, swimming and fishing with Schoatze, his classmate, and returned tense with health and enthusiasm to begin his work.

The red square broiled under the Maryland sun. Bill went in through the administration building where a gigantic Christ gestured in marble pity over the entrance hall. It was by this same portal that Bill's father had entered on his interneship thirty years before.

Suddenly Bill was in a condition of shock, his tranquility was rent asunder, he could not have given a rational account as to why he was where he was. A dark-haired girl with great, luminous eyes had started up from the very shadow of the statue, stared at him just long enough to effect this damage, and then with an explosive "Hello!" vanished into one of the offices.

He was still gazing after her, stricken, haywire, scattered and dissolved—when Doctor Norton hailed him:

"I believe I'm addressing William Tulliver the fifth——"

Bill was glad to be reminded who he was.

"—looking somewhat interested in Doctor Durfee's girl," continued Norton.

"Is she?" Bill asked sharply. Then: "Oh, howdedo, Doctor?"

Dr. Norton decided to exercise his wit, of which he had plenty. "In fact we know they spend their days together, and gossip adds the evenings."

"Their days? I should think he'd be too busy."

"He is. As a matter of fact, Miss Singleton induces the state of coma during which he performs his internal sculpture. She's an anaesthetist."

"I see. Then they are—thrown together all day."

"If you regard that as a romantic situation." Doctor Norton looked at him closely. "Are you settled yet? Can you do something for me right now?"

"Yes, indeed."

"I know you don't go on the ward till tomorrow, but I'd like you to go to East Michael and take a P. E. and a history."

"Certainly."

"Room 312. I've put your methodical friend Schoatze on the trail of another mystery next door."

Bill hurried to his room on the top of Michael, jumped into a new white uniform, equipped himself with instruments. In his haste he forgot that this was the first time he had performed an inquisition unaided. Outside the door he smoothed himself into a calm, serious manner. He was almost a white apostle when we walked into the room; at least he tried to be.

A paunchy, sallow man of forty was smoking a cigarette in bed.

"Good morning," Bill said heartily. "How are you this morning?"

"Rotten," the man said. "That's why I'm here."

Bill set down his satchel and approached him like a young cat after its first sparrow.

"What seems to be the trouble?"

"Everything. My head aches, my bones ache, I can't sleep, I don't eat, I've got fever. My chauffeur ran over me, I mean ran over me, I mean ran me, if you know what I mean. I mean from Washington this morning. I can't stand those Washington doctors; they don't talk about anything but politics."

Bill clapped a thermometer in his mouth and took his pulse. Then he made the routine examination of chest, stomach, throat and the rest. The reflexes were sluggish to the little rubber hammer. Bill sat down beside the bed.

"I'd trade hearts with you any day," he promised.

"They all say I've got a good heart," agreed the man. "What did you think of Hoover's speech?"

"I thought you were tired of politics."

"That's true, but I got thinking of Hoover while you went over me."

"About Hoover?"

"About me. What did you find out?"

"We'll want to make some tests. But you seem pretty sound really."

"I'm not sound," the patient snapped. "I'm not sound. I'm a sick man."

Bill took out a P.E. form and a fountain pen.

"What's your name?" he began.

"Paul B. Van Schaik."

"Your nearest relative?"

There was nothing in the case history on which to form any opinion. Mr. Van Schaik had had several children's diseases. Yesterday morning he was unable to get out of bed and his valet had taken his temperature and found fever.

Bill thermometer registered no fever.

"Now we're going to make just a little prick in your thumb," he said, preparing glass slides, and when this had been accomplished to the tune of a short, dismal howl from the patient, he added: "We want just a little specimen from your upper arm."

"You want everything but my tears," protested the patient.

"We have to investigate all the possibilities," said Bill sternly, plunging the syringe into the soft upper arm, inspiring more explosive protests from Mr. Van Schaik.

Reflectively Bill replaced his instruments. He had obtained no clue as to what was the matter and he eyed the patient reproachfully.

On a chance, he looked for enlarged cervical glands, and asked him if his parents were alive, and took a last look at throat and teeth.

"Eyes normally prominent," he wrote down, with a feeling of futility. "Pupils round and equal."

"That's all for the moment," he said. "Try and get some rest."

"Rest!" cried Mr. Van Schaik indignantly. "That's just the trouble. I haven't been able to sleep for three days. I feel worse every minute."

As Bill went out into the hall, George Schoatze was just emerging from the room next door. His eyes were uncertain and there was sweat upon his brow.

"Finished?" Bill asked.

"Why, yes, in a way. Did Doctor Norton set you a job too?"

"Yeah. Kind of puzzling case in here—contradictory symptoms," he lied.

"Same here," said George, wiping his brow. "I'd rather have started out on something more clearly defined, like the ones Robinson gave us in class last year—you know, where there were two possibilities and one probability."

"Unobliging lot of patients," agreed Bill.

A student nurse approached him.

"You were just in 312," she said in a low voice. "I better tell you. I unpacked for the patient, and there was one empty bottle of whisky and one half empty. He asked me to pour him a drink, but I didn't like to do that without asking a doctor."

"Quite right," said Bill stiffly, but he wanted to kiss her hand in gratitude.

Dispatching the specimens to the laboratory, the two internes went in search of Doctor Norton, whom they found in his office.

"Through already? What luck, Tulliver?"

"He's been on a bust and he's got a hangover," Bill blurted out. "I haven't got the laboratory reports yet, but my opinion is that's all."

"I agree with you," said Doctor Norton. "All right, Schoatze; how about the lady in 314?"

"Well, unless it's too deep for me, there's nothing the matter with her at all."

"Right you are," agreed Doctor Norton. "Nerves—and not even enough of them for the Ward clinic. What'll we do with them?"

"Throw em out," said Bill promptly.

"Let them stay," corrected Doctor Norton. "They can afford it. They come to us for protection they don't need, so let them pay for a couple of really sick people over in the free wards. We're not crowded."

Outside the office, Bill and George fastened eyes.

"Humbling us a little," said Bill rather resentfully. "Let's go up to the operating rooms; I want to convince myself all over again that this is a serious profession." He swore. "I suppose for the next few months we'll be feeling the bellies of four-flushers and taking the case histories of women who aren't cases."

"Never mind," said George cautiously. "I was just as glad to start with something simple like—like——"

"Like what?"

"Why, like nothing."

"You're easily pleased," Bill commented.

Ascertaining from a bulletin board that Dr. Howard Durfee was at work in No. 4, they took the elevator to the operating rooms. As they slipped on the gowns, caps, and then the masks, Bill realized how quickly he was breathing.

He saw HER before he saw anything else in the room, except the bright vermilion spot of the operation itself, breaking the universal whiteness of the scene. There was a sway of eyes toward the two internes as they came into the gallery, and Bill picked out her eyes, darker than ever in contrast with the snowy cap and mask, as she sat working the gas machine at the patient's invisible head. The room was small. The platform on which they stood was raised about four feet, and by leaning out on a glass screen like a windshield, they brought their eyes to within two yards of the surgeon's busy hands.

"It's a neat appendix—not a cut in the muscle," George whispered. "That guy can play lacrosse tomorrow."

Doctor Durfee, busy with catgut, heard him.

"Not this patient," he said. "Too many adhesions."

His hands, trying the catgut, were sure and firm, the fine hands of a pianist, the tough hands of a pitcher combined. Bill thought how insecure, precariously involved, the patient would seem to a layman, and yet how safe he was with those sure hands in an atmosphere so made safe from time itself. Time had stopped at the door of the operating room, too profane to enter here.

Thea Singleton guarded the door of the patient's consciousness, a hand on a pulse, another turning the wheels of the gas machine, as if they were the stops on a silent organ.

There were others in attendance—an assisting surgeon, a nurse who passed instruments, a nurse who made liaison between the table and the supplies—but Bill was absorbed in what subtle relationship there was between Howard Durfee and Thea Singleton; he felt a wild jealousy toward the mask with the brilliant, agile hands.

"I'm going," he said to George.

He saw her that afternoon, and again it was in the shadow of the great stone Christ in the entrance hall. She was in street clothes, and she looked slick and fresh and tantalizingly excitable.

"Of course. You're the man the night of the Coccidian show. And now you're an interne. Wasn't it you who came into Room 4 this morning?"

"Yes. How did it go?"

"Fine. It was Doctor Durfee."

"Yes," he said with emphasis. "I know it was Doctor Durfee."

He met her by accident or contrivance half a dozen times in the next fortnight, before he judged he could ask her for a date.

"Why, I suppose so." She seemed a little surprised. "Let's see. How about next week—either Tuesday or Wednesday?"

"How about tonight?"

"Oh, not possibly."

When he called Tuesday at the little apartment she shared with a woman musician from the Peabody Institute, he said:

"What would you like to do? See a picture?"

"No," she answered emphatically. "If I knew you better I'd say let's drive about a thousand miles into the country and go swimming in some quarry." She looked at him quizzically. "You're not one of those very impulsive internes, are you, that just sweep poor nurses off their feet?"

"On the contrary, I'm scared to death of you," Bill admitted.

It was a hot night, but the white roads were cool. They found out a little about each other: She was the daughter of an Army officer and had grown up in the Philippines, and in the black-and-silver water of the abandoned quarry she surprised him with such diving as he had never seen a girl do. It was ghostly inside of the black shadow that ringed the glaring moonlight, and their voices echoed loud when they called to each other.

Afterward, with their heads wet and their bodies stung alive, they sat for awhile, unwilling to start back. Suddenly she smiled, and then looked at him without speaking, her lips just barely parted. There was the starlight set upon the brilliant darkness; and there were her pale cool cheeks, and Bill let himself be lost in love for her, as he had so wanted to do.

"We must go," she said presently.

"Not yet."

"Oh, yet—very yet—exceedingly yet."

"Because," he said after a moment, "you're Doctor Durfee's girl?"

"Yes," she admitted after a moment, "I suppose I'm Doctor Durfee's girl."

"Why are you?" he cried.

"Are you in love with me?"

"I suppose I am. Are you in love with Durfee?"

She shook her head. "No, I'm not in love with anybody. I'm just —his girl."

So the evening that had been at first ecstatic was finally unsatisfactory. This feeling deepened when he found that for his date he had to thank the fact that Durfee was out of town for a few days.

With August and the departure of more doctors on vacation, he found himself very busy. During four years he had dreamed of such work as he was doing, and now it was all disturbed by the ubiquity of "Durfee's girl." In vain he searched among the girls in the city, on those Sundays when he could go into the city, for some who would soften the hurt of his unreciprocated emotion. But the city seemed empty of girls, and in the hospital the little probationers in short cuffs had no appeal for him. The truth of his situation was that his initial idealism which had been centred in Doctor Norton had transferred itself to Thea. Instead of a God, it was now a Goddess who symbolized for him the glory and the devotion of his profession; and that she was caught up in an entanglement that bound her away from him, played havoc with his peace of mind.

Diagnosis had become a workaday matter—almost. He had made a few nice guesses and Doctor Norton had given him full credit.

"Nine times out of ten I'll be right," Norton said. "The rare thing is so rare that I'm out of the habit of looking for it. That's where you young men come in; you're cocked for the rare thing and that one time in ten you find it."

"It's a great feeling," said Bill. "I got a big kick out of that actinomycosis business."

"You look tired for your age," said Doctor Norton suddenly. "At twenty-five you shouldn't be existing entirely on nervous energy, Bill, and that's what you're doing. The people you grew up with say they never see you. Why not take a couple of hours a week away from the hospital, if only for the sake of your patients? You took so many chemistry tests of Mr. Doremus that we almost had to give him blood transfusions to build him up again."

"I was right," said Bill eagerly.

"But a little brutal. Everything would have developed in a day or two. Take it gently, like your friend Schoatze. You're going to know a lot about internal medicine some day, but you're trying to rush things."

But Bill was a man driven; he tried more Sunday afternoons with current débutantes, but in the middle of a conversation he would find his mind drifting back to those great red building blocks of an Idea, where alone he could feel the pulse of life.

The news that a famous character in politics was leaving the Coast and coming to the hospital for the diagnosis of some obscure malady had the effect of giving him a sudden interest in politics. He looked up the record of the man and followed his journey east, which occupied half a column daily in the newspapers; party issues depended on his survival and eventual recovery.

Then one August afternoon there was an item in the society column which announced the engagement of Helen, débutante daughter of Mrs. Truby Ponsonby Day, to Dr. Howard Durfee. Bill's reconciled world turned upside down. After an amount of very real suffering, he had accepted the fact that Thea was the mistress of a brilliant surgeon, but that Dr. Durfee should suddenly cut loose from her was simply incredible.

Immediately he went in search of her, found her issuing from the nurses' ward in street clothes. Her lovely face, with the eyes that held for him all the mystery of people trying, all the splendor of a goal, all reward, all purpose, all satisfaction, was harried with annoyance; she had been stared at and pitied.

"If you like," she answered, when he asked if he could run her home, and then: "Heaven help women! The amount of groaning over my body that took place this afternoon would have been plenty for a war."

"I'm going to help you," he said. "If that guy has let you down——"

"Oh, shut up!" Up to a few weeks ago I could have married Howard Durfee by nodding my head—that's just what I wouldn't tell those women this afternoon. I think you've got discretion, and that'll help you a lot when you're a doctor."

"I am a doctor," he said somewhat stiffly.

"No, you're just an interne."

He was indignant and they drove in silence. Then, softening, she turned toward him and touched his arm.

"You happen to be a gentleman," she said, "which is nice sometimes—though I prefer a touch of genius."

"I've got that," Bill said doggedly. "I've got everything, except you."

"Come up to the apartment and I'll tell you something that no one else in this city knows."

It was a modest apartment but it told him that at some time she had lived in a more spacious world. It was all reduced, as if she had hung on to several cherished things, a Duncan Phyfe table, a brass by Brancusi, two oil portraits of the '50's.

"I was engaged to John Gresham," she said. "Do you know who he was?"

"Of course," he said. "I took up the subscription for the bronze tablet to him."

John Gresham had died by inches from radium poisoning, got by his own experiments.

"I was with him till the end," Thea went on quickly, "and just before he died he wagged his last finger at me and said, 'I forbid you to go to pieces. That doesn't do any good.' So, like a good little girl, I didn't go to pieces, but I toughened up instead. Anyhow, that's why I never could love Howard Durfee the way he wanted to be loved, in spite of his nice swagger and his fine hands."

"I see." Overwhelmed by the revelation, Bill tried to adjust himself to it. "I knew there was something far off about you, some sort of —oh, dedication to something I didn't know about."

"I'm pretty hard." She got up impatiently. "Anyhow, I've lost a good friend today and I'm cross, so go before I show it. Kiss me good-by if you like."

"It wouldn't mean anything at this moment."

"Yes, it would," she insisted. "I like to be close to you. I like your clothes."

Obediently he kissed her, but he felt far off from her and very rebuffed and young as he went out the door.

He awoke next morning with the sense of something important hanging over him; then he remembered. Senator Billings, relayed by crack trains, airplanes and ambulances, was due to arrive during the morning, and the ponderous body which had housed and expelled so much nonsense in thirty years was to be at the mercy of the rational at last.

"I'll diagnose the old boy," he thought grimly, "if I have to invent a new disease."

He went about his routine work with a sense of fatigue that morning. Perhaps Doctor Norton would keep this plum to himself and Bill wouldn't have a chance at him. But at eleven o'clock he met his senior in a corridor.

"The senator's come," he said. "I've formed a tentative opinion. You might go in and get his history. Go over him quickly and give him the usual laboratory work-up."

"All right," said Bill, but there was no eagerness in his voice. He seemed to have lost all his enthusiasm. With his instruments and a block of history paper, he repaired to the senator's room.

"Good morning," he began. "Feeling a little tired after your trip?"
The big barrel of a man rolled toward him.

"Exhausted," he squeaked unexpectedly. "All in."

Bill didn't wonder; he felt rather that way himself, as if he had travelled thousands of miles in all sorts of conveyances until his insides, including his brains, were all shaken up together.

He took the case history.

"What's your profession?"

"Legislator."

"Do you use any alcohol?"

The senator raised himself on one arm and thundered, "See here, young man; I'm not going to be heckled! As long as the Eighteenth Amendment—" He subsided.

"Do you use any alcohol?" Bill asked again patiently.

"Why, yes."

"How much?"

"A few drinks every day. I don't count them. Say, if you look in my suitcase you'll find an X-ray of my lungs, taken a few years ago."

Bill found it and stared at it with a sudden feeling that everything was getting a little crazy.

"This is an X-ray of a woman's stomach," he said.

"Oh—well, it must have got mixed up," said the senator. "It must be my wife's."

Bill went into the bathroom to wash his thermometer. When he came back he took the senator's pulse, and was puzzled to find himself regarded in a curious way.

"What's the idea?" the senator demanded. "Are you the patient or am I?" He jerked his hand angrily away from Bill. "Your hand's like ice. And you've put the thermometer in your own mouth."

Only then did Bill realize how sick he was. He pressed the nurse's bell and staggered back to a chair with wave after wave of pain chasing across his abdomen.

III

He awoke with a sense that he had been in bed for many hours. There was fever bumping in his brain, a pervasive weakness in his body, and what had wakened him was a new series of pains in his stomach. Across the room in an armchair sat Dr. George Schoatze, and on his knee was the familiar case-history pad.

"What the hell," Bill said weakly. "What the hell's the matter with me? What happened?"

"You're all right," said George. "You just lie quiet."

Bill tried to sit upright, but found he was too weak.

"Lie quiet!" he repeated incredulously. "What do you think I am— some dumb patient? I asked you what's the matter with me?"

"That's exactly what we're trying to find out. Say, what is your exact age?"

"My age!" Bill cried. "A hundred and ten in the shade! My name's Al Capone and I'm an old hophead. Stick that on your God damn paper and mail it to Santa Claus. I asked you what's the matter with me."

"And I say that's what we're trying to find out," said George, staunch, but a little nervous. "Now, you take it easy."

"Take it easy!" cried Bill. "When I'm burning up with fever and a half-wit interne sits there and asks me how many fillings I've got in my teeth! You take my temperature, and take it right away!"

"All right—all right," said George conciliatingly. "I was just going to."

He put the thermometer in Bill's mouth and felt for the pulse, but Bill mumbled, "I'll shake my ode pulse," and pulled his hand away. After two minutes George deftly extracted the thermometer and walked with it to the window, an act of treachery that brought Bill's legs out of bed.

"I want to read that thermometer!" he cried. "Now, you look here! I want to know what's on that thermometer!"

George shook it down quickly and put it in its case.

"That isn't the way we do things here," he said.

"Oh, isn't it? Well, then, I'll go somewhere where they've got some sense."

George prepared a syringe and two small plates of glass.

Bill groaned. "Do you think for a moment I'm going to let you do that? I taught you everything you know about blood chemistry. By

God, I used to do your lessons for you, and you come here to make some clumsy stab into my arm!"

Perspiring fluently, as was his wont under strain, George rang for a nurse, with the hope that a female presence would have a calming effect on Bill. But it was not the right female.

"Another nitwit!" Bill cried as she came in. "Do you think I'm going to lie here and stand more of this nonsense? Why doesn't somebody do something? Where's Doctor Norton?"

"He'll be here this afternoon."

"This afternoon! I'll probably be dead by this afternoon. Why isn't he here this morning? Off on some social bat and I lie here surrounded by morons who've lost their heads and don't know what to do about it. What are you writing there—that my 'tongue protrudes in mid-line without tremor'? Give me my slippers and bathrobe. I'm going to report you two as specimens for the nerve clinic."

They pressed him down in bed, whence he looked up at George with infinite reproach.

"You, that I explained a whole book of toxicology to, you're presuming to diagnose *me*. Well, then, *do* it! What have I got? Why is my stomach burning up? Is it appendicitis? What's the white count?"

"How can I find out the white count when——"

With a sigh of infinite despair at the stupidity of mankind, Bill relaxed, exhausted.

Doctor Norton, arrived at two o'clock. His presence should have been reassuring, but by this time the patient was too far gone in nervous tension.

"Look here, Bill," he said sternly. "What's all this about not letting George look into your mouth?"

"Because he deliberately gagged me with that stick," Bill cried. "When I get out of this I'm going to stick a plank down that ugly trap of his."

"Now, that'll do. Do you know little Miss Cary has been crying? She says she's going to give up nursing. She says she's never been so disillusioned in her life."

"The same with me. Tell her I'm going to give it up too. After this, I'm going to kill people instead of curing them. Now when I need it nobody has even tried to cure *me*."

An hour later Doctor Norton stood up.

"Well, Bill, we're going to take you at your word and tell you what's what. I'm laying my cards on the table when I say we don't know what's the matter with you. We've just got the X-rays from this morning, and it's pretty certain it's not the gall bladder. There's a possibility of acute food poisoning or mesenteric thrombosis, or it may be something we haven't thought of yet. Give us a chance, Bill."

With an effort and with the help of a sedative, Bill got himself in comparative control; only to go to pieces again in the morning, when George Schoatze arrived to give him a hypodermoclysis.

"But I can't stand it," he raged. "I never could stand being pricked, and you have as much right with a needle as a year-old baby with a machine gun."

"Doctor Norton has ordered that you get nothing by mouth."

"Then give it intravenously."

"This is best."

"What I'll do to you when I get well! I'll inject stuff into you until you're as big as a barrel! I will! I'll hire somebody to hold you down!"

Forty-eight hours later, Doctor Norton and Doctor Schoatze had a conference in the former's office.

"So there we are," George was saying gloomily. "He just flatly refuses to submit to the operation."

"H'm." Doctor Norton considered. "That' bad."

"There's certainly danger of a perforation."

"And you say that his chief objection——"

"——that it was my diagnosis. He says I remembered the word 'volvulus' from some lecture and I'm trying to wish it on him." George added uncomfortably: "He always was domineering, but I never saw anything like *this*. Today he claims it's acute pancreatitis, but he doesn't have any convincing reasons."

"Does he know I agree with your opinion?"

"He doesn't seem to believe in *any*body," said George uncomfortably. "He keeps fretting about his father; he keeps thinking he could help him if he was alive."

"I wish that there was someone outside the hospital he had some faith in," Norton said. An idea came to him: "I wonder——" He picked up the telephone and said to the operator: "I wish you'd locate Miss Singleton, Doctor Durfee's anaesthetist. And when she's free, ask her to come and see me."

Bill opened his eyes wearily when Thea came into his room at eight that night.

"Oh, it's you," he murmured.

She sat on the side of his bed and put her hand on his arm.

"H'lo, Bill," she said.

"H'lo."

Suddenly he turned in bed and put both arms around her arm. Her free hand touched his hair.

"You've been bad," she said.

"I can't help it."

She sat with him silently for half an hour; then she changed her position so that her arm was under his head. Stooping over him, she kissed him on the brow. He said:

"Being close to you is the first rest I've had in four days."

After a while she said: "Three months ago Doctor Durfee did an operation for volvulus and it was entirely successful."

"But it isn't volvulus!" he cried. "Volvulus is when a loop of the intestine gets twisted on itself. It's a crazy idea of Schoatze's! He wants to make a trick diagnosis and get a lot of credit."

"Doctor Norton agrees with him. You must give in, Bill. I'll be right beside you, as close as I am now."

Her soft voice was a sedative; he felt his resistance growing weaker; two long tears rolled from his eyes. "I feel so helpless," he admitted. "How do I know whether George Schoatze has any sense?"

"That's just childish," she answered gently. "You'll profit more by submitting to this than Doctor Schoatze will from his lucky guess."

He clung to her suddenly. "Afterward, will you be my girl?"

She laughed. "The selfishness! The bargainer! You wouldn't be very cheerful company if you went around with a twisted intestine."

He was silent for a moment. "Yesterday I made my will," he said. "I divided what I have between an old aunt and you."

She put her face against his. "You'll make me weep, and it really isn't that serious at all."

"All right then." His white, pinched face relaxed. "Get it over with."

Bill was wheeled upstairs an hour later. Once the matter was decided, all nervousness left him, and he remembered how the hands of Doctor Durfee had given him such a sense of surety last July, and remembered who would be at his head watching over him. He last thought as the gas began was sudden jealousy that Thea and Howard Durfee would be awake and near each other while he was asleep . . .

. . . When he awoke he was being wheeled down a corridor to his room. Doctor Norton and Doctor Schoatze, seeming very cheerful, were by his side.

"H'lo, hello," cried Bill in a daze. "Say, what did they finally discover about Senator Billings?"

"It was only a common cold, Bill," said Doctor Norton. "They've shipped him back west—by dirigible, helicopter and freight elevator."

"Oh," said Bill; and then, after a moment, "I feel terrible."

"You're not terrible," Doctor Norton assured him. "You'll be up on deck in a week. George here is certainly a swell guesser."

"It was a beautiful operation," said George modestly. "That loop would have perforated in another six hours."

"Good anaesthesia job, too," said Doctor Norton, winking at George. "Like a lullaby."

Thea slipped in to see Bill next morning, when he was rested and the soreness was eased and he felt weak but himself again. She sat beside him on the bed.

"I made an awful fool of myself," he confessed.

"A lot of doctors do when they get sick the first time. They go neurotic."

"I guess everybody's off me."

"Not at all. You'll be in for some kidding probably. Some bright young one wrote this for the Coccidian Club show." She read from a scrap of paper:

> "Interne Tulliver, chloroformed,
>   Had dreams above his station;

He woke up thinking he'd performed
His own li'l operation."

"I guess I can stand it," said Bill. "I can stand anything when you're around; I'm so in love with you. But I suppose after this you'll always see me as about high-school age."

"If you'd had your first sickness at forty you'd have acted the same way."

"I hear your friend Durfee did a brilliant job, as usual," he said resentfully.

"Yes," she agreed; after a minute she added: "He wants to break his engagement and marry me on my own terms."

His heart stopped beating. "And what did you say?"

"I said No."

Life resumed itself again.

"Come closer," he whispered. "Where's your hand? Will you, anyhow, go swimming with me every night all the rest of September?"

"Every other night."

"Every night."

"Well, every hot night," she compromised.

Thea stood up.

He saw her eyes fix momentarily on some distant spot, linger there for a moment as if she were drawing support from it; then she leaned over him and kissed his hungry lips good-by, and faded back into her own mystery, into those woods where she hunted, with an old suffering and with a memory he could not share.

But what was valuable in it she had distilled; she knew how to pass it along so that it would not disappear. For the moment Bill had had more than his share, and reluctantly he relinquished her.

"This has been my biggest case so far," he thought sleepily.

The verse to the Coccidian Club song passed through his mind, and the chorus echoed on, singing him into deep sleep:

> *Bumtiddy, bum-bum,*
> *Tiddy-bum-bum.*
> *Three thousand years ago,*
> *Three thousand years ago.*

THE FIEND

On June 3, 1895, on a country road near Stillwater, Minnesota, Mrs. Crenshaw Engels and her seven year old son, Mark, were waylaid and murdered by a fiend, under circumstances so atrocious that, fortunately, it is not necessary to set them down here.

Crenshaw Engels, the husband and father, was a photographer in Stillwater. He was a great reader and considered "a little unsafe," for he had spoken his mind frankly about the railroad-agrarian struggles of the time—but no one denied that he was a devoted family man, and the catastrophe visited upon him hung over the little town for many weeks. There was a move to lynch the perpetrator of the horror, for Minnesota did not permit the capital punishment it deserved, but the instigators were foiled by the big stone penitentiary close at hand.

The cloud hung over Engel's home so that folks went there only in moods of penitence, of fear or guilt, hoping that they would be visited in turn should their lives ever chance to trek under a black sky. The photography studio suffered also: the routine of being posed, the necessary silences and pauses in the process, permitted the clients too much time to regard the prematurely aged face of Crenshaw Engels, and high school students, newly married couples, mothers of new babies, were always glad to escape from the place into the open air. So Crenshaw's business fell off and he went through a time of hardship—finally liquidating the lease, the apparatus and the good will, and wearing out the money obtained. He sold his house for a little more than its two mortgages, went to board and took a position clerking in Radamacher's Department Store.

In the sight of his neighbors he had become a man ruined by adversity, a man *manqué*, a man emptied. But in the last opinion they were wrong—he was empty of all save one thing. His memory was long as a Jew's, and though his heart was in the grave he was sane as when his wife and son had started on their last walk that summer morning. At the first trial he lost control and got at the Fiend, seizing him by the necktie—and then had been dragged off with the Fiend's tie in such a knot that the man was nearly garotted.

At the second trial Crenshaw cried aloud once. Afterwards he went to all the members of the state legislature in the county and handed them a bill he had written himself for the introduction of capital punishment in the state—the bill to be retroactive on criminals condemned to life imprisonment. The bill fell through; it was on the day Crenshaw heard this that he got inside the penitentiary by a ruse and was only apprehended in time to be prevented from shooting the Fiend in his cell.

Crenshaw was given a suspended sentence and for some months it was assumed that the agony was fading gradually from his mind. In fact when he presented himself to the warden in another rôle a year after the crime, the official was sympathetic to his statement that he had had a change of heart and felt he could only emerge from the valley of shadow by forgiveness, that he wanted to help the Fiend, show him the True Path by means of good books and appeals to his buried better nature. So, after being carefully searched, Crenshaw was permitted to sit for half an hour in the corridor outside the Fiend's cell.

But had the warden suspected the truth he would not have permitted the visit—for, far from forgiving, Crenshaw's plan was to wreak upon the Fiend a mental revenge to replace the physical one of which he was subducted.

When he faced the Fiend, Crenshaw felt his scalp tingle. From behind the bars a roly-poly man, who somehow made his convict's uniform resemble a business suit, a man with thick brown-rimmed glasses and the trim air of an insurance salesman, looked at him uncertainly. Feeling faint Crenshaw sat down in the chair that had been brought for him.

"The air around you stinks!" he cried suddenly. "This whole corridor, this whole prison."

"I suppose it does," admitted the Fiend, "I noticed it too."

"You'll have time to notice it," Crenshaw muttered. "All your life you'll pace up and down stinking in that little cell, with everything getting blacker and blacker. And after that there'll be hell waiting for you. For all eternity you'll be shut in a little space, but in hell it'll be so small that you can't stand up or stretch out."

"*Will* it now?" asked the Fiend concerned.

"It will!" said Crenshaw. "You'll be alone with your own vile thoughts in that little space, forever and ever and ever. You'll itch with corruption so that you can never sleep, and you'll always be thirsty, with water just out of reach."

"*Will* I now?" repeated the Fiend, even more concerned. "I remember once——"

"All the time you'll be full of horror," Crenshaw interrupted. "You'll be like a person just about to go crazy but can't go crazy. All the time you'll be thinking that it's forever and ever."

"That's bad," said the Fiend, shaking his head gloomily. "That's real bad."

"Now listen here to me," went on Crenshaw. "I've brought you some books you're going to read. It's arranged that you get no books or papers except what I bring you."

As a beginning Crenshaw had brought half a dozen books which his vagarious curiosity had collected over as many years. They comprised a German doctor's thousand case histories of sexual abnormality—cases with no cures, no hopes, no prognoses, cases listed cold; a series of sermons by a New England Divine of the Great Revival which pictured the tortures of the damned in hell; a collection of horror stories; and a volume of erotic pieces from each of which the last two pages, containing the consummations, had been torn out; a volume of detective stories mutilated in the same manner. A tome of the Newgate calendar completed the batch. These Crenshaw handed through the bars—the Fiend took them and put them on his iron cot.

This was the first of Crenshaw's long series of fortnightly visits. Always he brought with him something somber and menacing to say, something dark and terrible to read—save that once when the Fiend had had nothing to read for a long time he brought him four inspiringly titled books—that proved to have nothing but blank paper inside. Another time, pretending to concede a point, he promised to bring newspapers—he brought ten copies of the yellowed journal that had reported the crime and the arrest. Sometimes he obtained medical books that showed in color the red and blue and green ravages of leprosy and skin disease, the mounds of shattered cells, the verminous tissue and brown corrupted blood.

And there was no sewer of the publishing world from which he did not obtain records of all that was gross and vile in man.

Crenshaw could not keep this up indefinitely both because of the expense and because of the exhaustibility of such books. When five years had passed he leaned toward another form of torture. He built up false hopes in the Fiend with protests of his own change of heart and manoeuvres for a pardon, and then dashed the hopes to pieces. Or else he pretended to have a pistol with him, or an inflammatory substance that would make the cell a raging Inferno and consume the Fiend in two minutes—once he threw a dummy bottle into the cell and listened in delight to the screams as the Fiend ran back and forth waiting for the explosion. At other times he would pretend grimly that the legislature had passed a new law which provided that the Fiend would be executed in a few hours.

A decade passed. Crenshaw was gray at forty—he was white at fifty when the alternating routine of his fortnightly visits to the graves of his loved ones and to the penitentiary had become the only part of his life—the long days at Radamacher's were only a weary dream. Sometimes he went and sat outside the Fiend's cell, with no word said during the half hour he was allowed to be there. The Fiend too had grown white in twenty years. He was very respectable-looking with his horn-rimmed glasses and his white hair. He seemed to have a great respect for Crenshaw and even when the latter, in a renewal of diminishing vitality, promised him one day that on his very next visit he was going to bring a revolver and end the matter, he nodded gravely as if in agreement, said, "I suppose so. Yes, I suppose you're perfectly right," and did not mention the matter to the guards. On the occasion of the next visit he was waiting with his hands on the bars of the cell looking at Crenshaw both hopefully and desperately. At certain tensions and strains death takes on, indeed, the quality of a great adventure as any soldier can testify.

Years passed. Crenshaw was promoted to floor manager at Radamacher's—there were new generations now that did not know of his tragedy and regarded him as an austere nonentity. He came into a little legacy and bought new stones for the graves of his wife and son. He knew he would soon be retired and while a third decade lapsed through the white winters, the short sweet smoky summers, it became more and more plain to him that the time had come to put an end to the Fiend; to avoid any mischance by which the other would survive him.

The moment he fixed upon came at the exact end of thirty years. Crenshaw had long owned the pistol with which it would be accomplished; he had fingered the shells lovingly and calculated the lodgement of each in the Fiend's body, so that death would be sure but lingering—he studied the tales of abdominal wounds in the war news and delighted in the agony that made victims pray to be killed.

After that, what happened to *him* did not matter.

When the day came he had no trouble in smuggling the pistol into the penitentiary. But to his surprise he found the Fiend scrunched up upon his iron cot, instead of waiting for him avidly by the bars.

"I'm sick," the Fiend said. "My stomach's been burning me up all morning. They gave me a physic but now it's worse and nobody comes."

Crenshaw fancied momentarily that this was a premonition in the man's bowels of a bullet that would shortly ride ragged through that spot.

"Come up to the bars," he said mildly.

"I can't move."

"Yes, you can."

"I'm doubled up. All doubled up."

"Come doubled up then."

With an effort the Fiend moved himself, only to fall on his side on the cement floor. He groaned and then lay quiet for a minute, after which, still bent in two, he began to drag himself a foot at a time toward the bars.

Suddenly Crenshaw set off at a run toward the end of the corridor.

"I want the prison doctor," he demanded of the guard, "That man's sick—*sick*, I tell you."

"The doctor has——"

"Get him—get him now!"

The guard hesitated, but Crenshaw had become a tolerated, even privileged person around the prison, and in a moment the guard took down his phone and called the infirmary.

All that afternoon Crenshaw waited in the bare area inside the gates, walking up and down with his hands behind his back. From time to time he went to the front entrance and demanded of the guard:

"Any news?"

"Nothing yet. They'll call me when there's anything."

Late in the afternoon the Warden appeared at the door, looked about and spotted Crenshaw. The latter, all alert, hastened over.

"He's dead," the Warden said. "His appendix burst. They did everything they could."

"Dead," Crenshaw repeated.

"I'm sorry to bring you this news. I know how——"

"It's all right," said Crenshaw, and licking his lips. "So he's dead."

The Warden lit a cigarette.

"While you're here, Mr. Engels, I wonder if you can let me have that pass that was issued to you—I can turn it in to the office. That is—I suppose you won't need it any more."

Crenshaw took the blue card from his wallet and handed it over. The Warden shook hands with him.

"One thing more," Crenshaw demanded as the Warden turned away. "Which is the—the window of the infirmary?"

"It's on the interior court, you can't see it from here."

"Oh."

When the Warden had gone Crenshaw still stood there a long time, the tears running out down his face. He could not collect his thoughts and he began by trying to remember what day it was; Saturday, the day, every other week, on which he came to see the Fiend.

He would not see the Fiend two weeks from now.

In a misery of solitude and despair he muttered aloud: "So he is dead. He has left me." And then with a long sigh of mingled grief and fear, "So I have lost him—my only friend—now I am alone."

He was still saying that to himself as he passed through the outer gate, and as his coat caught in the great swing of the outer door the guard opened up to release it, he heard a reiteration of the words:

"I'm alone. At last—at last I am alone."

Once more he called on the Fiend, after many weeks.

"But he's dead," the Warden told him kindly.

"Oh, yes," Crenshaw said. "I guess I must have forgotten."

And he set off back home, his boots sinking deep into the white diamond surface of the flats.

BABYLON REVISITED

And where's Mr. Campbell?" Charlie asked.

"Gone to Switzerland. Mr. Campbell's a pretty sick man, Mr. Wales."

"I'm sorry to hear that. And George Hardt?" Charlie inquired.

"Back in America, gone to work."

"And where is the Snow Bird?"

"He was in here last week. Anyway, his friend, Mr. Schaeffer, is in Paris."

Two familiar names from the long list of a year and a half ago. Charlie scribbled an address in his notebook and tore out the page.

"If you see Mr. Schaeffer, give him this," he said. "It's my brother-in-law's address. I haven't settled on a hotel yet."

He was not really disappointed to find Paris was so empty. But the stillness in the Ritz bar was strange and portentous. It was not an American bar any more—he felt polite in it, and not as if he owned it. It had gone back into France. He felt the stillness from the moment he got out of the taxi and saw the doorman, usually in a frenzy of activity at this hour, gossiping with a *chasseur* by the servants' entrance.

Passing through the corridor, he heard only a single, bored voice in the once-clamorous women's room. When he turned into the bar he travelled the twenty feet of green carpet with his eyes fixed straight ahead by old habit; and then, with his foot firmly on the rail, he turned and surveyed the room, encountering only a single pair of eyes that fluttered up from a newspaper in the corner. Charlie asked for the head barman, Paul, who in the latter days of the bull market had come to work in his own custom-built car—disembarking, however, with due nicety at the nearest corner. But Paul was at his country house today and Alix giving him information.

"No, no more," Charlie said, "I'm going slow these days."

Alix congratulated him: "You were going pretty strong a couple of years ago."

"I'll stick to it all right," Charlie assured him. "I've stuck to it for over a year and a half now."

"How do you find conditions in America?"

"I haven't been to America for months. I'm in business in Prague, representing a couple of concerns there. They don't know about me down there."

Alix smiled.

"Remember the night of George Hardt's bachelor dinner here?" said Charlie. "By the way, what's become of Claude Fessenden?"

Alix lowered his voice confidentially: "He's in Paris, but he doesn't come here any more. Paul doesn't allow it. He ran up a bill of thirty thousand francs, charging all his drinks and his lunches, and usually his dinner, for more than a year. And when Paul finally told him he had to pay, he gave him a bad check."

Alix shook his head sadly.

"I don't understand it, such a dandy fellow. Now he's all bloated up—" He made a plump apple of his hands.

Charlie watched a group of strident queens installing themselves in a corner.

"Nothing affects them," he thought. "Stocks rise and fall, people loaf or work, but they go on forever." The place oppressed him. He called for the dice and shook with Alix for the drink.

"Here for long, Mr. Wales?"

"I'm here for four or five days to see my little girl."

"Oh-h! You have a little girl?"

Outside, the fire-red, gas-blue, ghost-green signs shone smokily through the tranquil rain. It was late afternoon and the streets were in movement; the *bistros* gleamed. At the corner of the Boulevard des Capucines he took a taxi. The Place de la Concorde moved by in pink majesty; they crossed the logical Seine, and Charlie felt the sudden provincial quality of the left bank.

Charlie directed his taxi to the Avenue de l'Opera, which was out of his way. But he wanted to see the blue hour spread over the magnificent facade, and imagine that the cab horns, playing end-lessly the first few bars of *Le Plus que Lent,* were the trumpets of the Second Empire. They were closing the iron grill in front of Brentano's Book-store, and people were already at dinner behind the trim little bourgeois hedge of Duval's. He had never eaten at a really cheap restaurant in Paris. Five-course dinner, four francs fifty, eighteen cents, wine included. For some odd reason he wished that he had.

As they rolled on to the Left Bank and he felt its sudden provincialism, he thought, "I spoiled this city for myself. I didn't realize it, but the days came along one after another, and then two years were gone, and everything was gone, and I was gone."

He was thirty-five, and good to look at. The Irish mobility of his face was sobered by a deep wrinkle between his eyes. As he rang his brother-in-law's bell in the Rue Palatine, the wrinkle deepened till it pulled down his brows; he felt a cramping sensation in his belly. From behind the maid who opened the door darted a lovely little girl of nine who shrieked "Daddy!" and flew up, struggling like a fish, into his arms. She pulled his head around by one ear and set her cheek against his.

"My old pie," he said.

"Oh, daddy, daddy, daddy, daddy, dads, dads, dads!"

She drew him into the salon, where the family waited, a boy and girl his daughter's age, his sister-in-law and her husband. He greeted Marion with his voice pitched carefully to avoid either feigned enthusiasm or dislike, but her response was more frankly tepid, though she minimized her expression of unalterable distrust by directing her regard toward his child. The two men clasped hands in a friendly way and Lincoln Peters rested his for a moment on Charlie's shoulder.

The room was warm and comfortably American. The three children moved intimately about, playing through the yellow oblongs that led to other rooms; the cheer of six o'clock spoke in the eager smacks of the fire and the sounds of French activity in the kitchen. But Charlie did not relax; his heart sat up rigidly in his body and he drew confidence from his daughter, who from time to time came close to him, holding in her arms the doll he had brought.

"Really extremely well," he declared in answer to Lincoln's question. "There's a lot of business there that isn't moving at all, but we're doing even better than ever. In fact, damn well. I'm bringing my sister over from America next month to keep house for me. My income last year was bigger than it was when I had money. You see, the Czechs——"

His boasting was for a specific purpose; but after a moment, seeing a faint restiveness in Lincoln's eye, he changed the subject:

"Those are fine children of yours, well brought up, good manners."

"We think Honoria's a great little girl too."

Marion Peters came back from the kitchen. She was a tall woman with worried eyes, who had once possessed a fresh American loveliness. Charlie had never been sensitive to it and was always surprised when people spoke of how pretty she had been. From the first there had been an instinctive antipathy between them.

"Well, how do you find Honoria?" she asked.

"Wonderful. I was astonished how much she's grown in ten months. All the children are looking well."

"We haven't had a doctor for a year. How do you like being back in Paris?"

"It seems very funny to see so few Americans around."

"I'm delighted," Marion said vehemently. "Now at least you can go into a store without their assuming you're a millionaire. We've suffered like everybody, but on the whole it's a good deal pleasanter."

"But it was nice while it lasted," Charlie said. "We were a sort of royalty, almost infallible, with a sort of magic around us. In the bar this afternoon"—he stumbled, seeing his mistake—"there wasn't a man I knew."

She looked at him keenly. "I should think you'd have had enough of bars."

"I only stayed a minute. I take one drink every afternoon, and no more."

"Don't you want a cocktail before dinner?" Lincoln asked.

"I take only one drink every afternoon, and I've had that."

"I hope you keep to it," said Marion.

Her dislike was evident in the coldness with which she spoke, but Charlie only smiled; he had larger plans. Her very aggressiveness gave him an advantage, and he knew enough to wait. He wanted them to initiate the discussion of what they knew had brought him to Paris.

At dinner he couldn't decide whether Honoria was most like him or her mother. Fortunate if she didn't combine the traits of both that had brought them to disaster. A great wave of protectiveness went over him. He thought he knew what to do for her. He believed in character; he wanted to jump back a whole generation and trust in character again as the eternally valuable element. Everything wore out.

He left soon after dinner, but not to go home. He was curious to see Paris by night with clearer and more judicious eyes than those of other days. He bought a *strapontin* for the Casino and watched Josephine Baker go through her chocolate arabesques.

After an hour he left and strolled toward Montmartre, up the Rue Pigalle into the Place Blanche. The rain had stopped and there were a few people in evening clothes disembarking from taxis in front of cabarets, and *cocottes* prowling singly or in pairs, and many Negroes. He passed a lighted door from which issued music, and stopped with the sense of familiarity; it was Bricktop's, where he had parted with so many hours and so much money. A few doors farther on he found another ancient rendezvous and incautiously put his head inside. Immediately an eager orchestra burst into sound, a pair of professional dancers leaped to their feet and a maître d'hôtel swooped toward him, crying, "Crowd just arriving, sir!" But he withdrew quickly.

"You have to be damn drunk," he thought.

Zelli's was closed, the bleak and sinister cheap hotels surrounding it were dark; up in the Rue Blanche there was more light and a local, colloquial French crowd. The Poet's Cave had disappeared, but the two great mouths of the Café of Heaven and the Café of Hell still yawned—even devoured, as he watched, the meagre contents of a tourist bus—a German, a Japanese, and an American couple who glanced at him with frightened eyes.

So much for the effort and ingenuity of Montmartre. All the catering to vice and waste was on an utterly childish scale, and he suddenly realized the meaning of the word "dissipate"—to dissipate into thin air; to make nothing out of something. In the little hours of the night every move from place to place was an enormous human jump, an increase of paying for the privilege of slower and slower motion.

He remembered thousand-franc notes given to an orchestra for playing a single number, hundred-franc notes tossed to a doorman for calling a cab.

But it hadn't been given for nothing.

It had been given, even the most wildly squandered sum, as an offering to destiny that he might not remember the things most worth remembering, the things that now he would always remember —his child taken from his control, his wife escaped to a grave in Vermont.

In the glare of a *brasserie* a woman spoke to him. He bought her some eggs and coffee, and then, eluding her encouraging stare, gave her a twenty-franc note and took a taxi to his hotel.

II

He woke upon a fine fall day—football weather. The depression of yesterday was gone and he liked the people on the streets. At noon he sat opposite Honoria at Le Grand Vatel, the only restaurant he could think of not reminiscent of champagne dinners and long luncheons that began at two and ended in a blurred and vague twilight.

"Now, how about vegetables? Oughtn't you to have some vegetables?"

"Well, yes."

"Here's *épinards* and *chou-fleur* and carrots and *haricots*."

"I'd like *chou-fleur*."

"Wouldn't you like to have two vegetables?"

"I usually only have one at lunch."

The waiter was pretending to be inordinately fond of children. "*Qu'elle est mignonne la petite? Elle parle exactement comme une francaise.*"

"How about dessert? Shall we wait and see?"

The waiter disappeared. Honoria looked at her father expectantly.

"What are we going to do?"

"First, we're going to that toy store in the Rue Saint-Honoré and buy you anything you like. And then we're going to the vaudeville at the Empire."

She hesitated. "I like it about the vaudeville, but not the toy store."

"Why not?"

"Well, you brought me this doll." She had it with her "And I've got lots of things. And we're not rich any more, are we?"

"We never were. But today you are to have anything you want."

"All right," she agreed resignedly.

When there had been her mother and a French nurse he had been inclined to be strict; now he extended himself, reached out for a new tolerance; he must be both parents to her and not shut any of her out of communication.

"I want to get to know you," he said gravely. "First let me introduce myself. My name is Charles J. Wales, of Prague."

"Oh, daddy!" her voice cracked with laughter.

"And who are you, please?" he persisted, and she accepted a rôle immediately: "Honoria Wales, Rue Palatine, Paris."

"Married or single?"

"No, not married. Single."

He indicated the doll. "But I see you have a child, madame."

Unwilling to disinherit it, she took it to her heart and thought quickly: "Yes, I've been married, but I'm not married now. My husband is dead."

He went on quickly, "And the child's name?"

"Simone. That's after my best friend at school."

"I'm very pleased that you're doing so well at school."

"I'm third this month," she boasted. "Elsie"—that was her cousin—"is only about eighteenth, and Richard is about at the bottom."

"You like Richard and Elsie, don't you?"

"Oh, yes. I like Richard quite well and I like her all right."

Cautiously and casually he asked: "And Aunt Marion and Uncle Lincoln—which do you like best?"

"Oh, Uncle Lincoln, I guess."

He was increasingly aware of her presence. As they came in, a murmur of ". . . adorable" followed them, and now the people at the next table bent all their silences upon her, staring as if she were something no more conscious than a flower.

"Why don't I live with you?" she asked suddenly. "Because mamma's dead?"

"You must stay here and learn more French. It would have been hard for daddy to take care of you so well."

"I don't really need much taking care of any more. I do everything for myself."

Going out of the restaurant, a man and a woman unexpectedly hailed him!

"Well, the old Wales!"

"Hello there, Lorraine. . . . Dunc."

Sudden ghosts out of the past: Duncan Schaeffer, a friend from college. Lorraine Quarrles, a lovely, pale blonde of thirty; one of a crowd who had helped them make months into days in the lavish times of three years ago.

"My husband couldn't come this year," she said, in answer to his question. "We're poor as hell. So he gave me two hundred a month and told me I could do my worst on that. . . . This your little girl?"

"What about coming back and sitting down?" Duncan asked.

"Can't do it." He was glad for an excuse. As always, he felt Lorraine's passionate, provocative attraction, but his own rhythm was different now.

"Well, how about dinner?" she asked.

"I'm not free. Give me your address and let me call you."

"Charlie, I believe you're sober," she said judicially. "I honestly believe he's sober, Dunc. Pinch him and see if he's sober."

Charlie indicated Honoria with his head. They both laughed.

"What's your address?" said Duncan sceptically.

He hesitated, unwilling to give the name of his hotel.

"I'm not settled yet. I'd better call you. We're going to see the vaudeville at the Empire."

"There! That's what I want to do," Lorraine said. "I want to see some clowns and acrobats and jugglers. That's just what we'll do, Dunc."

"We've got to do an errand first," said Charlie. "Perhaps we'll see you there."

"All right, you snob. . . . Good-by, beautiful little girl."

"Good-by."

Honoria bobbed politely.

Somehow, an unwelcome encounter. They liked him because he was functioning, because he was serious; they wanted to see him, because he was stronger than they were now, because they wanted to draw a certain sustenance from his strength.

At the Empire, Honoria proudly refused to sit upon her father's folded coat. She was already an individual with a code of her own, and Charlie was more and more absorbed by the desire of putting a little of himself into her before she crystallized utterly. It was hopeless to try to know her in so short a time.

Between the acts they came upon Duncan and Lorraine in the lobby where the band was playing.

"Have a drink?"

"All right, but not up at the bar. We'll take a table."

"The perfect father."

Listening abstractedly to Lorraine, Charlie watched Honoria's eyes leave their table, and he followed them wistfully about the room, wondering what they saw. He met her glance and she smiled.

"I like that lemonade," she said.

What had she said? What had he expected? Going home in a taxi afterward, he pulled her over until her head rested against his chest.

"Darling, do you ever think about your mother?"

"Yes, sometimes," she answered vaguely.

"I don't want you to forget her. Have you got a picture of her?"

"Yes, I think so. Anyhow, Aunt Marion has. Why don't you want me to forget her?"

"She loved you very much."

"I loved her too."

They were silent for a moment.

"Daddy, I want to come and live with you," she said suddenly.

His heart leaped; he had wanted it to come like this.

"Aren't you perfectly happy?"

"Yes, but I love you better than anybody. And you love me better than anybody, don't you, now that mummy's dead?"

"Of course I do. But you won't always like me best, honey. You'll grow up and meet somebody your own age and go marry him and forget you ever had a daddy."

"Yes, that's true," she agreed tranquilly.

He didn't go in. He was coming back at nine o'clock and he wanted to keep himself fresh and new for the thing he must say then.

"When you're safe inside, just show yourself in that window."

"All right. Good-by, dads, dads, dads, dads."

He waited in the dark street until she appeared, all warm and glowing, in the window above and kissed her fingers out into the night.

III

They were waiting. Marion sat behind the coffee service in a dignified black dinner dress that just faintly suggested mourning. Lincoln was walking up and down with the animation of one who had already been talking. They were as anxious as he was to get into the question. He opened it almost immediately:

"I suppose you know what I want to see you about—why I really came to Paris."

Marion played with the black stars on her necklace and frowned.

"I'm awfully anxious to have a home," he continued. "And I'm awfully anxious to have Honoria in it. I appreciate your taking in Honoria for her mother's sake, but things have changed now"—he hesitated and then continued more forcibly—"changed radically with me, and I want to ask you to reconsider the matter. It would be silly for me to deny that about three years ago I was acting badly——"

Marion looked up at him with hard eyes.

"—but all that's over. As I told you, I haven't had more than a drink a day for over a year, and I take that drink deliberately, so that the idea of alcohol won't get too big in my imagination. You see the idea?"

"No," said Marion succinctly.

"It's a sort of stunt I set myself. It keeps the matter in proportion."

"I get you," said Lincoln. "You don't want to admit it's got any attraction for you."

"Something like that. Sometimes I forget and don't take it. But I try to take it. Anyhow, I couldn't afford to drink in my position.

The people I represent are more than satisfied with what I've done, and I'm bringing my sister over from Burlington to keep house for me, and I want awfully to have Honoria too. You know that even when her mother and I weren't getting along well we never let anything that happened touch Honoria. I know she's fond of me and I know I'm able to take care of her and—well, there you are. How do you feel about it?"

He knew that now he would have to take a beating. It would last an hour or two hours, and it would be difficult, but if he modulated his inevitable resentment to the chastened attitude of the reformed sinner, he might win his point in the end.

Keep your temper, he told himself. You don't want to be justified. You want Honoria.

Lincoln spoke first: "We've been talking it over ever since we got your letter last month. We're happy to have Honoria here. She's a dear little thing, and we're glad to be able to help her, but of course that isn't the question——"

Marion interrupted suddenly. "How long are you going to stay sober, Charlie?" she asked.

"Permanently, I hope."

"How can anybody count on that?"

"You know I never did drink heavily until I gave up business and came over here with nothing to do. Then Helen and I began to run around with——"

"Please leave Helen out of it. I can't bear to hear you talk about her like that."

He stared at her grimly; he had never been certain how fond of each other the sisters were in life.

"My drinking only lasted about a year and a half—from the time we came over until I—collapsed."

"It was time enough."

"It was time enough," he agreed.

"My duty is entirely to Helen," she said. "I try to think what she would have wanted me to do. Frankly, from the night you did that terrible thing you haven't really existed for me. I can't help that. She was my sister."

"Yes."

"When she was dying she asked me to look out for Honoria. If you hadn't been in a sanitarium then, it might have helped matters."

He had no answer.

"I'll never in my life be able to forget the morning when Helen knocked at my door, soaked to the skin and shivering, and said you'd locked her out."

Charlie gripped the sides of the chair. This was more difficult than he expected; he wanted to launch out into a long expostulation and explanation, but he only said: "The night I locked her out—" and she interrupted, "I don't feel up to going over that again."

After a moment's silence Lincoln said: "We're getting off the subject. You want Marion to set aside her legal guardianship and give you Honoria. I think the main point for her is whether she has confidence in you or not."

"I don't blame Marion," Charlie said slowly, "but I think she can have entire confidence in me. I had a good record up to three years ago. Of course, it's within human possibilities I might go wrong any time. But if we wait much longer I'll lose Honoria's childhood and my chance for a home." He shook his head, "I'll simply lose her, don't you see?"

"Yes, I see," said Lincoln.

"Why didn't you think of all this before?" Marion asked.

"I suppose I did, from time to time, but Helen and I were getting along badly. When I consented to the guardianship, I was flat on my back in a sanitarium and the market had cleaned me out. I knew I'd acted badly, and I thought if it would bring any peace to Helen, I'd agree to anything. But now it's different. I'm functioning, I'm behaving damn well, so far as——"

"Please don't swear at me," Marion said.

He looked at her, startled. With each remark the force of her dislike became more and more apparent. She had built up all her fear of life into one wall and faced it toward him. This trivial reproof was possibly the result of some trouble with the cook several hours before. Charlie became increasingly alarmed at leaving Honoria in this atmosphere of hostility against himself; sooner or later it would come out, in a word here, a shake of the head there, and some of that distrust would be irrevocably implanted in Honoria. But he pulled his temper down out of his face and shut it up inside him; he had won a point, for Lincoln realized the absurdity of Marion's remark and asked her lightly since when she had objected to the word "damn."

"Another thing," Charlie said: "I'm able to give her certain advantages now. I'm going to take a French governess to Prague with me. I've got a lease on a new apartment——"

He stopped, realizing that he was blundering. They couldn't be expected to accept with equanimity the fact that his income was again twice as large as their own.

"I suppose you can give her more luxuries than we can," said Marion. "When you were throwing away money we were living along watching every ten francs. . . . I suppose you'll start doing it again."

"Oh, no," he said. "I've learned. I worked hard for ten years, you know—until I got lucky in the market, like so many people. Terribly lucky. It didn't seem any use working any more, so I quit. It won't happen again."

There was a long silence. All of them felt their nerves straining, and for the first time in a year Charlie wanted a drink. He was sure now that Lincoln Peters wanted him to have his child.

Marion shuddered suddenly; part of her saw that Charlie's feet were planted on the earth now, and her own maternal feeling recognized the naturalness of his desire; but she had lived for a long time with a prejudice—a prejudice founded on a curious disbelief in her sister's happiness, and which, in the shock of one terrible night, had turned to hatred for him. It had all happened at a point in her life where the discouragement of ill health and adverse circumstances made it necessary for her to believe in tangible villainy and a tangible villain.

"I can't help what I think!" she cried out suddenly. "How much you were responsible for Helen's death, I don't know. It's something you'll have to square with your own conscience."

An electric current of agony surged through him; for a moment he was almost on his feet, an unuttered sound echoing in his throat. He hung on to himself for a moment, another moment.

"Hold on there," said Lincoln uncomfortably. "I never thought you were responsible for that."

"Helen died of heart trouble," Charlie said dully.

"Yes, heart trouble." Marion spoke as if the phrase had another meaning for her.

Then, in the flatness that followed her outburst, she saw him plainly and she knew he had somehow arrived at control over the situation. Glancing at her husband, she found no help from him, and as abruptly as if it were a matter of no importance, she threw up the sponge.

"Do what you like!" she cried, springing up from her chair. "She's your child. I'm not the person to stand in your way. I think if it were my child I'd rather see her—" She managed to check herself. "You two decide it. I can't stand this. I'm sick. I'm going to bed."

She hurried from the room; after a moment Lincoln said:

"This has been a hard day for her. You know how strongly she feels—" His voice was almost apologetic: "When a woman gets an idea in her head."

"Of course."

"It's going to be all right. I think she sees now that you—can provide for the child, and so we can't very well stand in your way or Honoria's way."

"Thank you, Lincoln."

"I'd better go along and see how she is."

"I'm going."

He was still trembling when he reached the street, but a walk down the Rue Bonaparte to the quais set him up, and as he crossed the Seine, fresh and new by the quai lamps, he felt exultant. But back in his room he couldn't sleep. The image of Helen haunted him. Helen whom he had loved so until they had senselessly begun to abuse each other's love, tear it into shreds. On that terrible February night that Marion remembered so vividly, a slow quarrel had gone on for hours. There was a scene at the Florida, and then he attempted to take her home, and then she kissed young Webb at a table; after that there was what she had hysterically said. When he arrived home alone he turned the key in the lock in wild anger. How could he know she would arrive an hour later alone, that there would be a snowstorm in which she wandered about in slippers, too confused to find a taxi? Then the aftermath, her escaping pneumonia by a miracle, and all the attendant horror. They were "reconciled," but that was the beginning of the end, and Marion, who had seen with her own eyes and who imagined it to be one of many scenes from her sister's martyrdom, never forgot.

Going over it again brought Helen nearer, and in the white, soft light that steals upon half sleep near morning he found himself talking to her again. She said that he was perfectly right about Honoria and she she wanted Honoria to be with him. She said she was glad he was being good and doing better. She said a lot of other things— very friendly things—but she was in a swing in a white dress, and swinging faster and faster all the time, so that at the end he could not hear clearly all that she said.

IV

He woke up feeling happy. The door of the world was open again. He made plans, vistas, futures for Honoria and himself, but suddenly he grew sad, remembering all the plans he and Helen had made. She had not planned to die. The present was the thing—work to do and someone to love. But not to love too much, for he knew the injury that a father can do to a daughter or a mother to a son by attaching them too closely; afterward, out in the world, the child would seek in the marriage partner the same blind tenderness and, failing probably to find it, turn against love and life.

It was another bright, crisp day. He called Lincoln Peters at the bank where he worked and asked if he could count on taking Honoria when he left for Prague. Lincoln agreed that there was no reason for delay. One thing—the legal guardianship. Marion wanted to retain that a while longer. She was upset by the whole matter, and it would oil things if she felt that the situation was still in her control for another year. Charlie agreed, wanted only the tangible, visible child.

Then the question of a governess. Charlie sat in a gloomy agency and talked to a cross Bernaise and to a buxom Breton peasant, neither of whom he could have endured. There were others whom he would see tomorrow.

He lunched with Lincoln Peters at Griffons, trying to keep down his exultation.

"There's nothing quite like your own child," Lincoln said. "But you understand how Marion feels to."

"She's forgotten how hard I worked for seven years there," Charlie said. "She just remembers one night."

"There's another thing." Lincoln hesitated. "While you and Helen were tearing around Europe throwing money away, we were just getting along. I didn't touch any of the prosperity because I never got ahead enough to carry anything but my insurance. I think Marion felt there was some kind of injustice in it—you not even working toward the end, and getting richer and richer."

"It went just as quick as it came," said Charlie.

"Yes, a lot of it stayed in the hands of *chasseurs* and saxophone players and maîtres d'hôtel—well, the big party's over now. I just said that to explain Marion's feeling about those crazy years. If you drop in about six o'clock tonight before Marion's too tired, we'll settle the details on the spot."

Back at his hotel, Charlie found a *pneumatique* that had been redirected from the Ritz bar where Charlie had left his address for the purpose of finding a certain man.

DEAR CHARLIE: You were so strange when we saw you the other day that I wondered if I did something to offend you. If so, I'm not conscious of it. In fact, I have thought about you too much for the last year, and it's always been in the back of my mind that I might see you if I came over here. We *did* have such good times that crazy spring, like the night you and I stole the butcher's tricycle, and the time we tried to call on the president and you had the old derby rim and the wire cane. Everybody seems so old lately, but I don't feel old a bit. Couldn't we get together some time today for old time's sake? I'ce got a vile hang-over for the moment, but will be feeling better this afternoon and will look for you about five in the sweat-shop at the Ritz.

Always devotedly,

LORRAINE.

His first feeling was one of awe that he had actually, in his mature years, stolen a tricycle and pedalled Lorraine all over the Étoile between the small hours and dawn. In retrospect it was a nightmare. Locking out Helen didn't fit in with any other act of his life, but the tricycle incident did—it was one of many. How many weeks or months of dissipation to arrive at that condition of utter irresponsibility?

He tried to picture how Lorraine had appeared to him then— very attractive; Helen was unhappy about it, though she said nothing. Yesterday, in the restaurant, Lorraine had seemed trite, blurred, worn away. He emphatically did not want to see her, and he was glad Alix had not given away his hotel address. It was a relief to think, instead, of Honoria, to think of Sundays spent with her and of saying good morning to her and of knowing she was there in his house at night, drawing her breath in the darkness.

At five he took a taxi and bought presents for all the Peters—a piquant cloth doll, a box of Roman soldiers, flowers for Marion, big linen handkerchiefs for Lincoln.

He saw, when he arrived in the apartment, that Marion had accepted the inevitable. She greeted him now as though he were a recalcitrant member of the family, rather than a menacing outsider. Honoria had been told she was going; Charlie was glad to see that her tact made her conceal her excessive happiness. Only on his lap did she whisper her delight and the question "When?" before she slipped away with the other children.

He and Marion were alone for a minute in the room, and on an impulse he spoke out boldly:

"Family quarrels are bitter things. They don't go according to any rules. They're not like aches or wounds; they're more like splits in the skin that won't heal because there's not enough material. I wish you and I could be on better terms."

"Some things are hard to forget," she answered. "It's a question of confidence." There was no answer to this and presently she asked, "When do you propose to take her?"

"As soon as I can get a governess. I hoped the day after tomorrow."

"That's impossible. I've got to get her things in shape. Not before Saturday."

He yielded. Coming back into the room, Lincoln offered him a drink.

"I'll take my daily whisky," he said.

It was warm here, it was a home, people together by a fire. The children felt very safe and important; the mother and father were serious, watchful. They had things to do for the children more important than his visit here. A spoonful of medicine was, after all, more important than the strained relations between Marion and himself. They were not dull people, but they were very much in the grip of life and circumstances. He wondered if he couldn't do something to get Lincoln out of his rut at the bank.

A long peal at the door-bell; the *bonne à toute faire* passed through and went down the corridor. The door opened upon another long ring, and then voices, and the three in the salon looked up expectantly; Richard moved to bring the corridor within his range of vision, and Marion rose. Then the maid came back along the corridor, closely followed by the voices, which developed under the light into Duncan Schaeffer and Lorraine Quarrles.

They were gay, they were hilarious, they were roaring with laughter. For a moment Charlie was astounded; unable to understand how they ferreted out the Peters' address.

"Ah-h-h!" Duncan wagged his finger roguishly at Charlie. "Ah-h-h!"

They both slid down another cascade of laughter. Anxious and at a loss, Charlie shook hands with them quickly and presented them to Lincoln and Marion. Marion nodded, scarcely speaking. She had drawn back a step toward the fire; her little girl stood beside her, and Marion put an arm about her shoulder.

With growing annoyance at the intrusion, Charlie waited for them to explain themselves. After some concentration Duncan said:

"We came to invite you out to dinner. Lorraine and I insist that all this shishi, cagy business 'bout your address got to stop."

Charlie came closer to them, as if to force them backward down the corridor.

"Sorry, but I can't. Tell me where you'll be and I'll phone you in half an hour."

This made no impression. Lorraine sat down suddenly on the side of a chair, and focussing her eyes on Richard, cried, "Oh, what a nice little boy! Come here, little boy." Richard glanced at his mother, but did not move. With a perceptible shrug of her shoulders, Lorraine turned back to Charlie:

"Come and dine. Sure your cousins won' mine. See you so sel'om. Or solemn."

"I can't," said Charlie sharply. "You two have dinner and I'll phone you."

Her voice became suddenly unpleasant. "All right, we'll go. But I remember once when you hammered on my door at four A.M. I was enough of a good sport to give you a drink. Come on, Dunc."

Still in slow motion, with blurred, angry faces, with uncertain feet, they retired along the corridor.

"Good night," Charlie said.

"Good night!" responded Lorraine emphatically.

When he went back into the salon Marion had not moved, only now her son was standing in the circle of her other arm. Lincoln was still swinging Honoria back and forth like a pendulum from side to side.

"What an outrage!" Charlie broke out. "What an absolute outrage!"

Neither of them answered. Charlie dropped into an armchair, picked up his drink, set it down again and said:

"People I haven't seen for two years having the colossal nerve——"

He broke off. Marion had made the sound "Oh!" in one swift, furious breath, turned her body from him with a jerk and left the room.

Lincoln set down Honoria carefully.

"You children go in and start your soup," he said, and when they obeyed, he said to Charlie:

"Marion's not well and she can't stand shocks. That kind of people make her really physically sick."

"I didn't tell them to come here. They wormed your name out of somebody. They deliberately——"

"Well, it's too bad. It doesn't help matters. Excuse me a minute."

Left alone, Charlie sat tense in his chair. In the next room he could hear the children eating, talking in monosyllables, already oblivious to the scene between their elders. He heard a murmur of conversation from a farther room and then the ticking bell of a telephone receiver picked up, and in a panic he moved to the other side of the room and out of earshot.

In a minute Lincoln came back. "Look here, Charlie. I think we'd better call off dinner for tonight. Marion's in bad shape."

"Is she angry with me?"

"Sort of," he said, almost roughly. "She's not strong and——"

"You mean she's changed her mind about Honoria?"

"She's pretty bitter right now. I don't know. You phone me at the bank tomorrow."

"I wish you'd explain to her I never dreamed these people would come here. I'm just as sore as you are."

"I couldn't explain anything to her now."

Charlie got up. He took his coat and hat and started down the corridor. Then he opened the door of the dining room and said in a strange voice, "Good night, children."

Honoria rose and ran around the table to hug him.

"Good night, sweetheart," he said vaguely, and then trying to make his voice more tender, trying to conciliate something, "Good night, dear children."

V

Charlie went directly to the Ritz bar with the furious idea of finding Lorraine and Duncan, but they were not there, and he realized that in any case there was nothing he could do. He had not touched his drink at the Peters', and now he ordered a whisky-and-soda. Paul came over to say hello.

"It's a great change," he said sadly. "We do about half the business we did. So many fellows I hear about back in the States lost everything, maybe not in the first crash, but then in the second. Your friend George Hardt lost every cent, I hear. Are you back in the states?"

"No, I'm in business in Prague."

"I heard that you lost a lot in the crash."

"I did," and he added grimly, "but I lost everything I wanted in the boom."

"Selling short."

"Something like that."

Again the memory of those days swept over him like a nightmare—the people they had met travelling; then people who couldn't add a row of figures or speak a coherent sentence. The little man Helen had consented to dance with at the ship's party, who had insulted her ten feet from the table; the women and girls carried screaming with drink or drugs out of public places——

—The men who locked their wives out in the snow, because the snow of twenty-nine wasn't real snow. If you didn't want it to be snow, you just paid some money.

He went to the phone and called the Peters' apartment; Lincoln answered.

"I called up because this thing is on my mind. Has Marion said anything definite?"

"Marion's sick," Lincoln answered shortly. "I know this thing isn't altogether your fault, but I can't have her go to pieces about it. I'm afraid we'll have to let it slide for six months; I can't take the chance of working her up to this state again."

"I see."

"I'm sorry, Charlie."

He went back to his table. His whisky glass was empty, but he shook his head when Alix looked at it questionably. There wasn't much he could do now except send Honoria some things; he would send her a lot of things tomorrow. He thought rather angrily that this was just money—he had given so many people money. . . .

"No, no more," he said to another waiter. "What do I owe you?"

He would come back some day; they couldn't make him pay forever. But he wanted his child, and nothing was much good now, beside that fact. He wasn't young any more, with a lot of nice thoughts and dreams to have by himself. He was absolutely sure Helen wouldn't have wanted him to be so alone.